THE LABYRINTH

by Bill Coulton

The motif of the hero's journey is exemplified by Theseus when he sailed to Crete, met Ariadne, and with her help, entered the labyrinth and slew the Minotaur. All of us must undergo similar journeys—both physically and metaphorically—in order to discover the hero that is within us.

—Elizabeth Wafford as recalled by
Ed Blakely aboard the *Sea Siren*.

THE MINOTAUR

Book II of The Labyrinth

by Bill Coulton

Nothing in the universe is lost. The answers to our questions lie all around us, but in forms we do not recognize. The wise man will touch earth and stone in reverence, the same as he would dare to touch the soul of the divine.
— An Afghani POW as recalled by Joachim Grenz

To Donald Cope —
After 45 years, we connect again! I hope you enjoy this book as much as I enjoyed writing it.
With Best Regards,
Your classmate,
Bill Coulton
3/19/98

THE MINOTAUR © 1997 Bill Coulton.

Book II of The Labyrinth.

All rights reserved. No part of this book may be reproduced or transmitted in any form or by any means, electronic or mechanical, including photocopying, recording, or by any information storage and retrieval system, without permission in writing from the copyright owner.

This is a work of fiction. Names, characters, places and incidents either are the product of the author's imagination or are used fictitiously, and any resemblance to any actual persons, living or dead, events, or locales is entirely coincidental.

This book was printed in the United States of America.

Xlibris Corporation
PO Box 2199
Princeton, NJ 08543-2199
USA
www.Xlibris.com

CONTENTS

Chapter 1	9
Chapter 2	21
Chapter 3	34
Chapter 4	43
Chapter 5	54
Chapter 6	72
Chapter 7	76
Chapter 8	83
Chapter 9	89
Chapter 10	94
Chapter 11	102
Chapter 12	113
Chapter 13	122
Chapter 14	136
Chapter 15	145
Chapter 16	154
Chapter 17	169
Chapter 18	183
Chapter 19	192
Chapter 20	205
Chapter 21	217
Chapter 22	220
Chapter 23	247
Chapter 24	259
Chapter 25	266
Chapter 26	280
Chapter 27	288
Chapter 28	300

Chapter 29	309
Chapter 30	325
Chapter 31	331
Chapter 32	339
Chapter 33	352
Chapter 34	374

FOR LUCIE

When I quit my job in February, 1996 to write full-time, my wife, Lucie Klein-Coulton, supported my ambition and shared my dream. It is with deepest gratitude that I dedicate this book to her.

Writing from five to sometimes ten hours a day is a lonely occupation. Magnolia Mae, our 92 pound yellow Labrador, made sure I was not alone. Unfortunately, I had to complete the final editing without Maggie; she developed cancer and died on 18 July, 1997. I miss her every day.

There are many people who help when you write a book. In particular, I want to thank my daughter, Valerie, for sharing her ideas and love. I thank John Feldcamp for his editorial assistance at Xlibris. I also want to acknowledge Mary Fowler and members of her writing critique group for their many suggestions.

Finally, I wish to recognize all of those people who are slowly becoming invisible in our society because they are no longer young or pretty or as strong as they used to be. I admire them for their courage and their desire to be of value. And that, after all, is what this book is about.

Bill Coulton
Atlanta, Georgia
26 September, 1997

CHAPTER 1

On to Crete

Blakely opened the ship's log. *28 March 1996. We weighed anchor at Piraeus, Greece, at 1105 hours this morning. Destination, Kastelli, located on the northwestern side of Crete, often called Kastelli-Kissamou. Weather moderate with some head winds. The sea is calm. Running under full sail and engine. Expected arrival at Kastelli 2300 hours. Chris and Justina Cunningham, archeologists, and Joachim Grenz consultant, came aboard for remainder of voyage.*

He checked his watch. It was 1512 hours. He picked up the phone.

"Tony?"

"Here."

"Want to be in on the Cunninghams' briefing? Leo or Mike can take over."

"I'll pass. Too beautiful a day. Leo's on watch. Mike's napping."

"See you." He hung up. Late again. He strode into the salon. Everybody looked like they were holding a wake.

"Why'd you pick Kastelli?" asked Marchese.

"It is surrounded by hills where Minoan artifacts have been found," said Chris. "Herr Grenz tells us Kastelli was where he and Heinrich von Etter were stationed together from May 30, 1941 until Herr Grenz was transferred in June, 1943. Our Greek friends you met last night, Neopolis and Santos, concur with Justina and I that this is the probable area to begin the search."

Harry was pouring a Greek wine and serving squares of goat

cheese with crackers. Justina and Elizabeth waved as Blakely sat at the dining table next to Jeremiah. It sounded to Blakely like there was a big glitch in the plan already, if Joachim was shipped out in 1943. Dead in the water before they got started. Wafford told them back in California that Joachim had been stationed with Heinrich until they were both transferred, meaning sometime around August or September, 1944.

Marchese raised a finger and slumped back in the sofa. "You say Mr. Grenz, here, transferred out in June, 1943?"

Joachim, sitting next to him, looked occasionally from one person to another. Between his poor hearing and absence of English, he probably had no idea what they were talking about.

"Yes," Chris replied. "He was sent to the Romanian oil fields."

Marchese put his hands behind his large head. "But this van Eller guy stayed at Kastelli?"

Chris pushed his glasses up on his nose. "It's von Etter. We presume so. He was on the island at least until ordered to Vienna in September, 1944."

Marchese was suddenly playing Mr. District Attorney. What business was it to him anyway?

"I guess what I'm getting at," said Marchese, looking at the ceiling, "is he could've changed assignments, right? I mean, there are other camps across Crete where he could have been transferred?"

Justina interrupted. "That's possible, Andy. And we may find documents on the island which show that. But based on what information we have, Kastelli is our number one target."

Marchese persisted. "You have orders on the guy telling him to report back to Vienna?"

"Yes," said Chris. "Issued by SS Colonel Eugen Horst."

"Well," said Marchese, shifting forward with a disagreeable grin forming, "what's van Eller's..."

"von Etter."

"Yeah, whatever. What's the guy's unit and address on the orders? Why beat around the bush? Let's go right to the last place he was assigned and go from there."

Marchese thinks he's got all the answers. Justina was shaking her head at Marchese.

"Not so simple," replied Chris, remaining incredibly patient. "The orders were sent to the commander of SS on Crete. It merely gave Heinrich's name, grade, and identification number. It was essentially a pick up and arrest type order."

Marchese slumped back again. "I understand."

Wafford drummed his fingers on the table. "Andy's got a point, professor. There's a space of one year between when Joachim was with Heinrich and when we know Heinrich received the shipment of jewels and gold."

Now Wafford had to get into it—and the glitch was his fault! Chris began rocking back and forth slightly. He removed his glasses, showing dark shadows around his eyes. He rubbed his eyes with his hand. "Yes, Louis. We didn't know that until we arrived here. Our interviews with Herr Grenz show he has no idea where Heinrich was stationed on Crete during the critical July, August, September 1944 period. We assume he stayed in Kastelli."

Wafford shifted his elbows to knees and rubbed his face in his hands. He was getting red around the gills. "In other words, we're taking a crap shoot going to Kastelli is what yer tell'n me."

Chris tried to keep a calm face. Wafford had taken a cheap shot. Chris put his glasses on. His eyes were blinking furiously. "No, Louis. I'm saying you did not inform us when we met in California that Herr Grenz was transferred off Crete a year prior to when Heinrich received the jewels shipment. Otherwise, I would not have agreed to join you at all. This bloody discrepancy came as a total shock. We must now do the best we can. So, we have to begin with what Herr Grenz remembers. We are taking him to the last place he was stationed with Heinrich."

"Louis," Justina chimed in, "why didn't you know about the discrepancy of time? You said you had an interpreter and interviewed him back last November!"

Wafford was sullen. "I can't remember," he groused. "Mebbe the interpreter did ask and we got no clear answer. I don't know."

THE MINOTAUR 11

Wafford's head lowered as though he were searching for the answer in the carpeting. "What about the fourth piece? With four out of five, will the marks on the back help any?"

Chris said, "They could mean nothing."

"Yer sure," Wafford asked, pointing at Joachim, "that the old man hasn't forgotten? Maybe he's mixed dates or something?"

"Dr. Neapolis and I spent two days going over the chronology," replied Justina, who sat, arms folded, a look of incredulity on her face. "Herr Grenz's memory puts him at the Ploesti oil fields of Romania during the first American bombing raids there. They occurred in August, 1943."

Blakely glanced at Joachim. So, the old Nazi was there when Luke got killed. Hell, Joachim could have been pulling the trigger that blew up Luke's bomber. This whole stupid adventure was unraveling. Wafford's hang dog looked out of options. "Sure they weren't in 1944?"

"Oh, come now, Louis," Justina pleaded. "Don't be ridiculous!"

"Couldn't Joachim have gone back to Crete after the bombing?"

Wafford wouldn't give in. It was a lousy try.

"Herr Grenz was moved immediately eastward to the Ukraine," said Justina, her eyes flashing daggers. "He describes his actions sufficiently that dates can be ascribed."

With all the discussion swirling around him, Joachim Grenz stared across at the bar and was filling the salon with pipe smoke.

Wafford was losing face. Elizabeth was looking at the tray of cards before her. They were arranged for a game of solitaire. Blakely couldn't allow the discussion to deteriorate any further. Bad enough they had only ten more days before they would abort. Worse, the Cunninghams were being attacked for something that was out of their hands. Blakely stood up, crossed the salon and leaned against the bar.

"We've heard all sides," said Blakely. "Why don't we let the pros follow their plan and we give them our total support? I can't imagine all you people up on the bridge telling me which course I ought to set or when to drop squares. Justina and Chris have spent their lives hunting for relics. I came on board thinking they were in charge of the hunt while the rest of us stayed out of their way. Why don't we keep quiet until they tell us how we can help them?"

Hands clapped. Mostly those of Elizabeth, Jeremiah and Justina.

"Amen to that, Edward," said Elizabeth heartily. "You hear what Edward's saying, Louis?

Wafford's face was fire red. Elizabeth wasn't giving him any latitude. He shot her the look of a wounded bear, but said nothing.

Elizabeth turned away from Wafford and raised her head. "And who, may I ask, is responsible for this wonderful wine and cheese? It is so delicious!"

"Thanks, Elizabeth," said Justina, who released the grip on her chair. "It was a gift from Professor Neapolis. I thought I'd share it with everyone."

Wafford and Marchese were silent. They were avoiding eye contact. Wafford hadn't touched his wine. Marchese got up and stretched, then sauntered out without a word. Wafford followed.

Elizabeth motioned Justina to come to her. She sat in Wafford's chair next to her. The two whispered quietly as the salon emptied. Chris motioned to Blakely to follow him. They went to Chris's cabin.

He searched for matches and lit his pipe. "I don't understand. Being second-guessed already, and we haven't even reached the bloody island."

He paced back and forth. One of Justina's gowns was neatly folded on the bunk. "It's what I said would happen, wasn't it? Back there in California. There is nothing substantial to go on. Louis has duped me into a bloody fiasco!"

"Yeah. Me, too."

"This Marchese chap. What's his background?"

"Ranger in Vietnam. Worked on a CIA mission to get mountain tribes to fight on our side. He's now a casino operator like Lou."

"So that qualifies him as an expert in archeology? As if we had made no preparations whatsoever. And did you hear him? The man cannot remember Heinrich's last name—after being reminded twice!"

Chris had a full head of steam going, pacing and puffing. "I've been blind-sided. Louis led us to believe Joachim Grenz was with Heinrich von Etter the entire time they served on the island. Now, we find he left the island in 1943. God knows where Heinrich might have been after that. And Marchese and Wafford are insinuating it is somehow our fault!"

He removed his glasses. His lips quivered beneath his mustache. "It's worse than I imagined, Edward."

"I know," said Blakely, thinking about the sale of the *Sea Siren* in two weeks.

"I'm quite afraid Grenz will prove totally useless. Unless we're very lucky at Kastelli, we are doomed to failure. Justina tells me Grenz is accurate in recalling some dates and places, but hasn't the foggiest about others. And as you are aware, I abhor failure. It is not in my vocabulary."

Blakely could not quite agree with him. But fatherhood was a separate issue from archeology.

Chris paused and put his hand on Blakely's shoulder. "I want to thank you for supporting us in there. I'm afraid if you hadn't broken in, either Justina or myself would have let Wafford and this Marchese chap have it."

Justina roared into the cabin, slamming the hatch. Her eyes were flashing black lightning. "Those bastards!" she hissed in German. "How dare they put blame on us before we begin. Tell me, Edward, why they do this in front of others?"

Blakely shrugged. "I don't know."

"Louis deceived us! Otherwise, we not be here. What do you want to do, Christopher? We can catch the ferry back to Athens tomorrow and go home."

"I suppose we should leave." He re-lit his pipe. "A damn bloody shame. There is a thousand to one chance Heinrich found the relic much earlier, say, in 1942 or 1943, while Herr Grenz was with him."

"I hope you will stay," said Blakely. "We're here. I'd like to see you guys do your thing."

Justina said, "I don't think it can work. I am not wanting to be around these stupid men, Andy Marchese and Louis Wafford."

Blakely said, "I'll hang in if you will. I'm willing to give it a few weeks. That's all anybody can ask for. Maybe I can run interference for you."

Chris shifted his pipe and glanced at Justina. "What do you say, Justina? I could do that."

"I don't know," she said. "Let us talk about it." She sat on the bunk and looked at Blakely. "I won't promise."

"I hope you stay." Blakely waved and left Chris and Justina to regroup. When he returned to the salon, Marchese was showing Elizabeth some card tricks.

"I can't do that," Elizabeth cried. She gave Blakely a glance that said 'get this guy away from me'.

"Yes you can. Easy, sweetheart. Watch my hands. See? I'm shifting the card in my palm?"

"Yes, I see. My hands aren't big enough for that. Please! I don't want to see any more of your card tricks. And I don't like to be called sweetheart!"

"Practice it. I know you can do it," said Marchese, seeming unoffended. "I'm going up on deck. Want to catch some air, guy?"

"Yeah, we could all use some fresh air," Blakely replied, winking at Elizabeth.

He watched as Marchese grabbed a slab of goat cheese and pushed it into his mouth, dropping crumbs down his chin. Bits of cheese collected in his chest hair above his running suit. He brushed daintily at his chin with a napkin, then took a swig of wine, leaving a white imprint on the glass and bits of cheese floating in the glass. He set the glass down and attempted to speak with his mouth full as Blakely accompanied him toward the aft ladder.

"As I told Gresh and them at our meeting last night, women love it when I show 'em card tricks." A wad of cheese was visible in his mouth as he talked.

"You mean the meeting you had with Homer and Lou?"

They crossed the deck to the Fife rail.

"Yeah, guy." He wiped his sleeve across his mouth. "Elizabeth's got some of them tricks down pat, so you better watch yourself, pal."

You'd better watch yourself too, pal, Blakely said to himself.

"I will." Blakely tapped Marchese's sizable stomach. "Watch the diet, guy. That cheese'll stick to you like glue."

Wafford hadn't mentioned Marchese was in their little meeting. Blakely ambled off to get his own fresh air. There was nothing to like about Marchese. He had been barely civil the entire voyage. He had done his own thing when they were at Trieste. He was interfering with the Cunninghams. Now, he was saying he was in on the meeting with Wafford, King, and McCloud. Everything about this trip was getting screwy. It stunk, and Blakely decided that if the Cunninghams pulled out tomorrow morning, he would pull out, too. If Tony, Leo and Mike wanted to stay on, then that was their call.

* * * * *

At 1600 hours, Blakely took the helm from Tony. The sun was white gold on aqua sea and the squares and staysails billowed in good air. He put on sunglasses. The winds were coming off the Libyan Desert.

Wafford came through the hatch at 1735 hours, still looking sullen. He sidled over to the console, rubbing his wrist, and said in a low voice, "Guess me and Andy kinda jumped the gun on the professor."

"They may be taking the ferry back tomorrow."

Wafford's eyes moved to Blakely. "You mean because of what we said, they'd up and quit on us?"

"Yeah. They feel betrayed. I do too, if you want to know the truth."

Wafford looked down at his shoes and started scoffing one across the toe of the other. "Damn. I guess it was my fault. I shoulda asked ole Joachim more questions. Woulda saved us all some grief."

"What will you do if the Cunninghams leave tomorrow?"

"Nothing to do, 'cept hire new ones. Archeologists are a dime a dozen around these parts. Get ole what's his name, Penopolis?"

"Neopolis."

"Get him to go with us. Wouldn't cost any more'n we're pay'n the professor and Miss Justina."

"So, you don't feel bad that they might leave?"

Wafford leaned against the console. Light patterns off the water danced on his pink jowls. "Course I do… But we got to go on. Can't fret 'bout prima donnas."

"We're not talking about prima donnas, Lou. You misled us."

He had a pouting expression and looked hopefully at Blakely. Blakely ignored him. He agreed with Justina. Right now, Wafford was a bastard first class. Blakely was determined to keep his mind on the helm. Several minutes went by while Wafford followed Blakely's slight adjustments of wheel and sail.

Finally, Wafford muttered, "Guess I oughta go down and apologize. Whaddya think?"

"Not bad for starters." Blakely punched the buttons to correct the angle of the spars to the wind. Wafford watched the luff disappear.

"You mentioned that meeting you and King and McCloud had after the party. How come nobody else was invited?"

Wafford gave him a quizzical look. "We're talking proprietary business. Were you thinking you shoulda been there?"

"Not necessarily. But why King and not Marchese, for example?"

Wafford cupped his hands on the console. "I don't decide who

Homer wants at a meeting. If he'd wanted Andy, he'd have invited him."

"So Marchese never met with you and King and McCloud last night?"

Wafford stared out the port windows. "I don't know what you're gettin at, Ed. No, he didn't."

"I wasn't getting at anything. A couple of hours ago, Marchese said he met with you guys last night. I guess he was mistaken."

"Yeah. He was." Wafford slunk toward the inside hatch without turning his head. The back of his neck was purple. "I'll pay a visit to the Cunninghams. See whether they'll stay."

So Wafford could lie, too. The sun and water were preparing the sky for a brilliant sunset. Scudding white puffs of cloud were already turning pink and orange, and the entire sea ranged from white gold to orange and pale aqua. All this beauty and all this stupidity. There was no reason for either Wafford or Marchese to lie. Who gave a damn whether Marchese attended the meeting? And how quickly Wafford was willing to dump the Cunninghams. Archeologists are a dime a dozen. If you've got the money, you believe you can buy anything or anybody. He muttered to himself, 'Well, ole buddy, he bought you, didn't he?'

* * * * *

After being relieved at the helm at 2000 hours, Blakely walked to the bow. The puffs had abandoned the sky to the stars. Soon, there ought to be lights off the starboard bow—the lights of Kastelli and Hania.

Marchese kept reappearing in his thoughts. The man was an enigma. He recalled that Marchese said he trained all those mountain people in guerrilla warfare. It came out later in the newspapers that the CIA was behind it. The CIA got these mountain tribes together, and they fought their own war against the North Vietnamese. Yeah. He remembered the whole effort was a fiasco. Another CIA disaster. Resulted in dislocating a couple million people from their homeland. Most were brought stateside to live in places like Minnesota, North Carolina and California.

He realized someone was standing nearby. It was the old Nazi. He was wearing one of those black headbands like Cretan men wore.

"You look at stars?" asked Joachim in German with a quiet gentleness. "Such star-filled night to talk with God."

"Ya. I should talk to God more often," acknowledged Blakely, thinking that fifty-three years ago, this old man and every other Nazi was his most hated enemy. "How come you are out so late?"

"Vas? Come round to my other ear. I have bad left ear!"

Blakely stood close to his good ear. "How come you're out so late?"

"I always spend time with stars." He pointed skyward. "From time I am a boy. Then, I attend parachute training. I learn all important stars. Polaris—the North Star—most important. We used Polaris to get our bearings, you know. The same way sailors do."

"Yeah?"

"That is so. When I work in Siberia, I learned through watching the stars to know my soul."

"I don't follow what you mean."

Joachim gazed at Blakely for a moment. "It is difficult to explain. You have to feel it. I only feel it after watching the heavens many, many years when I am alone."

"You discovered your soul?"

"Ya. I discover my soul and can now speak to God."

It didn't make any sense. The old guy must have been in Siberia too long. Him and McCloud ought to get together.

"What's the soul like?"

Joachim pointed skyward. "Like the stars, Edward. We have the same fire within us which stars have—and like stars, we burn until we are consumed. Our energy is released back to its source. My soul is the place no one can hurt or touch. It is God-given energy which nobody can harm."

Joachim pointed to his chest.

"No matter how difficult life becomes, the soul protects you."

"Is that how you survived all those work camps?"

"Ya. That is so. I look to the stars each night for help, and find I am one of them. It make me very peaceful with myself. I become a small part of great energy!"

Blakely could relate to that. Nights at sea, gazing at the stars, would often induce a feeling of kinship with the universe. Everything lived on sparks of energy.

"Interesting."

"Ya." The old man re-lit his pipe. "I was watching tonight the comet Hyakutake. Have you seen it?"

"Never heard of it."

Blakely knew many stars, constellations and comets, but hadn't heard of this one.

"I read about it in the German edition of the *Athens News* this morning. Discovered by young amateur astronomer, Yuji Hyakutake, January last. It is the brightest comet in two decades."

"Haven't seen it." Blakely gazed across the sky toward the west and south. "Where's it 'sposed to be?"

"Nein, you're looking the wrong way," the old man said, touching Blakely's shoulder. "Near the Big Dipper. There! There it is!"

And so it was. A burst of dusty white in a rounded shape with a diminishing tail. "What a show!"

"Ya," said the German, pipe clenched in his teeth as he looked skyward, a gleam in his eyes. "There are many wonders!"

"Yeah," Blakely replied, thinking how, every time you look to the heavens, there is the possibility of discovering a new thing that is very old. "There sure are."

CHAPTER 2
Kastelli

On the morning of 29 March 1996, Blakely wrote in the log, *the Sea Siren lay at anchor in azure water of four fathoms, off Kastelli, Island of Crete. The ship has passed inspection. The mountain Korikos rises up to the west along the forbidding Gramvousa Peninsula while to the east lay the Rodopou Peninsula with its several mountain peaks rising almost straight out of the Sea of Crete and casting long shadows across the calm water. Skies are clear. The early sun promises a warm day. This morning, our two archeologists decide whether they stay aboard and search for Minoan relics or leave the ship.*

Blakely bit the end of his ball-point. His description of the peninsulas was too flowery. And his statement about the Cunninghams didn't tell half the story. He felt torn between a desire to hang in and to escape. It was 0700 hours.

He went to the galley and poured himself some coffee. Harry flitted back and forth like a caged cat, deftly salting this and stirring that.

"What's breakfast this morning, Harry?"

"Shrimp omelet, biscuits, cous cous, fresh fruit, and apple pie."

Blakely passed the communications center. He could hear codes and voices like a song from outer space. Tobok was at it again. He climbed the forecastle ladder and went on deck.

Tony intercepted him. "You get my message?"

"No."

"Wafford said to tell you he and Marchese will be gone all day."

"Where to?"

"Some gorge in them mountains."

"Take Elizabeth?"

"No. Andy was in that climbing outfit again. Don't see how Wafford will keep up with his bad wrist and all."

"He say when they'd be back?"

"Late. It was hard to get much outta him. He ain't himself."

"How do you mean?"

"I heard him and Marchese arguing last night behind the pilot house. This morning, Wafford jumped all over Leo for not having the launch ready."

"So what happened?"

Tony pulled a punch at Blakely's midsection. "That's the funny part. Didn't want to wait on the launch. Settled for the dinghy. You oughta seen 'em in it. Not more'n three inches freeboard with Wafford sitting in the stern and Marchese trying to row. Looked like the owl and the pussycat, they did."

"What time did they leave?"

"0545 hours. I'd just come up from the galley with coffee for Leo."

"You say they were arguing last night?"

"Oh, yes. Mostly Wafford giving Marchese the what for. I couldn't hear what was said."

"Thanks for the info, Tony."

Blakely strode over to where Chris and Joachim were talking at the bow. The old man was pointing toward the Gramvousa Peninsula. Both were puffing furiously on their pipes.

"Morning, Edward. Herr Grenz recognizes several places where he and Heinrich installed defenses."

"Does that mean you are staying?"

Chris gave him a sardonic look. "We'll give it a go. Louis came by last night. We had a long talk. He apologized and assured us he and Marchese will stay out of our way."

"Good."

"I thought the four of us might spend the day looking about.

Obviously, there have been incredible changes here since the war. It will be very confusing to Herr Grenz. We shouldn't expect too much our first day. "

"Which four? Lou and Andy have gone mountain climbing."

"Really?" Chris seemed amused. "I meant you, of course. Justina, me, Herr Grenz."

"I'll be your driver. How about that?"

"Excellent. I should think we'll need a sturdy vehicle. The terrain is quite difficult."

Blakely scanned the stony mountains. They were bleak and naked. "We've got arrangements with a rental agency. I'll get Gregor to work on it."

He left them and went below. Codes and voices competed. Damned if he knew how Tobok tolerated it going on all at once. The hatch was locked and he didn't have his key. He banged on it. "Gregor, it's Blakely. I need to talk to you."

Jeremiah came down the passage with his Magic Johnson smile.

"You're wasting your time, skip. Gregor's got his earphones on. Only way to get his attention is by phone. Come on in the studio."

He followed Jeremiah and sat on a workbench next to the wall phone. "Is he still staying up all night, Jeremiah?"

Magic's smile grew wider. "Hey, I go to bed at night. All I know is he's there sometimes when I get up extra early."

"What's extra early?"

Jeremiah quit smiling. He hitched up his jeans. "Four? When I go on watch. Four thirty? You know, it varies."

"What do you think he does in there?"

Jeremiah raised his eyebrows and held out his arms. "Web browsing? Talking on the Ham? He's doing his thing!"

"What's the code I keep hearing?"

"Oh, weather, ships at sea, military. He showed me how to scan frequencies. You can pick up everything in there."

Blakely rang the comm center.

"Tobok here."

"Could you unlock the hatch, Gregor? I want you to make some arrangements for a vehicle."

"Yes, sir."

Blakely hung up.

"Is it okay if Harry, Gregor and I tag along today with our video equipment?"

Blakely thought a moment. "You better wait until the professor invites you. Your camera could make the old Nazi uptight."

"I understand. I thought the dining room was going to explode yesterday, didn't you? Uncle Lou kept persisting!"

"He's under pressure. Can you do me a favor?"

"Yeah. Sure."

"You, Harry and Leo. Take Elizabeth ashore and show her the sights, okay?"

Blakely pulled out his wallet and counted out five twenties. "Here. Buy a nice lunch. If Elizabeth sees something she likes, get it for her."

"Far out! Can we take our equipment? We need some local color shots."

"Why not. Have fun!"

Blakely stood before the comm room hatch. He was growing tired of Tobok's secretiveness. The cacophony of codes and voices went silent. The hatch clicked and swung open.

Tobok stood there, looking self-conscious.

"What were you listening to this morning, Gregor?"

Gregor stepped back to let Blakely pass. "A Ham out of Odessa. He's from my home town in Romania."

"Yeah? Able to talk to any relatives?"

"Not yet. He's working on it."

"I need you to call that contract agency and get us a vehicle for today. Have it delivered dockside by 0835 hours."

Blakely gave Tobok the details and then hustled to the dining room where Elizabeth sat alone.

"Morning, Elizabeth."

She looked up. The serenity he admired in her face was absent. Her attempted smile was frozen in silent despair. She put a toast end on her plate and glanced at the empty hatch before speaking.

"Louis is gone, Edward."

"What's that about?"

"I don't know." She looked down at her plate. "Andy Marchese called him at four a.m. Next I know, Louis is getting dressed and says they're going exploring. Then, he apologized to me for not being a better husband. He's in no fit condition to be traipsing around out there!"

It was bizarre! He considered asking her about the sale of *Sea Siren*, but thought better of it.

"Have any plans for today, Elizabeth?"

"I thought I would spend the day on deck, enjoying the scenery." She pivoted her wheelchair around, away from the table.

"How about joining Jeremiah for a tour of Kastelli?"

"That would be lovely." Her ebony face bloomed again. "Will you go with us?"

"Not today. I'm going with the archeologists and Joachim in search of the missing link."

"I'm glad they decided to stay, aren't you?"

"Yeah," he replied. And he was glad.

* * * * *

Blakely followed a shapely woman on a scooter around the square to the Venetian fortress. He dropped his passengers off at the entrance and parked.

When he joined them, Joachim stood on the battlements of the castle—or Kastelli—looking more like the tourist than the guide. Pigeons cooed and jostled for position near them.

"Can you see where your base camp was located, Herr Grenz?" asked Justina.

Joachim looked out at the jumble of pastel-colored commercial buildings. He took his pipe from his mouth and pointed with it. "Depot, along here. Tons and tons of materials. Many ships there." He pointed to where the *Sea Siren* lay at anchor. "We build fortification."

Chris asked, "Can you point to where you and Heinrich stayed? Did you live in one of those hotels?"

"Nein," said Joachim. "Tent. We stay in tent over there." He pointed toward the Gramvousa Peninsula.

"Where, exactly?" asked Justina.

The old man paused, then pointed with his cane. Justina stood behind him, looking down the barrel of the cane. "There... and there... and over there."

Justina and Chris looked bewildered. She rested a hand on Joachim's shoulder and asked, "You stayed at one work site, then moved to another?"

"Ya. We work. Complete fortification. Move tent."

"How many times?"

Joachim tapped the ashes out of his pipe against the stone wall. "Several. Ten? Twelve? I forget. Many times."

"And when was this?" Chris asked.

"Summer, 1941? 1942? It took many months!"

"Where was your permanent headquarters?"

The old man looked around in all directions, seeming confused. "We work there," he replied, pointing again toward the Gramvousa.

Chris asked, "You didn't have a permanent address where people sent you mail?"

"Ya. Hania. Hania a big base. They deliver mail to us from Hania. Near Souda. I leave here from Souda on ship to Romania."

"In May, 1943?"

"Ya. May it was."

"Why did you leave? Was your work completed?"

"Ya. We finish. They put guns there." He ran his pipe along the top of the peninsula where nothing except rocks was visible. "A big job. All done!"

"Where did Heinrich go from here?"

"Kastelli," replied Joachim.

"You mean here. Can you point out where in Kastelli that Heinrich was assigned?"

Joachim looked around. He scratched the white bristles of beard at his chin. "Nein. I go to Romania. Heinrich stay at Kastelli."

Chris sat down next to Blakely on the wall. "The old boy is consistent. He keeps to the same story he told Dr. Neapolis and Justina. Only difference is, he's isolated the area where he and Heinrich worked."

The three looked out at the desolate mountains, which were turning orange in the morning sunlight. Chris took out his map and studied it. "Phalassarna! On the western side of Gramvousa Peninsula. That's our best hope."

Blakely couldn't imagine what rationale Chris used for selecting that location from among others, but who was he to question the professor.

"Herr Grenz," said Chris, pointing to the map. "Did you ever stay in this vicinity?"

Joachim studied the map.

"Ya. We build fortification there," he said, striking the map with his finger repeatedly. "Ya, ya!"

Chris pushed his glasses up on his nose and nodded at Justina. "That's it."

"Wonderful," Justina exclaimed hollowly, "Let's be off!"

Phalassarna, Blakely discovered, was one of those nearby places it takes forever to reach. There was no direct route. Rather, they drove northwest to the little port of Trahilos, then turned southwest through small vineyards, past goat farms, monasteries, and tiny whitewashed villages to a larger village, Neo Horio, and across rocky mountains to Piperiana.

Chris and Justina were exceptionally quiet. He occasionally brushed at his mustache and studied the archeological map. She thumbed through books she had brought along, oblivious to the scenery they passed.

Blakely continued down a narrow road on the west side of the mountains overlooking the sea to a better road along the shore. Occasionally, he would catch Justina staring at him in the rear view mirror, and she would quickly look away.

"Turn right, here, Edward," directed Chris. Turning north, they drove along incredibly beautiful beaches between rocky bluffs and finally reached the empty ruins of Phalassarna. The only sign of life was three fishing boats working off the peninsula some three miles away.

Blakely parked the Rover at the edge of the ruins. Everyone got out and ambled toward the outlines of rock foundations still visible here and there. Blakely stretched. It was warm. He shed his windbreaker and shoved it through the window onto the front seat.

"This was once a thriving Minoan port city," said Chris, surveying the ruins. "See that line of cliff just below us?"

Blakely shook his head.

"An earthquake pushed up beneath the city, making it impossible for it to continue as a port."

"How long ago?"

"Sixth century AD."

Blakely looked across the ruins. He couldn't imagine what they would prove here. The place was desolate. Nothing visible except rocks and traces of foundations. It was a Minoan archeological site, which meant the pros—the grave robbers as he liked to call them—had already picked it over.

Joachim walked silently amid the ancient stones, looked in all directions, turned back toward the others, and shrugged his heavy shoulders. "I see nothing here that I remember," he said apologetically.

"Where would one put an anti-aircraft gun?" Chris asked nobody in particular, pulling binoculars from his canvas bag. Blakely checked the slope, looking for any tell-tales in the contours of the rocky slopes. The guy was stubbornly trying to invent something out of nothing, Blakely thought.

"Over there," Chris pointed at a pile of rocks, perhaps a hundred yards up the mountain. He started walking up the slope. Justina and Blakely stayed with Joachim, watching.

Chris disappeared behind some rocks and reappeared above them. He walked back and forth on a seemingly flat surface. "Concrete!" He shouted in German. "A gun emplacement!"

The words produced an immediate reaction in Joachim. "Ya! We build there!" He began to walk uncertainly up the difficult slope, probing with his cane for support.

"I am embarrassed to see Christopher play the fool in front of you," said Justina in a low voice. "He is better than this."

"What do you mean? I thought he's doing his archeology thing?" She looked sharply at Blakely, then began to follow Joachim.

"You know what I mean, Edward. You needn't be snide."

"Sorry. I didn't mean to be."

He lied. Chris was looking pathetic. He walked passed her and took Joachim's arm. They moved slowly up the rocky slope and around the pile of rocks.

A thirty foot square pad of reinforced concrete lay behind the stones. Evenly spaced orange indentations formed a circular pattern on the surface of the pad where a gun must have been bolted. Joachim was thrilled.

"I supervise here," he exclaimed. "Anti-aircraft battery!"

An empty pad of concrete, thought Blakely. Big deal!

"Yavoll," said Joachim proudly. "We construct many like this... Except, most have wall in front." He motioned with his pipe. "And net camouflage overhead."

Chris, Justina and Blakely followed his pipe as he spoke.

"Quite interesting," said Chris. He took out a piece of acetate from his bag. Blakely recognized it as the template. The prick marks and x and diagonal line had been copied onto the acetate from the backs of the four pieces of relic to form a whole. He laid it on top of a piece of white paper and held it out before him. He compared the few visible landmarks with the template.

"Nothing. Want to give it a try?"

Justina reluctantly took the template and turned it slowly,

comparing it with existing mountain peaks. She shrugged and in a tired voice said, "Nothing. Do you also wish to try, Edward?"

Blakely took it. He went through the motions, pretending to be serious. What was the point? Joachim and Heinrich—if they had been here at all—would have built the gun emplacement in 1941 or 1942. The cache of jewels was hidden probably in August or September, 1944. He turned the template a different way. Nothing among the marks lined up with physical landmarks.

"Being an engineer, Heinrich would have used obvious points of reference," Blakely said, attempting to play the game. "The only one I can figure is that mountain over there," pointing to Geroskinos Peak. "It doesn't jibe."

He handed the template to Chris, who slipped it into his bag. "Where did you stay while working here?"

Joachim looked perplexed. His blue eyes were barely discernible in the welter of wrinkles around them.

"There, I think."

He pointed to a sandy beach, which lay below the ruins.

"We have many tents there. Good swimming," he added.

Blakely was getting hungry.

"Let's have a look," said Chris confidently.

"A look at what?" asked Justina. Her tone was not enthusiastic. The guy was losing face with his own wife!

"The beach! Herr Grenz just said they camped on the beach."

Justina said, "Isn't it time for lunch? I'm starving!"

"We can drive down and picnic on the beach," said Blakely.

There was no point wasting anymore time here. The walk back was treacherous and required Chris and Blakely to assist Joachim. Blakely started the motor. He drove down the gravel slope to the beach and parked at the widest point of the natural harbor.

Blakely got out the food cooler. He spread lamb sandwiches, pickles, kiwi fruit, plastic cups and plates on the tailgate. He opened a thermos of iced tea. The four sat on the sand and ate.

"Look here," said Chris. He wiped sand away from a flat rock.

The rock had a black circle an inch in diameter with orange color leeching from it. "Perhaps the metal support for some structure."

Justina gave it a cursory inspection and sat back. She gave Blakely a quick glance. It was clear that she did not want Blakely to witness this travesty of archeological searching any longer.

Chris set his sandwich down on a napkin and pulled out the manila folder. "Worth checking," he said under his breath. He sat with the acetate template in his lap, turning it one way and another, studying the geographical features of the surrounding mountains. "No luck! Want to have a go at it, Justina?"

"No."

Chris wiped bread crumbs from his mustache and took off his glasses. "I know you must wonder why I am so persistent, Edward. I don't want to leave anything to chance. My theory is that Heinrich von Etter could have discovered the relic here at one of these sites in 1942, received the smuggled jewels in 1944, and returned here and hid them. I know it is a long shot, but it is all we've got going right now."

"Glad you explained it," said Blakely. Chris was blowing in the wind.

Blakely opened the plastic wrap and picked out a slice of Kiwi.

"I don't know what is with Harry," he said in German, laying back on one elbow. "Harry always has to have Kiwi."

Chris and Justina didn't reply. Joachim, sitting on the cooler, defended Harry. "Kiwi very good for you!"

The four of them continued eating in silence. He looked up the hill at the ruins of what was once a city and at where the gun emplacement had been. Only the rocks abide, and even they end up sand. He knew Chris and Justina were whipped. This was more than a long shot; it was a Hail Mary pass with no time on the clock ninety yards from goal, blindfolded, with nobody down field to receive it! And he knew also that regardless of how many construction sites they might visit on the Gramvousa Peninsula, the result would be the same: nada.

Looking across at the stark Korikos mountains, he found himself questioning why he was going along with it. Was this nothing more than another illusory experience? Justina's black wedge of hair and alabaster skin did not look half so warm and lovely as the remembrance of her that night in the snow. Her face was now sullen and unattractive. She was unhappily married and estranged from her two children.

He gazed at Chris, who was eating his sandwich and studying the rocks. The guy seemed oblivious to the realities of his life. Chris was marking time, avoiding the issues of relic, wife, kids, and future, in playing out a charade.

Joachim was lighting his pipe. An old Nazi. He had fought here, no doubt killing several British soldiers. Joachim had been at the Ploesti oil fields when Luke, his half-brother, was dropping bombs on it. No telling how many planes Joachim blasted to smithereens. A company of alienated strangers on a desolate island.

He laid back, feeling the warm sand on his back and the sun on his face. What did it matter? The Turkish proverb was true; they were all headed to the same destination, no matter which road they chose. He thought he had dosed off. Her voice seemed so distant.

"What are you thinking we should do?" she asked in a soft, low voice.

"It wouldn't hurt to have a look at one of those other places Herr Grenz pointed to this morning."

"You mean on the peninsula?"

"Yes."

"We can't get there unless we drive all the way back to that village in the mountains. It would take us several hours."

"Yes." Chris gave an audible sigh. "We should probably call it a day. Herr Grenz looks tired. We should get help from the anthropologist Santos recommended—that Kralos chap."

Justina said nothing.

"I think I'll have a look down the beach," Chris muttered.

Blakely could hear the sand scratch beneath shoes, as Chris

got to his feet. The sound of his footfalls grew faint.

"Meinen Gott!" whispered Justina under her breath. "The man has lost all reason. He is more stubborn than any German!"

Blakely opened his eyes momentarily. Justina had gotten up and was watching Chris walking along the thin crescent of beach. So much for togetherness among the archeologists. Joachim sat on the cooler, slumped over, fast asleep. His pipe rested in one fist on his knee. Blakely closed his eyes again and contemplated the idea that when you get really old, you sleep a lot. Was sleep an escape from illusion? Is that why cats sleep a lot? He dosed off. He was feeling like a cat must feel right now, warm and contented, lying in bright sun after eating, and trying to escape the illusion of his being.

He thought he heard Chris returning. The crunch of sand grew louder with each footfall. There were no words. He dosed again. Then, he heard rustling; Justina was collecting the plates, cups and napkins. He roused himself.

Chris sat in the sand cross-legged, stowing his map, template, and binoculars again. Apparently, he'd given the barren mountains one last study.

"Mind if I use the binocs a second?"

"Why no, Edward. Here." He handed him the binoculars.

Blakely focused the glasses and followed the sandy beach northward toward the Gramvousa Peninsula. The fishing boats were working along the water closest to the sheer cliffs some five miles away.

"Looks like a trail goes along the fault line, Chris. How about us following it a ways. It could be a shortcut to the eastern side."

He handed Chris the glasses.

"No sign that it turns up into the mountain. We were told that you must go by boat when exploring any point north of here."

"You don't want to give it a try? It could save us time."

"I think not," said Chris, with finality.

"So be it."

CHAPTER 3

Connecting

Dr. George Kralos handed Chris the piece of relic obtained at Trieste. "I've never seen any artifact such as this identified with Kastelli-Kissamou area. There are many caves to the south. Some have produced bronze, clay, and stone items. Nothing like this. If a person were to find such an artifact in this vicinity, I would say it was one in a million chance."

Kralos held out his glass. Elizabeth poured him more wine.

"I suggest," said Kralos, "that you consult with archeologists at Iraklion and Knossos. To my way of thinking, your chances are better there."

Chris folded his arms in front of him and stared at the carpet. "If only Herr Grenz had better memory."

Kralos asked, "Why here instead of Rethimnon? Why not start where Mr. Grenz and his friend first landed? Take him through the sequence of his experience?"

"We could have done that," replied Justina. "Except it would have taken several days. Probably with the same result. All of these cities are changed drastically from when Herr Grenz arrived in 1941."

"Exactly," added Chris. "We relied on two bits of information Herr Grenz repeatedly told us when Justina interviewed him in Athens: one, he and Heinrich von Etter were stationed at Kastelli together from 1941 to 1943. Two, Herr Grenz says that when he met Heinrich on furlough early in 1944, Heinrich still talked about being stationed at Kastelli."

Blakely turned to Kralos. "Are any records available on the island to verify Heinrich's assignment?"

"Most were burned by the Cretan resistance. There is Maleme, of course. The German cemetery has a registry."

"We thought we would take Herr Grenz to Maleme," said Chris. "It might remind him of something important."

Elizabeth refilled Blakely's glass.

' Chris said, "He and Heinrich wrote letters back and forth from 1943 through August, 1944. Heinrich must have told him what he was up to. Realizing, of course, Nazi censorship would have blotted out security information, such as his exact location."

"Ya," said Justina. "There was one time they were together on furlough. Vienna, I believe. Once, in 1944, in Portanone, Italy, they met accidentally while changing trains. Herr Grenz cannot remember details of these meetings. Perhaps you could jog his memory, Edward? He seems to like you."

"I might try, " Blakely replied skeptically. "I'm beginning to like the old bugger."

Justina looked disapprovingly.

"Sorry," he said softly.

Tobok knocked at the open hatch. "Excuse me, Mrs. Wafford. You have a message." He handed her a note. She read it, then shook her head in disbelief.

"Would you believe it? Louis and Andy are stranded in a place called Chora..."

Kralos asked, "Chora Sfakion?"

"Yes. Chora Sfakion. They have to stay there overnight. How could that happen?"

Kralos smiled knowingly. "It happens all the time," he commented. "Did they visit the Samaria Gorge today?"

Elizabeth shrugged.

"Probably," said Blakely. "My pilot said they were going climbing. How'd you know?"

"The Samaria Gorge is a very difficult journey."

Elizabeth's cocoa eyes and mouth opened wide. "How difficult?"

"Quite," replied Kralos, a grin playing at the corners of his mouth. "The path drops 1000 meters in the first two or three kilometers. It takes six hours to traverse the narrow gorge and finally reach Agia Roumeli on the coast. There are no roads there. The only way out is to return back through the gorge or else catch a boat. Boats operate from Agia Roumeli to Chora Sfakion. They apparently arrived there too late to catch the Hania bus."

Elizabeth held up the message. "Yes. That's what they did, all right. Their car is at Omalos. They're staying at Chora... Chora Sfakion?"

"That's correct," noted Kralos.

"... Chora Sfakion for the night. Plan to take the bus tomorrow morning. I can't see Louis and Andy doing this!"

"I can send Mike over early," said Blakely. "No sense in them having to take a bus."

"You don't think Andy and Louis deserve a nice long bus ride together, Edward? After what they pulled?" Elizabeth chirped. "I'd let them get back best way they can."

Wafford did deserve whatever he got. The man was losing it.

Blakely turned to Chris. "So what's your game plan for tomorrow?"

Chris crossed his legs and glanced at Justina. "Tomorrow we will take Herr Grenz to Maleme and Hania. If we develop no leads, then it may be best to lift anchor and go directly to Iraklion."

"All right by me," Blakely said.

"What shall we do this evening?" asked Justina. "Our first night on Crete!"

"I can recommend a restaurant not far above the harbor," said Kralos. "They have music. It is called The Grotto."

* * * * *

Their evening progressed from drinking Ouzo and eating mezedes on the plastic-enclosed patio to a full scale Greek dinner with an earthy red wine served in clay pitchers. By the time the music started, the group was in high spirits.

Blakely noticed a petite blond woman who reminded him of Jenny. German or Scandinavian. She was with another woman who smoked. The two women danced and sat down at a table across the room. When the music started up again, he excused himself and crossed the dance floor. The alcohol had not impeded his balance—at least yet.

He asked in German, "Would you care to dance?"

Without a word, the woman stood up and accepted his hand and arm in a slow dance. She was in her mid-forties, he thought. She was light and followed his steps easily. Her blue eyes studied his face. In English, she asked, "Are you a star?"

He was taken aback. Hair fell partially over her eyes so he couldn't read them. "A star? How do you mean?"

Her lips parted, showing nice teeth. "You would know, if you were a star."

"Are you looking for one?"

She released his hand to brush hair out of her eyes, then took it again. "Yes. I look for a star."

She had a musk scent. "Where are you from?"

"Mannheim, Germany. And you?"

"California. Here on vacation?"

"Ya."

"I'm curious. What do you mean by star? You don't mean movie star, do you?"

She touched her lips with her tongue. "Some men are ascending, like stars... I like only men who are ascendant."

"Winners."

"Ya, winners." She said it like she meant it.

"I understand now." He pulled her to him and they danced close. Her hair was thick and soft. It felt good to have her hair brushing his cheek and her body against his. He considered inviting himself to her table, but thought better of it. Go slow, Blakely. When the music ended, he escorted her back.

"You are welcome to join us," she said. "This is Hilda," pointing to another blond lady who sat smoking a cigarette, "and my name is Stephanie."

"Ed Blakley. Thanks, but I better stay with my group. Are you here for long?"

"We go to Iraklion day after tomorrow. Then to Chersonisou."

"We might see each other again. I'm on the tall ship in the harbor. Wherever you see it, that's where I can be reached."

"Ya? A beautiful ship!" Her face lit up. "Then you are a star!"

"Glad to meet you both." He turned and walked around the crowded dance floor, feeling everyone's eyes trained on him.

Chris looked like a lecherous voyeur. "Well done, Edward old boy! You will note, George, my friend Edward is... partial to blondes!"

Blakely sat down next to Chris and Kralos.

"I tell you, George," said Chris, who Blakely realized was slightly drunk, "I always remember Edward here... never shined his shoes. They were always dull! He was a total disgrace... to the Army."

George laughed loudly. He wasn't feeling any pain either. Justina and Elizabeth eyed the men and said something to each other.

"And this man, George... Went straight arrow by the book... He had..."

Someone's hand was on his shoulder. He looked up.

"Care to dance?" It was Justina.

He pushed his chair back and tested his weight on his feet. He was still okay. The dance floor was crowded. He held her in his arms. She looked up at him.

"You still wear a lavender perfume—after all these years," was all he could muster.

"You remember." Her eyes flashed like black coals. "How could you remember so long?"

"That night in Berlin," he replied. "It seems like yesterday. The dinner. Our walk in the snow. Saying good-bye."

They were moving rhythmically, moving into the depth of the crowd. "I haven't been able to forget your kiss, either."

She watched his mouth and looked into his eyes. "I was in love with you. Did you not know it, Edward?"

He wasn't believing what she was saying. "No. You're kidding me!"

She pressed her arm tighter against his neck. "I would not joke about love." A wistful look came into her eyes. "I tried every way I knew how to see if you also love me. And then I give up and take taxi."

Blakely's face felt hot. Waves of disconnected thoughts rushed through his head. Nothing made sense. He pulled her close to him, touching her fine hair with his lips. Perhaps it was better not to talk, not to think right now. They moved and occasionally bumped into other dancers. Men were damned fools, he thought. Just damned fools. They understood nothing about women or about themselves. He would never have thought she loved him—ever! It had all been an innocent flirtation. How could she have been in love with him?

Yet, now that he thought about it, there were times when he had come to the museum that she had seemed extra friendly. He had taken her to lunch one afternoon, and they had lingered over a second glass of wine. Damn! He hadn't a clue. How could he have been so dense? And why was she telling him now?

When the music stopped, they pulled away from each other slightly. She looked up at him and said, "Thank you for the dance."

He took her back to her seat. The music started again. Another slow song with a Bouzouki beat. Elizabeth gave Blakely one of her wide-eyed, skeptical looks and said, "You dance very well, Edward."

He sat down beside her. "Sorry we can't dance, Elizabeth. Or else I'd take you for a spin."

"I suppose I've been spun sufficiently for one day."

"You're worried about Lou?" he whispered.

"Yes, I am very much worried," she whispered.

THE MINOTAUR

"We'll have to talk more about this privately."

"It's Homer," she replied, seeming to want to talk. "Louis got some message from Homer yesterday. Made him all upset! The man will not leave Louis alone!"

"You know what it was about?" Blakely didn't remember a message coming in for Wafford. He would check the communication log in the morning.

"No."

The music stopped. Jeremiah sipped his Coca Cola. Harry's yellow eyes gleamed with delight. He was drinking tskoudia, a distilled grape drink which burned hell out of your throat.

"How can you drink that stuff?"

"Only like green peppers and cayenne," said Harry, pulling his normal grimace into a larger one. He held his hand to his throat. "Your throat gets used to it."

As if to show his prowess, Harry tossed down another gulp. What could he say? Blakely got up and sat down next to Chris.

"Tomorrow," said Chris, holding his pipe in one hand and his wine glass in the other. "Tomorrow, we go to Hania and Maleme... See cemetery... Show Herr Grenz all his dead brothers..." He laughed at his charnel house humor.

Kralos nodded sleepily. He, too, was drinking tskoudia.

"You go with us, Kralos? You find anthropo... anthropologic discoveries there?" Chris asked.

Kralos nodded again. "No. Hopefully not tomorrow. I go soon enough to my grave. No," he nodded, "You go, not me." He laughed at his own joke and his head bobbed heavily.

Everybody except Jeremiah and Elizabeth was out of control. Blakely gave Jeremiah a cut-sign with his fingers across his throat. It was time they returned to the *Sea Siren*. Jeremiah went to settle the bill and to bring the van around.

Blakely got up. First night on Crete and almost too much fun. Back in dangerous waters—like it used to be when he was racing boats. Women came out of the woodwork. Married ones, too. One night stands. Some lasted a weekend. He felt agitated and slightly wet. Yeah. Too much stimulation for one night.

* * * * *

It was 0130 in the morning. He found Joachim Grenz standing at the bow smoking his pipe and gazing at the sky. Joachim turned his head and lifted his hand in greeting. He didn't speak. The sweet scent of Turkish tobacco filled the air. They both watched the comet for several minutes before Joachim took his pipe from his mouth and spoke.

"Do you suppose that people are like comets?"

"In what way?"

"They come into this world with fire and light, then disappear out of it for many years, and return in the future again?"

"You mean death is like dropping out of sight for awhile? Your spirit hasn't died. It just reappears some day?" He thought about Jim Wafford and how, after forty years, Louis Wafford, his son, came into his life.

"Ya," said Joachim without turning his head away from the comet. "I worked with a man in Siberia who believed such a thing. An Afghani he was."

"Do you believe that?"

"I believe God can do what he wants at any time. How else do you explain a son dying and being resurrected, then passing into Heaven with the promise He will come again to the earth?"

"So, you believe the fire of the soul always burns and gives out light?"

"Ya. Like the comet, the soul disappears for a while out of view, then returns again, perhaps many times."

"Never thought about that," said Blakely, suddenly recalling a story Elizabeth had told him about Persephone, visiting the dead of the underworld in winter, then reappearing in the forms of flowers and leaves in spring, saddened by her own experience yet still beautiful. "Do you suppose we could have breakfast together tomorrow, Joachim?"

The old German turned to study Blakely.

"Oh, nothing serious." He laid a hand on Joachim's shoulder. "I thought we might go over some of your memories of Heinrich. What he did here on Crete. What he was like. Would that be okay?"

"Ya. That would be okay," replied Joachim, relaxing again. He tapped his pipe on the bow rail. "What time would we eat?"

"How 'bout 0600 hours in my cabin?"

"That will be fine." The old man leaned on his cane.

"Anything special for breakfast?"

"Oatmeal and coffee for me, please," Joachim replied, turning back to the stars.

"I'll see that its ready. Good night Joachim."

"Good night."

He left the old man standing alone on deck. Perhaps all of us come back, like he said, the same, yet different. Comet Hyakutake was a good example; the same comet, yet older than when last seen. Justina, like Persephone, had kissed him in the dead of winter forty years ago and returned in spring, older and the same, yet different, telling him she once loved him. And there was Elizabeth, who wanted to believe she was Ariadne—and she might be. Who knows? Elizabeth likened him to Theseus. Maybe somehow he was Theseus who had returned to earth to slay a Minotaur. And maybe the Minotaur, itself, was the same, yet different, too.

How would you know what a modern Minotaur looked like? He supposed you would simply know, just like that German woman, Stephanie, recognized a star when she saw one. The Ouzo and wine had affected him. He wondered what Jenny might be doing tonight. Or was it morning in California? He couldn't figure it out. It didn't matter.

CHAPTER 4

Homework

Harry knocked twice and automatically opened the hatch. Blakely glanced at the computer monitor. Harry was always on time; it was 0555 hours. He carried the tray on the fingertips of his left hand.

"How's your throat this morning, Harry?"

Harry set the tray on the table. "Fine."

His hand went involuntarily to his throat. His voice sounded like a frog's. Harry set out a bowl of sliced Kiwi fruit.

"How come you're so crazy about Kiwis, Harry?"

Harry arranged the silver, cloth napkins, cereal, and juice. He scratched his chest. "I don't know," he said sheepishly in his broken voice. "Guess I like them 'cause they're so different from all the rest."

"Makes sense. Thanks Harry. You can leave the hatch open. Joachim will be coming shortly." The kiwi was like Harry—very different. Yeah. Harry's own symbol of himself. Only difference was they were hairy little devils. Harry was an unhairy little devil.

Joachim stood in the hatchway.

"Come on in, Joachim. Have a seat."

He was a specter of black and white. Black pants and turtle neck sweater. Black headband. White beard. He propped his cane against the bulkhead and sat down across from Blakely.

"Nice quarters," said Joachim, eyeing the room from behind heavy wrinkles. The old man reached for the carafe of milk and poured some over the oatmeal. "When I shovel coal on boat, I have narrow berth." He held his hands apart to show the width. "Only mattress. No pillow or blanket."

"How did you manage not to get cold?"

Joachim's mouth gaped in a toothless grin. "I sleep next to warm boiler. When I get chill, I put great coat over me. Live very simply."

Blakely poured them coffee from the thermos pitcher. He poured milk over the cereal and both began to eat. The spoon looked small in Joachim's fist. He ate his oatmeal steadily until it was finished. Then, he tilted the bowl and spooned out the remaining milk. He sat back. "Das gut!" he exclaimed.

Where do you begin, Blakely mused. You begin with his passions, he concluded. He sipped the coffee. "You remember, Joachim, the other night? We spoke of Katrin."

"Katrin... Ya. Katrin von Shiller. Heinrich never marry her!"

"Yeah. You dated her before Heinrich?"

"Ya! She very beautiful. I become in love. Puppy love." He laughed. "I was a young puppy then."

"And later, you were in love with Heinrich's sister, Estel?"

"Ya. We love one another, but cannot marry."

"And why was that?"

"She come from aristocratic family." He fingered the handle on the coffee mug. "I come from merchant class. My father was a shopkeeper."

"So you could never marry?"

"Nein. Impossible."

"Were you ever in love again?"

The old man stiffened and reached into his pants pocket and pulled out his tobacco pouch and pipe. "No. I have only two women I love in my life. First Katrin, then Estel."

"You saw Estel in 1944? I believe you saw her put the piece of relic in a suitcase?"

The old man looked up at the ceiling, moving his mouth as he did so without saying anything. "September, 1944 it was. Ya."

"How can you be sure it wasn't July or August?"

He raised his eyes again and moved his mouth noiselessly. "Ya, September, it was."

"How do you remember?"

"My verses," said Joachim. He stuffed his pipe with tobacco and zipped the pouch. Blakely recalled Wafford mentioning Joachim used rhymes to remember.

"Can you tell me a verse?"

"Ya." The old man looked skyward again and recited, *"To Vienna went I to see my love, before to Ukraine I go, fifteen September of forty-four it was, that I last of Estel know."*

Joachim sat a moment and then lit his pipe.

"That's very nice, Joachim. Do you have verses about Heinrich?"

"Yavoll. Several."

"Can you recall any from 1944?"

He looked up again and mouthed unspoken words. "Ya. Heinrich von Etter, my comrade in arms, fell at Kastelli and broke his leg; recouping high above the farms, two months he lay without duty to undertake."

"When did that happen, Joachim?"

"Summer? I know it was in 1944, sometime."

"So Heinrich was in a hospital?"

"Ya! He tell me in letter. At Kastelli."

"Can you take me to it?"

"No. I don't remember hospital here. Only hospitals I remember were in Hania, Souda and Rethimnon."

The old man picked up the mug of coffee and put it down again. He looked up and began a silent recitation. "I remember another."

He held up his pipe as a baton and marked the syllables as he spoke them. *"Heinrich from the tower fell, the scaffold failed to hold, on furlough did he tell, of feeling death's hand cold."*

"This one about the tower..."

"Ya?"

"What kind of tower?"

"Ach so. I don't remember. Guard? Observation? I do not recall."

"Could it be a control tower for an airfield?"

"I do not know." Joachim wiped a bead of milk from his beard and put the napkin across his bowl.

"You mention furlough. Where was this?"

"Vienna. Ya. I meet Heinrich Vienna. Last time all of us together."

"When?"

"March 31, 1944. I am sure I remember."

"How are you sure?"

"Haydn's birthday. Heinrich, Katrin, Estel and I attend benefit concert. A string quartet." His eyes closed, and he began to wave his pipe back and forth. "I still hear the music. Wonderful!" He began to hum softly. Blakely silently filled in the words, *Deutschland, Deutschland Uber Alles...*

"The Nazis anthem."

Joachim opened his eyes abruptly and snapped, "First Haydn's music. Der Furher borrowed it. The music belong always first to Hayden and Austria."

Joachim still had some fire left in him.

"Could you do something for me?"

Joachim, still tense, replied. "Ya."

Blakely went over to his desk and opened a drawer. He removed a pocket-sized notebook and pencil. He laid them in front of Joachim.

"I'd like you to jot down any verses you remember about Heinrich. Tomorrow, we can have breakfast again. That suit?"

"Ya. Good! I like eating here with you."

"One more thing, just out of curiosity. Were you at Ploesti when the American bombers made that daylight raid in 1943?"

Joachim blinked. "Nein. I was lucky! I was in Bucharest on furlough."

"Glad to know that."

The old man stood up, shook Blakely's hand warmly, and

shuffled out the door using his cane for support. The monitor said it was 0715. He called the communication center.

"Tobok!"

"Gregor, this is Ed. I'd like to come by and take a look at the communications log."

"Very good, sir. The hatch will be open."

He strode past the dining room where Chris sat nursing a mug of coffee and a hangover. He looked haggard. Jeremiah was splicing videotape.

"You won't believe how photogenic Auntie Elizabeth is on video, skipper," said Jeremiah, sounding like a kid who had discovered a new starlet.

"Yeah. I'd believe it. Your aunt is a stunning woman."

The comm center hatch was open. No codes or voice communications going. Gregor sat in his swivel chair. There was a slight smell of vegetable soup in the room. "Do you eat in here, Gregor?"

"Sometimes. Harry brings me snacks."

"Soup?"

Gregor's eyes widened. "No. I don't care for it, actually."

The guy was putting on more weight around the middle. Too little exercise. A forty-five year old man can't sit around and eat and not expect to get out of shape.

"I suggest you use the fan. Clear the air in here. I want you to report to Leo for two hours every day, Gregor. You need to get some exercise."

Tobok looked at Blakely like he was crazy.

"I mean it. You need to do something physical instead of sitting here day and night. Okay?"

Tobok looked down. "If you say so, skipper."

"Yeah, I say so." Blakely picked up the communications log print-out. "Does this log include all communications sent and received during the past two days?"

"More than that," he replied. "All of our communications since we left Gulfport are there." He hesitated. "Did I do something wrong, Ed?"

Blakely ran his finger down the message entry dates. "You are part of my crew, Gregor. I've been telling you to get more sleep and not hang out night after night in here. You need a change of routine."

His finger stopped on the entries for yesterday. Elizabeth said Wafford received a message from McCloud. Nothing listed to or from either McCloud or Wafford.

"Thanks, Gregor. Check in with Leo every day at noon, starting today. Tell Jeremiah to take over for you while you're on exercise duty."

"Yes, sir." He left the room. Glad to get out into fresh air. It was body odor. The guy's not taking care of himself. He'll put Leo on Gregor's case. Shape the guy up before he rots! He poked his head in Jeremiah's studio. An idea was forming in Blakely's head.

"Can I see you in my cabin in five minutes?"

Jeremiah's Magic smile evaporated. "Sure, skip. I can come right now."

"Good."

The two men walked without words to Blakely's quarters.

"Have a seat. Anything to eat or drink?" Blakely noted that Harry had cleared the breakfast dishes.

"No. I just ate."

Blakely sat down across from him and crossed his legs. "I don't know quite how to say this..."

Jeremiah pushed his glasses up on his nose, like he was expecting worst news.

"I realize you are Lou and Elizabeth's nephew. What I'm about to ask you depends on whether I have your complete trust."

Jeremiah blinked his eyes at Blakely. He gave a weak nod. "Okay."

"What we talk about won't go further than the two of us?"

Jeremiah bit his lower lip. "No, sir."

"Even something that could involve your uncle?"

Jeremiah folded his hands together on the table. "I'm not sure I follow you, Ed." He tilted his head. "How would it involve him?"

Blakely scratched his head. "I don't really know. Just a gut feeling Gregor and Lou may be part of some clandestine deal. If that were the case, where would you stand?"

Jeremiah looked at the back of his right hand, then at his left. "You mean, if Uncle Lou and Gregor were into criminal stuff?"

"Yeah."

"I suppose I'd try to protect Auntie Elizabeth. I wouldn't want any part of some criminal thing. It would mess me up in television. I'd stand with you, Ed. I've trusted you with my life at sea. You got us through that storm. I trust what you say."

"Okay." Blakely looked across at the monitor. "I'll tell you my concerns. There are messages coming in and going out which are not recorded on Tobok's log."

"Not cool!"

"Yesterday, according to your aunt, McCloud sent a message to Lou. It doesn't appear on the log. I just checked. Gregor assures me every message sent and received since we came aboard is on that log. Gregor is either lying or else Lou is sending and receiving his own messages without Gregor knowing it."

"H'm!" Jeremiah leaned forward, putting his brown hands together.

"Now, that doesn't mean there's underhanded activity. It could all be confidential business between McCloud and Lou—totally above board. But why the deceit?"

"Yeah. It's like, Gregor locks himself in and sends and receives stuff all the time. I can see it, skip. Since we entered the Med, Gregor's been all to himself. A nice, cool guy and all, but not the same. So what is it you want me to do?"

"I'm thinking there is another communications level Gregor's using, which we can't access. That's where you can help."

Jeremiah sat up and thrust his hands out. "I'm not into hacking! I couldn't do Gregor's thing."

"No. I want you to use your long suit. You're the video expert. Could you mount a camera inside the comm room?"

The Magic reappeared across Jeremiah's face. "You mean a hidden camera?"

"Yeah."

"I can go one better. I've got an ultra-mini-cam with two lenses: one for wide angle and one that is up close and personal. Makes a split screen image."

"What about sound? I'd like to hear some of these conversations he claims to have with Ham buddies."

"If I can connect directly back to my studio, I can have it in stereo."

"How long could you record at any one time?"

"Continuously."

"Can you put it where Gregor won't find it?"

"I'd have to look over the possibilities. All those wall and ceiling insulation panels are independently fastened. Once I see where the camera needs to be, I can take a panel from my own studio and experiment. Then, all I have to do is exchange panels and run the connecting wire and cable."

"How long are we talking about?"

"To install and check out?"

"Yeah."

Jeremiah gulped and brought a slender brown finger to his lips. "Twelve hours? Fifteen? Give me fifteen after I check out the center."

"Tobok is assigned exercise duty with Leo this afternoon. I've ordered Tobok to have you cover the comm room. You'll have two hours to figure it out."

"Cool! What will we do with the recordings?"

"That's another challenge. If he's using special access, I want you to figure out Tobok's system and show me how it works. When you hear him saying something suspicious over the telephone or radio, tell me immediately. And you promise me that you'll say nothing about this to anyone?"

Jeremiah's face was still. "Yes, sir. You have my word on that!"

"I'm counting on you. You're the only man on board who can

do this without raising suspicions. Once you have a plan, let me know. Then, we'll find a time to install the camera."

"You've got it."

Jeremiah uncrossed his sneakered foot and stood up. He stretched, touching the ceiling with his hands. "Guess I knew something different was coming down. Sketchy stuff. I sorta felt it, you know?"

"Yeah. Same here."

Jeremiah left the cabin. Blakely threw one leg up on the bunk. Once you say your mind, you can't take it back. He had to take a risk, and Jeremiah was his best shot. What was it Christ said in Matthew? Turning relative against relative? Sons against parents? How did Jeremiah know Blakely wasn't using him for some bad purpose? Hell, secretly taping private communications might be illegal for all he knew. Not cool, as Jeremiah would say, but necessary. There was a light tapping on the hatch.

"Come in!"

Justina, wearing a blue jogging suit, came in and closed the hatch.

"Good morning."

Blakely got up out of his chair. "Morning. Have a seat." He beckoned her to the one already warmed by Joachim and Jeremiah. How about that? Three "J" persons sitting in the same seat today.

She looked anxious. "Why are you smirking, Edward?"

"Just thought of something silly. Sorry. What's happening?"

"I came to apologize for last night."

"How so? I don't remember anything you need to apologize for."

"Ya. I should never have told you. I am sorry."

He sat down. "In all honesty, I was shocked, Justina. You were truly in love with me?"

"From the first time you came to the museum. Do you remember?"

"Yes. It was before I met Chris."

"Ya. I took one look at you and was smitten! You were standing at my desk. I look up. There you were, reminding me of the American flyer, Lindbergh. Tall, blond hair, handsome. You had a shy confidence about you."

She got that seductive look in her eyes he remembered. He felt awkward.

"You were dating Chris then. How long had you been going with him?"

"Seven months, I think. Colonel Wafford sent him to me, you know."

"Yeah. Jim Wafford strikes again! Then he sends me in to check out what Chris had already reported."

"Ya." Justina shifted in the chair and crossed her legs. "Will you forget what I told you, Edward?"

"I can't forget it, but I won't tell a soul."

She brought her hand to her lips. "You don't have to answer this..." She touched her hair. Her face flushed. "Did you ever love me, Edward? Even a little?"

Her foot began to rock gently. Wasn't that what he had hoped for? He had felt her hand touching the side of his face for forty years.

"More than a little. After seeing you off that night in the snow, I went back to the Kafe and sat there thinking about you. God, I envied Chris. Still, I felt awful about kissing another guy's fiancé."

She glanced at the porthole. Age lines crinkled the skin around her eyes and mouth and beneath her chin. Her wedge cut did not belie her age, yet her slender neck was still smooth and alluring. A few crisscross creases showed above her collar. She held her hands in her lap. She sat there in silence for a time, avoiding his eyes. Her head turned slowly toward him and her face softened wanly.

"Is it so awful, Edward, to imagine what might have been?"

"No. I understand. I'm sorry, Justina."

"Ya. Me, too."

She got up and left him sitting there. As lovely as Justina had been in the snow that night, he couldn't fathom marrying her, then or now. It simply wasn't in his wildest fantasies of her. Had he married a German back then, it would have been Katrin, despite her age. Katrin he might have loved forever. Justina had been another woman Katrin would describe as being in love with for love's sake. Justina's passions were her manuscripts and relics; she was landlocked in a world of museum shelves and dusty artifacts. His was fast boats and the open sea. It never would have worked.

CHAPTER 5

The Return

Leo entered the pilot house where Tony was on watch and Blakely sat in the captain's chair. "Jeremiah said you wanted to see me, Ed?"

"Yeah. I want you to set up an exercise and diet program for Gregor. He's overweight and not taking proper care of himself. Take him for a jog every day. Get him good and sweaty so he'll shower. See that he gets sleep. Give Harry a list of foods and drinks the guy can have. No snacks. No alcohol. Weigh him in and keep a chart."

Leo stood before Blakely with muscled arms crossed. "What's with you, Ed? He's too old to join the marines."

"Needs shaping up is all. I want you to start today. Take a long walk. Give him two hours of your time. If he doesn't have proper jogging equipment, take him ashore and buy him some. One hour working out. The second hour can be maintenance jobs. Give me your schedule so I know where I can find him."

Leo winced. "Maintenance jobs?"

"Yeah. Like cleaning metal, repainting. Whatever will make the guy sweat. Put him in the bosun's chair. Those masts and cowls could stand cleaning and painting."

Tony whistled. "What'd he do to get on your list, Eddie?"

"Just need to put him on a short leash for a while. Make him feel he's part of our team instead of a solitary nerd. I want to see him doing a ten minute mile by the end of the second week."

"I'm not sure who's being punished, him or me," groused Leo, looking down at his jogging shoes. "How long do I have to work with him?"

"Until further notice. Can you arrange it between 1200 and 1400 hours every day?"

"I guess so. I prefer working out first thing in the morning."

"I'd appreciate your changing it to noon. Jeremiah will cover the comm center. Tell Harry not to feed Gregor lunch until after 1400 hours. Give him a chance to get hungry."

"So be it." Leo left the pilot house. He was ticked off. Blakely couldn't blame him.

"It's pornography, ain't it?"

"What?"

"He's addicted to cybersex, ain't he? Yer trying to cure him?"

Blakely pretended not to understand. "Leo? Nah!"

"I'm talking 'bout Tobok, Eddie. Like I said, the man's addicted."

"I would keep it hush, hush," Blakely whispered.

Tony's dark face looked empty. "Why?"

"Might agitate the women. Know what I mean?" He made a circle with his finger in the air.

Tony ran his hand across the dark stubble on his chin. "Yeah. I see yer point. The women could get scared of him. I'll keep it quiet."

Blakely went out on deck. It was 0945 hours. The Cunninghams, Joachim and Elizabeth were at the gangway waiting for Leo to man the launch. A surprisingly late start for Professor Straight Arrow.

"Well, how are the party animals this morning?"

"You're the one to talk," replied Chris with a smirk. "Dancing with all the ladies. I assumed you were still asleep."

"Up at the crack of dawn." He looked Chris up and down. "You are one sharp explorer this morning, Dr. Cunningham!" Chris wore a khaki outfit and one of those English slouch hats. Justina bit her lip and looked away.

"Are you out for some air, Elizabeth, or are you going on the expedition with these archeologists?"

"Justina was kind enough to invite me along. We're going to visit the German memorial and cemetery."

Chris said, "Thought we'd go to the cemetery, and then to Hania for a look around. There are Minoan ruins in the old fortress there—another kastelli. Could be coincidental. From what Dr. Neapolis told us, the fortress was heavily bombed by the Germans. Who knows? Perhaps Heinrich visited the ruins and discovered the relic lying about. I don't give us much hope of finding a cache of jewels, however."

"Why?"

"Following the war, archeologists sifted the ruins thoroughly. All historic objects have been recovered."

"I see." It sounded like another goose chase.

"Neapolis tells me that from the ruins, reference points such as mosques, churches, and the old light house are easily identifiable. It won't take us long to see if we are on target." He paused and puffed on his pipe. "I take it you haven't changed your mind?"

"No. I called George Kralos. I'm meeting him at 1100 hours." Blakely nodded toward the quay.

"Relative to Herr Grenz's verses, you mean?"

"Yeah."

"Appreciate your help. Good luck!"

Blakely returned to his cabin with a mug of coffee and switched on the computer. One message. It was from Jenny. "Dear Ed. I did it! We closed on the three-way yesterday. I deposited a six figure cashier's check. Also closed on a triplex in Huntington Beach. I'm rich again! Am shopping for the house on Balboa today! Wish you were here to celebrate! I might come to Crete for a brief visit!!! What do you think? Jen."

He sat back and reread her message. If he lived as long as Methuselah, he'd never understand women. It was over but not over. Amazing how a real estate sale can change Jenny from a cutthroat broker into a sex-starved kitten. Happened every time! He had to reply with congratulations. Then what? After last night, he felt as horny as he had in a long time. She was inviting herself over for a weekend of lovemaking.

He sat up and punched in a two fingered reply. "Dear Jen. Congratulations! You deserve seven figures for the work you put into it! We hope to be at Iraklion by tomorrow night. Let me know your plans. Again, congratulations! You did it! Ed."

He hit the fax send key and then the screen saver. His message would let her decide what she wanted to do. Put the ball in her court. His lust was beginning to focus again on the delights of Jenny—Jenny of the sweet stuff.

He keyed back into the message display and ordered a dozen roses from Pettigrew's in Carona del Mar to be sent to Jenny's office. He requested the card be 'To Jen from Bumper—with congratulations and love'.

*****

Blakely sat in the wire chair in front of the taverna watching the busy harbor. The *Sea Siren* continued to draw crowds of onlookers. Fishermen rowed their dories close-by for inspection. The lower fore-topsail billowed in the morning breeze. The round labyrinth logo looked great. He had gotten used to it. George Kralos appeared with an older man. Blakely stood up and greeted them.

"Sorry I am late, Edward. Nikos Patera, Edward Blakely."

"Nice to meet you, Nikos." They shook hands. "No problem, George. I just arrived. Have a seat." Kralos signaled the man in the taverna. He brought out cups of Turkish coffee.

Kralos said, "You wanted someone who knows hospitals in the area. Dr. Patera was director of surgery many years in Hania. He also was physician to Cretan resistance during the war."

The doctor looked like an old eagle, wide-eyed, bony hands, and hunched over.

"I'm trying to locate a place where a German soldier in 1944 might have recuperated from a fractured leg. Mr. Grenz describes the place as high above the farms at Kastelli. It sounds like it would be located in hills or mountains above here."

Dr. Patera listened closely. "No hospital at that time in these mountains. Perhaps he refers to a rest camp. The Nazis had several of those in mountains throughout Crete."

"Can you think of any in particular?"

"Not around Kastelli. As I recall, the rehabilitation centers were in monasteries. Otherwise, they weren't safe from resistance attacks."

"Such as?"

"Such as Hania, Rethimnon, and Iraklion. One would look, I suppose, at rest camps in these vicinities."

Kralos added milk to his coffee. He said, "Dr. Cunningham and you speak of kastelli. There are many here. That could be significant."

"How, George? I do realize kastelli means castle. In fact, Chris and Justina are checking out the kastelli in the old part of Hania."

"Yes. Exactly. I mention yesterday the unlikelihood of finding a wooden relic in this part of Crete. Could it be that this man found the relic at another kastelli?"

Blakely fidgeted and looked at the brown mud-like coffee. "It is beginning to look that way."

Dr. Patera began to laugh. "There are many kastelli on Crete. However, I do not believe your friends find any relic at Hania's kastelli. It was devastated by the Nazis. There was no rest camp or hospital at Kydonia—the name we call kastelli there."

"Yes, I agree with Nikos." said Kralos, "I don't see Hania as a likely place to find hidden jewels and artifacts. Every person search there after war."

Dr. Patera added, "One finds kastelli either along the shore protecting harbors such as this one, or high in the mountains, protecting roads and mountain passes."

"So you are suggesting," said Blakely, "that we should be looking for a castle in the mountains?"

"Perhaps," replied Kralos. "Who is to say? It would be logical to situate a recuperation center in a castle, no?"

"Yeah. That would be an ideal place."

"Your chances would improve greatly in central and eastern Crete."

"Why?"

Kralos responded. "More activity of Venetians, Saracens, Turks, Christians—all the invaders who built fortresses. There are such kastelli scattered throughout the mountains to the east."

Blakely sipped the bitter coffee. Three elements to build a profile: a hospital in a castle overlooking farms. He listened as Kralos and Patera discussed the possibilities of one kastelli over another. They could not decide where best to begin the search.

"Tell me, George," said Blakely, "are these castles listed on computer files?"

"Of course! I am certain of it. If not through the archeological museum in Iraklion, then through large travel agencies there. You would find all the famous castles on tour maps, too."

Patera slapped his hand lightly against the table and said, "Pediadas!"

"What?"

"There is a mountain village called Kastelli in the district of Pediadas" Patera explained. "A very old fortress village. The Nazis built an airfield above it. However, there is no castle left; only houses and shops."

Blakely leaned toward the old physician. "You know the place?"

"I visit some years ago. During war, great atrocities of villagers committed there."

"Yeah?"

"Yes. Retaliation for our resistance fighters killing Nazis pilots. I believe Resistance killed an SS leader there."

"And where is this?"

"Southeast of Knossos."

Blakely jotted down the information on a paper napkin. "Anything more you can add?"

Patera tossed down the last coffee. "The airfield is now a cadet

THE MINOTAUR   59

training base, I believe."

"I know the village," said Kralos. "A lovely view. One looks across the treetops."

"At farms?"

"Other mountains. Peasant huts. Perhaps tiny farms."

"Any other suggestions?"

The two men sat mute.

Blakely pushed the chair back and stood up. "Gentlemen, you've been very helpful. Thank you, Dr. Patera, for coming down here to talk with me."

They shook hands. Patera reached into his pocket. "Here is my card in the event you have other questions."

"Thanks. Sorry I can't stay for lunch. I have another appointment."

"We understand. Hérete! (Good-bye!)"

"Hérete!"

He left a wad of drachmas on the table and hurried to the quay. Leo was waiting in the launch. A crowd of locals watched as he boarded and sat down.

"Just about time for your workout, Leo," said Blakely. Leo looked away and shoved the launch into gear. The sudden lurch nearly flipped Blakely into the water. Some of the onlookers were clapping as Leo accelerated.

"For what it's worth," shouted Blakely over the engine noise, "I've asked Tony to give you the next three nights off. At least one will be in Iraklion."

"My payback?"

"Your payback. You have another three nights coming when you get Tobok running a ten minute mile."

Leo grinned. "I think we can do that. Thanks, skipper! Yeah, Gregor's going to be running like hell the next two weeks."

* * * * *

Jeremiah got up and took his glasses off. He cleaned them with a lens wipe and removed his white cloth gloves. The guy was meticulous about his work and himself. Always wore a denim shirt and jeans and high top black and white sneakers. His shirt had a rainbow across the breast pocket. The wall clock said it was 1215 hours. Gregor was ashore. Jeremiah must have read his thoughts.

"Would you like to see the camera?"

"Sure."

Jeremiah opened a drawer of his work bench. He removed a camera from an insulated nylon pouch and handed it to Blakely. The device was smaller than a baseball, egg-shaped, with a mounting bracket. Used mainly for industrial purposes, he supposed.

"Only problem is, once it is installed," Jeremiah said, "what it sees is what you get."

"You have to pre-set it?"

"Yes. It doesn't have the automatic features of a larger camera."

The thing weighed less than baseball. Two tiny lenses extruded like gun barrels from the body. He handed it back to Jeremiah who replaced it in its container and shoved the drawer closed.

"See these sound panels?"

"Yeah."

"I can make some of the holes a little wider on one of them and mount the camera behind it."

"Okay. Why don't we go next door and see what you have to contend with?"

Blakely unlocked the hatch. Tropical fish swam across the screen saver on the main monitor. Five other monitors were black. Jeremiah shoved his hands into his jeans and looked around. "Skip, could you sit in Gregor's chair and put your hands on the keyboard?"

"Sure." Blakely sat down, pulled out the keyboard, and locked it in position. He placed his hands lightly on the keys. They were satin smooth from Tobok's use. He watched Jeremiah's reflection in the dark monitor as he moved about, checking different panels and studying the angles. "I'll need my step-stool and viewer," he said, leaving the comm center for a few seconds. He returned and got up behind Blakely and looked through the viewer. "Getting a pretty good idea of where I need to put it," he mumbled. "Thanks, skip. I'm finished."

Jeremiah stepped off the stool. "This wall panel above the hatch has the perfect angle. What I'll do is simulate keyboard, chair, light, and distances over in my studio. I can mount the camera there and work on it 'til I get it right."

"Very good. Could you finish in two days?"

Jeremiah cracked a Super Magic smile and hitched up his pants. "Hey, man! How come you give me so much time?"

"That be enough?"

He shrugged. "I s'pose."

* * * * *

The clock on the monitor read 1547 hours. Tobok must have showered and finished lunch by now. Blakely rang the comm center.

"Tobok here."

Blakely held the phone in the crook of his arm while punching up the message screen.

"Mr. Tobok! How was your exercise?"

There was a pause. "It was okay. We walked to an interesting place down the beach."

"I've got a project for you. Five descriptors in priority order. I want you to come up with a list of castles on Crete which, number one, are located in mountains; number two, have a World War II airfield nearby, number three, have a hospital or medical clinic in close proximity; and number four, be near Minoan ruins. Got that?"

"Yes. What's the fifth?"

"Towns, villages, and castles called Kastelli, as in Kastelli-Kissamou."

"Got it. Have any sources of information?"

"Start with the larger travel agencies in Iraklion. Check Internet—whatever."

"Is that it?"

"One more project. I want you to provide me a list of German war document centers on the island such as museums, private collections, commercial or what. There's gotta be a document which identifies where Heinrich von Etter was assigned."

"What about German archives?"

"The professor's already checked German, Greek and American war archives on computer. All they show is headquarters, Crete. No specifics. I suggest you begin locally—on the island."

"Okay."

"Once you have a lead, check it out by phone. Find out what types of stuff they have. No use wasting our time on some guy who collects swastika arm bands and the like."

"What if they speak only Greek?"

"Get Tony to help you."

"Okay. I'll get started. When do you need the info?"

"ASAP."

Blakely hung up and began composing a message to Claudia. There was a knock on the hatch. "Come in!"

Lou Wafford stepped into the cabin with a drink in his hand. He looked like a shipwrecked sailor. His face was terribly windburned. His eyes were puffed, and he was unshaven. "Last time I go anywhere with Andy. Sombitch near killed us."

He limped across the room and slumped into the plush chair. From the sound of his voice, the drink may have been his second or third, and it was only 1600 hours.

"Mind if I take these shoes off? I've got blisters the size of quarters."

"Have Leo look at them."

Wafford pulled off shoes and bloody socks. He drew his left foot up and examined its bottom. It was a mass of broken blisters and raw meat. He held his glass out. "How 'bout joining me?"

"No, thanks."

He flexed his hand and rubbed his wrist. His fingers were cut and bruised. "Took us eight damned hours to go down into that Say-maria Gorge."

"What made you decide to go there? You left before daylight."

He took a sizable swig of whiskey. "Thought we caused you

THE MINOTAUR 63

fellas enough trouble. Wanted to keep outa the way." He paused and tapped his fingers on the chair arm. "Guess I didn't want to be around when the professor and Miss Justina left out."

"They're staying—at least for now."

"Oh?" Wafford looked up, then back at his foot. "How'd it go yesterday?"

"We eliminated several possibilities. Went to a Minoan ruin where Joachim and Heinrich had constructed a gun emplacement over on the west coast."

"Do any good?"

Blakely didn't want to be pressed to say no. "As I say, we eliminated places."

Wafford's eyes flicked around the room nervously. "Where's everybody?"

" Joachim, Chris, Justina and Elizabeth went to Maleme and Hania today."

"That where ole Joachim parachuted?"

"No. He jumped at Rethimnon. The decisive battle was fought at Maleme, though. The German dead are buried there. Should bring back plenty of memories for Joachim."

Lou sipped his drink. "How come you didn't go?"

"I had other things to check out."

"You say Elizabeth went with the professor?"

"Yeah."

Wafford ran the side of the glass along his forehead, trying to cool it. He seemed edgy and undone.

"You want a wet towel?"

"Naw." His eyes shifted to Blakely's. "What did Elizabeth do yesterday?"

"I sent her ashore with Harry and Jeremiah. They had a ball."

"Guess you know she's not speaking to me. Did she say anything?"

"No. What happened?"

"Same old business. She doesn't cotton to my associates." The swelling around his eyes made him grotesque.

"Marchese?"

"Andy, Homer, Gresh. All of 'em. Sez they're racists."

"Aren't they?"

Wafford drummed his fingers. "You and I've been through this. You know how I stand. I depend on 'em. It's more than them, though..." He looked at his bare feet. "It's been building up. Elizabeth and me don't see eye to eye on a lot of things." He took a large gulp of whiskey and swallowed. "Don't know I ever shared or not. Elizabeth and I haven't been together for 'bout ten years—if you understand what I'm say'n."

Maybe Wafford and Chris ought to switch partners awhile. Good for everybody's health. "How come?"

"A long story. I have to keep an eye out." He paused, and finished off his drink. "Can you have Harry bring me some ice and Jack Daniels?"

He sensed Wafford was going to get ugly drunk. He hadn't seen this side of him before—and he didn't want to.

"You don't want to get cleaned up first?"

"Naw! I'll fix up later. Just need a drink is all."

Blakely rang Harry and asked him to bring another glass, some ice, and bottles of scotch and whiskey. He punched the save key and screen saver on the computer and turned back to Wafford. Looks like it will be a long afternoon. "So, how come you have to keep an eye on Elizabeth?"

Wafford crunched ice. "She plays around on me."

"Yeah?" The idea of a black paraplegic woman confined to a wheel chair playing around on her white husband seemed ludicrous. Besides, Blakely had gotten to know Elizabeth and had the highest respect for her character.

"She had an affair ten years ago."

"I can't imagine her doing it."

"I finally hired a private investigator. Got pictures of her and this black man sitting on a balcony of a hotel down in Houston."

"Yeah?" Blakely didn't believe it. There had to be some reasonable explanation. Elizabeth was probably meeting with another mythologist or university professor.

Harry knocked twice and entered. He set the two bottles and ice on the table and placed the new glass next to Blakely's arm.

"Thanks, Harry." He waited until the hatch closed. "So how long did the affair go on?"

"I haven't one iota. Coulda been years. This man she went to Houston with—he kinda left her after that."

"There were others?"

"Never caught her..." He made himself another drink. "Musta been others by and by."

Blakely got up and made himself a light scotch and water. "Have you confronted her?"

Wafford stirred his drink. His puffed face looked defeated. "Naw. Saw no reason in it. Only lead to a bigger mess. Divorce is out of the question. Some ways, I still love her."

"Hell, Lou, you've got to talk it out! It's not fair to either of you. Ten years of deprivation? That's longer than some guys get for killing somebody."

Wafford touched the side of his face with the glass.

"So, what do you do for sex?"

Wafford blinked at him and took another large swig. "Lots of good look'n women for hire. I have one whenever I need to." He looked down at the carpet and mumbled, "Sometimes two or three."

"At a time?" Blakely could hardly believe this.

Wafford tapped on the chair arm and tried a hangdog grin. "You don't think I can handle three at a time?"

"Probably four. How would I know?" He couldn't figure why he was dumping all this on him. "You mentioned divorce is out of the question. Why?"

Wafford drew in a large breath and sighed. "Money. No way I could liquidate enough holdings to pay her what she'd want. And she's content to stay in the relationship. Elizabeth enjoys every luxury money can afford. She's happy."

Blakely was stunned. Elizabeth was anything but happy. He

sipped his scotch. There was an unpleasant aftertaste. He set the glass down. "I guess I'm wondering why you are telling me all this? Do you need me to help in some way?"

Wafford was looking at the bottom of his foot again. "I'm not sure why I came in here. Just feeling low's all." He paused without looking up. "Sometimes when I watch you and Elizabeth up in the pilot house carrying on, I wish I was more like you, Ed. You have a way of making women come alive. You bring out the best in Elizabeth. I don't know what it is..." He wiped across his mouth. "I noticed how Miss Justina looks at you, too. Women seem attracted natural to you."

He dropped his foot and took another slug of whiskey. He looked keenly at Blakely.

Blakely waited. Nothing. "Yeah? So?"

"You're not having sex with Elizabeth, are you, Ed?"

So that is what was behind this. His accusation didn't even make him angry. It was preposterous. He replied in a soft voice. "I can tell you this. If I want to take Elizabeth to bed, I'll sure as hell come and tell you before I do it. Is that what you want to hear?"

Wafford looked down at his lap and shook his head. "Guess I don't know what I want." He gave another sigh. A tear trickled down his red face.

"I don't want anything to come between us, Lou. I hope you'll tell me, if there's a way I can help you. Let's be clear with each other."

Wafford was shaking his head from side to side. "Nothin's clear, Ed, don't you see that? Nothin in life is clear—not even between you and me."

Wafford waved him away with his hand, adding, "And it can never be clear. Take that from a pro in such matters."

What was he saying? Was it a warning? Wafford's intoxication was making him belligerent. His voice was low and raspy. "Too much mess, Ed. Just too much mess."

Wafford was trying to tell him something. "What's too much mess? Can you tell me?"

THE MINOTAUR   67

His "no" was barely audible. Whatever was bugging him was lodged somewhere deep inside him.

"Sure you don't want to talk about it?"

"I said too much already."

"Let's get you cleaned up before Elizabeth gets back."

Blakely picked up the phone. "Leo? Can you check on Mr. Wafford's feet in a few minutes? He's going to take a shower. Got some bad blisters."

"His cabin or in the dispensary?"

"His cabin. And by the way, how'd the exercise go today?"

"Not bad. I think Gregor sees you have his interest at heart—that he's not being punished. We walked four miles along the coast."

"Good. That's exactly what I hoped would happen. Talk with you later."

"Okay."

Blakely hung up the phone. "Come on, Lou! Let's get you to your cabin. A shower will make you feel better."

Blakely went over to help him out of the chair. "I'm okay. Don't need your help."

Wafford's mood was resentful. He pushed Blakely's hand away. He slowly got out of the chair and unsteadily gathered his socks and shoes and sauntered out. More to it than Elizabeth. Wafford had come in to bare his soul and didn't get farther than his relations with Elizabeth. Too much mess, he had said. Too much mess—he'd repeated it. And what was it? Things couldn't be clear between him and Wafford? Was he saying Wafford shouldn't be trusted? Hell, he already knew that. Blakely picked up the phone and rang Marchese's room. No answer. He rang the bridge.

"Tony here."

"Did Marchese return with Lou?"

"No. Mike's here. Want to talk with him?"

"Yes. Put him on."

"Yeah, Ed."

"Marchese didn't come back with you?"

"No, sir. He was gone when I arrived. Mr. Wafford said they met some cavers last night. Marchese is going to spend the rest of his time in the boonies with them."

"Doesn't plan on coming back?"

"Mr. Wafford said he'd check in, in two or three days. He took a bunch of gear with him. Packed it down the gorge yesterday."

"So Wafford drove the rental back?"

"Yeah. He followed me. He's a total wreck! He could hardly walk from the motel to the car this morning."

"Yeah, I know. Thanks, Mike."

Blakely hung the phone up and went to Marchese's quarters. He unlocked the hatch and checked the locker. Still plenty of clothes folded in drawers. His black bathrobe hung on the shower door. Two climbing bags were stowed with gear. No personal toiletries or papers. He felt among the clothes and inside the climbing bags. Nothing suspicious. He closed the hatch behind him. He was just as happy Marchese was out of his hair. Too bad he doesn't fall down some hole he can't crawl out of.

Leo came out of Wafford's cabin carrying his paramedic kit.

"He okay?"

"More concerned with his dehydration than his feet. He should've been drinking water instead of all that alcohol. I put him to bed. I'll keep a check on him."

"Want me to stay with him?"

"Won't be necessary. He's already asleep," Leo said.

* * * * *

Blakely followed Elizabeth into the salon. Chris and Justina were sitting on the sofa.

"How was your trip?"

"Quite good, actually," said Chris. "Joachim pointed out an airfield where he and Heinrich did repairs. Seems Heinrich was something of a specialist in airfield construction."

That jibes with what Joachim's verse suggested this morning.

He was probably building a control tower in 1944. "Where is Joachim?"

"Resting. The old boy's had a difficult day. Many of the dead at the cemetery were from his unit. Seeing the markers brought it all back to him."

"Very sad," said Justina. "He wept when he read the names."

"You should go there, Edward," said Elizabeth. "There's a feeling of spiritual energy. Didn't you feel it, Justina?"

"Ya. Definitely."

The spiritual energy of what, Blakely wondered. Dead Nazis? Dead Germans? Simply dead men? Spiritual energy must be the same for good and bad men. Or was it the energy people brought with them to the cemetery? He had never felt a spiritual force in a cemetery. He poured himself a glass of orange juice and sat down.

"What about the kastelli at Hania?"

Chris pulled his glasses down on his nose and peered over them. "Cristos was right. Excellent landmarks. Unfortunately, none matched the template any way we tried the bloody thing."

Justina was avoiding his eye. Blakely looked at her and said, "Too bad."

"Otherwise," said Chris, pushing his glasses up, "there isn't much to report. I believe it is fruitless to drive about, hoping Herr Grenz will suddenly have a flash of insight."

Justina ran her hand through her hair. "Ya, Edward. We agree we should go now to Iraklion. We can obtain assistance from archeologists there."

They both sounded whipped again. And they should. They had no strategy.

"How was your day?" asked Chris without enthusiasm.

"George and Dr. Patera were helpful," Blakely replied. He shared what they had told him.

"Kastelli," said Blakely, "a fortress town southeast of Knossos, should be at the top of our list. It has an airfield built by the Nazis. I've asked Gregor to come up with some data."

"Good work, Edward!"

"Guess where we all decided to go tonight?" asked Elizabeth.

Blakely showed no change of expression. "I can't imagine, Elizabeth."

Pink rose up Justina's pretty neck.

"We all want to go back to The Grotto!" exclaimed Elizabeth. "And this time, Christopher promises us he'll dance, too."

CHAPTER 6

The Grotto

Lou Wafford's revelations weighed upon Blakely as he sat watching Elizabeth. Had she cheated on Wafford? What else? The mess he had mentioned. Frankly, Blakely hadn't really wanted to party tonight, but Chris, of all people, insisted he come along. Wafford, thank God, was sleeping off the alcohol and being attended to by Leo.

The music ended. Chris and Justina came off the dance floor. *At least Chris is paying attention to his wife for a change.* Blakely moved across and sat next to Stephanie.

"Would you like to go to real disco," Stephanie whispered.

"How far away is it?"

"Around corner. Half a block." She seemed to read his look. "Just the two of us."

"For an hour or so."

They excused themselves and left The Grotto. He felt everyone's eyes on him as he followed Stephanie up the steps. He draped her sweater around her shoulders. He could hear the din of Greek disco blaring before they reached the corner. "Sounds kinda loud for my taste," he said.

"We could go to my hotel. There is a bar with music. It is there." She pointed at a bright yellow four story hotel. They crossed the boulevard and entered the bar. A woman played a Greek lyre in the corner under a spotlight. A few couples sat at low tables in semi-darkness.

"You like this or shall we take drinks to my room?" Stephanie asked, shaking blond hair out of her eyes. She didn't waste time. He realized he had no condoms. Besides, she was too quick on the uptake. He could see himself getting rolled upstairs. "Why don't we have a drink here? The lady's playing nice tunes."

She brushed hair back. "Okay."

They both ordered scotch. A waiter brought two double shots, glasses, and a small pitcher of water on a little tray.

"I would like to visit your ship," she said, moving close to him. She was wearing the same musk scent as last night. He put his arm around her shoulder. "Our boss says I can't bring visitors aboard."

"Yesterday, I watch Greek man standing on deck."

"Oh? When was that?"

"Just before nightfall. Dark hair with glasses. He was with you last night at the Grotto."

"You mean George Kralos? A man in a blue suit?"

"Ya. That man."

"He had official business. He's an anthropologist."

"I have official business with you. You would show me your quarters, no?"

Her breath touched his cheek when she talked. He poured water into the scotch. "Here's to you and the stars!"

She leered. "To my star." They clicked glasses. "Probst!"

They drank. He pulled her close and tried kissing her lightly. He could feel her thigh against his. She put her hand at the back of his head and drew him against her mouth. She held on longer with her mouth than he wanted or intended.

When they separated, he asked, "How come you are so interested in the *Sea Siren*?"

"I'm not interested in ship. I'm interested in the ship's captain."

"You've been watching me?"

"Ya. Hilda sick today. We stay in room. I see you today meet

THE MINOTAUR 73

with same Greek man and an old gentleman at taverna. I later see you jog along avenue."

"You have nothing else to do than watch me?"

"Would you like to go to my room?"

She was in a rush. Not his style. "I'd rather stay here and finish our drink. After that, I'll say good night, Stephanie. I've had a busy day."

"You said you would disco an hour. It is only twenty minutes we are together."

He looked away. The woman playing the lyre changed melodies to one that sounded sad and somber.

"Yeah, well, those people back there are my responsibility. Maybe we can get together another evening. Dance and have dinner. You are very beautiful."

She leaned into him so that her dress gaped open. Two grapefruit-sized tan breasts peaked up at him. He kissed her and she responded. Her fingers found an opening in his shirt and stroked his chest hair.

She cooed hot breath. "You not like Stephanie?"

The more she tried, the more he resisted. "You are really lovely. Let's have a date later; maybe when we get to Iraklion."

She extricated her fingers. Her face changed sober. She looked down at her glass and ran her fingers up and down it, contemplating. Her face grew cold.

"I see you don't want to be a star after all. Excuse me, please."

She got up and left the bar. She hadn't finished her scotch. Blakely leaned his head back against the wall. He hadn't wanted to be rude. Hell, any other time, they'd be in her room hard at it by now—maybe.

Stephanie had come on too fast. Spying on him yet. She must have some agenda other than lovemaking. She must have a room upstairs with a balcony facing the boulevard. She'd be able to watch the *Sea Siren* and the taverna. Great looking breasts—larger than Jenny's. Probably about the same size as Elizabeth's and Justina's. Each woman is lovely in their own way. Why was it men were so hung up on breasts? Because they hung so prettily? Always comparing. When would he lose his lecherous feelings about women?

It would come soon enough, he thought. Some say the only way you know you are alive is when you are having sex. Was the last illusion of living, then, holding a woman in the final spasms of connection with... with the woman or with one's self? Or, were both possibilities simply illusory experiences?

The dark haired woman playing the lyre had wonderfully large and luminous brown eyes. She played gracefully and tried to make eye contact with her customers. She maintained a whimsical smile, all the while playing with gentle hands on strings and bow. Without realizing it, he was returning her smile. He drank the scotch and set the empty glass on the tray. He studied Stephanie's scotch a moment, then picked it up and drank it down. It's a sin to waste good scotch.

The young woman's touch on the lyre was soothing. He felt connected by the music to her. He waved at the waiter and held up two fingers. He would have another scotch for two by himself.

* * * * *

There was a message waiting for Blakely when he returned to the *Sea Siren*. It was from Tobok: a prioritized list of locations across Crete that fit the descriptors. At the top of the list was Kastelli—the place Kralos and Dr. Patera had mentioned. That had to be where Heinrich recuperated in 1944. If there was construction at the airfield, then it was likely he was a supervisor. All they needed was somebody who remembered when the control tower was built.

There was a note at the bottom.

"Still working on sources of German military documentation. One to check out is the Historical and Ethnographical Museum in Iraklion. There may be war-time photographs of interest there."

Gregor, he said to himself, you always come through when I need you!

CHAPTER 7

A New Game Plan

Joachim sat in the "J" chair eating his oatmeal. He had created three verses for Blakely in the notebook. Blakely read over them, deciphering the neatly printed German script. There was nothing wrong with Joachim's eyes or writing hand.

Only one of the verses had possible relevance. It read, *'Heinrich say he visit tomb, of ancient beehive shape; high above a logging flume, a crime did he investigate.'*

This one about the beehive tomb, Joachim."

"Ya?"

"What kind of crime was Heinrich investigating?"

"Courts martial, it was. He tell me in letter. Three soldiers set up machine gun inside tomb on mountain. They get arrested. It was criminal offense to damage an ancient ruin. Heinrich was one of officers on the review as I remember him saying."

"Can you recall a place on a mountain where there were tombs and a logging shoot?"

"No. It happen later. This was last letter I receive from Heinrich. No more after."

Joachim's eyes hid behind wrinkled lids as he slurped coffee and reached for his pipe. You could always tell when the old man was finished talking to you. His eyes receded and he turned you off. Almost like a turtle going back into his shell. The phone rang.

"Blakely."

"Skip? It's mounted and ready to install."

"You're a good man, Jeremiah!"

*****

Wafford, looking par boiled and weak, peeled a tangerine at the table. Everyone listened as Chris produced his game plan for the day. It sounded like an outing for tourists, which favored Blakely's own agenda.

"Today is essentially a travel day," Chris said. "Rather than journey by water to Iraklion, Justina and I believe we should use the opportunity to drive along the shore. Herr Grenz will likely recognize points here and there. We'll take the van and spend time at Rethimnon—the place where Joachim first landed. We'll see what he remembers. Unfortunately, according to George Kralos, there's little left from German occupation there. The Rethimnions erased every trace of the Germans ever having been there."

"Good for them," said Elizabeth. "They must be a proud people."

Chris brushed his mustache. "And brave. When the German army of occupation left Rethimnon in 1944, they attempted to take many of the women hostage for their retreat. Rather than be captured, the women jumped from the walls of the Venetian castle, killing themselves en masse."

"Oh, how awful!" exclaimed Elizabeth.

Chris nodded. He would make a great tour guide. Justina seemed to be looking absently at the middle of the table, engrossed in her own world.

Chris continued. "After lunching at Rethimnon, we'll take a leisurely drive, stopping at spots of interest along the way. We should arrive before dark at Iraklion harbor. Hopefully," he glanced at Blakely and winked, "the *Sea Siren* shall be waiting there for us. Justina and I shall contact archeologists there in preparation for tomorrow."

Wafford asked in a weak voice, "Mind if I go along? Once I get in the van, I'll be fine. I'd like to see that castle where the women jumped."

Chris said, "It's being reconstructed, I believe. We can stop there."

Elizabeth nudged Wafford. "What do you have in mind, Louis?" Wafford smirked.

"Are you up to it?" asked Blakely, hopefully.

Wafford pushed the tangerine peelings with a finger. "I feel lots better."

Great, thought Blakely, saying, "I'd like to give Gregor and Harry a day off. Gregor's in about the same shape you are, Lou. He's stiff from exercise yesterday. Do him and Harry good to get out. They can drive the Rover."

"Bring Jeremiah, too. We can make another tape," said Elizabeth, gleaming. It looked as though a truce had been struck—she was holding Wafford's hand. Both seemed in much better spirits.

"I need Jeremiah to cover for Gregor," said Blakely. "Tony, Leo and I will bring the *Sea Siren* around."

"That's fine by me," said Wafford. Elizabeth stroked his hand and looked at him encouragingly. Justina sat quietly, staring vacantly at her coffee. She seemed distant and uncaring.

"Miss Justina," said Wafford, trying to create a smile and failing terribly. "You haven't said a word this morning. What's your prognosis?"

She gave a little laugh. Her eyes were prepared for combat. "Of you or the search, Louis?"

He managed a grin. "The search. Do you agree with the professor?"

Elizabeth tilted her head and stared at Justina.

"Ya. Better chance there than here—that is for sure. Otherwise, Christopher and I might as well go home. And if I had my way, I would choose to go home today."

She wasn't exactly encouraging, although her rhyming was almost as good as Joachim's. She wanted no more nonsense. Chris looked down, then at Wafford. In a low voice, he said, "We will be going to Kastelli tomorrow."

* * * * *

Blakely stood on the bridge watching the van and the Rover disappear in the direction of Hania. Appropriate, he thought, it was April Fool's Day. Blakely hadn't any word from Claudia. Had she gotten his message? He felt very down. He would like to meet her in Athens or Rome after this fiasco was over. Seven days and he would be able to do what he pleased. He would no longer be skipper of the *Sea Siren*. He realized this short leg along the coast would probably be his last voyage at her helm.

He wished for a colossal storm so that both he and *Sea Siren* could be checked out once and for all. Just him on board her. Him and nobody else. He could almost feel her bucking under him and around him. She would squeal and scream and strain and hold him in her embrace, riding as one together, pitching and rolling in violent ecstasy, and then there would come silence and peace; the storm would be over. There was never a greater feeling of satisfaction than coming through a violent storm.

He wished for the kind of storm which just flashed out of clear sky as God's wrath—like in the old testament. Was that a death wish? Why did most people abhor a wish for death? What was the difference between a death wish and a life wish, if you had to die in order to obtain eternal life?

Christians were strange about that. They fought like hell not to die—instead of embracing death. They avoided the eternal life like the plague! Christians were quick to say, "He fought hard against death! Showed great courage at the end! You've got to admire him for that!" What was there to admire about fighting fate? Fighting against your Self? Fighting against your own salvation?

Doesn't matter, he reckoned. There's no good air today unless God creates one out of nothing. Fat chance of that. He opened the pilot house windows. Hardly any breeze. A smoky air hung over the water. If smoke goes low, watch out for a blow... Yeah, it could shower later.

He watched Leo and Tony securing the launch with a line to the stern. He gave two blasts of the air horn as the two mates went forward to weigh anchor. The horn's echo bounced between the two peninsulas and up the mountainside beyond Kastelli-Kissamou. A flock of goats on the far hill skittered. It was 0946 hours. Tony raised his arm. Anchor aweigh. He flicked on the monitors and instrument console.

He started the engine and swung the wheel over to starboard. Another blast of the air horn. He immediately felt a wave of happiness. Being under weigh dispelled all sadness. People along the shore waved. He couldn't be certain, but he thought he saw Stephanie and Hilda among the bystanders. He supposed Stephanie had found another star to bed down last night.

He dropped squares and set staysails, one after the other, and trimmed them by using the wheel. They were more for show than go. The Rodopos Peninsula lay to starboard like an impenetrable gray wall. Small whitewashed chapels dotted its scaly surface. A man in boots pulled a burro loaded with scraps of wood slowly toward a cluster of rock houses.

He pushed the throttle forward. He checked the monitors as Tony joined him. Tony's sleeves were rolled up and he was sweating. "Leo sez he has a job to do down below. Wanted me to stand watch for him."

"Yeah. We're playing shorthanded on purpose today." Blakely explained what Jeremiah and Leo were doing. "And I don't believe it has anything to do with Cybersex, Tony. Sorry to disappoint you."

Tony mopped his thinning black hair with a handkerchief. "I knew Gregor was into some illicit activity." He mumbled. "Still say he's Cybersexed."

The *Sea Siren* entered open sea beyond the point called Acra Spatha. The Sea of Crete stretched sublimely under a chalk sky, pale, nearly jade green with patches of slate showing currents and light air. One of the most ancient sea lanes in the world: a place where Ulysses plied; where Jason quested after the Golden Fleece; where Mycenaens, Egyptians and Phoenicians traded; and, where Theseus escaped with Ariadne under a black sail that would cause the death of his father.

Crossing their path two miles ahead was a large white ferry boat with a red stack headed in the direction of Athens. He checked a monitor. It must be the ferry between Souda and Piraeus.

On the night of 20 May, all across Souda Bay, English ships burned orange and red, as thousands of Englishers lay injured or dead.

Another verse from Joachim. 1941. The German invasion of Crete. He was learning them by heart. Ironic to be seeing the war from the opposite side—from an old Nazi.

Despite himself, he was becoming fond of Joachim. The past two mornings having breakfast with him were pleasant. The nights on deck together—watching the comet—were special times.

Joachim's verses. The guy had more tragedy stored up and memorized in verse than a fellow deserved. He pushed the throttle to three-quarters, and felt *Sea Siren* gracefully respond like a passionate woman being caressed.

*****

His watch read 1151 hours. Blakely turned the wheel over to Tony and picked up the glasses and scanned Rethimnon. A spike of white minaret looking like a NASA rocket ready to be launched stood high above the low-lying jumble of gray, blue and white buildings along the bay. A Toyota sign and another announcing Rooms for Rent showed above a frizz of palms. Gigantic gray mountains loomed in the distance, empty and foreboding, dwarfing the man-made structures. He supposed the tourist party from the good ship Lollipop would have a full day of sightseeing. He slipped the binoculars into their holder.

"Care to put in for a coupla hours, Tony? We've got plenty of time."

"I'd as soon get to Iraklion. I need to buy some Easter gifts for the family. Can you tell how far we got to go?"

Blakely punched up a coastal sector map and clicked the pointer on the cities of Rethimnon and Iraklion. A readout appeared. "Thirty four nautical miles."

"Piece of cake. We'll be there for lunch!"

The phone rang.

"Blakely."

"Skip, we've got the panel in and cable run."

"Great. Good sound and pictures?"

"Loud and clear. You can see the keyboard and screen perfectly. And the camera is totally hidden."

"What about on your end—in the studio?"

"No visible cable. It all looks normal."

"Be sure you leave the comm center just as you found it. No telltales."

"We've been very careful. Come down and have a look when you can."

"I will."

"Skip?"

"Yeah?"

"Check your messages. You've got one."

He cleared the sector map and punched in his name on the message board. It was from Jenny. 'Dear Bumper. Thank you for the lovely flowers and warm thoughts. Am arriving April 13 at Iraklion to visit your pal, Ed. More details later. Love, Jen.'

Well, well. What next? Maybe she and Stephanie and Hilda can share a room together. If Wafford can make it with three women at once, maybe it's time Easy Ed tried it. He rebuked himself for this blasphemy. Besides, Wafford's boast seemed to him a pathetic lie said out of desperation.

CHAPTER 8

Iraklion

The advantage of anchoring off New Harbor, thought Blakely, was it gave a wonderful perspective to the sweep of Old Harbor and the Venetian fortress—The Koules—guarding its entrance. Old Harbor was filled with fishing and pleasure boats of every description. Fishermen stooped over nets, pulling, separating, sewing, and sorting—preparing them for tomorrow's fishing. In New Harbor, two giant, three-story ferries were loading cars, scooters, and passengers.

Beyond New Harbor, Iraklion lay shrouded in clouds and pale sunshine. Modern glass and steel commercial buildings competed with Byzantine mosques, Venetian walls, Roman arches, and Greek Orthodox churches. Hotels lay stacked upon one another in white and gray rectangles, on the low hillside above the quay.

He stood at the rail, listening to the roar of traffic and watched O. Sophokles Venizelou—the main street beyond Old Harbor—for the blue van and the Rover. No sign of them. It was 1742 hours, and shadows stretching across the New Harbor promised a cool night.

Earlier, he had sent Jeremiah and Leo to check out the World War II photos and documents at the Historical and Ethnographical Museum. They had found nothing of consequence.

Tony had gone shopping and returned with red, blue and green seal stones of birds and dolphins for his children, a white flocati rug for his wife, and painted ceramic tiles for friends.

When Tony got back, Blakely went exploring. He turned into

Epimenidou Street, attracted by a sign announcing Candia Tours. A hand painted sign in German boasted in typical American hyperbole: BEST GUIDES FOR SEEING KRITI. A pretty young woman with sandy brown hair and blue eyes greeted him. "Guten tag."

Blakely responded in German. "Guten tag!" He turned, pointing at the sign in the window. "Your sign says you have the best guides on the island. Is that true?"

"We like to think so." She gave a little laugh.

"Wonderful! I'll tell you. I am trying to locate a particular kastelli on the island. Kastelli Pediadas. Would you be able to direct me?"

"Yes. I know of it. A lovely village, but there is no castle left."

"I understand."

"It is some twenty five kilometers from here. Not far. I show you. One moment, please."

The woman pulled out a map from below the counter and spread it before him. She took a red grease pencil from a cup, and began to trace streets and roads.

"You are here, see?"

She pointed to Iraklion. "Follow the signs to Knossos…"

She marked the directions and gave him the map. He left the shop thinking he should buy some trinkets. But for whom? Jim Willis, for taking care of Bumper? Old Guthrie, for keeping an eye on *Easy, Too*? Claudia? Jenny? He couldn't see buying tourist stuff for them. There was nobody else left in his life to buy remembrances for. They were either dead or out of his life. Maybe he could find a gift Joachim would enjoy, but he couldn't imagine what it might be. He felt the onset of a black mood. Actually, it had begun when they first arrived in port.

When he had ordered Tony to drop anchor off New Harbor, it was as though the anchor chain was attached to Blakely. He was tethered to land again. His sadness returned. The black ship with the dripping black sails drifted through his thoughts as though he were dreaming it. A daymare? The shrouded figure standing in the gloom, faceless, seen but not seeing, turning aside as the boat veered soundlessly and moved away, yet lingered in the shadows of his mind. Perhaps the figure was himself. Death instead of Father No-Name, a specter looming, hovering about him in this ancient harbor and burial place of ships and men.

He returned to the ship and found himself at the rail, watching and waiting. What was he waiting for? It seemed that when he was in port, he was always waiting for someone or some thing. First Jenny. Now, Chris and Wafford. You can't wait, Blakely, he said to himself. You've got to do what you have to do. There isn't time to wait. Don't wait for them. Don't wait for anybody—ever again. Lift anchor! Get your innings in before the game ends! A shudder whisked through him. He zipped up his windbreaker, asking himself what his inner voice was telling him to do. The Rover appeared, and behind it was the blue van. There was no longer any need to do anything for the moment, except to assist Leo with the launch.

* * * * *

"Ole Harry knows how to cook fish," said Wafford, patting his stomach and sitting down on the sofa in the salon with his bourbon and water. Pink windburn marked the pads beneath his eyes.

Blakely asked, "Where'd Harry and Gregor get the knives?"

Each had returned with an intricately tooled leather sheath in which was a bone-handled, folding knife.

Wafford looked down and swirled his drink. A little grin was forming. "Guess I'm responsible. It was me wanted to stop. A little knife and gun shop in Rethimnon. They make 'em there. Fine craftsmanship."

"You buy one for yourself?"

"Naw. I'm not into that."

"Frankly, Lou, I don't like any crew members having weapons on board."

Wafford's blue eyes flickered. "I saw no harm in these, Ed.

These are what every Cretan man carries. No different as weapons from all the knives Harry keeps in the galley. Course, you can put 'em in the ship's safe 'til it's time to vacate, if you feel different."

Blakely considered. Yeah, he's right. It would be a stupid idea to take their knives. Only serve to create a morale problem. Chris entered and sat across from Blakely. "We've made an appointment for tomorrow at ten with Dr. Nicolas Paulas."

Blakely asked, "Who's he?"

"The archeologist Santos recommended. We'll spend the morning with him. Perhaps take him out to lunch."

The casualness of Chris was beginning to irritate Blakely. They only had six more days until Easter! He got up and made a scotch and water. He realized Mediterranean protocols required a laid-back approach, but they had a solid lead. Why not go for it? He turned and asked, "Mind if I do my own thing tomorrow? I'd like to check out that Kastelli place. It's at the top of the list in Gregor's computer."

Chris took off his glasses. He shifted and crossed his legs, looking challenged and uncertain. "Why, no, Edward. Do what you like. The whole point of meeting with Dr. Paulas is to determine the likelihood of Minoan artifacts in that vicinity. Justina and I planned to go to Kastelli in the afternoon. I just assumed we'd all go together."

Blakely said, "Will you need Joachim to go with you to meet this guy?"

Chris blinked and put his glasses on. "No. We hadn't planned to take him to the museum with us."

"Good. I'll take him with me."

Chris seemed nonplused. "I thought you would want to see the other parts of our relic. They are on display there at the museum."

Blakely shrugged. "I can see them later."

Wafford said, "Elizabeth said she wants to see them Minoan art treasures. You mind if she tags along, professor?"

"You are coming with her, Louis, aren't you?"

Wafford grinned. "If it's all the same to you, I'd like to go with Ed and Joachim. That okay with you, Ed?"

"Sure."

Wafford and Blakely exchanged looks. They were agreeing, for a change. The phone rang.

"Blakely."

"Got somebody want's to talk with you, skip," said Gregor. "Your daughter's on the Ham."

"Be right down!"

He hung up the receiver. "Claudia's on the ham," he explained, dashing toward the comm center.

He put on earphones and held the mike. "Hello! Claudia?"

Crackling static. "Hi, there! what's up?"

She sounded terrific. "We're in Iraklion. How are you?"

"Oh, I'm fine. Just got back from a four day assignment. Mostly interviewing Moslem and Bosnian leaders for PR. It's pretty chaotic here. How about you? Finding any lost treasures yet?"

"No. Any chance you can come over for Easter holiday?"

"As a matter of fact, I'm coming to Athens Monday after Orthodox Easter on assignment. Could you meet me there?"

"Yeah. How long will you be in Athens?"

"Only a couple days. From there, I go to Macedonia. Wish you could come along. It's a working vacation."

"That might be possible. I'll have to let you know later. Where will you be staying in Athens?"

"St. George Hotel."

"Good. I'll leave a message there."

"I'd love to see you. Guess you know I miss ya!"

"Me, too."

"How's Jenny and Bumper Dog?"

"Both fine. I have a lot to tell you."

"Uh, oh! Is Easy Ed on the prowl again?" She giggled.

He laughed. "Could be."

"Good old Dad! The peripatetic adventurer."

"Yeah. That's me, I guess—whatever peripatetic means."

THE MINOTAUR 87

She giggled again. "Yeah, Dad. That's you! Well, I guess I'd better hang up now. I'm sitting here next to a very nice Bosnian man—the Ham operator. He's spent hours looking for me. I brought him a can of American coffee and a pound of sugar. He's very appreciative. Anyway, I'm looking forward to seeing you in Athens."

"Can't wait."

"Me, too. Love ya!"

"Love you, too. Good night, Claudia!"

She clicked off. He removed the earphones and handed them to Gregor.

"You've made my day, Gregor!"

Tobok sat pensively in his chair, resting his hands on the computer keyboard. "Glad I could make the connection. It took long enough!"

"Thanks. A big load off, knowing she's all right."

"Could I ask you a favor?"

"Sure. What is it?"

"Would you mind if I skipped the workout with Leo tomorrow? I'm still stiff as can be."

Blakely couldn't help but smile. "Yeah. Why not?"

Tobok's brown eyes brightened. "Thanks, skip!"

CHAPTER 9

A Lead

It was 0700, 2 April 1996, Blakely mused. He went topside. Old Joachim was already there, gazing seaward. He held his pipe away from his mouth.

Blakely realized, as he approached, that the old man was mumbling to himself, saying phrases with catchy rhythms, rhyming couplets. He was going over his verses. He thought he heard Joachim mention Estel's name at least twice.

"Good morning, Joachim. Reciting your verses?"

"Ya, that is so." Joachim's left eye told him he was violating private space.

"Sorry. I didn't mean to intrude."

Joachim leaned both elbows on the rail and looked down into the slick. "That is okay." He paused, then said in a low, misbegotten voice, "We were forbidden that most precious gift."

"What is that?"

"Marriage and children." Joachim took his cane in his hand, turned away from the rail, and looked squarely at Blakely through watery eyes. "Do you know what it is like never to have been married? Never to have had children? No one to receive your love or your name?"

They were shaming questions. Blakely felt sad and embarrassed. "No, Joachim. I cannot imagine how that would be."

They said nothing for a long time. Blakely watched the latebirds—the last of the fishermen—navigating under power out of

Old Harbor. Their diesels chug, chug,-chugging, like John Deere tractors.

"Like to go with me into the mountains this morning, Joachim?"

The old man's head turned. The blue eyes squinted and the whiskers parted into a round hole he took to be a smile. "Ya, Edward. I look forward to seeing mountains with you."

"We'll leave about 0930 hours. Lou will be going with us."

"Good." The old man patted Blakely on the shoulder. "Good," he repeated, putting himself in motion toward the aft companionway, shuffling across the deck, hunched over his cane. "I go to breakfast now."

* * * * *

Blakely helped Joachim into the back seat of the Rover. Wafford climbed in beside Blakely. He handed Wafford the map with the marked directions. "You play navigator, this morning, Lou."

Wafford looked down and moved his fat finger along the colored trail. His finger stopped. He said, "Kastelli Pediadas."

"Kastelli," Joachim replied. "Different kastelli?"

"Right, Joachim," said Blakely. "A different kastelli. This one is supposed to be like the one in your verses. It is high up, with a piazza, and an airfield."

"Yavoll." The old man seemed confused but hopeful. "Too many kastelli," he mumbled.

Blakely drove the Land Rover to the outskirts of Iraklion. The landscape turned dusty, with small housing developments. They passed the sign for Knossos and entered a countryside where large plantings of olive trees were interspersed with rows of grape vines and truck gardens. Plane trees shaded whitewashed cottages with blue and red tiled roofs.

"Slow down, Ed. We're coming to where you need to turn."

After the turn toward Agia Paraskie, the road was narrower, windier, and the country grew quite primitive. They passed small ramshackle farmhouses. Goats and sheep grazed behind crude stick fences similar to what Blakely had seen in the poorest parts of Mexico. An occasional farmer in black hat, dark clothing, and boots, walked beside a donkey, paying no attention to the Land Rover or its occupants. The whole atmosphere reminded Blakely of the Baja, where you'd see old Indian women walking along, watching you with those dark eyes and creased faces that didn't change expression. He recalled as a teenager hell-raising with his friends in an open jeep through the hills of Baja. They tried to get a rise out of the natives. Whatever they did, wave, smile, stick out their tongue, make a face at them or what, there was no response. The peasant faces remained mute, unchanged. That stuck in his mind. Those primitive people were much wiser than the smart-assed kids in the jeep. They knew the jeep had to come back on the same road; they knew they could gather stones and pelt the hell out of them when they returned. But they didn't. He guessed those poor Indians knew it was just stupid kids. Another cruel sport he had overcome, he thought. Now, he could look back to those people with admiration.

Inscrutable, that was the word. No show of suffering, or joy. That was probably how these Cretan peasants were.

He glanced in the mirror. Joachim was sound asleep. Joachim the old man, who liked to watch stars with him, who shared stories about love, was becoming a friend—a father-figure. Life is a mixed business, he thought. Love and hate don't mean anything unless there is a context. Your enemy yesterday is your friend today.

Still, there was this problem inside him. How could he hate Nazis and like Joachim? Joachim was a Nazi. The authorities were still bringing old Nazis to trial. How did he know Joachim hadn't committed heinous crimes? Just because you were old didn't absolve you from guilt or sentence. The Russians kept him a prisoner for over forty years. Maybe they had good reasons.

The country was getting rougher with more hills and fewer dirt roads off to the sides. Everything was dusty. The landscape changed into thickets of pine with only an occasional break where barren earth surrounded a makeshift barn next to a stone well. A few chickens and a staked goat searched for anything edible. No kids—goat or otherwise. All old people. The kids and grandkids must have high-tailed it down to the coast to work in restaurants and hotels, he guessed, leaving the old folk at home to feed the chickens, milk the goats, and sit around a wood fire.

The Land Rover crossed a stone bridge, and began to climb a series of switch backs through woods, eventually heading up a steep grade toward a pile of stone buildings. Houses had been constructed over an ancient stone gate. The sunshine disappeared when they entered the fortress village.

He turned on the headlights and down-shifted. The Rover whined shrilly as it climbed along the winding passage over tessellated gray cobbles with high stone walls on either side.

Blakely shifted to lowest gear as the Land Rover labored up a very steep and curved grade onto a level square, coming out into sunshine again. There was the piazza, surrounded on two sides by shops and stone buildings. Blakely pulled to a stop.

Wafford looked at Blakely. "This it?"

"Believe so." They looked across the piazza.

A cluster of eight or nine blond women sat in one corner, drinking from small glasses. Two ragtag children ran about, laughing. A black and white dog lay curled up next to a man sprawled in his chair, asleep. A truck beeped behind them. Blakely glanced in his mirror. A military vehicle. He released the brake and moved the Rover to the curb. The gray truck passed by and disappeared around the corner.

The three climbed out and walked to the edge of the square.

"How's this for a view, Joachim?"

"Wonderful!"

The air smelled of pine and Rosemary, of earth and fresh straw. The cooling breeze stirred the tops of trees in currents of movement far below. To the north, you could see the hazy blue of the Cretan Sea; and looking west, gray and bald mountains loomed in the distance.

"Ever been here before?"

"Nein. I would have remembered this place in my dreams!" Joachim walked to the very edge and looked across the void.

Wafford pointed. "Lookit those eensy-teensy trees. There's a farm so pismire tiny you can hardly see it. No bigger'n an ant."

Blakely followed Wafford's finger. Yes. There were peasant huts and brown barns and patches of farmed land and vineyards—if you looked closely among the trees. It fit with Heinrich's description.

Joachim stood looking and slowly removed his Greek hat and held it to his chest. In a low, modulated voice, he began to recite. *Heinrich from the tower fell, the scaffold failed to hold, on furlough did he tell, of feeling death's hand cold... Heinrich von Etter, my comrade in arms, fell at Kastelli and broke his leg; recouping high above the farms, two months he lay without duty to undertake...*

"What's he saying?" whispered Wafford.

"His verses. The same ones we translated."

Wafford scratched at loose skin on his nose.

"I don't know about you," said Blakely, hitching up his sailing pants, "but I think this place has possibilities."

"What do you say we have something to eat? Maybe a drink, too?"

"Where would you like to sit?"

Wafford eyed the blond tourists sitting all to themselves.

"Over there?" Blakely pointed to a table near the women.

"Anywhere will do," said Wafford, walking to the table nearest the women.

CHAPTER 10

Max Brings Greetings

They ate from the mound of green and red pepper and onion rings, tomato slices, tiny brown olives, and block of Feta, slathered in olive oil. Breaking a piece of bread from the uncut loaf, Blakely watched Joachim dip a chunk of bread into the oil, take it into his mouth and chew contentedly. He followed the old man's example, washing it down with beer. Wafford did the same, while eyeing the young women at the other table. The ladies were speaking Danish.

Three more blondes arrived. Real dishes, sporting tight leotards, thin blouses, and tans that came out of a jar. Too much make-up. The three caught Wafford's attention. He wasn't listening when Blakely asked him a question. So, he asked again.

"If this were to be our work site, Lou, would we drive back and forth to the *Sea Siren* or what?"

Wafford glanced around at the buildings. He nodded. A small sign over a doorway said simply, HOTEL. He wiped his mouth with his hand.

"We can stay right there, I 'spose. No use driving back and forth. Lose too much time." he replied, looking past Blakely to the women again.

Joachim ate and stared out across the mountains. It was almost like the man had finally come home. Blakely hoped—for Joachim's sake—that this was where Heinrich had stayed.

Two air cadets in blue uniforms sat down next to them.

Blakely said, "The airfield must be nearby."

Wafford leaned toward Blakely "Why don't you ask them if they can give us directions."

Blakely got up, went over, and asked in English and German. Both answered negatively. Blakely turned, shaking his head. He knew he couldn't use his limited Greek. He tried using mime, waving his fingers and shaping them like an airplane. The shorter cadet pointed back over his shoulder, where the road turned up a hill behind the row of shops. He then gesticulated with his own fingers and hands, showing the road was guarded or blocked. Blakely returned to his chair.

"They tell me the air field is approximately four kilometers above the piazza. From what I gather, it's a restricted area requiring a special pass."

Blakely looked down the row of storefronts. One had a Greek flag over the door. It was probably where the mayor hung out. He nodded over his shoulder.

"Why don't we go over there? We can ask if somebody can arrange a visit to the air field?"

Wafford looked for a moment, then concentrated on picking out the tiny olives from beneath the rings of peppers and onions. "Let's wait 'til we're finished. Plenty of time. No hurry."

One of the cadets left the table and went over to the office. A stocky man in a brown suit and open white shirt came through the door, followed by the cadet. He walked directly over to where they were sitting. The cadet returned to his own table.

"Can I be of assistance to you gentlemen?" He spoke good English and had a friendly, puffy face. "My name is Max Padopolis. I am administrator for the Pediadas constabulary."

Blakely stood up. "Glad to know you, Mr. Padopolis. These are my friends, Joachim Grenz, and Louis Wafford."

They shook hands. Padopolis lit a Marlboro, tossing the match on the concrete. He nodded toward the cadets.

"I am told you have an interest in the air base above our village."

"Yes," said Blakely, pointing to Joachim. "Joachim's friend may have been stationed there during the war. Perhaps he helped build it. We'd just like to take a look, mosey around, see if this is the place."

Padopolis's small, dark eyes watched Blakely's face as he explained. He did not appear impressed.

"This word mosey. What does it mean?"

"Oh, sorry. Actually, we'd like to take a tour—an escorted one, if possible."

Padopolis looked from Wafford to Joachim to Blakely and back to Joachim. "You are telling me this man's friend was stationed here during World War II? Fifty years ago? I'm not sure I understand the connection."

Blakely knew he was treading water. How could he explain? Joachim wouldn't be any help. And Wafford? Wafford was still ogling the blondes. He'd come about and try it the Greek way, he thought, slowly, one step at a time.

"Would you have time to sit with us while I explain?" Blakely asked. "I'd like to buy you a beer or something."

Padopolis shrugged and drew on his cigarette. "I've got lots of time," he said, blowing smoke. "I'll have Oozo."

Padopolis signaled the waiter, went over to the cadets, asked them something in Greek, and dragged the extra wire chair back close to Blakely. He swung the chair around, straddling the seat so that he rested his massive stomach against the back, folding his arms on the top. He leaned his head forward, drawing on his cigarette, holding it inside his palm with his fingers.

"Now tell me again your interest in our military bases, sir, for I do not understand."

The waiter brought the Oozo. Padopolis took the glass of clear liquid and sipped.

"Well, sir," Blakely paused.

He was going to explain they were looking for a relic, but realized immediately this heavy breathing bureaucrat would never believe what he was about to say.

"Well, sir," he began again, "do you know the man who works

at the Iraklion museum, Professor Nickolas Paulas?"

"No." Padopolis squinted displeasure.

Wafford laid a hand on Blakely's arm. "Let me explain, Ed."

Padopolis shifted his eyes toward Wafford. "Mr. Wolfert, is it?"

"Wafford!"

"You are American?"

"Yes, sir."

"Please explain."

Padopolis looked grimly at Wafford. Wafford's face was already warming pink beneath peeling skin.

"We are really looking for Minoan relics which could be hidden some place near here. There was a German officer who we think was stationed here during the war. We believe he found one in this vicinity. We think the man was supervising construction of the airfield in 1944."

Padopolis's glum expression had not changed. He took another healthy swig of Ouzo. "I see."

"We brought some archeologists from Berlin to help us," Wafford added.

Padopolis looked around on all sides. "I do not see them. Where do you keep them hidden?"

Wafford's face was breaking out in a sweat. He looked exasperatedly toward Blakely.

Blakely said, "They are with Dr. Paulas at the museum in Iraklion. They'll be coming here this afternoon."

Padopolis glanced at Blakely and then resumed staring at Wafford. This was not going well at all. Joachim stopped eating and started loading his pipe.

"You have passport, Mr. Wolfert?"

Wafford began hauling passport, driver's license and credit cards out of his travel pouch.

Padopolis thumbed quickly through the passport, comparing Wafford's face with his I.D. picture. He squinted at his Mississippi driver's license. He took each credit card, turning it this way

THE MINOTAUR 97

and that, holding it up to the sunlight. He handed everything back to Wafford except his passport.

Padopolis turned back to Blakely. "May I see your passport?"

Blakely handed him his passport. Padopolis thumbed through each page, examining the various stamps of South American and South Seas countries. "You are a military pilot, Mr. Blakely?"

"No, sir. I'm a sailor. I have raced internationally. Nick Serpanos in Athens can vouch for me. I've raced against him."

Blakely knew that was stretching it! Nick was an internationally famous twelve meter skipper. He and Nick had been casual friends ten years ago. The guy probably wouldn't remember. How dumb!

Blakely added, "You can also contact Zebulon Transport in Piraeus. Zebulon is sponsoring our expedition here."

Padopolis tilted his head and frowned.

"I still don't understand this matter of the air base, and this gentlemen's friend, being here fifty years ago. What's all that to do with here and now?"

Before anyone could answer, he turned to Joachim. "May I see your passport, please?"

"He speaks no English," explained Blakely.

He translated Padopolis's request, but it wasn't necessary. Joachim had nervously set his pipe down and was already pulling from his pocket a tattered leather case. He removed some folded papers and handed them over. Padopolis shuffled through them, seeming not to understand them. He held out his hands over the unfolded papers.

"What am I to do with these? He has no passport?"

Joachim understood. "Nein."

Joachim's hand was shaking. Maybe this reminded him of the Gestapo or Russian interrogators. Wafford wiped sweat from his upper lip and attempted to explain.

"Joachim recently arrived from Russia, sir. He'd been in a Siberian labor camp. You can see from his papers that he is a ward of the International Red Cross. A displaced person. He's been given permission to travel by the Greek government. It's on one of those papers there."

That's all they needed, thought Blakely—to give the impression they were somehow connected to Russia!

Padopolis collected Joachim's papers and placed them with the passports. He raised his hand in the air, motioning to the waiter. The waiter leaned down. He whispered. The waiter went over to the sleeping man stretched out in the chair and tapped him on the shoulder. The large man came awake, looked around, saw Padopolis, got up, and came over, stuffing a white shirt tail into his pants as he did so. He did not seem happy that Padopolis was there on what appeared to be official business.

"Alex, introduce yourself to these gentlemen and stay with them while I make a telephone call."

Padopolis climbed out of his chair and said to Blakely. "Please do not wander off while I am gone. I'll try not to take too much of your valuable time."

Wafford, now bright red, called after him. "Sir. If you would call the '*Sea Siren*'—it's a ship anchored at Iraklion—and ask for Tony Zeno, the pilot. He can explain our trip and who we are. Or call the museum and ask for Dr. Christopher Cunningham. I know it sounds complicated, but it really isn't. We're basically just tourists here to see your village."

Padopolis shuffled back to the table and put his hand on Wafford's shoulder. "I understand your concern, Mr. Wolfert. But you must understand our security concerns. When foreigners come to this place asking strange questions about a military base of highest security, then we must take all precautions."

Padopolis strode off toward his office.

"What a pismire!" mumbled Wafford; sweat poured down his face.

Alex slumped in the chair and looked at Wafford through sleepy eyes.

Hot damn, thought Blakely, they might see the inside of a Greek jail unless the wind changes. He ordered another round of drinks, including a beer for the man called Alex. The guy was almost asleep again. Joachim's hand was shaking as he lifted his pipe to his mouth.

"Nothing's going to happen, Joachim," Blakely said, patting his arm. "Just got hit with some red tape is all. It might take an hour or so, but we'll be okay. Maybe even get to see the air base before dark. What about that, Joachim? Would you like that?"

"Ya, I guess so," mumbled Joachim. "Kastellis not much fun," he said. "We should go next time to see the windmills."

Blakely glanced at Wafford. His eyes and mouth were open extra wide. He turned his head to see what Wafford was ogling. The Danish women lifted skirts to climb into their Volkswagen bus. At least the anatomical scenery was entertaining. A man with a dilapidated wood and brass box camera on a tripod had set up shop in the corner of the square. The three blondes were getting their pictures taken. Joachim had turned to watch them.

"How about it, Joachim? I'd like to get a picture of you. Want to?"

The old man turned back and held out a hand. "We don't have to."

"You want to, Lou?"

Wafford shifted in the chair. "Naw. Ya'll go on and do it. I'll stay here."

Blakely stood up. "Do you mind, Alex, if we go over there and get his picture taken?"

Alex waved his hand without looking up. "No problem."

"Come on, Joachim. Let's do it!"

"Okay."

Joachim followed Blakely over to where the photographer was using a brush to fill in tints of color on the sepia prints. He finished and handed them to the women. They pointed at the pictures and laughed as they left the square.

"I want you in picture, too, Edward," said Joachim.

"All right. Let's have two prints, then," said Blakely to the man who was lining them up in the view finder.

"Be very still," said the voice in German as Blakely held his arm around Joachim's shoulders. "Very still..." The photographer removed the lens cover and exposed the film. "There!" He shifted plates. "And again..."

They watched him process the photographs. After applying fix and tint, the man handed them two prints. It showed Joachim and Blakely standing side-by-side with Blakely's arm draped over Joachim's shoulder. Blakely was smiling. Joachim had his pipe planted firmly in his mouth, and his wizened eyes peered out of leathery wrinkles.

"A good likeness of my friend," said Joachim. "I keep it always."

"Me, too."

They returned to the table where Wafford sat, pink and taciturn. "Turn out okay?" he asked.

Joachim offered him the print.

Wafford took the picture and held it away from him and studied it. "The two musketeers!"

Wafford's tone was bitter. He handed the picture back to Joachim and resumed his gloomy expression. Blakely opened his wallet and slipped the photograph behind the window normally reserved for Jenny. Wafford was in a funk, suddenly, and Blakely wasn't interested in working him out of it. This kind of misunderstanding happens when you visit foreign countries. No big deal! There was nothing they could do, except to be patient. Worst case, they would have to sit on this beautiful piazza a few hours drinking beer and Ouzo until Chris and Justina arrived.

CHAPTER 11

Colonel Dimitrius Stupak

The cadets had finished their beer and left on motor scooters by the time the big brass arrived in two official blue cars. The two men looked in Blakely's direction and got out. The driver of the first car entered Padopolis's office while the other walked immediately toward them.

The officer was tall and broad-shouldered in his sky blue Greek Air Force uniform. He carried his cap in hand. Blakely reckoned he was thirty five or so. He smoothed his short black hair and a broad, friendly smile spread across his craggy features as he came closer. He stretched out his hand to Blakely.

"Welcome to Kastelli Pediadas. I'm Colonel Dimitrius Stupak, base commander."

With the sound of Stupak's voice, Alex awoke, got up quickly, and offered him his chair.

Blakely shook the colonel's hand and introduced Joachim and Wafford.

Stupak graciously nodded at each man, got out a pack of Camels and lit one. He gestured toward the chair. "Do you mind if I sit down, gentlemen?"

Wafford replied. "Go right ahead, colonel. We're glad you arrived."

Alex retrieved another chair and sat down in it behind Wafford.

Stupak flicked an ash and leaned back. His blue eyes moved from one to another. Blakely realized the guy looked like Gamal Abdul Nassar—he could have been his brother.

Stupak said in a soft voice. "I understand you are having some little problem with identification and that you wish to visit our installation?"

Blakely tried a new tack.

"Joachim, here, is a veteran of the Seventh Division paratroopers, sir. He was stationed on Crete with his friend Heinrich von Etter during the occupation. The two guys got separated. Heinrich talked about building an airfield at Kastelli. We were wanting to find out whether there were any documents around to confirm he was here back in 1943 or 44."

The colonel studied Joachim as Blakely explained. The waiter came over. Stupak looked up. "A beer for me, George."

Stupak drew his chair around so he could address Joachim directly. Joachim's hand was shaking again as he held the pipe to his mouth.

"So, you were a paratrooper of General Kurt Student?" he asked in German.

"Yavoll," Joachim said with pride, holding his pipe shakily in front of his mouth. Joachim's eyes grew alert.

"What was your military occupational specialty?"

"Engineer. Civil Engineer I was."

"I also am civil engineer," said Stupak in a kindly way, attempting to draw the old man out. He shifted his chair closer, put his elbows on the table, and looked into the old man's face.

"Tell me... Is it Herr Grenz?"

"Ya. Joachim Grenz," said Joachim.

"Yes. Tell me, Herr Grenz, what were your duties while stationed here?"

The old man livened. He pointed his pipe toward the distant horizon and waved across its length.

"I arrive at Rethimnon, May 20, 1941."

"The invasion, yes?"

"Ya. Me and Heinrich. We built many defenses along the northwest part of Kriti, around other Kastelli," he replied.

"And where were you based?"

"In western mountains near Kastelli. I was transferred to Romania in 1943, leaving Heinrich here on the island."

Blakely sat listening, intrigued with how Joachim's verses and all the recent discussions had pulled events together so that he could now speak of the past coherently.

Stupak drew on his cigarette and asked, "So Heinrich, you believe, was the engineer who constructed the base here?" He pointed back over his shoulder.

Joachim shrugged. "I know nothing of that."

Joachim looked at Blakely for help. "Herr Blakely believes so. For me, there are too many kastellis. I am an old man. I get confused about these things."

Alex was nodding off, his head bobbing. Padopolis and the other officer came out of the building, walked across the piazza, and stood next to the group. The officer was carrying their identification papers. Without getting up, Stupak opened his hand toward the officer and introduced him.

"Gentlemen, this is Captain Sal Lutra. He is in charge of base security. Sal, this is Herr Joachim Grenz, a former officer in the German Army. An engineer like myself. Edward Blakely from California, and... Louis... Wafford, from Mississippi."

Stupak was impressive. The guy remembered their names and gave the oldest one proper place in the pecking order. Not only that, he had background information on each one. Evidently, Padopolis had given him names and addresses out of their passports by telephone. Blakely liked him. Lutra was darker, more reserved, nodding at each introduction and handshake. He returned their documents without comment.

Alex shuffled to his feet and brought another chair over, then walked stiff legged in the direction of the office. Everyone sat down.

"You are from that beautiful sailing vessel anchored off Iraklion, yes?" Stupak asked.

"Yes," Blakely replied. How did he know?

"Such a beautiful ship. Our wing commander was immediately attracted to it when it approached the Bay of Kissamou last

Thursday. You have many sophisticated electronics aboard, not true?"

Wafford shifted in his chair. He waited for Blakely to answer.

"Yes, sir," said Blakely, "the *Sea Siren* is state of the art all the way around. Owned by Zebulon Transport Company."

"I am familiar with Zebulon. You are here, I understand, to make programs for television and to search for ancient relics?"

Blakely and Stupak locked eyes. They both smiled.

"How'd you know?"

Stupak dropped his cigarette butt and ground it beneath his shoe. "We do background check with Athens. We learned something about each of you. Whenever a ship with such communications devices comes into our waters, we are put on alert. We have watched you for some days, getting daily reports. We used your activities as part of our training exercise. The superintendent of the cadet academy takes full advantage of such opportunities."

"So we've been under surveillance?"

"Yes. It is routine."

The waiter brought a round of drinks without anyone ordering them, setting down the colonel's beer first.

"And you are a professional racer of sailboats, I believe?"

"I haven't been lately," Blakely replied, wondering how detailed his background check must have been. "But that's been my passion, you might say."

"Yes. Mine is flying, but I unfortunately have the wrong specialty for it. Like Herr Grenz, my responsibilities are to see that the plumbing works, that nobody gets beyond our security, and that our cadets like the food we serve."

He glanced at Lutra.

"Then, with help from Captain Lutra, I also have to keep our boys from getting into trouble. You might call it being a private hotel manager."

He broke into another broad smile, reached into his pocket, and offered everyone a Camel cigarette before lighting one for himself.

THE MINOTAUR

As if reading Blakely's thoughts, he said, "The American base. My position affords BX privileges there."

He lifted his glass.

"I welcome you to Kastelli, gentlemen. May you find us always ready to assist you!"

"Thank you," said Blakely. They raised their glasses and drank.

"You show good Southern hospitality, colonel," said Wafford, giving Stupak his grandest hang-dog grin. "My daddy was a military man—and my granddaddy before him. Want you to know you're always welcome to come down to Biloxi and stay a spell."

Stupak nodded. "That would be very nice."

He turned to Joachim, speaking again in German.

"Herr Grenz, you may be interested in seeing some memorabilia from the war. We have documents and photographs giving some history of the base."

"Ya?"

"Yes." Stupak put his arm on the back of Joachim's chair. "We have many photographs, some of them having to do with construction. There is flying paraphernalia, various things. Would you like to see them?"

"Yavoll. That would be wonderful."

The colonel pushed his chair back. "I must tell you, however, that I cannot vouch for the condition of these materials. They are stored in a damp basement."

Blakely said, "We don't care about the condition. This is exactly what we've been looking for."

Stupak stood up. "In that case…" He scratched his head. "Why don't Herr Grenz and I ride in my staff car while you two gentlemen ride with Captain Lutra?"

****

The vehicles pulled up before a two story building. Everyone got out. Stupak pointed toward a distant control tower to the far left side, which was protected by chain link fence and razor wire.

"That is the flight section, our highest security area. You would not be allowed there unless we obtained for you special permission from Athens. The wing has its own commander who is in charge of all air operations."

An American F-14 Fighter with Greek markings blasted off the runway and disappeared in the sunlight. Stupak said something to Lutra, who nodded and left the group.

"Come with me, please. I have asked Captain Lutra to have my clerk open the basement room for us. To the right, gentlemen, is the cadet academy. You can see the dormitories, recreation hall, classrooms. That, too, is operated separately under a commander."

He turned and moved toward the closest building. Everyone waited until Joachim got himself in motion and followed the colonel.

"Come with me, Herr Grenz. In this building we have personnel, engineering, a wing for infirmary, a general mess, officers quarters, and many other elements."

Two young men in work clothes were washing the front windows. They stopped and saluted. The colonel saluted and held the door open for Joachim to pass. They entered into a foyer lined with photographs of the various base officers, including those of Stupak and Lutra.

Joachim removed his hat and pointed with his cane at the photograph of Stupak. He exclaimed. "Colonel Stupak!"

"Yes, Herr Grenz. Let's go this way."

They followed. The green and yellow paint, brown tile floor, and smell of disinfectant mixed with floor wax reminded Blakely of the Gutleut Kasserne where he was billeted in Germany. Down the hallway, blue uniformed clerks whisked back and forth between offices. Stupak paused, waited for Joachim to catch up, placed a hand on the old man's shoulder, and led him through an empty room to a narrow stairway.

"This is what I wanted you to see, Herr Grenz. We must go down these stairs." He stood aside and let everyone pass by him. They entered a large, musty room which had glass topped display tables and cases filled with various objects. Everything was in disorder. Stacks of framed photographs and documents rested on the cases. The place reeked of old paper, mildew, and disuse. The walls were covered with photographs of people, construction, and aircraft. Bookcases were stuffed with black binders and tattered file folders. Every surface was dusty. Apparently, nobody ever came in the place.

"I must apologize for the conditions here," said Stupak. "We closed our museum upstairs some five years ago and moved it over to the cadet classroom building. What you see here is the excess—all the items the superintendent did not think were useful. I admit, this place is not good for documents. They get moldy and decay. But... I offer these to local library and schools, and nobody want them. Cretans are selective in the culture of invaders—they choose to burn documents rather than keep them for their children to see." He threw up his hands. "What can I say? They are better here than throwing them out, no?"

A glass cabinet drew Joachim's attention. He leaned down, studying a pair of rotted, German parachute boots and broken goggles. He moved to another cabinet where the bent barrel of an engineer's level lay, glazed over with green oxidation.

"Look, Edward!" Joachim exclaimed. "We used these to lay out a construction site!"

He tapped on the glass. "And here, these are what I wore when I parachuted."

Wafford leaned closer. "My, my."

The old man shook his head, "I never thought to see such things again."

Stupak crossed his arms and said to Blakely. "They found a lot of Nazi equipment when the base was taken over by the Resistance. Kind of a hodgepodge of memorabilia. We've dug up some of these items over the years, such as that donkey level. You know how it is. We'll be repairing a sewer line or something and dig up part of a mess kit or a helmet. You never know. Clean it up. Let the superintendent decide if it goes to cadet museum or put here."

Wafford picked up a moldy leather binder off a counter. He thumbed through a few pages and put it back. He wiped his hands across his windbreaker. "Ever find any ancient things, like Minoan artifacts?"

Stupak touched his chin with his fingers. "They tell me that in 1880's, a bronze spear head was found. That is the only ancient item anyone recalls. It was turned over to the museum at Iraklion. Otherwise, no. We mostly find shell casings, belt buckles, and cannon rounds from Turks. An insurrection by local farmers occurred in this vicinity a century ago."

Blakely walked to the bookcase where black leather notebooks were arranged. Some bore swastikas on the spines. "What are these?"

"Herr Grenz will be interested in those," Stupak replied. "Some have photographs of construction. There are flight logs. Others contain orders and various plans. Herr Grenz!"

Joachim shuffled over. Stupak looked along the row, selected a binder, and brushed mold off the leather back, explaining, "Try as we will, these old ones get moldy. It's the thick concrete walls you know. Not enough fresh air."

He carried the volume to a glass counter and opened it. Black and white photographs were arranged in brittle cellophane pockets. "Here you are, Herr Grenz. These are about the construction of the base, September, 1942 through November, 1944, I believe. Let me get you a chair. I'll be right back."

Stupak went through a doorway and returned with a chair. He placed it before a table and removed stacks of manila folders. "There. A more suitable place, eh?"

Joachim carried the album to the table and sat down. He turned the pages slowly, looking at photographs of foundations being poured, walls being laid up, roof beams being lifted into place.

Blakely and Wafford looked over Joachim's shoulder.

Blakely said, "Did they used Cretan labor?"

"Yes," responded Stupak. "The Nazis relied on the local population to do the heavy work. It was easy to conscript labor because workers received food rations. Many were already members of the Cretan Resistance. So by the time construction was completed, the Resistance knew everything about the base. If you want to hear some very gruesome tales, buy Alex's father, Paul, a few drinks of Ouzo. He will tell you how they would lay in wait for the drunk German pilots and ground crews to return to base late at night. Suddenly, puff! Nobody knew what happened to them. They just vanish into the night!"

Stupak gave a boisterous laugh and slapped Wafford on the shoulder.

"After some hours of searching, the matter would be turned over to the SS. There was a very nasty man in charge of SS in this sector. A major named Gustav Kemft. You mention his name in the village and they will spit upon the ground in hatred. He..."

"Ha!" cried Joachim from his chair. "It's Heinrich! Here, standing on flight line with others!"

They looked over Joachim's shoulder at a tall, athletic, blond haired man in military dress uniform on crutches, raising a toast along with fellow officers.

"You're sure that's Heinrich?" Blakely asked.

"Ya, that is Heinrich!" There was no doubt in Joachim's voice. He turned the page.

"Und here is another!" Joachim cried. It was the same guy, this time in fatigues and working cap, without crutches, standing next to a Messerschmitt 109.

Blakely checked his watch. 1631 hours.

"Well, Joachim, you've located your old buddy after all. How 'bout if we call the *Sea Siren* and tell them the good news. Old Joachim came through for the home team!"

"Yavoll," mumbled the old man. He could not tear himself away from the pages.

"So..." said Stupak, looking from one to another, "Is this it? You need nothing more from here, then?"

"We hope it's the beginning," said Wafford. "Now we know

Heinrich von Etter was based here, we can begin looking for Minoan artifacts."

Stupak seemed amused. He blew smoke above Wafford's head. "I see."

Wafford said seriously, "Well, ole Heinrich found one and split it into pieces and sent parts of it to friends in Germany. Must be more where that came from. Might even find other valuables."

The colonel laughed. "The other valuables being jewels and gold, perhaps?"

Wafford's mouth opened. "How'd you know about it?"

"An American named King."

"Gresham King?" Wafford asked without enthusiasm.

"Yes. He was quoted in Athens newspapers—saying you hoped to find smuggled jewels and gold belonging to the von Etter family. It was on television last night."

"Yeah?" Blakely glanced at Wafford, who looked stunned. Why would King announce publicly anything pertaining to jewels and gold? It would bring every two-bit hoodlum and entrepreneur out of the woodwork.

"I can't believe it," said Wafford, shaking his head. "Gresh and I agreed we'd mention only the search for relics!"

"You saw it on TV?" asked Blakely.

"No," Stupak replied. "It was mentioned in communiqués I received from Athens and Iraklion today. "You and your expedition received good publicity." Stupak laughed. "Not to worry, gentlemen. I won't tell a soul about what you find here!"

He laughed again. Obviously, Stupak didn't think much of their chances. Maybe all the crooks will feel the same way.

Wafford collected himself. "Is there any way we might come back tomorrow and bring the whole team? Spend the day going through your materials here?"

Stupak spread his feet and held a flat hand against his left jaw. "And what would be the purpose, now that you know von Etter was assigned here?"

"Well," said Wafford, looking at Blakely, "we may find documents and such that pinpoint where to search. I mean, what can we lose?"

Stupak moved his hand to his chin. "I suppose no harm could be done. How many are your team?"

"Six, including us."

"No problem. I take it you wish to stay over at the village tonight, eh?"

Wafford shrugged. "A mighty fine idea. Is there room for us down there?"

"Of course. This is off-season. The hotel has plenty of rooms. A nice place. You will like it."

Wafford turned. "Suit you, Ed?"

"Sure."

"Why don't you call Tony. Have Leo throw some clothes into a couple bags fer all of us? Mike can drive down and get them."

"Suits me."

"The professor and everybody oughta be at the square by now." Wafford broke into a wide grin. "Won't they be surprised?"

Stupak put his hands on each of their shoulders. "I tell you what, gentlemen," said Stupak, "I will join you this evening. Everyone can meet for drinks on the piazza! What about that? After sufficient refreshment, we eat! We go to fine restaurant. Their house specialty is escargot—as only Cretan cooks can prepare them. You will help boost the economy of Kastelli! What do you say?"

Wafford grinned. "Sounds nice."

Stupak turned to Joachim. "Herr Grenz, take that album to the hotel with you tonight. Enjoy it to your heart's content. Bring it back tomorrow. All right?"

Joachim carefully closed the book and got up, bowed to Stupak, and shook his hands. The old man had been weeping. His face was wet with tears.

CHAPTER 12

The Piazza

Three old Greek men sat down in the lighted corner of the piazza and opened cases. Two of them tuned lyres. The third played part of a scale on his flute. At a nod and stamp of a foot, they fell into a rhythmic tune that was lusty and mournful. The music had an inevitability about it—each note destined to follow the next in an ancient cadence, reminding Blakely how it was to jog along the edge of Newport Bay.

He looked across the abyss, from the unguarded edge of concrete. Tiny lights appeared, one after the other in the growing dusk. Soft, yellow flickers of light which appeared and disappeared in an instant, probably from kerosene lamps, flashing cook fires where mutton fat dripped, lanterns of peasant farmers returning from makeshift barns, and night fires on corner stones to warm a room.

Like Mexico. Like any place there are peasants, he thought. All the people of higher rank come and go; the peasant survives, stays lean and ready, and doesn't tell what he's thinking.

Wisps of smoke curled from the valleys like thin gray snakes stretching and reaching until their heads evaporated in twilight. The cool night air was settling upon the gathering on the piazza. The dark undulations of mountains suggested the humped backs of many small and large serpents getting nested, cuddling, waiting for the dawn.

Wafford spat an olive seed on the concrete, following the example of Max Padopolis. The piazza was peppered with black pits, looking like droppings of birds. Padopolis was attempting to convince Wafford about the merits of drinking Ouzo clear, without water. Adding water changed the powerful liquid to milk color and diluted the anise flavor.

Elizabeth and Justina were conversing with Colonel Stupak about the prospects for peace in Bosnia. George served large platters of Greek salad and baskets of bread.

Blakely stared at Chris. The guy had gone into relapse—back to the conservative professor Blakely had met at Berkeley. It was the result of their visit to the Archeological Museum. Apparently, Nick Paulas had talked Chris and Justina out of thinking positive. By the time they arrived at Kastelli—at nearly 1700 hours—they had convinced themselves they were on a 'goose chase.'

What does Chris want, for crying out loud? You put the guy in the ballpark, and he says the whole project is a dead dog. Chris had stopped listening. He didn't want to hear any more. He sounded like Justina did the other day.

Not only that, Chris and Elizabeth got into it over the history of Egypt, and Justina had entered into the argument and crossed swords with Elizabeth.

"White history," Elizabeth decried when she and Blakely shared a Coke on the hotel patio after they had gotten registered. "Would you believe these people see the culture of early Egypt as pure white? They give no credence whatsoever to black African culture. It had great impact on Egyptian civilization. It's all in their education, Edward! They received a white elitist education. It is as though the black peoples of the upper Nile—including my Nubian ancestors—never existed."

Blakely had sat there listening as Elizabeth ventilated. He didn't understand much of what she said about Nubians, but his gut told him Elizabeth had a reasonable claim. After all, she was as much an expert in mythology and her own history as they were authorities in Greek archeology.

He sat, watching Chris. They were both brooding and mentally stalking, waiting for the next bitter words to fall. They had

had words, and Blakely was steeling himself against having more words, because the Ouzo and the music were taking effect.

Finding evidence of Heinrich von Etter's existence today had been exhilarating. Then, the Cunninghams had to come along and degrade their accomplishment. Wafford, he noticed, was staying away from the Cunninghams. He supposed Wafford was afraid of what he might say after what Elizabeth had told him.

Chris sat mute, elbow on chair arm, stroking his mustache. Blakely felt sorry for him, yet he also was disgusted by the man's lack of imagination. Blakely's anger was rising despite his resolve.

"I don't get it," Blakely finally said in a harsh whisper. "How can you say there's nothing you can do? We've put you on top of the mountain where von Etter spent practically every waking minute of his time from spring 1943, until he was arrested in September, 1944?"

Chris blinked his eyes. "You don't know that, Edward. As Professor Sibley once said—and you were there when he said it—this von Etter chap could have obtained the relic anywhere. Remember? He said it might have been found accidentally after a rain shower. Dirt washed off it. There it was, lying on the ground.

"Now, we find von Etter has been constructing an air field on top of a mountain where there is no evidence—except one bronze spear point found a century ago—that Minoan artifacts exist. Justina and I talked at length with Paulas about it. He confirmed what Colonel Stupak told you. There simply isn't any evidence of Minoan activity on this mountain! Now, Edward, let's suppose the best case."

Here he goes again, thought Blakely, taking a large gulp of Ouzo. History lesson number one thousand forty-five about to begin. "Yeah?" was all Blakely could muster.

"Yes. Suppose the best case."

Chris leaned elbows on knees, looking intently at him in the half-light. All Blakely could see now was his silhouette against the shop lights behind him. "What is our best case, Edward?"

Hell! Why is he doing this? If the all-knowing professor doesn't know the answer, how was he, the peon student, supposed to know?

Blakely said, "I think we've given you best case, thanks to Joachim. When you go to the air base tomorrow morning, you are smack-dab walking on von Etter's turf. What else could you ask for?"

"Precisely! Von Etter's turf! Where he supervised construction of an air field and half a dozen buildings. Dug ditches, dug pits for garbage, dug cesspools, ran water lines—all these things involved digging, Edward! And out of all this digging atop the mountain, what did he find?"

"The relic."

"Yes. Heinrich von Etter found one solitary bit of history—and nothing more."

"Like the spearhead that was found a 100 years ago."

"Yes. Von Etter found the relic and what did he do next?"

Pedantic. That was the word Blakely was looking for. Pedantic son of a bitch. Or maybe Didactic. Was that it? A combination. Professor Cunningham was a god damned pedantic didactic person with bad breath covering his thousands of words and excuses for not seeing more than what he had ever read about in books. Wrong. More correctly, he was a sour-breathed didactic pedant, which isn't too far removed from a pederast, if you consider, which he had, that neither can be cured by any medicine or therapy known to man. He glanced over at Justina. Her form in the semi-darkness made her appealing just now.

"Edward?" Chris tapped his arm with his pipe hand. The smell of old pipe was strong.

"Edward. Perhaps you didn't hear. I was asking what you thought von Etter would do after he had dug up everything and found the relic? What would he have done next?"

He wanted to punch him. It was Blakely's third Ouzo and Chris didn't get it. This was not the night to talk in negatives after such a goddamn great discovery. This was a night to celebrate! Yes, Heinrich von Etter, Nazi officer and parachutist, engineer extraordinaire, did exist, once upon a time. And they had prima facie evidence of it! And his old buddy Joachim proved it. Chris hadn't touched the Ouzo, had ordered a beer, and hadn't touched that either.

"What would he do?" mused Blakely, making a stab at playing the professor's rhetorical little university of perversity game. "Hell, Chris, I don't know what he'd do. If it were me, I would fill in all the god damned holes I'd made."

Chris nudged him on the arm. "Yes!" He shouted. "Precisely, old boy! That's what von Etter did. What's more, he covered all the filled-in holes with concrete runways, thick foundations, concrete slabs, fuel dumps, barracks, administration buildings, hangars, and towers. I'm saying it would be impossible to locate the source of a relic that is one-of-a-kind because it is no doubt under all the concrete and steel."

Blakely listened, hearing an echo of Chris's protestations up at Berkeley. He glanced toward Justina. She seemed to be looking at him.

"I vaguely remember you said the same thing to me that night at the Faculty Club. You thought it then; you know it now. I guess I'm a little bit confused. If you really feel this way, why the hell are you here?"

Chris didn't seem to recognize Blakely's anger. He responded as though it were a reasonably asked question.

"Well, Edward, I've been asking the same question these past several days. I don't suppose there is a reason for me to continue, is there? You've brought me here to this mountain top, and I've found the truth of it: there is nothing here to discover."

"You aren't even wanting to check out the template against landmarks at the base? How does an archeologist make such deductions, site unseen, if I may be so bold to ask?"

Blakely marveled at his own play on words and prepared for deduction lesson number four-fifty-three, page two-twenty-eight in your philosophy tract, paragraphs one-eighty through two-thousand-and-twenty.

Chris fumbled for his tobacco pouch. "Quite simple, Edward."

The guy was seriously trying to answer him.

"Nick Paulas confirms that records show no significant archeological finds in this area directly related to Minoans. There are significant Roman, Byzantine, and Venetian artifacts associated with some of the ancient churches scattered through the valleys. Nothing here at Kastelli, except recent Turkish and German items from the occupations."

"So, the books win again. If it isn't in the record book, it can't be found?"

Chris lit a fresh pipe. The smoke was one of those aromatic blends that made a nice stink for everybody in the vicinity.

"You have a point, Edward," Chris continued. "Like Louis and his casino friends, we work with odds. If there aren't favorable odds that we'll find something, there is no reason to dig. You follow me?"

"Yeah." He dug what he was saying. He wanted to argue. He was feeling righteous, smart-assed, wanted to be a little mean—maybe because he disliked guys who quit before they even got their hands dirty.

He'd seen it in racing. A day of light air and no chance to set a new elapsed time record and two or three guys would immediately bow out, thinking the race wasn't worthy of their talents. Hell, the air can change suddenly. The odds can shift with a flick of your tiller. Except for Atlanta, he couldn't remember a time he'd just up and quit something and walked. It wasn't the way he was inside. The Greek musicians began a livelier tune that was syncopated, so that your foot insisted on keeping time.

Blakely said in an off-hand way, "I guess, following that theory, there wouldn't be many things discovered the first time, since the record showed zilch. A guy would never have crossed an ocean, flown an airplane, or rode a damn rocket to the moon."

"Look how many men died in the efforts? The odds of doing it successfully made them long shots. Besides, each of those efforts cost enormous amounts of resources. In archeology, we must always be concerned with resources. We're not likely to have unlimited money to spend just digging hither and yon."

"Except on this trip," Blakely said flatly. "You don't have a budget on this one. You can dig up the whole island of Crete if you want to. Lou doesn't care what you or I spend."

"If you'll pardon me, Edward, I think you're being bloody intrusive about this. I don't believe you've heard anything I've said to you. Otherwise, you would understand there is nothing more for me to do here."

"Then why the hell don't you pack up and go home?"

The syncopated music was getting louder and the tempo faster. Two Greek men were dancing in a circle of lamplight, holding hands, bowing, pawing, and moving like crabs with side-steps and back again.

"You mean that, don't you?" Chris was finally angry. He leaned in so that his tobacco breath covered Blakely.

He hissed, "You do mean that. You don't bloody well understand anything I'm about, do you? You never could—even when I tried to keep you out of trouble time and again. And here you are, forty years later, an arrogant sailor attempting to tell me how I should conduct a search—something which you know nothing about! You haven't the least respect for what Justina and I stand for. You liken us to grave robbers! Even Paulas heard about that gaffe! You're quite right. I should go home. If you will excuse me, I'll say good night. I suppose Mike would be available for us to collect our cases so we can catch the ferry."

"Come on, Chris! Give me some sea room!" Blakely hadn't meant to stir him that much. "Hell, I'm truly sorry. I was out of bounds. Stay here. Forget what I said. Have a beer with me! Enjoy the music!"

The two men stood up. Blakely held Chris by the arm. Wafford came over. "What's all the fuss?"

"Please, Edward," said Chris in a low tone while pulling away. "No harm done, really. I'd already told myself there was nothing

THE MINOTAUR   119

for us to do here. Justina agrees. Why should we linger when there is so much to do at home?"

"It's your choice," Blakely said, "but I'd like for you to stay."

"He's leaving?" asked Wafford, showing no real concern.

"Justina and I will discuss it. I'll let you know later."

Chris waved in Justina's direction, then walked over and leaned down. Her silhouette drew back in surprise, then rose.

"Excuse us, everyone," Chris announced. "We shall retire to our room, now."

Justina followed her husband toward the hotel. Blakely sat down again, feeling lousy that he had pushed Chris over the edge.

Wafford sat down. "What happened?"

"He's giving up. Wants to go home. I told him, if he feels that way, he should get the hell out! I'm sorry, Lou. That should be between Chris and you—not me."

Wafford got up and gave Blakely a pat on the shoulder. "Not your fault the professor's got no guts. We'll do it ourselves, if we have to."

"Yeah." He watched Wafford return to his chair. 'Do what ourselves,' he wondered. Chris was right. Hell, he had history books and all the bookies in the world on his side. This was a wild crapshoot. What would they look for tomorrow? Only five more days and it would all be over anyway!

He looked across the darkness, watching the bright flickers, thinking about the peasants there, and what they must be doing. Some making love, maybe; others eating a supper of roasted mutton with onions and green peppers; a mother nursing a new baby; an old one dying. Hell, those people have lived as long as man without checking the records to see if what they wanted to do could be done. They just god damned tried it. If it worked, they did it again. If they liked it, they did it more often. Yeah. They were the people who made record-keeping necessary in the first place. Records were the results of people who tried things—took chances—and found out what worked best—like making love the first time or sailing uncharted waters.

Christopher Cunningham would never find much of value, he thought, because he wasn't willing to look in places where the rewards weren't guaranteed. What happened to his passion? Christopher, St. Christopher, Christopher Columbus, Cristofer, Christo, Christ, Christ the Son—the Son of the Father.

Christopher the archeologist was trained to quest, armed with abilities to read signs—like a sailor is trained to read stars, wind, and water. What happened to all that? Once you know how to sail, you don't consult the record book to check the odds. You get in your damned boat, check your gear, the wind, the tide, the swells, and get the hell out in it and do the best you can. Otherwise, you stand safely on shore and watch and laugh at the crazies challenging a Force Six.

Stay on the lecture circuit, man. Stunt the growth of all those budding archeologists until they're so damned tired of hearing your pedantic didacticism that they'll quit school and run off some place where nobody has dug before, and there aren't any books to consult, and they'll use their instincts, apply basic training, learn by doing, take a new slant to problem solving, maybe use a photo of earth from outer space—and lo and behold—they discover buried beneath fifty feet of swirling sand the ancient silk route Marco Polo traveled—or some other damned thing.

Blakely stretched his legs out and looked up at the stars. Or maybe, you take chances of wasting precious time by looking through binoculars every night at the stars because it is your passion to do so. And one night, one night in 10,000 years, you discover a comet nobody on earth has seen except you, and it is named after you.

Joachim says Hyakutake will not come again for 17,000 years. A snowball of a jillion bits of ancient fire. It will have disappeared but not perished, staying lit, hot with energy, lighting the sky for anyone left on earth who might dare to lift their eyes some night and see it. And 17,000 years from now, some other guy will discover it again, and the comet will be named after him in his honor.

George poured Ouzo into Blakely's empty glass.

CHAPTER 13

A Helluva Party

Wafford came over and sat down beside Blakely after wheeling Elizabeth over to the hotel. "Elizabeth got a little chilly out here in the night air. The Ouzo kinda got to her, too. Made her tired, she said." He paused. "You okay, Ed?"

"Yeah. I'm okay."

"I noticed ole Chris had a burr under his saddle when they arrived this afternoon. Even had Elizabeth agitated. Something about Egypt and black history. Guess she told you."

"Yeah."

"Elizabeth's mighty proud of her people. Knows probably more than most 'bout the Nubians. That's her people, you know."

"She told me."

"You think they'll really leave?"

"Chris has given up. So, yeah. We'll be minus two archeologists tomorrow morning."

"Well, I declare," said Lou without any emotion. "Seems they've been chase'n their tails anyway. I guess I don't understand how these fellas operate."

"Tell me about it," Blakely responded. "Joachim puts them on target and the guy doesn't even want to visit the damned air base. All he wants to do is fold up his tent and go home. I know it's not my place to make judgments, but I say the hell with him. Let them go back to Berlin. You need a grave robber? You got plenty. They're runn'n over with 'em here. There's this guy Nick Paulas. There's the ones from Athens... what're their names?"

"Angelo and Kristos."

Blakely knew he was sounding like Wafford—about archeologists being a dime a dozen. Wafford's right after all! When money's no problem, you can buy whatever or whoever you need.

"Yeah, ole Angelo and Kristos, the really big grave robbers."

Blakely took another drink of Ouzo. He felt Wafford's eyes on him.

"Miss Jenny's arriving soon. She on your mind, Ed?"

"Not on my mind," Blakely retorted, trying to see Wafford's face in the gloom. His head told him he was out of control, but he was enjoying the heat in his bowels. He wouldn't mind picking a fight—something he hadn't thought of doing in years—except maybe with Gresham King. Why couldn't Chris duke it out—even verbally—and have a drink and forget their differences? Stick around, celebrate, get drunk and trade insults. Instead, the guy runs away in a damn huff. Like Wafford says, he has no guts.

"Why isn't anybody celebrating?"

"Dunno, Ed."

"Where's my old buddy Joachim?"

"Up in his room. Wanted to be by himself with that picture book. Max had the cook send up food. I believe ole Joachim's a little tuckered out after all the excitement today."

Max Padopolis, thought Blakely, trying to separate the events of the afternoon in the alcohol haze of faces, Greek names, and sounds. Padopolis almost put them in jail as spies today. Now, he's all sweetness and light. "What the hell is Max, anyway?" asked Blakely in a belligerent tone.

Padopolis turned in his chair to look, then resumed talking.

Blakely stared across at Max sitting, spitting olive pits, talking with Stupak. "Administrative constabulary—whatever that was, host to the lost and desperate, gate keeper for the Greek Air Force, chief cook, bottle washer. What doesn't the guy do around here?"

Wafford touched Blakely's arm. "Sounds like you're pretty angry. Want me to leave you alone?"

"Sorry. Stay with me. Just need George to fill my glass is all. I thought we were gonna celebrate our discoveries. You want to celebrate with me, Lou?"

"Hell yes. Let's celebrate! First I better check in with Chris and Justina. See what they want to do tomorrow. I'll be back in a few minutes."

Wafford walked across to the hotel. Blakely sat there listening to the music. Four men were doing a line dance beneath the street lamp. Alex said something about Nazis. Blakely tried to shake himself awake. Probably insulting his buddy Joachim!

Max called to Blakely. "Come join us!"

Blakely stood up and checked himself. A little wobbly, but he was okay. He looked down into the black valley. Fewer yellow lights flickered. The good people of the earth are going to bed while the bad ones stay up and get drunk, he thought, finding the idea funny. He carried his empty glass with him, and sat down next to the colonel.

Stupak said, "We were just talking about the occupation. You remember my telling you about the Cretan Resistance this afternoon. When the Resistance killed a Nazi from the air field, all the civilians would be brought to this piazza. Major Kemft would point to this one and that, line up eight, ten, sometimes twelve of the men here at the edge. They would be shot. The villagers call this piazza the place of martyrs."

Blakely thought about Elizabeth and her King Minos story and the sacrifice of the Athenian men and women to the Minotaur. Good old Theseus! Times hadn't changed. Alex was speaking to him.

"The edge you see here," Alex stood up and swayed as he pointed down, "there was always blood. If the bodies did not fall over the edge, the damned Nazis would order us to throw them off the side. As a boy, I witnessed such atrocities."

Padopolis said, "You never knew when the SS would blow their whistles. That meant you must come here. Otherwise, they sent out search units. Persons hiding would be shot on sight. I would stand with my parents, hoping the SS would not point in the direction of my father. One day, however, after three pilots were found shot to death, my father was chosen for execution. He was one of twelve who stood right here."

Blakely shivered. Was it different for the son, Blakely wondered, when the father was forcibly taken from you? How must it be to witness your father's execution? Christos upon the cross wasn't the Son after all; it was the Father incarnate. Christ the Father was executed slowly--tortured on the cross. The son of the Father was the Father of the father. How could Christopher, the father, run out on his son Thomas? How could Chris leave Blakely before their business was finished? It was all a betrayal! Nothing made any sense. Padopolis waved his glass along in front of him.

"I'll never forget, August 17, 1943 it was. I could not bear to watch, yet I could not take my eyes from my father's face. Major Kemft gave the order. My father stood there, looking straight ahead, without emotion, even as the bullets struck him, making holes in his chest, until he fell upon this slab. I was sick in my stomach, but I could not cry.

"From that day until the Nazis left, I carried messages for the Resistance, counted aircraft taking off and landing each day, tried to help any way I could. I would have pissed in their beer, had I the chance!"

Blakely was roused, shaking off the effects of too much Ouzo. So it was the same bitterness, whether it was about Father No-Name or losing your father to an enemy's bullet. The bitter feeling of loss and desire for retaliation were there. At least Alex had his father's murderers to retaliate against. He tried to speak, realizing his tongue was not cooperating.

Blakely sat up straighter, trying to sober up. "Did they ever kill the major, this Gustav Kemft guy?"

"There are certain mysteries the Resistance leaders would never explain," replied Stupak. "Everyone is sure Resistance lured Kemft into some sort of trap, killed him, and buried his body secretly. Nobody will say for sure, but he one day disappeared like other Nazis, and was never heard of again. A reward was posted. SS began systematically shooting larger groups of people in an effort to force out the truth. After a hundred or so people were murdered, they gave it up. Is that not right, Alex?"

"Yes, that is so."

"Increasing the reward did no good either," said Padopolis. "The Nazis eventually took down the reward signs, because these became a symbol of how strong the underground really was."

Blakely watched Stupak. Handsome bastard, even in his civilian clothes. The new soldier! Always relaxed and in control of himself, yet vigilant. The Ouzo made Blakely want to challenge him. Wafford stood in a frame of light at the hotel. He had changed his shirt. The musicians struck up another dance tune, and three old men stood apart and began to move in time.

Wafford approached. "Looks like you boys are settling down for the evening!"

George brought them fresh glasses of Ouzo, more bowls olives and crackers. The music was growing louder. Several Greek men were dancing and singing. It was 2215 hours. There was no sign that anyone was ready to eat dinner.

"Alex, I don't recall your last name?"

"Vanos."

"And you are Max's assistant?"

"Yes, I help Max. I also own the Kastelli cab company."

Alex pointed toward a beat up yellow Volkswagen van which Blakely had noticed earlier parked at the corner of the square beneath a plane tree. The van's rear end looked like somebody had taken a sledge hammer to it; the dusty surface was totally bumps and ripples and gouges. Two side windows were cracked.

"Alex is my brother-in-law," Padopolis said, his voice hinting that it was a mixed blessing.

"Where's Mike?" asked Blakely, aware he hadn't seen his second mate since he returned with the luggage from the *Sea Siren*.

Wafford looked around. "Musta gone to bed."

"Not to worry about him," Padopolis said, laughing knowingly. "He is down the way at our disco. Young men have the power to sniff their way to the girls, if you know what I mean."

"He's been sniffing since about 1900 hours," replied Blakely. "I think he'll have more than a snoot full, if one of those Scandinavian women gets hold of him. Are they staying here tonight?"

"They are here," Alex noted. "Same hotel where you stay. Maybe you will be lucky tonight."

"Too much for me," Blakely chuckled. He thought about Stephanie calling him a star and wondered whether she had looked for him in Iraklion tonight. At least, Stephanie was closer to his own age. "Those chicks aren't interested in any man over thirty, unless he has lots of money to spend."

"You'd be surprised, Ed," said Stupak seriously, spitting out a pit in the direction of the valley. "These women come here for one purpose, and that is to get laid. True. Of course, they also come to get a sun tan, see historic ruins. Sure. They do all that in one or two days. The rest of their vacation—maybe here for a week, ten days, more—they lay around naked and look for guys to screw them. And for variety, they often like men of experience such as yourself."

"What are you saying, Dimitrius?" Blakely munched down on a pit and spat it out. "You mean they take on graybeards like me?"

"Yes, of course. You know damned well they do!" Stupak grinned, clapping Blakely on the back. "Hell yes. You want to get laid, my friend? Crete is the place. All beautiful German, Scandinavian, some English, a few French, mostly blondes under thirty five."

Wafford pulled his chair closer. "They charge or do it free gratis?"

Stupak called. "Over here, George! Another round!"

Stupak punched Wafford on the shoulder. "Are you serious? There is so much foreign nookie here, it is all gratis!"

"Except you must be very careful where you go to pick these ladies up," explained Alex. "Above all, you must not intrude on the territory of our young men who consider these women as strictly theirs."

THE MINOTAUR 127

"How do you mean?" asked Blakely.

Stupak rested his elbows on his knees so his face was immediately in front of Blakely. "If, say, you were to try dancing with these ladies at a disco in such places as Malia, the local boys would be most upset. They might not challenge you at the moment you asked the pretty lady to dance, but they might surprise you on your way home."

"Kinda like the Cretan Resistance?" Blakely noted. "So what happens?"

Alex downed his Ouzo and set the glass carefully on the table. "They just beat the piss out of you, that's all. You end up in hospital a few days."

He said it matter-of-factly, without any emotion. George poured Ouzo in all the glasses.

"If you want a nice blond for tonight, Ed," said Alex, "there's some to be had at the disco."

Wafford whispered, "Why don't you, Ed? It'll do you good. We could go down together."

"I myself go there from time to time," confided Stupak, "but only when I am extra horny. Otherwise, I am more prudent and go to special places."

Blakely listened to them declaiming on the possibilities ahead. A bunch of horny mountain goats, he thought. Like all those erotic little statues he saw in the curio shops this morning. Satyrs, they were called. He looked over at the shadow of Wafford, sitting there, drinking quietly. Wafford seemed to be waiting for Blakely to say he would go the disco.

"Hey, Ed," said Wafford, "we forgot to celebrate!"

"Yeah."

It was growing late and Blakely was feeling heavy and tired. He wanted to go to bed.

"Celebrate?" Stupak stood up. "Lou is right. We haven't celebrated! Get up everyone! Let's celebrate! Mikos! Play something lively! Play Zorba!"

The three musicians began a boisterous rendition.

"Come, gentlemen. On your feet!"

Stupak grabbed Blakely's arm and hauled him up and took Wafford by the other arm. They sauntered toward the lamp light, under which several men were dancing. They formed a line with Stupak in the middle and Alex anchoring Blakely and Padopolis on the outside of Wafford.

Stupak held Blakely and Wafford in his strong arms and moved them about, leading, and giving direction, as the music's beat helped them to move their feet in time.

"Now, gentlemen, let us move, this way, and this way, and this way again; now, other way, other way, and other way again; and, forward step, another step, and still another one; and, backward step, backward step and step once again, now right, to the right, to the right a-gain. Good! Very good! You were meant to dance, Lou!"

Wafford was laughing so hard he was like a marionette held between Stupak and Padopolis.

"Now, raise your arms, gentlemen," said Stupak, "and place them on the shoulders—like this!"

Blakely hung his arms across the shoulders of Stupak and Alex and immediately felt lifted and connected, and it was easier to follow the dance steps—especially moving from side to side.

"Keep going!" shouted Stupak to musicians. "Play it ten times over, Mikos!"

The musicians watched as the line of dancers began to sidestep with Padopolis leading.

"Follow to the right, Lou," commanded Stupak. "Follow Max!"

And they moved to the right, neatly, slowly, and Max joined arms with four other men who continued curving, slowly, sidestep, side-step, until they joined arms with Alex, forming a circle, and they continued dancing in the same direction, circling, until Stupak shouted, "Now to the left!"

And they circled to the left. "Now forward!"

They stepped, and stepped, and again took a step, "Now back!"

They were one, Blakely thought, feeling the movement, watching the Cretan men across from him, following their rhythms and lightness. It was beautiful. He couldn't have imagined the oneness he felt as they moved in unison—like a strong yet delicate animal with many parts. The music stopped suddenly, and everyone clapped and shouted.

"Every man was put on this earth to dance," Padopolis announced to Wafford with great solemnity. "You dance well for a man not in practice."

Stupak raised his hand. "Another round, George, before we go to dinner!"

They sat down and were joined by the other men.

Alex explained. "Here are Stepheno, Nick, Costos, and Pedro. They speak no English, but they wish to have drink and share dance with you, our guests."

Wafford whispered, "What does that mean?"

"Dunno," said Blakely.

The four men stood up and held their hands out and waved for Blakely and Wafford to stand up. Stephano said something to Mikos, and the musicians started up another lively tune. They took Blakely and Wafford and formed another line and began to dance.

"Looking very good!" shouted Padopolis from his chair. Alex whistled.

Others joined, until everyone on the patio had formed a large circle and danced as one. The music lasted a long time, and Blakely found his steps becoming natural, so that he could enjoy the undulations and movements of the men joined together. And when it stopped, he wanted to dance again.

They drank the Ouzo and listened to the increasingly raucous music. One of the Greeks who spoke no English was attempting to explain something to him. The face faded and then Blakely could no longer hear what the man said. Wafford's voice said something to Stupak, and he could not understand Stupak's reply. Someone tapped him on the shoulder.

"Would you be ready for dinner?" asked Padopolis. "I believe it is waiting for us."

Blakely tried to get out of the chair. The guys who didn't speak English were out dancing again. He noticed Wafford and Alex had the same problem getting up. Damned Ouzo. He wobbled, got control of himself, balanced his weight evenly on his feet, and put himself in motion. Stupak reached over and helped Wafford. Max listed to port, but pushed himself off the chair in the direction of the cobbled street.

The five men joined arms and walked uncertainly down the narrow street, turning into an alley lit by gas lamps, bumping against the stone walls on either side, moving uncertainly even as Padopolis, pointing the way, turned and crashed into some parked bicycles. He extricated himself only with help from Alex and Stupak. They arrived at a wide wooden door, where light was glowing through the cracks. He could smell onions cooking. The clock above the piazza chimed softly. 2400 hours, thought Blakely, counting the twelve strikes to check his sensibility.

The door opened into what appeared to be a one room restaurant with several long tables in front of a low, wide hearth. Old and middle aged women greeted Padopolis, nodded at the Americans, and went into a kitchen as the men sat down. The women reappeared with fat brown pitchers of wine, heaping bowls of French fries, and metal trays with slabs of what Blakely thought were beef steaks with onions.

"Here is to our American friends," said Stupak, raising a glass of straw colored wine. Everyone drank.

Wafford stood up, uncertainly, "Here's to our Greek brothers," he said in good down-country fashion. Everyone drank. Wafford nearly missed his chair when he sat down.

Blakely grinned at Wafford, considered getting up, but thought better of it. Padopolis, however, would not be denied opportunity.

"Gentlemen," he began, "as an official of this ancient district, I am so very pleased to have you and the other members of your party as our guests. It is not every day that we are so greatly honored. We are blessed with the presence of a famous American yacht captain and an entrepreneur who operates a famous wagering establishment, the epitome of the American dream of a successful man in America. Gentlemen, it is our pleasure to have you here with us. We hope you will stay a long time. And we hope you spend lots of American money while you are here!"

Everyone laughed. Padopolis was no fool, thought Blakely. The guy knew how to pile it on and make fun of you at the same time.

"Where do you raise the beef?" Blakely asked.

Alex looked perplexed, then laughed. "You are eating fine lamb steaks, my friend. We do raise beef on the island, but that isn't what you are eating."

A hefty dark woman with black hair over her lip brought out a round flat serving dish piled high with snails in snail shells. They were a golden, gelatinous mass. Blakely sure as hell was glad he had drunk lots of Ouzo now. This wasn't exactly French escargot.

"This, a specialty," Padopolis said, emphasizing it by waving his fork.

The woman pushed about two dozen of the snails onto Blakely's plate, an equal amount on Wafford's. They wanted their guests to be given best treatment—perhaps too good, thought Blakely.

"Taste them," Alex said, watching Blakely toy with a snail shell. "Take the little fork and dig them out," he directed.

Blakely held the snail shell with his knife and dug the critter out, eating it with one gulp.

"Delicious," reported Blakely. The snails had the same earthy flavor as the wine. Another drink of wine. He wondered whether peasants in the valley ever ate this grandly.

"Did I tell you the good news, bad news, Ed?" asked Wafford from across the table.

"Not sure whether you did or not, Lou. There's been so much of each lately." He really didn't want to hear it.

"I spoke with Miss Justina and Chris tonight." Wafford was slurring his words. "Good news and bad news. Miss Justina is going to stay with us. Chris is leaving tomorrow morning."

"Which is the good news and which is the bad news?" asked

Blakely, who felt his mind fog, trying to see Wafford's face above the fried potatoes and steaming mutton steaks.

"You'll have to judge that for yourself," Wafford said with a leer, gravy running down his chin. "I think Miss Justina has a gut feeling we're onto something here."

"Maybe she knows something I don't."

"You two musta been plenty chummy back in Germany."

"Not that good."

Wafford must be drunk. He was using sexual innuendo. Maybe he's got a letch for Justina. Must be tough, not having a woman who can move her legs for you the way you want. He tried to imagine Wafford and Elizabeth making love, but couldn't.

"How can a Christian man such as yourself get ideas like that, Lou?" asked Blakely, trying to keep from slurring his words. "She's a married woman."

"Marri... married or not, I saw a gleam," Wafford said, his face pink and showing sweat.

Stupak was listening. Blakely pointed toward Stupak with his fork, "I think Justina has the hots for Dimitrius. Notice how attentive she was, hanging on his every word. That's who she was thinking about, ...not me."

Stupak laughed, tilted his head back, and laughed again. "Good looking for her age," he said. "She has a nice shaped bosom, too, for one so past prime."

"What do you mean, so past prime?" challenged Blakely. "You're only past prime if you feel that way. I sure don't feel that way. You agree, Lou?"

"My granddaddy live to be 85," replied Wafford. "He'd em... embarrass me sometimes, talking about his sexual prowess. Claimed he could still do it at 81. He enjoyed look'n at all the women 'til the day he died. Would even pat 'em on the behind once in a while."

Blakely was finding it more difficult to hear. The voices grew distant, and he concentrated on eating. He tried to eat all the escargot, but the woman with the mustache kept putting more on his plate. So he reluctantly gave up, concentrating on finishing the wine in his glass. That too, was a lost cause. He would forget, then open his eyes, and find the glass was full.

He took another swig, found he was being helped out of his chair, opened his eyes wide, and saw he was shaking hands with the woman who'd been serving the escargot. He started to give her a kiss, but Stupak pulled him toward the door. Wafford was supported by Padopolis and Alex. The five weaved along the narrow entry, which was totally dark. Stupak fell over the bicycles, dragging Wafford with him. Stupak swore, got to his feet again, and put his arm over Blakely's shoulder for support. Wafford was pulled to his feet by Alex. They stumbled along, concentrating on staying upright, finding it easier footing on the cobbles leading up the steep hill toward the hotel.

Wafford tried to sing a German song his daddy had taught him. "Nach housa, nach house gehen..." Blakely knew the song. Wafford couldn't seem to remember the words. Hell, he said to himself, anybody would know that song.

Blakely tried to help. "...wir sichted.. Nach hau, geht wir sicht." He couldn't remember either.

Blakely pointed to the yellow Volkswagen van, and tried to explain to Wafford that it belonged to Alex, but couldn't get the right words out. The men stood next to it. "Ni... Nish pent job," he said, leaning against his buddy Alex. Alex nodded, looking grim, like he was viewing the body of a dead relative. Alex patted the dented, yellow side, leaving print marks in the dirt coating it. Stupak was relieving himself on the front, agreeing. "Good pant job. Good pant job." He zipped up, staggered over, and joined them.

Padopolis had his arm around Wafford's neck.

"Too late for disco, my frien?"

"Toooo late," whispered Wafford.

And like a drunken chorus line, the five men listed to starboard, setting themselves as one in a side-ward scuttle, then in forward motion and meandered across the empty street. They shuffled into the hotel. A sleepy clerk came around the desk and helped carry Blakely up the stairs.

CHAPTER 14

The Morning After

Blakely awoke to the sound of a horn blaring. Where was he? Whitewashed room, an open window, brown curtains flapping. Not on the boat. A bell tolled. He picked up the count at three. 0800 hours. Damn. He was at Kastelli! He rolled out of bed, stood, feeling the floor shift beneath his feet, gained balance, and moved carefully down the hall to the shower. Cold water always felt good. Helluva party. It started to come back. Couldn't imagine how Max and Dimitrius held all that alcohol.

He toweled off, threw on a CAL sweatshirt, sailing pants, and boat moccasins. He checked the contents of his canvas shoulder case. Cellular phone, tablet, pens, sun glasses, and two packs of gum. What else? He threw in a pack of TUMS. He tried running down the tile stairs. His head reeled. Find the banister. Walk, guy.

"Where's everybody?" he asked the clerk. Manolis pointed toward the rear of the hotel. He went down the hall and onto a patio where grape vines formed a canopy over tables. Elizabeth, Wafford and Justina were sitting at a table having coffee over empty plates. His appearance drew stares of disapproval from Elizabeth and Justina. Well, heck, he couldn't be the most popular guy in class every day!

"Good morning!" He tried. "How's every body this morning?"

His own words hurt his ears.

"Hey, guy," he said to Wafford, trying to raise some enthusiasm with a Marchese impression, "you look like you had a celebration last night."

Wafford tried to smile, but it looked more like he was about to cry. He grinned at the coffee cup, not saying anything. He actually looked awful, with bloodshot eyes, dark circles, a swollen lower lip. His face was one big peel of dead skin.

"You must have had some party, Captain Easy," Elizabeth said, a bit of dry humor creeping into her eyes and playing at the edges of her pretty mouth. "It took three men to get Louis up the steps, undressed and put to bed. What did you mean, staying out until all hours?"

Elizabeth was at least conciliatory. Justina turned back to the papers she had been studying, seeming to ignore Blakely altogether.

"It's the Greek way, Elizabeth! Some nights, the men dance with the men and forget about the women. You should have seen your husband out there—a Greek Gene Kelly with sore feet, yet, doing it with his Greek buddies!"

"Spare me the lurid details, Edward!"

" Actually, Lou and I went looking for women last night, Elizabeth, but Lou decided none was as beautiful as you, so we were good boys and came home to bed."

"How nice of you!"

She laughed hollowly. Justina would have laughed too, he thought, except she pretended not to hear and was biting her lip.

"Lou, I don't remember anybody punching you last night, but you've got a fat lip. Was Elizabeth getting back at you this morning?"

Wafford touched the swollen place with his fingers.

"Think I got it trying to help Dimitrius, after we fell over them bicycles. I leaned over and he raised up. Bumped me in the mouth with his head."

"You men! You are all disgusting!" Elizabeth shook her head. She nodded toward Wafford.

"He wouldn't tell me what happened. I thought he'd been in a fight for sure."

"Well, he tried, Elizabeth, but Dimitrius backed down."

THE MINOTAUR 137

Blakely turned to Justina, acting innocent. "Where's Chris this morning?"

She looked up, paused as if to say, you ought to know all about it, you SOB. But she didn't say it. Her voice was restrained.

"Mike took him to the boat to get his cases. He is returning home."

"You decided to stay on?"

Blakely was pressing. But why not?

"I wanted to keep my bargain with Louis. If I can still be of help, I will. When I see I can't, I also will go home."

Her eyes said to him, it has nothing at all to do with you, you egotistical bastard. Okay, he thought, what's your agenda?

"So, how are you planning to help?"

Her black eyes blinked uncertainly, then locked on his. "I wish to cooperate, if that is what you are asking. Otherwise, I have no plan before I see the situation. Once I make an assessment, I determine whether I can do archeology here or not."

A good answer. He realized Joachim wasn't there.

"Joachim out taking a walk?"

"Not feeling well," Wafford replied. "Stayed up too late with the picture book. He stopped by this morning and spoke to Justina. Then he went back to his room."

"I hope you don't mean anything serious?"

Blakely was concerned about Joachim. The day before yesterday, he had been to Maleme and, from what Elizabeth said, had cried at the cemetery. Yesterday, he had been very emotional—first on the piazza, and later, at the air base when he found photographs of Heinrich. The strain of it all could be too much for him.

"Is he eating?"

"The waiter took him some fruit and a roll." Wafford said. "He was eating. He had some coffee."

"Rolls aren't his thing. He's got to have oatmeal. I'll get the waiter to take him some."

"Joachim will be okay," Justina added softly. "Perhaps you can see him before we go to the air base this morning."

"Yeah."

Good, he thought. Justina's looking forward to visiting the base. The waiter brought Blakely coffee and breakfast cakes.

"Lou, can Elizabeth join us today?"

Elizabeth drew back. He had said it wrong and knew it the moment Wafford's name came out first.

She feigned hurt, pretending to glare at Blakely. "Why are you asking Louis what I can do and can't do, Captain Easy? Are you striving to become a Greek?"

He smirked. God, his head was pounding! "Sorry." He would try again. "Elizabeth? Can you give us a hand today?"

"Certainly." She touched her neck with long fingers and extended her black arms on the ceramic surface of the table. "I would enjoy it. You just tell me what you want. I'll do whatever you say."

"Do you have all the documentation on the relic, Justina?"

She reached down and pulled up a black leather case. "All here."

He finished eating the cake, took another swallow of coffee, and pushed back his chair.

"I need to warn Stupak we're coming, so he can have passes ready. I'll stop by Joachim's room, too. See if he needs anything."

He stood up and checked his watch. 0845 hours. "Can we meet in front of the hotel at 0900 hours?"

They nodded. He left them to take care of business. Elizabeth could be a big help. If only Joachim were feeling better. He stopped in the hallway and removed his cellular phone and dialed the *Sea Siren*.

"*Sea Siren*. Communications Center. Gregor Tobok. Can I help you?"

"Hi, Gregor! How's it going?"

"Fine, skipper. Are you up at Kastelli?"

"Yeah."

"I found out there's a war museum at the Greek Air Base above the town. They say you'll need a clearance from their headquarters in Athens."

THE MINOTAUR 139

"Good work, Gregor. Fortunately, we've got that covered through the base commander. We were up there yesterday."

"Oh, good."

"Anything else?"

"No, except Jeremiah wants me and Harry to help him do some taping at Kastelli tomorrow."

"Fine. Can you ring Tony?"

"Sure."

"Pilot house. Zeno speaking."

"What's happening, Tony?"

"Nothing here, Eddie. Sounds like all the happenings are up there on the mountain top! Understand you and Mr. Wafford kinda made a night of it. Dancing with all the men. Cavorting to all hours!"

"Mike's got a big mouth! What else is going on?"

"I see the professor is leaving with Leo in the launch. He's taking the ferry back to Piraeus this morning. His missus staying on?"

"Yeah. For awhile."

"Be careful up there, Eddie boy!"

"Thanks for all your moral support, Mr. Zeno. Talk with you later!"

He punched the power off button and climbed the stairs. His head throbbing with each step. He knocked. "Enter!"

He opened the door. Joachim lay dressed on the bed with two pillows propped under his shoulders. The album of photographs rested on his chest.

"Good morning, Edward," he said weakly, trying to smile.

Blakely crossed the room and glanced at the food tray on the night table. One bite out of a breakfast cake. Hardly any fruit gone. Most of the black coffee still in the cup.

"Good morning, Joachim. You haven't touched your breakfast."

Joachim pulled himself into a sitting position and looked scornfully at the tray. "I do not feel so strong today."

"What if I got you some oatmeal?"

Joachim shook his head slowly. "Ya. That would be better. Oatmeal is good for the soul."

His voice was barely more than a whisper.

"What's wrong? Does your head or chest hurt?"

"No. I feel tired is all."

"You aren't in any pain?"

"No, Edward."

"Any numbness? Feet or hands?"

"No."

"Can you see okay?"

"Ya."

Joachim rubbed his eyes and dropped his hand to his side.

"I want you to stay here and rest today, Joachim. Get strong so you can help us tomorrow. Okay?"

"Ya." He opened his eyes wide. "I want to be strong for tonight. There is to be an eclipse of the moon. Chance to see Hyakutake best. Maybe last chance we have."

Joachim pushed the album down off his chest.

"Let me take that," said Blakely, removing the album.

"Many pictures of Heinrich there. I want to see the other books, see more of Heinrich and others."

"Stay resting today, Joachim. And tomorrow, you can look through the other albums."

"That would be good."

The old man reached around, looking for something.

"What do you need?"

"My pipe and tobacco," replied Joachim, seeming confused. He looked around the room. "I don't know where I left them."

Blakely opened the bathroom door.

"Here they are. On the toilet."

He brought the pipe and tobacco to Joachim.

"Where are your matches?"

"Look in my other pants, hanging on the hook there."

Blakely found the box of matches and handed them to Joachim.

He filled the pipe, tamped it with his index finger, struck a match, and puffed until the pipe sputtered with each draw.

"If I am able," Joachim said, "could we watch the eclipse together?"

A rush of warmth swept through Blakely. "Sure, Joachim. We sure can."

"See the Hyakutake for last time?"

Joachim was looking intently at Blakely with watery blue eyes. His voice sounded low and distant, like his thoughts were coming from far away. Blakely tried to be cheerful.

"Who knows, Joachim? We might see the comet several more nights. How can you say 'for the last time'?"

Joachim disregarded his question. "It is supposed to be visible to the northwest tonight, when the eclipse is full."

He took the pipe from his mouth, looked at it in his thick fingers, and handed it slowly to Blakely.

"The pipe does not taste so good this morning. Would you mind bringing the ashtray from the bathroom and putting it here where I can reach it?"

"Not at all."

Joachim must really be sick, not to want his pipe or even a cup of coffee. He returned with the ashtray and placed the hot pipe in it.

"What else can I get you?"

Joachim looked around again. "My notebook and pencil. They're in my coat pocket—on the hook there—the left one."

Blakely dug into the pocket and removed the spiral pocket notebook and pencil.

"Where would you like them?"

"Here, next to my pipe will do. Thank you."

He put the notebook and pencil down. "Now, what else? Need a glass of water?"

"Nothing," he replied, reaching out his hand. Blakely sat on the edge of the bed and took his hand. It felt rough and cold.

"You are my best friend, Edward. You like stars the same as I do. We are the same in many ways."

"How 'bout if I arrange for a doctor to look at you today?"

"Not today. Maybe, if I don't feel better, tomorrow. Not today," he said weakly.

Blakely let go of Joachim's hand, got up, and pulled a quilt down from the closet shelf. "Let me put this over you, Joachim. Your hands are cold." Blakley touched the old man's bearded cheek and forehead. They were cool.

"Thank you, Edward," he said. "The blanket feels warm and good."

"Will you eat some oatmeal if I send some up?"

"Tell them I'd like oatmeal for lunch. I think now I want to take a nap."

"Mind if I take this album back to the air base?"

The old man nodded.

"Take it. I've memorized all of the pictures of Heinrich. I don't need it any more."

"Can I take one of these pillows out so you can lie flat?"

"Ya. That would be good."

Blakely removed the extra pillow, helping Joachim to move down further on the bed.

"Sure you are all right?"

"Ya! I rest now so we can stay up tonight. Watch Hyakutake." His eyes closed.

"See you later, Joachim," said Blakely as he walked toward the door.

"You are a good man, Edward," Joachim whispered. Blakely opened and gently closed the door.

He went down the stairs and ordered the oatmeal. He didn't want to leave Joachim by himself. He had a premonition that Joachim was dying, and he wanted to be there, to hold his hand and to comfort him. Just hang on, Joachim. He was filled with anguish. May thy will be done, God. May thy will be done!

He went out into the street. Alex was cleaning the windshield of his van.

"Can you do me a favor, Alex?"

"Any thing you ask!"

His eyes were bloodshot, too.

"My friend Joachim is up in room four. He may be very sick. Could you arrange for a doctor to look in on him?"

"Of course. The old German man, you say?"

"Yeah."

"Our physician lives down the way. I'll go there now."

"Thanks, Alex."

CHAPTER 15

Scavengers

The colonel was in high spirits for a guy still suffering the effects of Ouzo. Stupak was wearing extra large bags under his bloodshot eyes. He pushed Elizabeth's wheel chair down the hall.

"Your husband Lou is—how do you say it in America—a big party animal!"

Elizabeth was reluctantly enjoying this suave Greek. He turned the corner into the room where the stairs led to the basement.

"I tell you, ladies and gentlemen, this room is yours. Much more convenient than the moldy one downstairs, not true?"

He stepped around Elizabeth and pointed. "See what I have for you? My men brought up all those documents and cleaned them. Nice for you to touch, eh? They still smell, but you can't have everything, no?"

The bookshelves and their contents had been brought upstairs, cleaned, and arranged in neat order. There was a small table to one side with a coffee maker, a bowl of fruit, some breakfast cakes, napkins, cups, and a pitcher of water. There was also a large work table and chairs for everyone.

The colonel put his hands on his hips. "What do you look for this morning, if I may ask?"

"We're not sure," replied Blakely. "We're going to survey what is here. We hope to find a document showing the arrival of a shipment from Trieste to Major von Etter. We're also looking for maps or photographs which might correspond to the template."

"No maps there. We continue using the German engineering

maps. They are very accurate. I can get them for you, if you like."

"Please," said Blakely.

"And what is this template?"

Justina opened her case and removed the template. She handed it to Stupak. He held it in both hands to the light.

"These are the marks you find on the relic?"

"Yes," said Wafford. "That's the composite."

"I see. And what do you believe these marks indicate?"

Wafford pointed to the X mark. "We know Heinrich received a shipment of jewels and gold from Trieste in August or September, 1944. That X might be where they're hidden. The other marks could be landmarks which would pinpoint the exact location."

Stupak looked amused. "You truly believe you'll find jewels and more relics on Kriti?"

Wafford tilted his head and shifted from one foot to the other. "We might. Never can tell."

Stupak touched his chin. "Very true."

Stupak turned to leave. "Help yourself to the documents. If you need anything, use the telephone there," nodding at the black phone. "My extension is 24. Now, I will try, myself, to work hard today, unless the little drums in my head continue to beat like Indian tom toms. And you know, ladies?" He tapped Blakely on the chest. "It was all his fault that we stayed out so late. He simply refused to go home until we literally had to carry him to his bed!"

Justina laughed this time. He closed the door behind him. The place was dead quiet.

"Smells old enough," commented Elizabeth, "if that means anything." She poured herself some coffee. "Anyone?"

Blakely raised one finger. Elizabeth poured another cup. Blakely took a swig of coffee.

"Maybe we could divide up the work so we can make the most of our time," he said.

Justina came over and leaned against the shelves. She had changed her lipstick from bright red to a mauve-pink, which suggested to Blakely another part of female anatomy. The dark liner accentuated the fullness of her lips. Wearing one of those, what do they call them? Banana boat outfits? Khaki pants and shirt, kind of military, except hers was open at the neck a couple buttons more than SOP, showing un-military dark cleft between snow white swells.

"Those leather bound volumes behind you, Justina," he said, pointing, then walking over and running his hand along them, "all contain paperwork. Everything from work orders and requisitions to reconnaissance reports and pilot logs. I thought you might start with those. There might be something that could point to a fake shipment and its destination."

"All right."

She turned and pulled four of the volumes down and placed them on the table. Blakely turned to Elizabeth and Wafford.

"This is the photo album Joachim was looking at yesterday." Blakely turned the pages. "Here's a photograph of Heinrich von Etter in fatigues."

Blakely took a paper clip from a bowl on the table, and attached it to the page.

"Here is one of Heinrich in his dress uniform using crutches."

He pointed to the smiling young face in the photograph, then put a paper clip on it.

"I suggest you look through this album and put a paper clip on every picture where you can identify Heinrich. Besides that, if you see any unusual photographs which make you ask, 'what is that doing in here?' let Justina know so she can take a look. Okay?"

Justina looked up. She seemed pleased.

Elizabeth took the album and placed it on her lap. "All right."

"Lou, here are two shelves of albums to check. All the ones with pictures of Heinrich, just stack in a pile. The rest can be put back on the shelf."

"Okay. Think we can open the door and get some fresh air? This place stinks."

Blakely opened the door.

"While you guys are doing that, I'll be looking over these gen-

THE MINOTAUR 147

eral command orders."

He pulled two binders of orders down, and carried them to a seat adjacent to Justina.

"Wonder what the oldest thing in here is?" he asked her. She looked up, broke into a big smile and said, "You."

"Thanks," he said.

"You're welcome."

They set about their tasks. At least she had her sense of humor back. Everyone was being very polite under the circumstances. The chance of finding any useful information in this heap of rotting paper was about the same odds as discovering a new comet. He reminded himself that he was sounding like Chris.

"This is interesting," said Justina. "A damage and casualty report for August 29, 1944. Bombing and strafing attack by sorties of British and American bombers and fighters. It gives a listing of losses. Two ME-109's, one Stuka, three staff cars, a half-track. A wing of the barracks damaged. One fuel dump destroyed. There are ten people listed killed, six injured. Reported missing are a Corporal Stefan Helgar and SS Major Gustav Kemft."

"Kemft is the guy Dimitrius was telling about. Stupak thinks the Resistance killed him and hid his body. An allied bombing attack would be a perfect cover for picking him off. Maybe that corporal was his driver."

"Interesting coincidence," said Justina. "We'll have to mention it to Dimitrius."

"He could have been blown up by a bomb," said Blakely. "Nothing left to find."

"Ya," replied Justina. "That is true."

They continued sorting through the materials without saying very much during the next three hours. A tapping at the door. Stupak poked his head in, smiled broadly, looking much more sober. "A studious group! May I interrupt to invite you to lunch? Afterward, I will show you the grounds."

"I knew you would rescue me sooner or later," said Wafford.

"Ole Blakely here is 'bout to work us to death. We could use some lunch. A siesta wouldn't go badly either."

*****

Blakely checked his watch. It was 1630 hours. The commotion he heard outside was troops being let off duty and others reporting. A growing stack of albums next to Elizabeth confirmed von Etter had good press relations. He was in many of the construction photographs, but none of the pictures seemed relevant. Justina also was being skunked. Mundane stuff. Von Etter's signature for material. Orders to von Etter showing transfers of men under his command.

The walk after lunch was also negative. Comparing the template with landmarks such as the control tower, flag pole, and water tower showed no relationships which they could decipher.

"A shame we can't go over there," Justina had said, looking across the open area to a high fence with Greek guards and dogs patrolling it. "If all else fails, we can always request the special pass. Stupak didn't tell us what our chances of getting one are."

The afternoon search revealed nothing linking von Etter to the shipment of June 27, 1944. Nor was there additional information regarding SS Major Gustav Kemft. Still, there were several more shelves to check.

At 1530 hours in the afternoon, Blakely called Alex. Good news. The doctor said Joachim was weak, but would be okay if he rested. He left some medicine with the old man, too.

"Why don't we quit for now?" asked Blakely, anxious to see Joachim. "It's 1630 hours. We've put in a busy day."

"I enjoyed looking at these photographs," said Elizabeth.

"Glad you did. If you can stand it, you can look some more tomorrow."

"How long do you think it'll take us to go through all this?" asked Wafford, waving his hand at the four tiers of shelves.

"Three days?"

"Three days is nothing," responded Wafford, the lump on his lip still prominent. "Let's do it. Whatever it takes."

"Ready for a night on the town, Lou?" asked Blakely teasingly.

"Tonight, let's me an' you go down to that ole disco Alex was tell'n us about."

He had as much of a leer on his face as his swelled lip allowed.

"Would you really want to go there, Louis, at your age? With everyone else under twenty-five?" asked Elizabeth.

Wafford scowled. "Naw! Not really. I was just kidding."

Wafford reached down and kissed her on the mouth.

Blakely leaned against a cabinet and surveyed the room. What were they missing? He remembered the case showing German engineer's tools and a pair of binoculars downstairs. Joachim. Binoculars for Joachim!

"Why don't you get ready while I let Dimitrius know we're finished for the day."

He left them and walked down the hall. A clerk in the outer office took him back. The colonel was sitting behind a handsome wood desk. He looked up.

"Come in, Ed. How can I help you?"

"I noticed the German binoculars in one of the cases downstairs. Any chance I could borrow them for tonight?"

Stupak rose up, scratched his neatly combed hair. "Why would you want them, if I may ask."

"My friend Joachim. Tonight there's an eclipse of the moon, he tells me. Says the comet will be visible again."

"I've got a much better pair, 80 power. Let's go back to the engineering department."

They walked down the hall and into a room with a drafting table, blueprint drawers, and shelves containing survey instruments.

"I seldom use the glasses. Air exercises, mostly. You're welcome to them."

Stupak reached up, pulled a leather case down, and removed a large pair of binoculars.

"Hardly been used," he commented, replacing them in the

case and handing them to Blakely.

Looking around the room, Blakely noticed several aerial photographs lying on an adjacent table.

"Do you do your own aerial photography?" Blakely asked.

"We have a special aircraft. We can request any we need. They are useful. We sometimes use the negatives as overlays to confirm the accuracy of our topographic maps here in these drawers." He pointed to the blueprint file cabinet.

"Are any topos left over from the German occupation?"

Stupak said, "Oh, sure. The Germans were map crazy. They kept very accurate topographic maps of the entire island. Would you like to see some?"

"Yeah. They aren't in the room."

"Yes! You did mention this morning wanting to see maps. I'm sorry! I completely forget. They're right up there."

Stupak pointed to another shelf lined with leather-bound books with a swastika symbol on each. He walked over and opened a black binder. He handed it to Blakely.

"The Germans used a good scale for sector maps. This is the Neapolis Sector, just northwest of here."

Blakely thumbed the worn map pages. "You've got sector maps of the whole island, including the Kastelli district?"

"Sure, sure," said Stupak. "If you think they are of any value, I'll have them moved to your work room. They'll be waiting for you tomorrow."

"Good. I'd like to go through them." He put the map book on the shelf. "Can you think of any other German military documents lying around that could be useful to us?"

Stupak touched his chin and reflected. "Not off hand."

"Well, I appreciate the binoculars. I'll bring them back tomorrow."

"No problem. Use them as long as you like. Glad to help," said Stupak. They left the engineering room and walked to the front of the building. "I see our pretty archeologist is without her husband. Is he ill?"

"Chris left this morning. Going back home to take care of business."

"I see. Pardon my saying so, but my impression is he's something of what we in the military call a tight-ass, is that not true?"

Blakely smirked, trying to think of a good comparison. "I think you could characterize him as the kind you would get if you bred a fighter wing commander with a cadet academy superintendent."

Stupak laughed loudly and placed his hand on Blakely's shoulder.

"You are very observant. You have experience with tight-asses! This archeologist, Chris. Why does he leave his charming wife here with a horny old man such as yourself?"

"I can't say."

"Take her to the disco tonight. Enjoy a drink or two of Ouzo, dance with her. You'll see this lady is not the tight-ass like her husband. Trust me. I study women. She is the open one. Already she is melting for you—oozing delicious honey!"

He overlooked the sexual hyperbole. "What about yourself? Will you be around tonight?"

"No," Stupak replied, scratching his chin, "too much Ouzo. I will go home tonight, and be a good husband."

For all his bravado with Stupak, Blakely did not look back on his behavior last night without remorse. He was ashamed and saddened. He had purposefully driven Chris away for no good reason. He had drunk too much and knew he was getting nasty in the process. Hell, he had picked on Max Padopolis, a man who meant no harm to anyone.

He had shown Wafford how bitter he could be. It was self-loathing, he guessed. Striking out at everyone else so he didn't have to look inside himself. Is that what he had traveled over 5000 miles to accomplish? Self-loathing? When you self-loathe, then you loathe others. Wasn't it possible he could slay his dragons on this journey? Or would this be one more wasted opportunity—another illusory experience? No. He had no hope of overcoming self-loathing. Not so long as he turned the dragons loose on others before facing them within himself. Yet, how could he do that?

Now that Chris was gone, he realized Chris would have continued going through the motions—pretending there was something to find—until Wafford and everyone else agreed there was nothing here. It had been a difficult pretense on Chris's part—one which was against every principle the man stood for—and Blakely now believed Chris had played the charade so he could stay with the group and enjoy the camaraderie.

Justina hadn't understood that, either. She, like Blakely, could see only weakness and stupidity. She must have hated the prospect that Chris could actually rise above the man she loathed in her own way. Wasn't she the one who first wanted to quit? It had been Chris who had begged her to stay on—even when they both knew the search was flawed.

Justina and Blakely had without words conspired to defeat his effort.

They were the superior ones. Chris was the inferior one. They made him feel like the small, professor-pedant he no doubt knew in his heart he had become, behind his wall of blue smoke and bad breath. Betrayal takes many forms.

CHAPTER 16

Eclipse

Blakely carried Stupak's binoculars into the hotel. The clerk, Manolis, waved.

"You have two messages, Mr. Blakely."

One was from Tony. Call him ASAP. The second was from Tobok. He was about to go upstairs when he saw Joachim in the sitting room at the desk writing in the spiral notebook.

"You must be feeling better."

He nodded, taking his pipe from his mouth.

"My strength return, Edward. We see eclipse and Hyakutake tonight?"

"Can't wait! What time are you having dinner?"

The old man turned in his chair and blinked. His eyes showed a happy resolve.

"I was thinking I might eat supper late—with you—unless you have plans."

"What's your pleasure? Fish? Lamb?"

"I let you choose. You always surprise me with good food."

Joachim turned again to his work, dismissing further discussion. The stub of pencil in Joachim's fist moved with steady strokes. It appeared he had filled over half the pages in the notebook. Blakely returned to Manolis at the desk and ordered dinner and a pitcher of beer to be delivered at 2000 hours on the piazza.

He went to his room and punched in the *Sea Siren*'s number on the cellular phone.

"*Sea Siren*, Comm Center, Tobok here."

"Good afternoon, Gregor. Did you get some exercise today?"

"Yes, sir. Leo's got me jogging. You need to talk with Tony, right?"

"Yeah."

"After you get finished, I've got two more messages which arrived today."

"Just give them to me, now, before you transfer."

"Okay. One is from Jenny in California. Says she will arrive in Iraklion Saturday morning at 0800 hours, 13 April, on overnight ferry from Piraeus. Please arrange for someone to meet her and a friend."

A friend. "Okay. And the other?"

"It's from your daughter, Claudia, in Rome. Says she's attending a conference there. Athens and Macedonia confirmed. Love, Claudia."

"Well," said Blakely happily, "when it rains, it pours! Anything else, Gregor?"

"No, sir. We're running smoothly. We got some great video footage yesterday. "

"All right. Can you put me through to Tony?"

"Hold on. He's in his cabin."

"Zeno."

"Tony! What's happening?"

"We got company, Eddie boy. Two of your favorite people."

"Who?"

"King and Marchese. They called around 1330 hours wanting the launch to pick them up."

"What's their business?"

"Talking about doing a test. Mr. King wants us to strike canvas and rig the black 'uns. We're supposed to get the ship SOP, then stand clear so they can calibrate and test the equipment."

"When?"

"Friday night's what I understand. He wants Jeremiah to set

THE MINOTAUR 155

up a broadcast on your mountain there and do it live all the way to Atlanta."

"I see. I don't want you to do anything until you hear back from me. We don't answer to King. I'll talk with Lou. If he says to strike the sails, we'll do it."

"Suits me. I assume you'll be coming down?"

"Whenever Wafford wants me to. Anything else?"

"I spose you'd like to talk to Jeremiah. He's been putting in special overtime lately."

"Yeah. Put him on."

"Television studio. Jeremiah Wilcox speaking."

"Too bad you weren't up here last night, Jeremiah. You could have done a special feature on Greek music. Your uncle does a pretty fierce line dance!"

"Far out! From what I hear, skipper, you guys are having a blast."

"Gregor says you're editing today?"

"Yeah. Got some great footage at Knossos. I have a whole program on Minoan ruins—including the throne room and the labyrinth. It's perfect! Also did an interview there with an English archeologist who is into this Linear A and Linear B language? Really far out! I want to transmit the finished tape by tonight."

"Good. How's your research project coming?"

"Super, but it'll take some time."

"How long?"

"A couple days. By the way, how is Mr. Grenz? Is he okay?"

"He's better. We plan to watch the eclipse and comet tonight."

"Oh, too cool! Wish I were there!"

"Is Tony letting you work on the project instead of pulling watches?"

"Yes. He has Harry and Leo on watch at night. It works!"

"Good. See you later."

"Right, skip."

Blakely put the phone into his bag and sat there. Jenny was arriving with a friend on the thirteenth. He might not even be on

Crete then. He would see Claudia in Athens on the fifteenth. How long had it been? Seven? No. Eight months. Too long!

He needed to speak with Wafford immediately. Manolis pointed toward the patio. Wafford was sitting by himself eating a meat pie with Ouzo. He had the haggard look he often got after talking with McCloud or King. Blakely decided to act innocent and let Wafford tell him.

"You're having quite a food and drink combination there, Mister Lou. Must be famished!"

Wafford chewed a chunk of pastry without looking up. "Ole Gresh called me 'bout another change in plans."

"Where is Mr. King? In Athens?"

Wafford flicked his tired eyes at Blakely before lowering them and concentrating on capturing a piece of pastry on the tines of his fork. "Naw. Him and Andy came in today. Gresh caught the ferry yesterday from Athens to Souda. They drove up from Hania this morning. They're at the *Sea Siren*. It's going to change our plans tomorrow."

"How so?"

"Gresh wants us to change out the sails and put them receptors up so they can do a test Friday or Saturday night. It'll depend on the weather."

"I see. So what's the video going to be for the test?"

Wafford looked away. "Nothing's been talked about that I know of. I'm 'sposed to be in charge of that end of the project, and I haven't one iota what we'll do. I didn't get any advance notice. Gresh thinks up here would be as good a place as any. Jeremiah can probably think of something."

"I just talked with him. He's got footage from Knossos. I know he'd like to interview Justina. Why don't we bring that square with the logo up here and use it as a backdrop? He could interview her on the piazza. Maybe have those Greek musicians playing in the background?"

Wafford had a pouting expression. "You handle it, then. Sounds like you got a plan."

"What about clearing the ship?"

"We'll move the crew out when the schedule's set. King wants us to spend most of tomorrow and Friday getting the ship SOP in case the buyers come by to inspect the boat. We may need to do some painting—whatever. Your boys can spend nights either up here or down in Iraklion—whichever you prefer."

"I like having Tony, Leo and Mike staying in sight of their ship, unless you see a problem with that?"

Wafford shrugged without looking up. He was stabbing bits of pastry with his fork. "Whatever."

"Easter weekend. King wouldn't expect the crew to work Easter Sunday, would he?"

"Is that a problem?"

"Yeah. It will be for Tony. He'd like to go to church. There might be others who'd like time off."

"Find out and let me know. I'll take it up with Gresh."

"Is everyone expected to work on the *Sea Siren* tomorrow, or can some of us work at the base? I don't see why Elizabeth, Justina and Joachim can't continue searching documents, do you?"

"That'd be fine, I guess. Is old Joachim up to it?"

"Yeah. He's much better. We're having dinner together tonight."

Wafford had that taciturn look about him like he did the day he came back from the hike with Marchese and got drunk. There was a brooding, bitter quality which hovered around his mouth and eyes. He was forcing himself to answer Blakely's questions, and only grudgingly sharing information which pertained to normal routine. He avoided eye contact and kept stabbing at tiny pieces of pastry flakes and devouring them one at a time.

Blakely asked in a soft voice, "Anything you'd like to talk about, Lou? You seem pretty upset this evening."

"Naw." He rubbed his wrist. "I'm having Mike drive me down to see Gresh in a little while. Need to iron the mess out. Taking Elizabeth along for the ride. I'll see more what Gresh has in mind. Probably have dinner in Iraklion before we come back."

Wafford set the fork on the empty plate and concentrated upon the glass of clear Ouzo, which he now held in both hands.

"Want me to come along for support?"

Wafford peered out, a hurt look in his eyes.

"I can take care of Gresh. I'm only concerned there's a lot to get ready on the ship. There's personal stuff to clean out, too. Especially with Elizabeth, Miss Justina, and ole Joachim not around tomorrow to help."

"I thought you would want them to keep looking. If you'd rather, we can all go down and work on board tomorrow. I don't see that changing out sails and picking up our personal gear is a big deal. The vessel is close to shipshape. Tony's kept her in good order. And getting Jeremiah set up with his equipment is no big deal either—we can all help him."

Wafford's face was perspiring. He wiped across his brow with a napkin. He was like an old alley cat prowling, looking for a fight, yet knowing he was going to be defeated when he found one.

"It isn't a big deal, Ed. I originally thought we'd all go down together. Now, you say some should stay. You seem to have it all figured out ahead of me. You and Gresh share that in common. Always thinking. Always a step ahead. Ya'll do whatever. Nobody listens to me any more. What I say doesn't count one iota."

"Hey! Come on! Loosen up! You and King have a another falling out?"

"Never you mind, Ed. I'll handle my own affair with ole Gresh."

Wafford wiped across his mouth and gulped some Ouzo. "Just a mess is all—when nobody goes by the plan... and calls their own shots."

Wafford was talking "mess" again. Apparently, King had changed everything without informing Wafford. Or maybe McCloud had pushed Wafford's button. Whatever it was, Wafford's frame of mind was as low as Blakely had ever seen it.

"What can I do to help?"

"I say, Ed, I don't need no help. I'm just a might upset is all.

THE MINOTAUR

Give me—how do you say it? Sea room? I need some sea room right now."

Blakely got up. "Okay. We all need it now and then. After you guys decide what you want to do, you might give Tony the go-ahead to get started tonight. It would save us time tomorrow."

"I 'spose."

"Just let me know how I can help. If you need me tonight, Joachim and I will be on the piazza watching the eclipse."

Wafford gave a hollow hang dog grin. "You and Joachim are into that, too?"

He is bitter as hell. He drank the rest of the Ouzo.

"Yeah. We're into that, too."

"How will Elizabeth and all get to the base, if we take the van tomorrow morning?"

"They can take Alex's taxi. Be a new experience for them, riding with Alex."

Wafford looked at the empty glass in his hands. He was sweating profusely. His voice was hollow and low. "Everybody's got all the answers 'cept ole Lou."

"What'd you say?"

Wafford half turned his head. "Nothing important. I'll see you and Mike out front at quarter of six tomorrow. That okay?"

"Fine."

* * * * *

Manolis cleared the table of the dinner dishes and carried them on a tray back to the hotel. Blakely looked across the valley from the darkest corner of the piazza. "You sure you're okay out here, Joachim? After this morning, I don't want you getting sick. You would tell me, wouldn't you?"

"Ya. I am fine."

"I've been reading that the ancient Greeks thought the world was coming to an end when they saw a lunar eclipse," said Blakely, watching Joachim hold the binoculars with elbows braced on a chair back.

"Ya, many still believe such a thing."

Blakely looked up, watching the moon for a minute, looking away, checking back. The dark edge was growing. The mountains and valleys below were half-lit by the moon. Joachim drew back from the binoculars, handing them to Blakely.

"You look awhile. My arms get tired."

Blakely held the glasses up, focused, and saw the edge of shadow had moved again. "Good binoculars," he said. "You can see the mountains and craters of the moon tonight, Joachim."

"Um," said Joachim, making his pipe crackle. The pipe smoke was stronger, less sweet smelling than Chris's. Joachim removed his pipe and mumbled a verse to himself, saying something like, "And Katrin kissed me upon my lips...". He couldn't catch more of it. Joachim put the pipe back in his mouth.

Out of curiosity, Blakely shifted from the moon down to the valley, scanning for lamp lights. He saw a yellow flicker and held the glasses steady. Something passed in front of the light. Probably an open window, a person walking across a room, perhaps someone with binoculars looking up, sharing the same experience. He set the glasses down on the table. There was no hurry. It would take a while for the shadow to cover the whole moon. Joachim huddled in the chair as though he were cold, holding the glowing pipe in his right fist, gazing skyward.

"Was your friend Heinrich a good person, Joachim?"

"Ya, Edward. Like you, a good man. He was like my brother," he said, not taking his eyes away from the moon. "We were very different. He came from noble family, I came from middle class; he was university, I from institute. He a philosopher, me a draftsman. He a politician, me a technician. He a Catholic, me a Lutheran. You see? Very different. That's how we get along so well."

"How did you meet?"

"A student engineering conference in Frankfurt. Wrote back and forth. He was in Berlin, I in Frankfurt. We formed a club of engineers. Took holidays mountain climbing, skiing. When we saw war was coming, five of us volunteered as officers in the paratroopers."

"Was Heinrich a favorite with the Nazis?"

"Never. He was a count; the Nazis hated noble families. He was a Catholic; that was against him. No, Heinrich always under suspicion—even as a war hero."

The old man's strength had come back. His voice sounded strong and regular. "How do you mean, war hero?"

"When we drop on Holland, the group he was leading captured a section of Rotterdam without anyone wounded or killed. Later, when he himself was wounded, he continued fighting until the city was won. His superiors gave him high praise, a quick promotion."

"Alex and Max say there were lots of atrocities here during the war. Many civilians were shot on this slab of concrete. Do you think Heinrich participated?"

"Never! He had honor. He would take his own life before committing such cowardly crime."

"Tell me more about Katrin."

Joachim turned. "Katrin?"

"Yeah. She told me about you, and how difficult it was for her when you fell in love with Estel."

Ironic, how two men so different in age and experience could have slept with the same lovely woman. And he thought Katrin had never quite gotten over her love for Joachim; it was memories of Joachim which brought tears to her eyes when Blakely and Katrin talked about her experiences before the war.

"Ya. She and Heinrich became engaged a few months, then broke off. Not the same when a woman is loving two men."

He tapped his pipe on the side of the chair. Sparks danced to the concrete. He looked across. "Different with men, don't you think, Edward? Men can easier forget?"

"Probably. Hard for me to know what women feel, Joachim. All I know is you can hurt them even when you don't want to."

Blakely wondered what Jenny was doing right now. Probably already starting to pack for her trip.

Joachim picked up the binoculars and pointed them towards the moon, which was mostly in shadow now.

"You tell me Katrin is dead?"

No matter how often Blakely told Joachim what he knew about her death, the old man didn't seem to remember. Maybe he was putting the memory into verse and required the repetitions. He tried to answer with the same information every time Joachim asked.

"Lou tells me she died not long ago. He tried to contact her. She worked for years with the Catholic Relief Agency, helping to place children in foster homes."

"It is nice she should help children. We spoke of having children together, Katrin and I."

"Yeah."

"Sorry to hear she is dead." He turned. His mouth formed a gaping semblance of smile. "Our histories always end the same. We end up dead."

He handed Blakely the binoculars.

"That doesn't sound like my friend Joachim talking. I thought you believed that souls don't die; they just disappear and reappear like Hyakutake."

"Ya, that is true. I was thinking more of Katrin's beauty. The flesh withers and dies. It is no longer the lovely house of the soul," Joachim said quietly.

Blakely shifted to the northwest, scanned, and found the comet. Tonight, it was a bright burst of dazzling bits of light, and you could clearly see a tail trailing the dusty ball.

"There it is, Joachim, clear as a bell."

Joachim blew out bits of tobacco from the pipe stem, and began packing tobacco for another smoke.

"Go ahead and watch, Edward. I will light another pipe. I can see it now without binoculars."

Joachim just isn't feeling good, thought Blakely. He put the binoculars down. It was 2130 hours and they were the only ones on the piazza. Alex's taxi was gone. He guessed Alex and Padopolis were being good boys like Stupak, staying home with their wives. He looked across at the hotel. No activity. The round globe above the door cast a somber, white pallor upon the white plaster.

Wafford and Elizabeth must have had a row, because he noticed him and Mike had left without her around 2015 hours. Poor Elizabeth!

Where was George tonight? They need a drink and there's not hide or hair of George.

"I'll get us some more beer," he said to Joachim. Blakely walked over to the hotel and knocked on the Waffords' door.

"Yes? Who is it?"

"Me, Elizabeth."

"Come in, Edward. It's not locked."

He opened the door. Elizabeth sat in her wheelchair at the far side of the room. She had been crying.

"Louis is beyond my help, Edward."

"Do you have any idea what's going on?"

She wagged her head slowly and began weeping.

"No. Only that they are killing him slowly."

"Why don't you both leave? Get away from all this."

"I've already been through that with Louis. I begged him to leave tonight."

"He won't?"

"He's bent on staying."

"Then why don't you go by yourself?"

"I have been considering it."

He patted her on the shoulder. "Can I do anything for you? Get you anything?"

She put her hand over his. "No, Edward. I need to be by myself. You get back to Joachim. I'll be okay."

"You know where I am, if I can help."

It was difficult for him to figure how he could help Elizabeth, unless she did agree to go home. Both Wafford and Elizabeth seemed paralyzed. Neither seemed willing to break out of their circumstances.

"Thank you. I know I can count on you."

Blakely shut the door. He stopped by his room to get an extra jacket, then got two beers and three bags of pretzels from the bar, and carried them to where Joachim sat in the darkness.

"Got some pretzels, Joachim. They'll go good with the beer."

"Ya." Joachim put the binoculars down and opened one of the bags. They sat, not saying anything for a long while, passing the glasses back and forth, sipping beer, and watching. The moon was coming back again, brighter, higher in the night sky.

The three German women Blakely noticed yesterday came up and stood behind them. Dressed for disco, probably early twenties. He thought of Jeremiah and what a great job he could do with a video production here on the piazza. Lunar Maidens visit Satyr and Sage on Mountain During Eclipse. Seek Advice About Having Sex on Crete, possibly on Concrete. Full Story at Eleven on Channel Ten.

All three were in white, like they were Athenian maidens ready to be sacrificed to the Minotaur or any other horny creature that might be convenient for the purpose. All wore sheer white blouses with tiny sequins that glistened. What stood out, besides their pert breasts, were their dark aureoles and nipples, announcing each lady was the same but very different.

The one with the biggest breasts with silver dollar-sized aureoles leaned over Joachim's shoulder, looking in the same direction his glasses were pointing. Her long blonde hair brushed Joachim's arm for a moment before she stood upright again, pushing back her hair from her face. She spoke with the icky north German accent. "What are you watching?"

Joachim pulled the glasses away, turned toward her, then pointed skyward. "We are watching the passing of Hyakutake, a comet not seen since the ice age, 10,000 years ago."

"Really!" exclaimed the one with the longest hair, shortest skirt. "May I see?"

Joachim gave her the binoculars, pointing to the vague, distant ball of dust.

"Ya! Neat!"

She sounded like Jenny.

"Let me see," said the shorter one in white leotards, shoat-sized breasts jiggling. She took the glasses, looked for maybe five seconds, and passed the glasses to another.

"Cool!" the third one said, handing the glasses back to Joachim.

"Danke!" they chimed, heading for the disco, all twittering at once like song birds, then breaking into squeals of uncontrollable laughter which echoed across the piazza.

Joachim looked over at Blakely, a grin on his face.

"They smell nice. It is a very long time since I smell perfume like that. They look nice, too, don't you think? Katrin always look nice and have sweet fragrance. Young ladies just not interested in same thing as an old man."

Katrin, again. He agreed with him. Katrin always looked lovely and had a sweet scent—even without perfume.

"Been there, done that—the slogan of today's youth, Joachim," replied Blakely, putting his feet up on a chair and taking a deep swig of beer. Ah, the rites of Spring. Same everywhere. He wondered whether those pretty Nordic maidens ever looked up at anything higher than a bedroom ceiling. It was hard not to be judgmental.

Being out here on the piazza with Joachim in the quiet night looking at Hyakutake transcended time. Behind them and below them were vestiges of civilization, while above was an eternal showplace of fire and light, of violent birth and destruction—the magnitude of which was unrealizable by mere man. They had a front row seat to the universe.

The eclipse had passed. A Greek word, eclipse. He had asked Padopolis what it meant. He answered with a shrug and said, "To cover, I suppose." Blakely looked the word up in his dictionary. Eclipse meant 'an abandoning,' related to ekeipein, to leave out, to fail, to pass over. For Greeks, it was a dreaded omen of darkness to come. For Jews, to pass over meant a new beginning.

Joachim sat hunched in the chair, looking small and cold.

"Here, Joachim. Put this over you."

"Danke!" Joachim put on Blakely's extra jacket.

Blakely thought again about Chris, and wondered how he must be feeling, flying back to a different vestige of civilization. It must be very sad for him to open the door and hear the sound of an empty house, and to realize why Justina chose not to go home with him.

And he thought, too, of the hollow sounds inside *Easy, Too*, when the tidal water slapped her bow in the dark of night. She sat alone, now, like an unplayed, high-strung instrument which had been cast aside. An empty boat sound was the saddest sound of all in the world. It must be like a person's emptiness when they feel they have no soul. He couldn't bear to think about *Easy, Too* in this way, for a boat can also be a sacred thing. Every vessel needs caring and love and protection and use. It must be allowed to burn itself out like men and stars do.

He realized he would never go back to Newport Beach. It was like an outgrown shell, which he must cast off now because it no longer fit. The vestige had no value except its memories. And like Joachim, he had all the pictures memorized. There was no need for the artifacts of his former life to exist anymore.

He had made up his mind. He would sell *Easy, Too*. He would send a message to Jim Willis to put her up for sale, or perhaps he should wait until Jenny arrived. They could talk about it. Maybe he could sell the whole kit and caboodle—his boat, his business, the property, and the Morgan—as one big package. It was not a thought which made him sad. Rather, he felt an urgency to get it accomplished so that all of it would be only a rich memory and not a nagging responsibility. Strange, how, suddenly, he could shuck off his earthly treasures. He got up out of the chair and stretched.

"Would you like another beer, Joachim? It would be good for

you."

The old man took the glasses from his eyes and turned his head. The white beard parted and formed a small, black crescent in the half-light—one of Joachim's happiest smiles.

"Ya! Another beer would be good, Edward. Maybe more! We toast Hyakutake tonight, my son!"

CHAPTER 17

Clear the Brigantine

Blakely formed two work parties. Jeremiah, Tobok and Swann opened the packages and brought the black receptors topside. Leo, Mike and Tony struck the regular sails and stowed them in numbered bags in the sail locker. Wafford and Marchese stood informal watch while Blakely manipulated the auto-furlers from the pilot house. Blakely was determined to finish installing the receptors by 1200 hours, if possible.

King watched vigilantly as the black sails were unfolded and prepared for rigging. There was air today. He came into the pilot house and expressed concern about whether the wind would be too strong to set the receptors. Blakely was tempted to remind him that the bridge was off limits to King, but held his tongue. His cologne was so strong Blakely could taste it.

"Once them black receptors are hoisted, I'd appreciate you furling them. Keeps them out of the wind. We don't want 'em damaged."

"Okay."

King leaned against the forward window and watched the activity on deck. He reached into his breast pocket and brought a tooth pick out, examined it, and put it in his mouth.

"Can you spare Harry and Gregor through the weekend, Mr. Blakely?"

He knew why, but he asked anyway. "For what reason?"

"I want them on board for the test. Depends on weather as to when we'll do it. Expect it'll be tomorrow night or sometime Saturday."

"That's fine."

King had a kind of sneer on his face.

"Just can't abide that boy handling those receptors with long finger nails. They're damned expensive. I don't want him to mess up and tear one."

"Who do you mean?"

"Why, the black boy yonder, Wilcox."

Blakely watched the three men unfolding the black receptors. Jeremiah was, in fact, more careful than either Swann or Tobok.

"Jeremiah won't hurt them any more than Harry or Gregor. If he does, I'm sure there's insurance to cover damage."

He sensed King's dislike for Jeremiah, but wasn't sure why. King's gray eyes looked steadily at Blakely. "You kinda favor that boy, don'tcha?"

"I'm not sure what you mean, Mr. King?"

King smirked. "I'll see to him myself, then."

Before he could reply, King had closed the hatch and was hurrying down the outside ladder. Blakely felt sweat break out on his neck. He wanted to have one good punch. Just one! Deck that snide, self-righteous bigot. King crossed to where Wafford and Marchese were standing. He pointed toward Jeremiah and said something to Wafford. Wafford glanced toward the pilot house and then went over to Jeremiah, said something, and they both walked through the forward companionway.

Blakely picked up the phone.

"Tony, I'd like you to replace me on the bridge."

Tony waved from the bosun's chair half way up the main mast. He came down in seconds and ascended the ladder. Blakely didn't wait for him. He left the bridge and strode down the passage to the television studio. Wafford leaned against a bench talking with Jeremiah, who was preparing a video camera. Neither of them seemed upset. Blakely stepped through the hatch. "What's up?"

"Oh, hi, skip. Mr. King wants me to do a video of the black

sails going up. Is that okay with you? I know it means you'll be shorthanded, but it shouldn't take too long."

So, King was pulling Blakely's chain just for the hell of it. He calmed himself and nodded at Jeremiah.

"Great idea, Jeremiah. You agree, Lou?"

Wafford was still sweating. He seemed totally preoccupied. Maybe King had said something nasty to Wafford, too, and it was Wafford's idea to diffuse the situation with the videotape ploy. Wafford said in a low voice, "Fine. It'll make a nice feature."

"Yeah," said Jeremiah enthusiastically. He obviously had no knowledge of King's innuendo. "I thought I could do a voice-over about how they're used and bring in that stuff about Theseus and the black sails and the Minotaur. You know? It would be so cool!"

"Yeah," said Blakely, admiring Jeremiah's innocence. "Really cool!"

Blakely had always been aware that Jeremiah did have a feminine way about him—an affectation of hands and body movements—and he did have longer, neatly shaped fingernails than most men. He also had a wonderfully creative and sensitive nature, which resulted in excellent video productions. And he had never met a brighter, cheerier, or more decent young man than Jeremiah Wilcox. If he was gay, that was his business. And he would stand up for him against anybody. As far as he was concerned, Jeremiah probably had more character than Marchese, Wafford, McCloud, and King put together.

"How about us having lunch at a little taverna, today, Jeremiah?"

Wafford tilted his head and looked peevishly at Blakely. "Not inviting me along?"

"Sure. Didn't mean to exclude you. Come on along! I was wanting to talk with Jeremiah about video cameras. I'm thinking of buying one. I thought we'd stop in some of those shops after lunch and price the different models."

Wafford ran his hand up the side of his face. "In that case, include me out. I'd just as soon eat here with Gresh as look at cameras."

* * * * *

An exceptionally large crowd had gathered on the New Harbor and Old Harbor quays to watch the black receptors being lifted and set in place. A military staff car was parked in a restricted area of the harbor. Two uniformed men sat inside. One of the men on the near side using binoculars looked like Captain Lutra.

"Need an extra hand?" Blakely called to Leo, who was in the ratlines of the foremast rigging the last black square. Jeremiah was busily taping the process from the bowsprit.

"I've got it, Ed. Hove to whenever you want."

Blakely crossed the deck and entered the pilot house. He furled the remaining black sail. He picked up his own eighty power glasses and focused them. It was Lutra. The other officer was using a car phone. They could expect Colonel Stupak to appear within the hour. He replaced the glasses in their holder and went on deck. He had an idea. He approached Wafford, Marchese, and King, who were in a huddle amidships. Jeremiah waved a hand at Blakely as he carried his mini-cam and battery down the forward companionway.

"Thought I'd give you advance warning, Lou. Our friend Captain Lutra is over there in a staff car watching us with glasses with another officer. I imagine Colonel Stupak will be down here to check us out. He'll want to come aboard."

Wafford looked down at his shoes and scuffed the deck with his foot. His face was turning a bright red.

"Who's Stupeck?" snapped King.

"Base commander," said Wafford, sullenly. "Up on the mountain at Kastelli."

"He has no authority here," said King, touching his toothpick with his fingers. "I'd tell him this is proprietary business relative to television transmissions. Leave it at that. Has nothing to do with him or the military."

Blakely said, "A matter of protocols, Mr. King. You've been around military people enough to know they expect red carpet treatment—especially when a tall ship comes to port. You might save yourself some grief by allowing him on board for a few minutes. He's allowed us inside a highly secured fighter base. We've got Justina, Elizabeth and Joachim there right now. If we don't reciprocate and give him a cook's tour, it will make him think we're hiding something."

King chewed on a toothpick and took it from his mouth. He nudged Marchese's arm. "Andy? Whatcha think?"

"I agree with Ed. But wait until the guy asks. If he does, bring him on board. Show the guy some cabins and take him to the salon. Put on that tape Wilcox made in Trieste. Give him a drink. The guy will be a happy camper and leave."

King looked steadily at Blakely. "What's he like?"

"Easy-going. He likes to feel he's in charge. Likes to do favors. He's been great to us."

"A fine man," Wafford mumbled, still scuffing with his foot.

The tick in King's jaw began to twitch. He picked his nose. "I spose these black receptors was bound to bring us some attention. Them people yonder have never seen the likes of this ship before. All just standing there gaping at us. Let him come on, then."

Blakely seized the opportunity. "Then I say, let's initiate it by inviting him. He expects us to invite him. Remember, Lou? He didn't wait for us to ask him to visit the base? He took the initiative?"

"Yes. Very hospitable to us," said Wafford in a meek tone.

Marchese shook his head negatively. "No, guy. Don't ask for problems. He doesn't ask to come on board, he don't come."

King put his hand on Marchese's shoulder. "More I think about it, Andy, the captain here has a point. These here Greeks ain't like most people you run across. Been my experience they'll give you the shirt off their back, if you want it. If like the captain here says,

THE MINOTAUR   173

ole Stupeck's done 'em favors, he expects something in return. Right, captain?"

"Yes."

"Let's make him feel we're treat'n him right." King nudged Blakely's arm. "Why don't you call Stupeck and invite him down here? What time is it? Ten twenty. He can make his visit and be gone afore lunch time."

Blakely nodded and left Marchese and King discussing the pros and cons. Marchese didn't like Blakely's second-guessing him, but he had accomplished his purpose. Stupak was no fool. If there were more to this testing than televised pictures, Stupak would probably recognize it. He entered the pilot house and called the base.

"Colonel Stupak, please."

"Dimitrius Stupak."

"Colonel. This is Ed Blakely. How are your guests doing today?"

"Ah, they are very happy. The old one has discovered more photographs of friends. And Mrs. Cunningham has identified certain orders of this von Etter. Yes. They are happy. We plan an excellent lunch today, Italian spaghetti. And what about you, my friend? Will you join us?"

"I'm aboard the *Sea Siren*. I'd like to invite you to come down for a tour this morning, if you have time."

"Splendid! Tell me what time and I shall be there."

"1115 hours?"

"Excellent. I understand you change from white to black sails." He laughed. "Am I to believe Theseus has been slain by the Minotaur?"

"News travels fast! No. The black sails are only coincidental."

"I see. Would you mind that I bring along an adjutant who likes tall ships?"

Must be a signal officer, Blakely surmised. Probably the guy with Lutra using the phone. "By all means. Bring him and Captain Lutra, too, if you would like."

"Yes, Ed." His voice had a conspiratorial quality like Stupak had caught on to what Blakely was up to. "I'd like to do that. See you soon."

He hung up the phone. Mission accomplished!

* * * * *

The three Greek officers sat on the sofa watching Jeremiah's production about Trieste with fascination. The so-called adjutant was named Galvanos—the same guy Blakely had seen in the car with Lutra. Marchese, Wafford, and King waited expectantly as the logo appeared and the music came up with the credits. The officers clapped. Lutra grinned.

"Excellent! A Hollywood quality film," exclaimed Stupak. "And you do it all here on this ship?"

King replied. "Oh, yes, sir-ree. From the television studio. This entire vessel is a state-of-the-art floating television station, you understand. Tomorrow night, we plan a live telecast from... what's the name?"

"Kastelli," said Wafford.

"Kastelli!" Stupak punched Lutra in the side and said something in Greek to him. "I just told him, finally television crew comes to Kastelli! We must be sure there is dancing and music, is that not correct, Lou?"

Wafford forced a smile. "Yeah."

"This studio," said Major Galvanos, setting his beer bottle down on the coffee table, "would I be permitted to see it?"

King glanced at Marchese. "Sure. Would all you gentlemen like to see it?"

Stupak and Lutra got up.

"Yes," replied Stupak. "I'd also like to meet your technicians who do such fine work."

King sniffed and stood up. "Come this way, gentlemen."

King led them down the passageway and knocked on the tele-

THE MINOTAUR   175

vision studio hatch. Jeremiah opened it and immediately stepped aside.

"This here's the boy that did it," said King, sounding like Jeremiah had been guilty of a crime. He didn't introduce the boy.

"Dimitrius Stupak." Stupak held out his hand.

Jeremiah gave him his super Magic smile and they shook hands. "Jeremiah Wilcox, sir."

"And this is Major Galvanos and Captain Lutra."

They shook hands.

Stupak was already looking closely at the equipment. "So, this is where you produce the videotapes. You do a wonderful job. If you get tired of working for Mr. Wafford and Captain Blakely, you come work for me, eh?"

Stupak laughed loudly. Jeremiah looked uncertain.

"I am totally serious!" said Stupak. "We could produce wonderful training video with your talents. We have a cadet academy audio technician. But he does nothing of this quality. Of course," Stupak extended his arms toward the stacks of monitors and editing equipment, "he does not have such advanced technology that you have... But you know something, Mr. Wilcox?" Stupak paused and pointed to his head, "I think big difference is what you have up here. You must be very bright, if I do say so."

King shifted his weight and took a deep breath. Jeremiah leaned against his work bench, his confidence swelling. "Thank you, sir."

Galvanos was examining the equipment closely. He raised up from a recorder and looked at King. "Excuse me, but tell me once again how your remote telecast works?"

King described how the receptor materials assisted in receiving live television signals generated remotely and how the signal was regenerated, using boosters and satellites, to distant television stations for live broadcast. Galvanos examined the transmitter, control boards, monitors, recorders, and the small, networked computer attached to Jeremiah's central control board.

"But I see no large computer here, only this personal computer which appears connected to others," Galvanos said, looking around him and tapping thick cables which ran from the computer through the bulkhead. "I assumed there would be computer control of reception and transmission."

King blinked and his jaw twitched. "Yes, sir. Our comm center is next door. Like I said, some of this equipment you are looking at is proprietary secret—we just don't show it to anybody. Our competitors get hold of them black receptors, for instance, and our company loses its advantage. Same with our computer. It's bigger'n most."

King glanced at Marchese, whose heavy breathing had accelerated.

King said, "Come this way."

Music from the Trieste tape could be heard inside the comm center. King rapped hard on the hatch. The music was turned down and Tobok opened the hatch. His cherubic mouth gave no hint of what he was thinking. His eyes settled on Stupak, then Galvanos.

Stupak nodded and strode past Tobok and stood in the center of the room, pulling up his pants, and glancing around. On Tobok's main monitor was playing the Trieste program.

"This is our communications technician, Gregor Tobok," said King, introducing the Greek officers to him.

"Tobok," repeated Stupak, placing his hand to the side of his face. "Tobok is Bulgarian, no?"

"No, sir. Romanian."

"Ah, so it is."

Galvanos stooped down and ran his hands over the disk ports, switches, and assemblies of the two large computer cabinets. His eye followed the cables connected between the two main computers.

Galvanos looked up at Tobok. "You have two computers instead of one?"

"Yes, sir," replied Tobok. "One is for back-up."

Galvanos glanced at Stupak. "They are tied together. Can they be used in tandem?"

Wafford's cheeks were sanguine. Tobok's cherubic mouth flattened slightly. "Yes, sir. They can be used together, but I use the second to down-load as a secondary hard drive storage file."

"Both computers are identical?"

"Yes, sir."

King stepped closer and squatted down next to Galvanos. His face was set in a squint. "On a floating studio like this one, there's got to be a back-up unit in case one goes down. You have no other choice."

"I see." Galvanos stood up. He looked at the sonar and emergency radio equipment stacked to the left of the console where Tobok normally sat. Galvanos nodded silently at Stupak.

"Thank you for your time," said Stupak, extending his hand to Tobok. "You must be computer genius to operate all this. I don't believe we have better computer on the flight line at my base, do you, major?"

"No," Galvanos replied. He shook his head in awe. "Perhaps not in Athens, either."

"Anything else you'd like to see?" asked King, his squint fixed and stony.

"You have been most hospitable, Mr. King," said Stupak. "We will let you get back to your preparations. If I or Major Galvanos or Captain Lutra can be of assistance when you make tests, please let us know."

Stupak grabbed Blakely's arm. "Are you coming to see us this afternoon, Ed?"

"Yeah. I'll be coming over to the base around 1400 hours."

"Good! I look forward to seeing you then."

He gave a little salute and led his men toward the aft companionway. They followed the officers topside and stood at the rail watching as Leo took them in the launch to the dock.

"Well, well," said King under his breath. "They saw what they came to see. That Galvanos fella must be a signal officer. He didn't miss a thing. You see him looking over them computer hook-ups?"

"Anybody would be curious," said Wafford. "I would be, too."

"I guess they're satisfied," said Marchese. "The colonel seemed impressed in a positive way."

"What we should do," said Wafford, showing a bit of energy for the first time today, "is get them fellas into our videotape show tomorrow night. Make an extra copy of the tape for each of them."

"Good idea," said King, looking Wafford up and down. "You must be feeling better. Hate to see you down in the dumps, Lou. It's not like you. You been downright out of sorts."

Wafford reddened and scratched his ear. "Well, you know how it is, Gresh. I just don't like to be blind-sided like I was last evening. You'd feel the same, if I did it to you."

King put his elbow on the rail and toyed with his toothpick, shifting it from one side to the other with his tongue.

"Got to stay flexible, Lou. Got to roll with the punches! Speaking of which... We've got them Greeks stirred up. I'm thinking we oughta change the timetable. Maybe postpone it a week 'til Orthodox Easter. Whaddya think, Andy?"

Blakely stood behind them, listening to their conversation, and realized they had forgotten he was there. Marchese turned, saw him, and asked, "Hey, guy! This Kastelli place. Any good mountains to climb up there?"

Wafford and King turned. Blakely stepped over next to King, leaned over the rail and dropped a ball of spit into the water.

"Not the kind you want. There's bigger mountains south of there, I believe."

He looked at Wafford. "Need me any more, Lou?"

Wafford didn't look up. "Naw. Go do what you need to do."

"If you'll excuse me, gentlemen, I'll check with my crew. I want to finish up so I can go back up to the base this afternoon."

The three stood watching Blakely as he turned away. A motley bunch, thought Blakely. King is running the show and wants to postpone the test. Wafford is scared or angry. And Marchese has more say in what happens than he had guessed. They are hiding something, and judging by the close inspection Galvanos had given the computers, the Greeks think so too.

* * * * *

"So," said Blakely, "you're into his code?"

"Yeah," replied Jeremiah. "It's like, there are key words and a bunch of coded symbols, you know? Like using asterisks, parentheses, and the pound sign, and maybe five or six 'at' symbols in a row followed by the percent sign. And once he does all this and presses enter, a file opens up, and there are code names which he can put the icon on, and he uses the mouse to open up the messages."

The street noise of the outdoor cafe made it difficult for him to hear what Jeremiah was saying, which was perfect. Blakely had selected a table along the ancient Venetian wall where they had a perfect view of the *Sea Siren* and anyone coming to the dock in the launch. "Can you access these files?"

Jeremiah leaned in, his arms folded on the edge of the ceramic table. "I think I can. I've got the access code memorized pretty well. Gregor sometimes uses a file with blocks of numbers. He'll point the icon to a box above the block of numbers and activate it. I think what it does is to encrypt his messages somehow."

"Yep. That's exactly right, Jeremiah. I used to see that kind of code back in Germany years ago. Blocks and blocks of nothing but numbers on a page. We had guys who could crack a code like that in a matter of a few days."

"Too much! Really?"

"Yeah. They lived and breathed that stuff—just like Tobok. Has there been much activity the past two days?"

"Yes. I've watched what he does. He is using codes and then putting them on the Internet. Like, I don't think he's used the same address twice."

"Any recognizable people or places mentioned?"

"Yeah. There's Zeb. I think that stands for Zebulon. Most are addressed by a code name. There are lots of messages going back and forth. Most traffic is between two and three in the morning.

I've got a date and time clock set and the time is being recorded on the tape file every second it is operating."

"That's the kind of detail I would never have thought of. What's your impression now, Jeremiah? Is this stuff just regular confidential business communications?"

Jeremiah scratched his head. "I can't tell. It's all too sketchy! Gregor is really far out with this stuff. I can't tell what is normal routine and what may be clandestine, you know?"

"It doesn't look like we'll be able to get into the comm room until King finishes his test. They're talking about changing the test date."

"I should have the access code figured out by tomorrow night."

"Any chance you can make a sample tape of those messages so I can play it on a VCR?"

"Sure."

"Pick out something you can do quickly. I don't want you getting caught at it."

"How 'bout first thing this afternoon?"

"Lock yourself in with the DO NOT DISTURB sign on your door. I'll see that everybody is topside."

Jeremiah touched his lips with his fingers. "How long should the segment be? Fifteen minutes be enough?"

"That's plenty."

"All right."

"You are certain nobody can detect what you are recording in your studio?"

"No way, skip. I follow my normal routine. I keep all my stuff turned on—including test monitors, and I have a big sign which says DO NOT TOUCH! The actual camera feed into my powerbook doesn't show—it comes in through the bulkhead cable space directly into my work cabinet. I keep the powerbook inside a locked cabinet drawer. I also keep the studio locked when I'm not there."

"Your powerbook isn't connected with anything else?"

"No. I've detached it from the network and removed the telephone connection."

"Good. My expectation is that King and Marchese will look for signs of eavesdropping. That's why I think they want us off the ship when they're doing this testing business."

"But why all the secrecy? A live, remote transmission of a broadcast isn't like a big secret to anyone."

"That's all the more reason I think this is more than just testing equipment. Maybe Tobok's messages will tell us. Why don't you plan to haul some of your gear to Kastelli tonight? Throw a VCR in. I want to view the tape as soon as possible."

"Will do."

Blakely got up and stretched. Pigeons crowded around his feet, searching for scraps. He emptied the crumbs on his paper plate on the ground, causing a skirmish of fluttering, making him wish he hadn't done it. He was engulfed. Pigeons were all over his boat shoes, making marks.

"Nice show, skip." Jeremiah emptied his plate, causing another frantic skirmish—mostly toward Blakely—as Jeremiah's Magic smile spread across his face again.

CHAPTER 18

A Match

Blakely watched as Wafford sullenly carried another pile of photo albums to the table where Elizabeth and Joachim were working. He set them down without a word. Wafford's gloom was infesting everyone. Stupak entered the room and threw an arm around Wafford's shoulder and whispered loudly, "Watch the captain's expression, Lou!"

In a louder voice, Stupak announced, "That beautiful, young waitress, the widow—the one called Anna—asked about you last night, Ed. She wanted to know where you were staying. I gave her your hotel room number. Did she come visit?"

Stupak tilted to look into Wafford's face. Wafford's attempted smirk was filled with sadness. Stupak removed his arm and reached toward Elizabeth. "Is it not true what I say, Elizabeth? You heard her ask me!"

"Shame on you, Colonel!" said Elizabeth, hardly more effusive than Wafford. "Anna is a very nice lady. She would be quite unhappy to know you made fun of her."

"Yes," Stupak sighed. "That is true. I should not make jokes about nice ladies."

"No, you shouldn't," replied Elizabeth seriously. She resumed her work. The exchange stopped further conversation. He left the room without attempting a retort.

Minutes later, a clerk entered, carrying a stack of black notebooks. Stupak followed, carrying a similar stack. Stupak set the pile of notebooks down and went over to Joachim. He put his hand on the old man's shoulder and made another attempt at joking.

"I am so glad to see the boss has joined the peons today. Yesterday, they not work very well in your absence. They goof off! They require constant supervision. Do your workers give you much trouble, Herr Grenz?"

"They good workers," he said, smiling up at the colonel. "I see many photograph of my friend and others I knew," Joachim continued, pointing to the album. "It is nice to see Heinrich still young and smiling."

Stupak leaned over. "Which one is he?"

"There, in the middle."

"Yes. A handsome devil. Did he survive the war?"

"No. Edward tells me he died at the hands of the SS. Murdered."

"H'm. Too bad." He patted Joachim on the shoulder. "Well, ladies and gentlemen, I shall leave you again to your work. Those are the maps you asked for, Ed"

Stupak was on his way out the door when he stopped and came back to where Blakely was sitting.

"I should tell you, these German sector maps are not in the best condition because we've used them so often over the years."

Stupak left. Justina got up from the table and came over to Blakely.

"May I look at one?" she asked.

"Help yourself. Dimitrius told me yesterday they are numbered according to sector. Maybe the first one will have a sector key."

The two examined the black leather spines and began sorting them in numerical order.

"Here is number one," said Justina. She opened it to the second page. "It shows each of the four major sections of the island is subdivided into ten sectors, so there are forty sector books in all."

"Okay."

"Any particular book you would like to see?" Justina asked,

sitting down across from him.

"Why not start with home base, Kastelli?"

Justina ran her finger down the list. "Kastelli, Sector Book Number 28." She reached over, found number 28, and handed it to Blakely. The black leather was worn and dog-eared from use. He opened it and examined the subsector listings. There was a ten-square grid overlaying the villages and towns in the Kastelli sector, numbered, so you could turn to the sub-sector page and find a larger map of the same place. The village of Kastelli was located in subsector seven. He carefully turned the fragile pages. Map seven was in tatters, held together with yellowed and semi-sticky tape. The red lines of roads and black topographic contour lines were barely discernible.

"Son of a bitch," said Blakely under his breath, but loud enough that Justina heard him. "Come over here, Justina. Bring your one-to-one template."

Justina retrieved the negative template, and came around to Blakely's side of the table.

"See what I see?"

She leaned over. Lavender scent enveloped him. He waited for her to see what he saw.

"No."

"Look at this. The handwritten notations and the symbols. See? And here! The arrows point to the actual symbols on the map."

"The two pencil marks. One horizontal, the other perpendicular. They are the same as on the relic. Ya?"

"Yes!"

"What do the notations say?"

She attempted to read the faded notes printed with lead pencil.

"I can't make them out," said Blakely. "This one begins with 'FUEL' so we might assume it has to do with fuel storage. Maybe Joachim can tell us. Joachim? Come over here for a second. We have a topo map with some German script."

THE MINOTAUR   185

Joachim came over, took one look and exclaimed.

"An engineer's map!"

"Yes, Joachim. That's what we wanted to know. What does that note mean there?"

He pointed to the horizontal line.

Joachim put his own scarred finger on the note.

"The engineer who used this was identifying the location of underground fuel storage for air field. See there? The writing. It begins FUEL. The words tell type of tank and capacity."

Joachim moved his finger to the perpendicular line and notation.

"Here, a runway. The little arrow above the runway symbol indicates normal wind direction."

"What about this notation with the bigger arrow pointing to the runway?"

Joachim leaned closer, studying the finely printed German script. He shook his head.

"I cannot read it. I know, however, it describes runway length, width, probably materials, weight capacity. We would remind ourselves of those things, sometimes. Make notes on maps. Easy reminders. Those you think written by Heinrich?"

"Could be, Joachim. Watch what happens when Justina overlays the negative. Lou? Elizabeth? You've got to see the moment of truth. Justina and I think we've got a match that you won't believe!"

Wafford wheeled Elizabeth over. They watched expectantly as Justina took the clear acetate showing the black dots and two lines and cross mark, and placed it on the map. She moved it so the lines fell exactly on those of the fuel dump and runway. As she did so, the black dots of the prick marks fell into place exactly on nearby villages. The X fell on a contour line at 25 feet, approximately 100 meters from a curve of road leading to Kastelli. Justina pulled her hands away, leaving the overlay in place.

"Meinen Gott! Wunderbar!" she exclaimed. She grabbed

Joachim and planted a kiss on his cheek, leaving lipstick on his white whiskers.

"Ya! Is this Heinrich's Karte Buch?" he asked, happy, but totally confused.

"Ya," cried Justina, "I do believe as God is in Heaven, this was Heinrich's Karte Buch."

"God damn! Son of a bitch! We did it!" cried Blakely, then was immediately conscious of Elizabeth. "Sorry!" He looked at Elizabeth. "Just couldn't help myself."

"I understand, Edward! Not to worry!"

Wafford leaned closer. His eyes were rimmed with water.

"Can you do it again, Miss Justina? I want to experience it again. I don't believe what I've just seen. Do you, Elizabeth?"

"I don't. How could you know they would match, Edward?"

"When I saw these two symbols on the map in the same relationship as on the template, the two had to be identical. They were in the same scale."

"Well, I swear," said Wafford, watching as Justina moved the acetate off the page, then back on, adjusting it perfectly. "What you're saying, then, is the X tells us what we thought all along— the place where Heinrich found this relic?"

"Maybe," replied Blakely, feeling his ego puff the size of the room. "Or where he hid the jewels. Could be either one or both."

Justina lifted the map page, feeling along its back. "Here is how he did it," she said, her voice barely under control. "You can also see very tiny holes. The slit marks for the lines have been repaired with sealing tape. Heinrich laid the relic face down beneath the map so it was under the area he wanted, then he used a cutting tool to make the marks on the back."

"So much for the dart theory," said Blakely.

"A drafting tool, perhaps," she replied. "One of those drafting compasses with the sharp point."

"Excellent job, Miss Justina. You and Ed oughta be mighty proud," Wafford said, patting Justina on the back and leaving his hand on her shoulder. "So what should we do now?"

"I think we need to make several copies of the template on the map," said Blakely. He got up, called extension 24, and asked for Stupak.

"Good news, colonel!" He could not keep the elation from his voice. "We've found what we're looking for."

"Congratulations," he responded. "I'll come over."

He hung up the phone.

"Goal dang it, Ed," said Wafford. "You know, in all honesty and fairness, I didn't think after the last few days we had a snowball's chance in Hades of figuring it out," Beneath his words, the deeper sadness remained. "Truly, did you, Elizabeth?"

"Oh ye of little faith, Louis!"

She wheeled her chair closer to the table.

"At least," she said dryly, "Edward and Justina have vindicated your father for you."

"Yes," replied Wafford, smirking. "They vindicated my daddy's name." He looked toward the ceiling. "You hear that, James Wafford? You were right! And I intend to tell the whole world you were right! You hear?"

Stupak came through the door.

"What's all the commotion in here? You look like you've found King Minos alive or something!"

Wafford went over to Stupak and grabbed him by the arm and said in a low voice, "We did it, Dimitrius. We got a match, thanks to you having these ole map books—and these two here," pointing to Justina and Blakely. "They match!"

"I don't understand. You mean those two are getting married?" asked Stupak in mock surprise. Everyone laughed.

"Seriously, what did you match?"

"The marks on the back of that ole relic down in the museum with one of the map pages you gave us," said Wafford. "Justina, show the colonel how it works."

"Sure. We take the acetate..." said Justina.

"You've got to see this," said Wafford, grinning from ear to ear, nudging Stupak with his elbow. His pride was overcoming the sadness. "Never seen anything like it in all my life."

"...And we do this," said Justina. Stupak watched as Justina fit the overlay perfectly.

"I'll be damned. Oh, pardon..." he said, already starting to apologize when Elizabeth interrupted.

"Not to bother, colonel." said Elizabeth demurely. "Everyone has been doing it"

Blakely said, "What we need, Dimitrius, are some copies of the composite. If they could be enlarged, that would be great."

"I can use our drafting enlarger. How many copies will you need?"

"What do you think, Justina?"

"Since there is the possibility of finding Minoan artifacts, we will need to share the information with various officials. I suppose twenty five, thirty copies?"

"I'll have my clerk make fifty," said Stupak.

He picked up the map book and negative and left the room.

Blakely leaned back in his chair. He looked at Justina sitting next to him. Her face was reminiscent of the young woman he once knew. He wanted to kiss her, and she seemed ready—her lips were parted and her dark eyes held him. He broke the spell by touching her on the arm and saying, "Well, it took forty years, but we solved it!"

"Ya. We did it together."

Blakely looked around, feeling Elizabeth and Wafford were watching them. They were.

"Lordy, lordy," said Wafford in a whisper. "Just wish my daddy coulda been here to witness this. He wasn't crazy like people thought he was. Lordy, lordy! Out of all the mess... comes the unexpected. A little victory."

It was the mess again. A little victory. What did he mean? Wafford sat, elbows on knees, covering his face and weeping. Elizabeth patted his back and stared ahead, seeming to be into another world of her own—her face masked like those of the peasants.

THE MINOTAUR

Joachim whispered something, sounding like he was having a private conversation with Heinrich. His thick fingers grappling the cellophane pages, tried to turn them. Joachim craned over them as though looking to discover some secret meaning in the grainy, black and white photographs.

Wafford reached over and grasped Elizabeth's hand. Everyone fell silent, each handling the moment of connection and expectation quietly.

Blakely went over the sequence in his own mind, reliving the moment when he knew they had put it together. Good old Fort Riley, Kansas. Were it not for military intelligence school, he couldn't have put together the marks, template, map, and logic of it. Now, he was feeling the excitement you get after you've hit a jackpot on a slot machine, but you're not sure what the payoff will be—only that you've been damned lucky. It had been a wild crap shoot from the very beginning.

Joachim mumbled to himself as he attempted to grasp a page. Elizabeth released Wafford's hand and moved her chair over to where Joachim sat. Without saying anything, she helped him to turn the fragile cellophane photo pages.

Wafford raised up. His sadness had returned. He sat, looking waxen, numbly staring at Elizabeth as she spoke softly to Joachim, turning the fragile pages like a kindergarten teacher helping a first-day pupil.

A dark shadow of black hair fell across Blakely's eyes as lavender scent descended and soft lips planted a kiss on his mouth and Justina's hand held his.

"We did it!" she whispered, then let go before he could respond. Her face was flushed.

The same words Jenny used in her message about the three-way deal. "Yeah." he grinned at her. "We did it!"

He recalled the many times he had heard those words in sports and competitions over the years. An exultant feeling of overcoming great odds and sharing in a wave of camaraderie and celebration. Why couldn't Wafford break through and feel the joy of winning? It is so rare you can truly say, "we did it!".

CHAPTER 19

Site Visit

"I got a favor to ask," said Blakely, watching the guards waving the procession through the gate and off the base.

"Anything you want," replied Stupak.

"Those pictures of Heinrich. Could I make a paper copy of some of them for Joachim? I was thinking I'd buy a nice album and put them in it so he would have them to look at."

"Hell, they are duplicates of what we have in the museum. Take what you want. What use are they here? Nazis! Another invader of Kriti. Funny, I just last week thought of throwing out the whole smelly lot of them."

"Sure?"

"Absolutely."

"I'd like to have the ones Lou and Elizabeth paper clipped. There are thirty five or so."

"I'll have my clerk gather them for you."

Stupak drove slowly down the hill, checking to be sure Mike was still behind him. "As a matter of fact, we have plenty of vinyl albums at headquarters. I'll get one for you. What else do you need, my friend?"

"That's it," said Blakely, as they passed through the square. "You've been very cooperative, Dimitrius. If you hadn't shown us those sector maps, we'd never have found anything."

"Well, since you mention this, you must know myself and Greek military have a national interest in this archeological scavenger hunt. You believe we will find a treasure at the bottom of this mountain?"

"Who knows? It could all be von Etter's little joke. We may find a case of schnapps he wanted to stash."

"That would be good! We could have a big party, then."

They came around a hairpin curve. An old man walked slowly up the hill, not raising his eyes as they approached.

"One of the old ones," Stupak said. "You don't see many of them anymore, unless you come to the mountains."

"Yeah. I saw a man wearing the same outfit in Iraklion the other day. Selling stuffed dogs."

"I know the man you speak of. He has been on the street in front of the mosque many years, selling now and then a dog. The orange and white one nobody wants to buy."

"What is that they wear around their heads?"

"They are called mandilli. Black lace, often with small black beads. You not familiar with this?"

"Joachim has a plain one."

"Part of how the old ones dress. A warrior costume. Ready to fight. Always high black riding boots called stivania, riding britches we call vraches. Most wear a cummerbund into which there is always a knife."

"Yeah. I know about the knives. Two of my crew on the *Sea Siren* bought knives like that in Rethimnon the other day. I guess they are for collectors?"

"Oh, of course. But also for your protection. The knife is the weapon of choice among Cretans. You will seldom find a Cretan without a knife. And believe me, he is ready to use it. A little song goes, 'He wore at the waist a silver knife, A knife such as that one Nowhere will be found...'"

Stupak laughed aloud. "You like my singing voice, no?"

Blakely grinned at this affable, open man who seemed more intent upon turning his head and talking than watching the road.

"I tell you, Ed, the Cretans of this island are the best soldiers in the Greek army."

THE MINOTAUR

"Why?"

"They are so damn ferocious. They hold vendetta, they seek revenge. You kill someone here, their grandsons and cousins will track you down, carry the blood of their grandfather with them until you die." Stupak braked for a sharp curve, then resumed speed. "That is just how it is."

A flock of goats was crossing the road ahead, attended by a young boy with a scraggly black and white dog. Stupak stopped the car at a safe distance. They watched the procession.

Stupak scratched his chin. "Tell me something... Your boss, Lou? What is in his head today? He look like the world has come to an end."

"Yeah. I don't know. It has to do with the man you met this morning, Gresham King, and the big man, Homer McCloud."

"I hear of this McCloud. A general friend in Athens tell me this Homer is as mysterious as the original—people know of him, but do not know him. He drift in to Athens and Piraeus and out again—like a cloud which comes and goes. McCloud is over all of Zebulon Transport Company, eh?"

"Chairman of the board."

"Yes. The company is very big... and Lou Wafford, he seems to me a man who is suddenly made very unhappy—yesterday a big man, today a small boy. His wife, too, is unhappy. I do not understand this."

"I don't know. I have the impression Wafford is about to get fired."

Stupak watched the goats crossing. "This ship of yours—the *Sea Siren*. I think there is more here than a television studio. Can you tell me more about the computer we saw this morning? Nothing was mentioned about special software or how this transmission booster apparatus operates. And these sails of black material. We were not offered the opportunity to examine them."

"Yeah. Well, King says all of it is proprietary. Company secrets."

Stupak adjusted the rear view mirror. "That is interesting! These black receptors. Where do they come from?"

"King told me the material was developed for NASA. The army signal corps tried using it for communications, but they found it was too fragile. I understand the government released control and production to private companies some time back."

"They pass customs inspections?"

"Oh, yes. Customs and military. We were stopped by a UN gunboat in the Adriatic Sea—on our way to Trieste. They checked everything—including the electronic stuff on the masts. The inspector took one of the black sails back to the admiral's flagship for examination. When we came back down from Trieste, they gave it back. No problems at all."

"Trieste? And what did you do in Trieste?"

"We bought the fourth piece of the relic from a dealer there."

Stupak squinted at the windshield. "So, your boat pass successfully through the blockade?"

"Yeah. Why? Did you think we were carrying contraband?"

"No, no, my friend." He touched Blakely's shoulder. "From my observations, I believe you are an honest man. But I tell you..." He scratched his chin. "How should I say? My people monitor communications, and occasionally we've been getting unusual signals between your *Sea Siren* and unidentified sources. Sometimes they happen at strange hours. It makes me wonder, that is all. Would you know about such communications?"

Blakely hesitated. How best to answer?

"You met Gregor Tobok. He's a cyberspace cadet. He stays up 'til all hours talking on the Internet with his buddies. I know he listens to all kinds of stuff. He also uses Ham radio to talk with people. He's been doing it ever since we set sail. Nothing out of the ordinary that I know of."

He couldn't share his suspicions with Stupak. By doing so, Stupak might use the information to seize the vessel and its crew until the whole business could be investigated—and that could take months. No. He couldn't risk sabotaging whatever King and Wafford had going. Hell, it could be a covert CIA operation for all he knew. As much as he disliked Marchese, the guy did have a past connection with CIA.

"Ah! You have cyberspace cowboy!" He laughed. "I am sure that explains it."

A horn beeped behind them. Blakely looked back. Mike waved.

Stupak swung his hands to the wheel. "The goats are all across!"

He released the emergency brake, and they proceeded down the grade and around a curve. They descended another hill. The road leveled out, made a sharp turn close to the mountain, and crossed a stone bridge. Stupak slowed the car, glanced at his topographic map, and pulled the car into the grass before the bridge.

"We are here," he said.

They climbed out just as the van arrived.

Stupak oriented his map to match the contours of the mountain and stream crossing the road. Justina and Wafford came over to where the two men stood.

Blakely asked, "Who owns this land, Dimitrius? Do we need permission?"

Stupak waved his hand. "No permission. Public land maybe? Who knows?" He pointed to Justina. "She may need special permission to explore archeology here, but today we are doing no harm, eh? It should be in this direction, approximately a hundred meters."

He turned and walked, map in hand. The group followed. Blakely checked the turns of the dry stream bed, trying to match those with the line marking it on the map.

"Reminds me of places along the Delta back home," Wafford said, making an attempt to be talkative. "Got any cotton mouths here, colonel?"

Stupak stopped and looked back.

"I don't understand what you say."

"Snakes," explained Wafford. "Are there poisonous snakes in here?"

"One poisonous, but he always escapes. I have never seen one," Stupak replied, turning and lifting a branch out of his way.

They had walked approximately a hundred yards from the road. Blakely and Wafford cracked off limbs, making it easier for Justina to follow. Stupak stopped, shifted his map so it paralleled the curves of the stream bed, looked toward the rising hillside, and pointed to thick brush on a gentle rise beyond which the mountain rose sharply.

"Twenty five meters elevation from this point should be right there." Stupak ascended the gentle slope to the mountain wall, pushed back the thick limbs, and held them until Blakely, Wafford and Justina passed.

"This is the location, maybe ten feet either direction. Soil, mountain rock, lots of bushes," he said, letting the limbs fall back in place. "It will take cutting these away, some test digging here and there. Is that not correct, Justina?"

"Ya. No visible openings. That is good. Nothing has been disturbed here for many years."

Justina stepped back a few paces and held her hand above her eyes. She turned, moved farther down the slope, turned again, studying the terrain.

"Something happen here," she said, pointing. "You can see the mountainside is different in front of you, more vertical than at either side. There is also a dish pattern of earth at the base. You are standing on the outside edge of it."

The three men walked down to where she was standing.

Stupak put his hands on his hips.

"A bomb crater. A bomb must have exploded there."

He turned to the group. "Many bomb craters here and there. You can see them best in winter, just across the bridge and on the mountain approaching the air base. Most have been filled in by farmers, so you do not see them any more."

He turned toward the site and pointed.

"Probably a bomb struck the mountainside, removing tons of earth and rock."

Wafford looked around. "That's one bomb pretty well off the target, wouldn't you say?"

THE MINOTAUR 197

Stupak shrugged, looked at his map, then glanced back toward the road.

"I've seen bomb craters near where my car is parked. Perhaps the bombs were aimed at a convoy on the road. Now and then farmers will discover in this area a Nazi truck or motorcycle buried in the dirt."

"A bomb, then, could have burst there, exposing a cave or burial crypt," said Justina. "Or, the bomb may have exposed the relic, and it was found by Heinrich von Etter when he came out to assess damage."

"Sounds logical," said Blakely.

"If you wish to dig here, it will take several strong workers and good equipment," said Stupak. "It won't be difficult to get labor. I may be able to arrange for my own engineers to assist you. We call such work missions of good will to America!"

"Good," said Justina. "I suppose what we need to do now is make our search legal. You said you didn't know who owns this property?"

"No," replied Stupak. "However, archeology is always number one priority on Crete. It takes precedence." He glanced toward the site. "I don't think anyone cares about you digging here. You would destroy nothing. When through, you put the earth back as you found it. No problem!"

They walked toward the road. Justina spoke over her shoulder.

"I will call Nick Paulas. He can get us the permissions we need."

She put her hand on Wafford's shoulder. "At last I can become useful!"

"You've been plenty useful, Miss Justina," Wafford replied. "Never mind about that! Thank goodness you didn't go back with the professor."

She didn't reply. They came out on the road next to the staff car.

Justina waited for Wafford to catch up.

She said, "Louis, if you don't mind, I'll ride back with Dimitrius and Edward. I would like to start planning the work for tomorrow."

"Sure. Fine by me," said Wafford with a frown, turning to the van. "See you back at the hotel."

Blakely crawled into the back seat, giving Justina the front one next to Stupak. She turned in the seat.

"I thought we should talk privately about this. Dimitrius, what are the resources here for security, in case we were to find a store of ancient artifacts?"

He held his hands open above the wheel.

"You have the very finest security in the population of Cretans," he replied. "None more fierce. However, if it is a really big deal, then the Greek state uses any resources necessary. We have plenty trained guards at the airfield, more at the base at Iraklion—including United States Air Force. What can I say? Are you expecting to discover the tomb of Zeus?"

Justina laughed. Stupak started the car.

"Seriously, I try to think of what would happen if we should find something important. I didn't want to say anything in front of Louis, but I think he would announce any discoveries on television to the whole world before we have adequate security. This place could be swarming with people."

Stupak pulled out, backed, and headed up the winding road. Mike followed slowly with the van.

"No doubt," Blakely added.

"Security you can depend upon" said Stupak. "Believe me, I have the best security force on the island."

They arrived at the piazza.

"I'll bring those photos and album when I leave work," said Stupak, as Blakely got out of the car.

"Appreciate it."

The piazza was lively. Bouzouki music blared across the square from the taverna. The three German women were sitting with others in a little circle, drinking bottled juices.

"Can I buy you a celebratory drink, Justina?"

"Ya," she replied, heading toward a table with two empty chairs. They sat down.

Mike pulled up in front of the hotel in the van. Wafford and Mike shifted Elizabeth into her chair as Joachim stood by. Blakely and Justina watched them enter the hotel.

"What is wrong with Louis?" asked Justina. "Elizabeth was most upset last evening. She tell me over supper that Louis is totally pulled inside like a snail hiding in his shell."

"I think he's lost a power struggle with King, which puts us all in a bad position. Whether we like it or not, we may not be working for Lou anymore."

"But we have contracts with Louis and Crete Enterprises. We have no contract that involves Gresham King."

"Yeah. True." Blakely didn't want to make a big to-do and get Justina worked up. "Maybe with our discovery today, Lou will snap out of it. I've tried to cheer him up, but you see what happened when Stupak joked. It's like Stupak said, the guy is acting like the world is coming to an end. Let's hope he feels better tomorrow."

Justina leaned back and gave a sigh and pushed against the shiny wedge of hair with her hand.

"At least I know I am not responsible for his bad feeling. Thank God," she said, "At last! I do something real!"

Blakely looked over at her and said in English, "Can you believe it? We damn well did it!"

"Ya, Edward," she replied in Berlin English. "We damn well do it!" They laughed. He held up a hand to George. The waiter came and leaned down to hear Blakley above the din of music.

Blakely asked, "What'll you have, Justina?"

"A glass of white wine?"

"Hell, why don't we get a bottle?"

"Hell," she replied, "und why not?"

"A bottle of your best, George!"

"Demestica?"

"Yes. And could we have real wine glasses, please?"

George nodded grimly. "I try. I know we have some."
George went off.
He turned back to her. Her face was flushed. She was resting her head against the chair back and her eyes were closed. Her white jogging shoes were stained green from the foliage. She looked incredibly happy.

"Going to call Chris tonight and invite him back for the excavation?"

He wasn't sure it was a smirk or a wince as she opened her eyes and looked toward the open valley. Her full lips parted. She answered in English. "No."

"Mind if I ask why not?"

"Because..." She crossed her legs, letting her left foot rock up and down in rhythm. "If we dug there and found nothing, Christopher would be angry and say I brought him back here for another chasing of goose. If he were here and we did find something, he would immediately want to take the credit."

"Why?"

"Because he is a man and we are in Greece. Men come especially first here. He also would want the celebrity."

"So you want the celebrity?"

The foot was moving faster. "Ya, perhaps."

She smiled, turned serious again.

"I help to get Christopher his professorship at the university. Later, I help to obtain special chair for him there. I take off from my duties at the museum to raise children. I cannot now see my grown boys because it is his wish that I not do it. I always do what he want. But not anymore."

She wiped across her nose with her hand.

"Now, it is my turn. Christopher has had his chances. Forty years of opportunities."

Blakely said, "Good for you."

He reached over for her hand. She moved her arm so he could take her hand in his.

Blakely squeezed her hand and said, "I say damned good for

you."

She was looking off in the distance through half-closed eyes.

"After all, it was Christopher who chose to go home. It was I who insisted on staying. So now I have something exciting to stay for. Let him stay at home!"

She pulled Blakely's hand closer toward her and stroked his arm with her other hand. They said nothing else. George came with the wine and a bowl of olives. Blakely released her hand and watched as George set the two glasses and the bowl on the table. He poured the wine and set the bottle down.

"Anything else?" he asked in German.

Blakely gave him some drachmas. "No. Thanks, George."

"To a future celebrity," Blakely said, raising his glass to hers.

"To successful dig." The glasses clicked and they sipped the cool, astringent wine. She looked hopefully at him.

"Have you ever in your life made a radical decision, Edward?"

"Radical?" Blakely looked at the wine before answering. "Yeah. Sometimes sailing, you hafta say, 'what the hell,' and do something radical. Is that what you mean?"

"I mean a decision which changes your whole life and outlook?"

"Yeah. Agreeing to come on this trip was one. Last night, I decided I would sell out my boat, office, business—lock, stock, and barrel—and not go back to California."

She looked more hopeful, and sipped her wine. "What will you do?"

"I'm not sure. Right now, my future is a clean slate, ready to write plans on. Is that where you are, Justina?"

"Her eyes flickered and then grew determined. "Ya. Except my slate is not so clean. All I know is that from this moment forward, my life will be very different than it was yesterday." She looked away. "I can't tell you more than that."

He sensed that Chris leaving and the discovery of the site today might have given her false hopes. And he especially hoped she was not planning her future to include Ed Blakely as her partner. He glanced at her and their eyes met.

"Will you help me with Paulas?" she asked.

"I don't follow you."

"Nick Paulas also will want to take over, and do the excavation his way. He no doubt will bring Angelo Santos and Cristos Neopolis in from Athens. There is also an English archeologist at Knossos who may wish to barge in."

"You really are expecting to find something big, aren't you?"

She sipped the wine. He refilled her glass.

"I am merely planning for any eventualities. Archeologists spend most of their lives preparing for the one moment of major discovery. Heinrich von Etter had his reason for putting the code on the back of the relic. I believe we may find other relics. Will you help me if it happens?"

"Count on it," said Blakely. The woman is seriously covering the bases, he thought. She intends to hold these other guys at bay. Hell, she's playing on their turf. Why wouldn't they steal the limelight? These are the professional archeologists everybody listens to when the subject focuses on Greek antiquities. At least that's what Chris told him.

He watched Justina's foot moving up and down. Jeremiah Wilcox and CDN News. If Wafford could maintain control over the publicity, then he could also designate the spokesperson. Keep the other archeologists off television and radio. Keep Justina in the limelight. They would have to come to her hat in hand. Greek television wouldn't mean didley. Seeing how relaxed she is, Justina had probably thought of the same strategy.

She's getting ready to take on the competition. He liked that. Just so she didn't grow too attached to him in the process. They sat without saying anything. Blakely had closed his eyes and felt the spring sunshine warm his face and watched the white particles dance and skitter inside the red of his eyelids like minuscule water skates which, when you looked at them, immediately darted away.

He finished the glass of wine and opened his eyes. Justina had finished her second glass to his one. He poured them another. Without opening her eyes, she said, "Thank you, Edward."

She opened her eyes long enough to raise the glass and drink half the wine before putting it down again. She gave him a curious smile and closed her eyes again. Probably fantasizing about becoming a star archeologist with her name flashing around the world. Why not? She would be a star!

The green stained jogging shoe began to twitch back and forth slowly. He watched it holding a nice rhythm that jiggled her leg slightly. Something erotic about that. He took a swig of wine. He leaned back and closed his eyes and rested his arm on the table. A hand touched and then closed over his open palm and held it gently.

CHAPTER 20

Passover

Blakely and Justina walked back to the hotel. It was probably the wine, but Justina's eyes had taken on a sultry look. He hadn't seen her with bedroom eyes since the Minderhof Kafe. Actually, he was feeling a little drunk. It was all too much on an empty stomach.

"Can we meet for dinner, Edward?"

"I think Lou and Elizabeth said to be in the lobby at 2100 hours."

She looked uncertain then. They entered the hotel.

"I don't want to be around Louis tonight," she said. "He is sulking. Why don't we go out ourselves to another place? I want to celebrate!"

"There's a restaurant a couple blocks down the hill. Alex says they have a terrace. Want to meet here in the lobby at 2045 hours?"

"I'll meet you in the piazza."

She paused in the doorway of the sitting room where the black telephone sat on a table.

"I have a telegram to send, and I must call Nick Paulas," she said.

"Okay. See you outside at 2045 hours."

She entered the sitting room and sat down next to the phone. Blakely picked up his key at the desk. The desk clerk reached down behind the counter and placed a brown package before him.

"Colonel Stupak requested I give you this."

"Thanks."

He carried the package to his room and sat down with it on

the bed. He reached for his cellular phone and dialed.

"*Sea Siren*, Tobok here."

"Any messages, Gregor?"

"No, sir."

Tobok sounded tired. Leo must be working him hard.

"Can you reach Jeremiah for me?"

"Yes, sir. Just a sec."

"Television studio. Jeremiah speaking."

"Change of plans, Jeremiah. We think we've found where Heinrich hid the cache of jewels!"

"No joke?"

"No joke. It's at the bottom of the mountain not far off the road. We'll be starting the dig as soon as Nick Paulas can get here with letters of approval."

"Wow! That means we've got a major story for CDN!"

"It means you have a major story, Mr. Journalist."

"Too much!"

"Will you be bringing stuff up here tonight?"

He heard a sigh. "Can't, skip. Mr. King wants to wait on equipment transfer 'til tomorrow. It doesn't look like the test will happen until Saturday night."

"How come?"

"Don't know. It's good in a way because now I can use Harry and Gregor to help me do the on site camera production tomorrow."

"Okay. I'll call you when we get the green light. Stupak's offered use of his troops to help us."

"Far out! That's the kind of footage I need. Is Uncle Lou paying them or what?"

"Stupak volunteered them. A gesture of friendship between Greece and America, he says."

"Fantastic! I want an interview with him with some of his men in the background working."

"I'm sure he'll oblige. You saw this morning—he's no wall flower."

"Interesting expression." He chuckled. "You'll have to tell me what it means sometime."

"All right, junior. Don't knock our lingo and we won't knock yours."

"Touche'!"

"Stay out of trouble."

He folded the phone and tucked it away. He was disappointed Jeremiah couldn't bring him the videotape of Gregor's communications, but one day wouldn't make any difference. He was feeling like he had had two bottles of wine rather than half of one. A grumpiness was coming on.

He lay back on the bed. He was beginning to feel adversarial within himself. The demons within were making him feel hot and uncomfortable—for no apparent reason. He could feel the beginning pangs of anger and couldn't understand why he should be angry. Just like the other night on the piazza, when he ran Chris off. He raised up and looked at the neatly sealed package, knowing what was in it.

He tore off the brown paper. Fresh plastic photograph holders punched for a three ring binder were stacked on top of all the black and white pictures of Heinrich von Etter. And underneath them was a new, gold embossed leather photo album.

Stupak is remarkable, Blakely thought. No vinyl for the former enemy! Only the best leather would do. He had never known any people so generous and at the same time so ready to be withholding as the Greeks he'd met here. They'd do anything in the world for you. Just don't cross them accidentally or otherwise.

If Joachim had murdered some Greek guy—even accidentally—when he was stationed here, there would probably be grand children and all their cousins still looking for Joachim right this minute, hoping to get their revenge. Helluva tradition that is! Vendettas. Just what the world needs.

Wasn't that what the ancient Gods and Goddesses did? Everything was a vendetta. Theseus trying to get back at King Minos. Nothing learned in how many thousands of years? For Christ's sake! Still an eye-for-an-eye. The mythologists—including Elizabeth—say people can't do anything about it, though. Whatever happens is fate. The comet comes round again.

He began sliding the photos into the holders and looking at the Nazis in their uniforms, with their iron crosses, swastikas, batons, and big bastard smiles. The holier than thou conquerors swaggering in the photographs were savage killers.

He stopped. What in hell's name was he doing? Stupidest goddamned thing he'd done yet in his whole life. Making a scrapbook of Nazis for a guy who, if he'd been in Joachim's way in 1944, would have shot hell out of him. Besides, Joachim worked at Ploesti oil fields trying to make all the pumps operate when his own half-brother, Luke, was flying over in a goddamn B-24 Liberator and the goddamn Germans on the ground were firing at Luke as his buddies tried to drop bombs, and the bastards shot Luke's plane down. Luke was dead.

So, here he was, Ed Blakely, sixty damn years old, a veteran of the United States Army who served in Germany, sitting here in a little hotel room on a Cretan mountain top without a telephone or private bath, making up this picture book of the enemy to give to an old bastard who lived only to watch stars, smoke his pipe, and recite verses of his own miserable history. Talk about illusory experiences!

He sat back, looking at the photographs he had sorted next to him on the bed. What the hell was it about Joachim? He's like them damn peasants you see in the valley, he thought. Inscrutable. Undeniable. Why hadn't he just gone off somewhere and died instead of surviving all these years? What was it he said? Something about the oppressed? As long as you hold freedom in your soul, it is the oppressor who is the oppressed? And last night, Joachim and he had gotten a little high on beer and sat watching the eclipse—and Joachim called him 'my son.'

He picked up a photograph showing Heinrich lifting a glass along with the other Nazis officers. Count Heinrich von Etter. What else could he do but toast along with the other bastards?

Shoot himself? From what Joachim says, Count Heinrich was a hero with the German general staff and an enemy of the Nazis. What a helluva marriage that must have been!

Then this other count comes along, Count von Stauffenberg. He tries blowing Hitler to kingdom come, and all hell blows loose. The Nazis round up all the suspected general staff and smaller counts like this guy Count von Etter and torture them a while before putting them out of their goddamn misery.

Amongst all this are the majority—the uncounts, the un-Nazis, the no-accounts, the uncountable millions of sorry-assed victims. All the ones caught in the middle of a goddamn mythology being carried out by would-be Gods who don't give one damn who gets hurt, killed or what. Part of a greater plan at work. All the people, merely petals falling off the tree of life to be replaced after a winter, like millions of flowers living one minute, and dying the next—Persephone and Hyakutake all rolled into one.

He paused and considered his thoughts. The wine had opened up his bitterness again. Why was he so bitter? What was going on inside him that he raged on like this? It always came on him unexpectedly and with a fury far beyond the immediate cause, as though his anger waited, simmering, for just the right trigger to set it off in a flood of vituperation. At least he was by himself and wasn't hurting anyone!

Elizabeth spoke of it as his conflict, where Easy Ed and Edward tried to kill each other. She might be right. Then, there was Captain Easy, the man Easy Ed always wanted to become. They were like dragons, coming out of hiding when he least expected them to, causing inner conflict and outer grief. Yeah. Easy Ed and Captain Easy ganged up on Edward and told Chris to get the hell out. Go home! And it must be the boy, Easy Ed, who was making such a big deal about Joachim being a former Nazi because the man of feeling and reason—Edward—considered Joachim as a loving friend and an old man he wanted to take care of—the only man who had ever called him 'my son.'

When he really thought about it, he could understand it all.

THE MINOTAUR

And maybe it was this effort to understand which would be the beginning of a new Ed Blakely. He laughed at himself and his efforts with the photo album. He resumed his work.

He placed each of the plastic holders into the binder, following the arrangement which seemed to show the progress of the construction. When he finished, he looked around for his pen. He fished it out of his travel bag.

How do you express true feelings to an old man who had more than anything wanted to have a son? He thought about his own grandfather. He'd never given granddad a book of any kind. Maybe that was it. God was giving him a chance to make amends with an older one—a Father man, a God father—and say what was in his heart.

He wrote: 'To My Best Friend Joachim Grenz, who loves God and the stars in a way I hope to, someday. Love, Edward.'

Blakely capped his pen, then set the album and pen on the dresser. Damnedest gift in the world to be giving your best friend, he thought, lying back down. He remembered Joachim saying that when he looked at the photographs, his friend Heinrich was young and smiling again. He guessed that when Joachim looked at the smiling face, he, too, was feeling young again. And when he did that, it renewed the possibilities of a future.

He undressed and slipped on his robe. He went down the hall to the bath. It was warm and humid. A lavender scent. Justina must have been there before him. He showered, shaved and returned to his room. Justina was feeling her oats, and he had responded—even as his gut told him not to. He decided to take a nap before meeting her for dinner. He would have plenty of time. He stretched out and pulled a sheet over him. He dosed.

A knocking sound.

"Yeah?" His watch said it was 1825 hours. "Who is it?"

Justina's voice said, "May I come in?"

He pulled on his robe and opened the door. Justina stood before him in a black silk robe holding a tray of wafers, bread, cheese, and a bottle of red wine.

"Would you like to share a special moment with me, Edward?" He was so shocked he hardly knew what to do. He stepped aside. She walked passed him into the room. Lavender and fresh soap filled the air. He closed the door. She sat down on the bed and placed the tray on the bedside table. Her robe had opened above her knees and the top gaped. She held the bottle in both hands on her lap, looking up at him as though waiting for him to say something—anything. He sat down next to her. His mouth was dry.

They sat looking at one another. He asked, "What brought this on?"

She dropped her eyes to the wine bottle.

"I have sent a telegram to Christopher. I told him I want a divorce. You are the first to know."

She looked up. "We came out here with hopes we could begin again. You could see it was no good—from the very beginning."

He didn't understand. She read his look.

"The night of the party in Athens, when I learned of Christopher's deception about Thomas, any chance of reconciliation was doomed." She sighed. "And so, after almost forty years, I get the courage to do what I should have done when Christopher proposed."

Tears streamed down her face. So, Blakely thought, she was saying it was Blakley's message that night about Thomas that had wrecked their chances? Damnedest thing about people with problems—they like to push the blame on somebody else.

"Would you celebrate my courage with me, Edward? Have a glass of wine with me? Hold me and make me feel I am not dead inside? It has been so long!"

The messenger of bad fortune gets to share the fruits of disaster. "Excuse me, I'll be right back."

Blakely got up and returned with a dampened cloth from the lavatory. He sat next to her and daubed her eyes and cheeks with it. She took the cloth from his hand and put it down next to the tray.

THE MINOTAUR   211

"I didn't come here for your pity, Edward." She shook her head so that her wedge of hair bounced slightly. Her eyes flashed at him.

"Just trying to help, Justina." He looked around the room. "Afraid I don't have any glasses. I can go down and get some."

"Please, Edward. This is not easy. Stay here and be with me!"

She reached for his hand and drew it up to her mouth. She kissed each knuckle and opened his hand and kissed it inside. Her eyes were closed. He reached and drew her against him. She set the wine on the bedside table and fell back on the pillow, drawing him down with her.

* * * * *

A knocking sound. Probably the clerk coming to remind him the gang was waiting to go to dinner. No. Wouldn't be. He switched on the light. The bottle of red wine and hors d'oeuvres were there—untouched—next to the dampened cloth. Justina was gone. What time was it? 2230 hours. He swung his feet off the bed and rubbed his eyes. Maybe she was coming back.

"Come on in. Door's unlocked."

The knob turned. Wafford peered around the door.

"Come on in, Lou. Overslept. Sorry I missed dinner."

It was a lie, but Wafford didn't say anything. He came over and sat next to Blakely on the bed, looking long faced. Probably more changes in the test schedule. King had a way of constantly twisting Wafford's tail.

"Don't know how to say this, Ed."

"What do you mean?"

Blakely was still groggy. Had somebody seen Justina come to his room in her robe? She left about the time everybody was supposed to be at the Blue Dolphin restaurant. Her room was across the hall. Wafford put his arm around Blakely's shoulder. His eyes rimmed with water.

"Our old friend died."

"What old... Joachim?"

"We came back from supper. I thought it was odd not seeing you two watchin' the stars on the square. I asked the desk clerk. He said Joachim hadn't come down for dinner. So he went up and knocked on his door. He didn't answer. The clerk went in. He was slumped over in his chair by the window. Musta been look'n at the moon rise. The clerk called the doctor. He pronounced him dead."

Blakely felt a rush of guilt. He hadn't thought to make plans with Joachim for tonight. He'd totally forgotten him. Damn it all! God hadn't wasted any time with his payback. Hell, he didn't even have a chance to say good-bye. He glanced toward the dresser. He got up and went over and touched the album.

Wafford asked, "What's that'cha got?"

"Nothing." Blakely slipped the album into the dresser drawer.

"Guess you need some time to yerself. I see you got some food and drink. I can getcha more, if you'd like."

"No, thanks."

"I'll be going now, unless you need something."

Wafford got up, walked to the door.

'Where is he? I want to go see him."

"Still in his room. Doctor was just coming out when we arrived. Alex is arranging to have him taken down the way to an undertaker. If you want to join us later, we'll be on the hotel patio."

"All Right."

Blakely watched the door close. There was silence. No Bouzouki music. He stood up, walked over to the window, and swung it out. A clear night. Full moon. He looked toward the northwest for Hyakutake, knowing even before he did so that the comet would be gone. Joachim knew that last night, but hadn't told him. 'Goodbye old man!' he whispered.

By the time Blakely got dressed, three men with a wooden litter had arrived. Blakely went with them to Joachim's room. He was stretched out on the bed beneath a sheet. The four carried the draped corpse down the curving stairwell and out past the empty piazza and down the winding street and into a narrow alley which opened onto a cobbled square. The double wooden doors of the undertaker's stood open. A gray, heavy-set man with glasses waited in the yellow light and pointed them to a wooden table. They laid the body on it. The men left without a word. The undertaker turned up a gas lamp and said something about needing to leave. He nodded and left Blakely standing beside the table.

Blakely pulled the sheet back from Joachim's head and chest. As in life, Joachim's eyes peered out from deep beneath heavily wrinkled skin in death. His mouth was slightly open. He was wearing his dark gray coat. Blakely slid his hand into the inside jacket pocket and pulled out a tattered leather wallet. In it were the folded papers he had shown Padopolis the other day and the photograph of him and Blakely. He replaced the contents and slid the wallet inside the pocket again.

In his right lower jacket pocket, Blakely touched his tobacco pouch, pipe, a box of matches, and bits of loose tobacco. In his left pocket, there was a lead pencil, a small pen knife, and Blakely could feel the spiral wire of the notebook he had given Joachim. He put the penknife in his sail pants. He pulled the notebook out and opened it. He turned the pages, seeing the neatly printed German script and feeling the impressions of the pencil on the thin paper. The pages were filled with Joachim's verses. The last entry was inscribed, 'To Edward.' And below it was a four line verse. *'We shared the comet Hyakutake, my friend Edward Blakely and me, of what was once and what will ever be, a power, a spirit, a God in eternity.'*

He closed the book and put it also in the pocket of his sailing pants. He looked up. "I never got to give you your present, Joachim. I'm really sorry, but I hope you know how much I cared! I truly love you!"

He leaned over the grizzled head and kissed Joachim's forehead. Tears dropped on the old face as Blakely looked a final time at all the lines and scars, the pug nose, and deep-set eyes, and the mass of white beard and gray hair.

"Joachim," he said aloud, "wherever you are, I want you to know you were a fine man and would have made the damnedest-best father."

He pulled the sheet back over Joachim's head and turned down the gas light. He closed the double doors and walked slowly back to the hotel.

He went to his room and sat on the bed. It was 2315 hours. He drank some of the wine from the bottle and tried to eat the now dried crusts of bread, and wafers, and cheese. He found it difficult to swallow the food. He took another swig of wine, and gazed out the open window. Somewhere far off, a dog barked. Joachim was gone.

He took another swig and looked at the label on the bottle. Castel Danielis, Red Dry Wine, Achaia-Clauss, Peloponnese, 1992. Compliments of Justina. He drank again, remembering how she had pulled him down and held him and began to cry softly, and how he had stroked her hair and comforted her, and kissed her tears and eyes and lips. They lay together holding one another for a long time without moving. He ate another wafer with the wine.

Finally, she said, "As much as I want to, I cannot do it yet, Edward. I want you to just hold me. Hold me tight so I know you care!"

And he did, and she wept quietly, and he had stroked her hair again until she was calm. He raised up on one elbow and looked closely at her face in the lamplight. There were many more crinkles and lines than he had noticed before, yet there was a bloom about her that reminded him of the young woman he had known in Berlin. He had stroked her cheek and her eyes closed softly.

Her robe had come undone and her left breast was partially exposed—full, lovely, creamy white with faint blue veins and tipped with salmon. He had reached across and pulled her robe over it, covering her again, and then had touched her lightly on the cheek. Her eyes slowly opened. She looked at him without expression and then opened like a fragile flower into the same wan smile she had given him the morning she had come to his cabin on the *Sea Siren*.

She had removed his hand and gotten up slowly, becoming modest, clutching the front of her robe in her hand. He got up, too, and tightened his robe. She looked up into his eyes.

"Thank you, Edward, for holding me and loving me. I think I will go to my room and sleep now."

She reached and kissed him gently on the cheek and left his room.

He took another swig from the bottle. He ate the stale bread and the crackers, chewing slowly, thinking how he had tried to give back to Justina a gentle warmth of his hand to her cheek like she had given to him forty years ago on that snowy night. He drank the remainder of the wine with the last wafer.

CHAPTER 21

Bad News on Good Friday

Blakely asked, "Is it possible Joachim could be buried in the German cemetery at Maleme, Dimitrius?"

"That would be lovely," said Elizabeth, looking hopefully at Stupak through red, swollen eyes.

Stupak mashed the stub of his cigarette into a saucer, pursed his lips and nodded. "I will check it out. I regret he cannot be buried here, but our people have strict rules."

"Better with his own," said Wafford. "He'll join all his buddies there."

"The undertaker hasn't any way to keep him here more than today and tomorrow," said Blakely. "My thought is to have him cremated. I've made arrangements to take him to Iraklion this afternoon. The undertaker will have his ashes back here in a couple days. Worst case, we can scatter them at sea. How would you feel about that?"

Everyone nodded sadly.

"Would it cost very much?" asked Justina.

"No, said Blakely. "I'll pay for it."

"Needn't do that," said Wafford. "Crete Enterprises brought him here, and it can cover it as another expense."

"I'd rather pay for it myself, Lou. This is between me and Joachim."

"So be it," replied Wafford, fingering his spoon. "Just wanted to help out is all."

Blakely looked at his watch. It was 1345 hours. Justina, sitting next to him, must have read his thoughts.

"I don't know where he is. Nicholas said he would meet us here at one o'clock."

Justina put her hand on his arm. "Are you going with the undertaker when he takes Joachim?"

Blakely shifted. "Joachim and I have said our good-byes. I think my best tribute to him is to finish what we came here for. That would please him most."

A slender man appeared in the doorway.

Justina waved. "Over here, Nick."

Following introductions, Nick Paulas sat down. He reminded Blakely of Cristos Neopolis, the Scythian grave robber. He was fit, tan, wore glasses, and sported an expensive suit. He obviously didn't intend to do any digging today.

Paulas said in English, "Perhaps I should have called you rather than coming here. I have applied to the Governor for your permits to dig in Pediadas, but his staff tells me he and his deputy are out of the office until Wednesday of next week." Paulas smiled and raised his eyes to Justina's. "You must wait until then. I am sorry."

Justina was furious. "Surely, there is someone else to sign off the papers, Nick. That's five days! Can you not get someone to sign for the Governor?"

Paulas chuckled. "Yes, of course. And they signed them—as well as my supervisor—but they do not become official until properly stamped by the Governor's office. There's no one there to do that."

"Meinen Gott!" said Justina in disgust. "I should have gone with you this morning. Why don't we appeal to authorities in Athens for special consideration?"

Paulas strummed his fingers on the table. "That would not be wise. I could not personally risk going outside proper channels. And this is essentially my project. Sorry, Dr. Cunningham, but you must wait. I would advise you against setting foot on the site until you receive proper authorizations."

Paulas was enjoying it, thought Blakely. Justina was almost in tears. Stupak pushed his chair back abruptly and stood up. "I must inform my men that they won't be needed today. If you will excuse me, I will go to my office."

Stupak left without shaking hands.

"I need to return to Iraklion," said Paulas, getting up. "Again, I am sorry for the delay. Had you gotten your request in by noon yesterday, the Governor was there and could have given approval."

Everyone watched Paulas exit through the doorway.

"I kick myself that I didn't go with Paulas!" said Justina, pounding the table with her fist. "There must have been someone to approve this. Nick Paulas is deliberately dragging our feet!"

"Never you mind," said Wafford sadly. "Not the only bad news. Gresh says the test is postponed 'til next weekend, Orthodox Easter."

"How so?" asked Blakely, remembering King's mentioning a change in schedule.

"Oh," Wafford shrugged, "just some bureaucratic snafu."

"Does Gresh have that kind of authority?" asked Blakely.

Wafford's face reddened. "He got the word from Homer."

Wafford tried to be nonchalant by stretching. "We can use the time to perfect our videos and help Jeremiah best we can. Anybody wants to can go to Easter service on Sunday, if they can find the right church. No use worrying 'bout things you can't control."

Elizabeth eyed Wafford critically. "Do you really believe that, Louis?"

Wafford scowled. "Well, sure I do."

THE MINOTAUR 219

CHAPTER 22

Taking Charge

Finally, at 0900 hours, on Friday morning, 12 April 1996, Justina received a faxed copy bearing the Governor's stamp. And now, all hell was breaking loose at the bottom of the mountain! It was unbelievable. Joachim would have loved it. Chain saws whined and had, within minutes, brought the peasants of the valley to the site. By 1035 hours, a crescent of people stood along the curved edge of road at the bottom of the mountain watching a dozen Greek Air Force engineers in fatigue uniforms clearing a swath through the underbrush. Stupak, looking larger than his six foot two inch frame in his fatigues and boots, directed operations, moving to point here, wave there. A dozen farmers under the direction of Padopolis loaded brush onto carts drawn by burros.

A back hoe operator moved his heavy tractor this way and that, pulling out stumps, smoothing a path using the front-end loader, and pushing rocks out of the way. Off toward the bridge, Jeremiah had set his video camera on a tripod, sun to his back, so he could capture the event on tape.

Paulas drove up. He was the consummate archeologist in khaki with a bag of tools. He presented Justina with the hard copy letter from the governor giving her authority to dig. Almost before he had gotten out of his car, Paulus reminded Justina that anything they might find was the property of Greece. No artifacts would be permitted to leave the country without permission.

Suddenly, there was silence. A bird chirped. Stupak came over, smiling, his orange sunglasses flashing, beads of sweat glistening on his forehead.

"You can come now. All is ready."

The sloped area in front of the mountain wall had been cleared of all vegetation. Justina explained to Paulas what they had concluded yesterday. Paulas walked to the vertical wall, removed a pick hammer from his belt, and dug into the earthen wall at eye level. It struck stone. He turned, said something to Stupak in Greek. Stupak turned, motioned to two of his men holding mattocks to come forward.

Paulas and Justina stood back while the two men began scraping earth from stone along the face of the mountain. Stupak came over.

"You take everything in stride, don't you Dimitrius," said Blakely.

Stupak planted his large hand on Blakely's shoulder. "We take pride in our hospitality. You tell me how I can help you, I help you. Everybody here believe same way. We are here on earth only to help one another."

"Thanks for the leather binder. You didn't have to do that."

"Ah, what the hell? I saw it on my work table. I thought, why not? The old man deserves a nice gift."

"Unfortunately, I never got to give it to him."

"That is very sad. So what did you do with it?"

"I'll put it on the bonfire tomorrow night."

"A good place. Added sacrifice in the name of your friend. What better thing to do at Easter?"

The engineers' mattocks clanged against rock. Justina pointed to a break in the stone. The two men used their mattocks more delicately now, pulling clinging earth from around stones which looked as though they had been piled into a cavity in the face of mountain.

Harry was manning camera, while Jeremiah, microphone in hand, was 'reporting for CDN news from the archeological site in a valley below Kastelli, Island of Crete.'

THE MINOTAUR   221

A break in the mountain wall was discernible, approximately five feet high and four feet wide, filled with large and small stones. Justina and Paulas were standing close together, speaking Greek, gesturing to one another and toward the various stones. Stupak went over to them, said something. He called one of his men over. The man nodded, and began to run back toward the road.

Blakely approached Justina. "Can I do anything to help?"

"Perhaps you can. Nick and I will take over from these men. If you wish to join us, I must tell you beforehand it is meticulous. You cannot be in a hurry."

"Okay."

"I will invite Colonel Stupak to join us also."

An engine whined. A military truck came around the bend and stopped at the edge of the clearing. The driver got out and unloaded an array of small tools, leather and canvas gloves, and plastic goggles. Other men removed saw horses and planks and set up a makeshift table where the tools were dumped out of a canvas bucket. Screw drivers, cold chisels, brick hammers, spikes, and pieces of rebar clanked onto the table. Folding camp chairs were placed around. Stupak thinks of everything, thought Blakely.

"I suggest you both use these screw drivers to begin cleaning the earth from around the rocks. Colonel, if you would work this side," Justina pointed to the left side. Paulus was already chipping dirt from the middle section. "Edward, you can start on the right side, here."

Justina used her trowel point to work the area next to Paulas. They picked and scraped, Justina concentrating on a smaller stone near the top of the cavity which she loosened and carefully removed.

"More stones and earth behind it," she said, tossing the rock toward the dirt pile. Paulas lifted out a large rock, carried it to the side, and dropped it. The hole showed more stones behind it.

They worked silently. The sun was up high above the clearing now, warming Blakely's neck as he carefully removed one stone after another, watching the others do the same.

They had removed rocks and earth to a depth of two feet along the top third of the cavity. The work wouldn't be difficult, thought Blakely, except for the conditions imposed. It had taken them two hours to remove the fill, virtually a tablespoon at a time.

"A cavity," said Paulus to Justina in a calm voice.

He pointed to a narrow space between two stones, showing darkness. His eyes showed excitement as he turned and looked at her. She held both hands around the small trowel and made little jumps.

"Wonderful! Now we must be extremely careful," she cried. "Let's stop a moment and decide how to proceed."

Stupak and Blakely followed Paulus's hand to the hole. It was less than an inch wide and three inches tall. What was there to decide? You simply keep on removing stones!

"What is it?" asked Elizabeth

"Pay dirt," said Blakely, smiling down at her. "There's a pocket of air behind the stones Nick just took out. Could be a tomb or cave."

"Oh, how exciting!"

She touched his arm. "I feel so sorry for you, Edward. I know how much you cared about Joachim. The other night, I watched the two of you out of the window. You stayed up very late."

"Yeah, we got to know each other pretty well," he replied. He squatted down and whispered. "How are you holding up?"

She took off her straw hat and ran her hand over her cropped hair. "I'm okay. I just need to decide what I'm going to do."

"Lou any better?"

The life in her black face evaporated. Tears welled. "No. And I can't reach him."

She dabbed at her eyes with her fist and took a deep breath. "I don't know what all this is about, but he is not taking this black woman down with him—marriage or no marriage."

"We need to talk more—maybe tomorrow. I may have some answers for you then. Unfortunately, my gut tells me it won't be pleasant news."

"My inner voice tells me that Louis Wafford is a doomed man. He's given up, Edward. And no Theseus or Ariadne can help. He won't talk about it and says he doesn't want any help."

"Yeah."

"What has he done, Edward?"

"I don't know. It seems like King has Lou by the neck."

Wafford was watching them.

"We can't talk anymore now."

"Louis watching doesn't bother me none, Edward. It might wake him up to living again!"

Blakely went back to the wall where Justina and Paulas were examining the stones near the hole.

"Let's take this one out first," Justina seemed to be saying in Greek. Paulas began working on the stone she was tapping with her gloved finger. She worked one side while he worked the other. Paulas said something. She looked, turned, and asked Stupak something. An engineer brought a crowbar. Paulas was working the hole larger, pulling the dirt toward him, keeping it from falling inside the cavity. The hole was now one inch by five inches vertically. He placed the hooked end of the bar into the hole, turned the hook horizontal, and pulled steadily against the stone, easing it toward him. It fell into Stupak's hands. He carried the rock to the pile.

Paulas and Justina were now able to take advantage of the larger opening, using the curved bar as well as hands to pull the rocks and earth out. The hole had grown sufficiently wide enough for them to peer inside.

Stupak called for lamps. Large flashlights were brought. Justina took one, switched it on. She reached in with the light and put her head into the opening. "Gott im Himmel," she cried, sounding muffled yet shocked. She drew back.

"What is it?" cried Stupak. Paulas took the flashlight out of her hand, poked it into the opening and looked for himself. "Christos!" he cried.

She held her gloved hands to her face, eyes wide, mouth open.

"It was so unexpected," she whispered. "But I'm all right now."

Paulas pulled himself away from the hole, taking a deep breath of air, and handed the light to Stupak. "There's skeletal remains of a human. Still see parts of a uniform."

Wafford came over. "What's going on, Ed?"

"Some dead guy in there, Lou. Scared Justina half to death."

Alex appeared in the clearing, tucking in his shirt. "Ladies and gentlemen, lunch is served." He walked over to the trestle table. "Could we set it up here for you? It will be buffet today: lamb, salads, red and white wine, and special cakes from the baker made just for you this morning. So, here okay?"

"That will do fine, Alex." said Stupak. "Any where'll do fine."

Three grim-faced men placed trays of food on the table. Stupak handed the flashlight to Blakely.

"Take a look."

Blakely held the flashlight inside the hole, and peered down. Lying eight feet away from his lamp was a skeleton still dressed in bits and pieces of uniform. The skull was turned away, facing the wall of the cave. Tatters of black cloth, leather belt and boots were frosted with mold. That's no Minoan or Turk. He's German, not knowing precisely why he thought so. How did he know? The buttons and collar. They were like those in the photographs he had put in the album. The air was too stuffy.

He pulled out into the sunlight and took several deep breaths. Stupak was waiting for his reaction. "German. It's a German in there," was all Blakely could muster.

Stupak lit a cigarette. "The worst kind. SS."

Paulas pointed over his shoulder to the opening.

Justina looked again through the opening using the lamp. She turned to Paulas. "I see no reason to delay removing these stones. It does not appear there are any things of value here."

"I agree," replied Paulas.

Stupak motioned to three of his men. They began removing the stones and earth, using picks, shovels, and mattocks.

Blakely stood next to Jeremiah, munching a pita bread sand-

THE MINOTAUR 225

wich of lamb and tomato salad.

"Looks like you've got an exclusive story here, Jeremiah. Going to send it to Atlanta this evening?"

He smiled broadly. "You know it!"

Blakely swallowed the last piece of lamb, washed it down with red wine and joined the non-eating archeologists. Blakely peered in. Natural light exposed the dead guy's right boot, which still showed some black color beneath a white film, but the leather heel had disintegrated into layers like flaked pastry.

Finally, the way was clear. The body was exposed to light. It lay in a tunnel six feet high and, Blakely thought, nine feet in diameter with passages at each end. Obviously, the break in the wall was not the cave entrance. It must lay at the end of one of the two passages.

The back of the skull was shiny above frayed pieces of black uniform with silver trim. The two archeologists stepped into the cavern with their flashlights. Stooping down, they checked out the dirt floor. They moved slowly across, examining the surface.

"Just as I imagined," said Paulas. "Nothing here. Archeologically sterile." Justina now and then pushed her trowel into the powder dry dust and let it fall. "Ya. Only surface dirt and rock beneath it."

Paulas moved closer to the body.

"You are correct, colonel," Paulas noted, without looking back at Blakely and Stupak. "This man was an SS officer. Wish Dr. Skyros were here. A paleoarcheologist would be..."

He stopped talking as he leaned over the body, looking at the front of the skull.

"Would be what?" asked Justina.

"A bullet hole," said Paulas. "The man was shot in the frontal lobe."

"What?"

Justina moved past him so she was standing above the skull, flashing her light down.

"Ya. It can't be anything else. A cleanly made hole."

She was cool and professional.

"Puts us in a dilemma, does it not?" asked Paulas. "A question of protocols."

"What do you mean, Nick?" asked Justina.

Paulas smiled. "Isn't it appropriate to bring in some forensic people before anything is disturbed?"

"Forensics we don't have at my base," sighed Stupak.

Paulas turned toward Stupak. "Ours are not so sophisticated at Iraklion. I suggest we bring someone from Athens."

"But why?" asked Justina. "Nick, this man's been dead for over 40 years. Look at his uniform. What would be gained by having forensic scientists hold us up here? Who is to argue over what happened to him? There was a war! The man was shot or committed suicide. The matter of forensics is moot!"

Paulas raised a hand. "We need an official opinion."

Justina's mouth hung open. "Are you telling me we should not continue exploring this cave until the body has been examined by authorities?"

"Yes, Dr. Cunningham" replied Paulas. "We should not disturb the area until a forensic examination has been conducted."

Justina sat back against the wall. "Why can't we work around him? Explore the passageways without disturbing anything?"

"We would possibly be trampling upon evidence."

"Evidence of what?" asked Stupak.

Justina roused to her feet and touched Stupak's sleeve. In an even voice, she asked, "How long will it take to get permission to remove the remains?" asked Justina.

"With the Easter holiday, it would probably be next week. However, actual removal would have to be done by proper investigators. You understand, Dr. Cunningham, ancient remains you and I could remove. Remains which are recent with a bullet hole—this requires specialists of a different sort."

Paulas, hands on knees, wagged his head back and forth, then proceeded to examine more closely the dead man, shining the flashlight along the skull, neck, and down to the belt. Paulas didn't appear to have any feelings one way or another about Justina's disappointment. It looked like he was purposely throwing up a road block.

"The Americans have forensics specialists at their base, I believe," said Stupak, who seemed to read Paulas's scheme. "Frankly, I don't know what it is you wish to show by forensic examination, professor."

Stupak scratched his head and pulled off his sunglasses.

"Could I have a look?"

"Yes. Come on in."

Paulas looked at Blakely. "Would you be so kind as to bring me my canvas bag? It is on the other side, leaning against a tree."

"Sure," said Blakely. He found it, and reached it into the entrance to Paulas. The archeologist opened it, pulled out a flash camera and made adjustments to it. Stupak and Justina moved out of the way. Paulas fired off nine or ten frames from various angles. He replaced the camera in the bag and resumed examining the remains with the flashlight.

Stupak knelt down above the dead man's skull, leaned over close as Paulas played the light on the frontal lobe. "Small caliber bullet," said Stupak knowingly. He looked up at Blakely. "Like the 30 caliber carbines your American Army carried. This perhaps smaller. They make a clean hole."

Blakely, without invitation, entered the cavern and took a look for himself. "What about identification? The Germans carried an I.D., didn't they?" he asked.

"Officers carried identification papers. Everybody had metal tags," said Stupak. He took his finger and pushed back the tattered collar of the uniform. There was a metal chain visible around the neck vertebrae. "I don't dare touch it, though," he said with a sarcastic tone, "if you intend to have forensics examine him."

"I think it best," explained Paulas. "I don't want to be accused of robbing a grave."

The bastard gave Blakely a knowing look. Paulas was getting back for his buddies, Santos and Neopolis. Grave robbers stick together. Blakely feigned innocence, "What's the next step, professor?"

"I will report what we have found. It will then be a matter of jurisdiction here."

"Eh? Jurisdiction?" Even Stupak was angry. "Give or take a few feet, this man may be within my jurisdiction," replied Stupak. "If not mine, then it is under the jurisdiction of the Pediadas constabulary, Max Padopolis. Why don't we discuss this matter with some wine. Do you agree, Justina?"

"Ya," she said. "There have to be other alternatives."

Paulas shook his head negatively. They walked over to where Wafford and Elizabeth were sitting.

"Professor Paulas tells me," said Justina, "we cannot explore the cave passages until proper authorities are contacted about the soldier in there. It will be a matter for authorities to decide what next should be done with the remains."

"How long will that take?" asked Wafford.

Paulas shrugged, smiled. "Who knows? Sometime after Easter holiday."

The guy was enjoying the payback, thought Blakely, and it was his fault. "So, it looks like we're held up until Dr. Paulas finds out for us," said Justina.

"How do you think that German soldier got there?" asked Wafford.

"It appears he was shot by someone. The killer saw the opening in the mountain, dragged him into it, and sealed up the hole," Justina said.

"Resistance," Stupak said. "That is work of Cretan Resistance. They hide their work very well."

"Or Heinrich," said Blakely. "Maybe that's what the code on the relic was all about."

"Dr. Paulas," said Wafford, "who do you intend to call about this?"

"I shall report to my superiors in Athens. "

"I see," said Wafford, pushing dirt with his foot. "No way to

THE MINOTAUR 229

proceed without having to go through all these channels and red tape?"

"No."

"No other reasonable way of handling this?" Wafford squinted, appearing to grow pink around the gills. "Maybe, like, a donation of money to your museum for a quick decision?"

"No. I cannot do that. It is out of my hands."

"Well, then," Wafford looked at Justina, "I suppose you have to make your call and do what's best."

Everyone nodded agreement. Paulas slung the canvas bag over his shoulder. "I will return to the museum."

"Why not use the phone in my truck?" asked Stupak. "Feel free to use it. Save time."

"No. I may have to make several calls," said Paulas, backing away. He turned and left. They watched him in disbelief.

"I suppose there is nothing more here to do," said Justina, as she looked at the gaping hole in the mountain.

"You haven't eaten anything," said Elizabeth. "Why doesn't everyone have some of this wonderful food? Make everybody feel better."

"I'm not very hungry, thank you," said Justina.

The men walked over to the table. There was much food left. Blakely poured a cup of wine. Wafford turned to Blakely. "Pardon my saying so, but that fella is a royal sombitch. Can't play second fiddle to a woman."

Wafford carried a tray of salad to Elizabeth. Blakely and Stupak were left alone.

"I am truly happy to see Paulas leave," said Stupak. "Now, we can decide how to get on with our little scavenger hunt."

Stupak began pacing back and forth, holding his forehead in the same hand in which he held his cigarette.

"To my way of thinking," he said, "this is a military matter. A German national in uniform has been shot. It is immaterial when it happen. Yesterday? Fifty years ago? What does it matter? A military crime has been committed here. I think it is my duty to obtain authority to take command of this incident and do whatever is required. Do you agree or disagree with that, Captain Blakely?"

"I heartily agree." replied Blakely, removing the cork from the bottle and pouring Stupak a cup of wine.

"Fact is, you've got a very delicate situation of a murdered German soldier on Greek soil," said Blakely. "How would you go about getting permission to take charge of such a matter?"

"Probably one phone call to Athens," said Stupak, "which I intend to make as soon as I drink this wine."

They laughed heartily. "I think you would enjoy seeing me pull one on Nick Paulas, wouldn't you?"

"Yeah, I would." Blakely looked over at Justina. "Is it your considered opinion that Paulas is a glory seeking tight-ass?"

"Seems to run in the profession," replied Stupak, reaching for the bottle and pouring Blakely and himself another cup. "I think I should rescue this matter out of the hands of such individuals," Stupak said. "I know just who to call in Athens."

Blakely looked around. He suddenly became aware that Greek peasants were standing among the thickets watching all that was going on. They had evidently been watching since early this morning. Stupak followed Blakely's eyes. He beckoned the people to come closer.

"They see everything, my friend, and tell nothing! With them here, we need no guards. They will see our work is not disturbed—until there is something they value, in which case, it will disappear." He laughed. "Ah, well! That is why we have guards."

Stupak laughed again and ambled toward the military truck. "I must make a telephone call, if you will excuse me." Stupak opened the door on the passenger side, pulled a portable phone out, dialed, and began speaking into it.

* * * * *

Stupak replaced the cellular phone, hitched up his fatigue trousers with both hands, and swaggered back to the group.

"I have good news for the lady archeologist here," he said, patting Justina on the shoulder. "Within a few minutes, you may continue your exploration."

Justina's mouth opened. "What do you mean?"

"I mean," said Stupak, "I have been given responsibility to look after our departed one there in the cave. Athens Headquarters Command is sending right now an order to my office and copying it to museum authorities in Athens and Iraklion. I am to use my own discretion, provided I do not cause any damage to antiquities. I called my office to be sure the clerk will deliver the order to me immediately. Once I have it in hand, I can act."

"What will you do?" asked Justina, beginning to be amused as Stupak shifted his weight from one foot to the other, his chest puffed out to the fullest.

He motioned toward the truck.

"I also call the American base to speak with my friend Major O'Donnell there. He is arranging for a forensic team to come out this afternoon to pick up the dead one, take it back to the base, do a full examination, and report their findings back to me."

"Dimitrius," said Wafford, giving way to a slight hang-dog grin, "I can't imagine why you're not a general instead of a colonel."

Stupak laughed and patted his own stomach. "I am young enough for that to come, but I must behave better."

He laughed again.

"We wait, then, for the Americans to arrive?" Justina asked.

Stupak held up his index finger. "Remember, Dr. Cunningham, who is in charge of this strictly military matter. We wait for nothing! The Americans may not arrive for three or four hours."

He looked at the black dial of his watch. "1432 hours. We will remove the inconvenient remains so that you may proceed with your archeological hunting."

She laughed, stood up, and kissed him on the cheek.

"For another, I do anything you ask."

She kissed him again. Everyone laughed.

Stupak turned. The engineers, sitting in a long row at the far side of the clearing, were laughing and slapping each other on the back. He said something. Two of them got up, went to the truck, and returned with a roll of construction plastic.

"We do two things," Stupak said, holding up two fingers. "We try to remove the dead one without disturbing him so badly he wake up. Second, we lay down a material on the cave floor to preserve any forensic or ancient materials, no? In this fashion, Professor Paulas cannot accuse us of destroying evidence."

"Cool," said Jeremiah, moving his camera from one face to another. Swann carried a sound boom and Tobok carried a battery pack.

Stupak waved his flashlight at Blakely. "Ed, if you would assist me, please."

Blakely followed Stupak into the cave. They knelt down next to the skeleton. Stupak flashed the light on the dirt floor next to the remains. "You know, I thought we might roll him onto the plastic sheeting, but I'm afraid this Nazi would not be up to it. He'd fall apart. It really makes no difference, I suppose, but I try to be neat when handling the dead—especially at Easter time. Any ideas?"

Blakely smirked. "We could take him apart and put him back together again on a plank or something."

Stupak laughed. "You like human jigsaw puzzles, eh? I think I may have a piece of plywood or sheet metal in the truck which we could slide under him"

They walked to the truck where Stupak rummaged among ceiling tiles, and concrete forms. He pulled out a two foot wide by eight foot long scrap of half-inch plywood.

"How would this do? This comes from your American base. "

"Perfect."

They knelt down and slowly pushed the scrap of paneling partially beneath the remains. The skeleton and tatters of uniform failed to cooperate, however. Pieces began to shift and drag.

"Stop!" Stupak said, leaning back. Blakely sat on his haunches.

THE MINOTAUR 233

"Even in death, these SS bastards are difficult! We must apply delicate pressure to the departed. Convince him to cooperate, eh? Lou, would you mind getting one of the planks off the table for us?"

Wafford left the cave and returned with a two by six by eight foot board.

Stupak handed one end to Blakely. "We shall say nothing about this delicate intrusion upon our departed one, eh? This will be our own little secret. Ed, if you will assist me, we will position the board on the other side so none of him can escape. Then, we push the plywood under him."

Blakely pressed the edge of two by six against the cave floor and with his left hand worked the panel beneath the boots and legs.

"He is crowding himself into a straighter man, I believe," said Stupak. "And what is that sound?"

It sounded like a marble in a hubcap, coming from the skull or upper body, thought Blakely. They listened as the little rolling noise diminished and ceased.

"Hand me your light, please," said Stupak to Wafford. He flashed the light into one of the eye sockets. "Evidence of murder or suicide," he said. "The bullet is inside the skull. I now qualify as a military forensic specialist, gentlemen."

Stupak stood up and handed the light back to Wafford. He moved to the end of the panel.

"He shouldn't be so heavy we cannot lift him. Ready, Ed?"

"Sure."

The two men carefully lifted the panel and parts of the skeleton began to slide. They put it down again.

"Our deposed one still is trying to escape! Let's put the panel on the plank for support, eh?"

They slid the panel onto the plank and lifted. The remains were hauled out into the sunlight, showing gruesome teeth with gold fillings, a patch of skin and hair still attached to the side of the skull, a gold ring still on... Blakely thought a minute about that one...the ring bone, connected to the...?

"Over here," nodded Stupak. They carried the skeleton to the sawhorses and placed it next to the remains of the feast as Jeremiah and his crew recorded the proceeding. The bullet rolled again, slowly coming to a stop. Elizabeth held both hands to her mouth, watching as they left the German lying uncovered.

"Shouldn't you put something over it?" Elizabeth asked.

Justina came over, looked at the remains, and said wistfully, "I wish we could check his identification papers. It would be nice to know if we have here a friend of Joachim's and Heinrich's."

Everyone gathered around the skeletal remains, examining the bullet hole in the skull, the leather belt and holster which still held a rusted pistol. Jeremiah continued recording. Blakely watched the young Greek engineers who were at once attracted and repulsed by this anomaly of partially uniformed skeleton. The men pointed to the skull, nudged each other in the ribs, and joked; their expressions quickly changing from lightness to sardonic grimness as they perhaps imagined themselves in a similar condition, dead without rites or grave—the skeleton mute testimony to violence and defilement.

Blakely took a piece of opaque plastic and covered the body, weighting down the corners with wine bottles.

"Thank you, Edward," said Elizabeth. "I wasn't sure anyone heard me."

"The Americans will be able to tell us, probably in a few hours, who the soldier is," said Stupak. "Perhaps, Dr. Cunningham, you would like to examine the cave floor before we place this plastic down. You may find something useful."

"Ya. Would you like to help me, Edward? Lou? Bring the flashlights."

The three got down on hands and knees, checking the floor for anything that wasn't dirt. They found nothing except flaked leather, threads, and patches of cloth from the dead Nazi. Stupak's men rolled out plastic and spread it across the cave floor. A driver arrived and delivered the faxed orders to Stupak. He read them over.

"These give me full authority to do what we just did," he announced proudly.

"In that case, may I proceed with exploring the cave?" Justina asked, eyes full of excitement.

"Of course," replied Stupak, grinning, "unless you wish to wait for your colleague Dr. Paulas to return."

"No, no! I want to begin this minute."

"Before we do so, however," said Stupak, "I should caution everyone. How many have experience with caves?"

Nobody said anything.

"Skip," whispered Jeremiah. "Is it okay if I ask Mike to go back to the *Sea Siren* and get me some lights? I'd like some interior shots. I was thinking of doing an interview with Justina in there."

"Sure."

Blakely thought about Marchese. Just when you need the guy, he's not around. Mike could bring him back with him. On second thought, he'd just as soon keep Marchese out of it.

"How many have experience with Kriti caves?"

Wafford said, "We have a man you met yesterday, Andy Marchese—the heavy-set fella with all the curly hair?"

"Yes," said Stupak.

"He's a spelunker, if you need one. Been in all sorts of caves."

Justina scowled. "I would prefer, Louis, that we not involve Andy unless we absolutely need his assistance."

Wafford looked down, and said in his pouting voice, "Only trying to help, Miss Justina. Thought he might be useful is all."

Stupak looked from one to the other, and continued. "Then I must tell you. We have to go very slowly, making sure there are no surprises around bends in walls, such as deep drop-offs or poison gas. Okay?"

"Ya," said Justina. "I must admit I am not used to cave exploration."

"Yes. Why don't I have my men obtain proper ropes, harnesses, and head lamps for us for tomorrow? I believe we will need them. Today, we see how difficult it is inside the mountain."

"All right."

Stupak gave one of his men orders. Another returned with a gas testing device.

"We will carry this with us meanwhile."

Blakely flashed his light along the cave walls. Two passages, one ascending to the left and another ascending to the right, each approximately ten feet in height and four to five feet in width. It was impossible to know which passage led to the cave's mouth—if one existed—and which led to the bottom.

"Right or left passage?" Justina asked Blakely.

"Left" he replied, for no particular reason, except that he was left-handed.

"Left it is."

Justina led, carrying the bright flashlight, followed by Blakely, Stupak and Wafford, who also carried lamps. She had not gone more than twenty feet in the curved passage when she stopped.

"A metal box just ahead of me."

Stupak came up and flashed his light. "A German ammo can. World War II. I see many of these."

Justina squatted down and tried to lift it. "Heavy!"

"Rusty, too," said Blakely. He knelt down and flashed the light along the bottom.

"Bottom might drop out if we're not careful. Want to use our dead soldier technique?" he asked Stupak.

Stupak barked an order back over his shoulder. A two foot piece of panel was passed up to Blakely.

"We'll both tilt it up slightly to your side, Justina," he said, "while I slide this under."

"Okay."

The panel slid beneath the can. Blakely grasped the edges of the panel and lifted. The thing must weigh forty pounds. Like a sack of concrete. Everyone backed out of the passage, enabling Blakely to carry the rusted can out of the cave and set it on the

THE MINOTAUR 237

table. Stupak put his hands on his hips. "What do you think, Dr. Cunningham? Want to try opening it?"

"Well," she shrugged her shoulders, seeming unsure what to do. "As Dr. Paulas is quick to say, an ammunition can from World War II is not quite ancient archeological material, is it?"

"Then you've made the decision for me as a professional," said Stupak. "It is in my domain of authority as the investigating officer of a criminal case to follow your decision. I say open it!"

Blakely gripped the rusted handle on the ammo can lid and pulled. It came off in his hand.

"So much for the soft approach."

He picked up a screw driver, and pried on the lid. It would not budge. He looked at the bottom. "What if we turned it upside down and opened it along this rusty seam?"

"Excellent idea," said Stupak.

Blakely leaned down, picked up a canvas tool bag from the grass, and placed it over the top of the ammo can, held the sides, and flipped it. Before he could set it down, the lid burst off, emptying the contents into the bucket with a dull clicking sound of pieces of metal and stone. He removed the empty can, looked in the bucket and whistled. Damn! There were gold jewels, pearls, diamonds, rubies, broaches, bracelets, necklaces, and Lord knows what, shining in a thick, congealed pile.

He reached in and pulled out a gold chain necklace.

"Oh, my word!" exclaimed Elizabeth.

"Mein Gott!" cried Justina. "What else can happen today? The von Etter fortune!"

"Far out!" Jeremiah exclaimed from behind his camera. "Hold it up a little higher, Skip, and turn it towards the camera."

Blakely held it for a few seconds and then handed the gold chain necklace to Justina and drew out a string of pearls. "Jewelry for Elizabeth this evening?"

Stupak peered into the bucket and laughed. "Incredible! I suppose this is better, Ed, but a case of schnapps would have been good, too!"

"I'll buy you one," said Blakely, looking in the direction Stupak pointed. The peasants stood among the trees without words or expressions, waiting, seeing, and perhaps hoping—for what, he didn't know.

Stupak put his hands on his hips. "The Resistance would not have left this treasure. There must be some other explanation."

"Look's like von Etter might have been surprised by the SS guy and shot him and sealed him and the jewels up together."

"Could be," said Stupak.

Wafford put a hand on Blakely's shoulder.

"Reach in," said Blakely, looking at the pile of jewelry in the canvas bucket. "Grab a handful of the von Etter jewels for Elizabeth."

Wafford pulled out a wad of gold, silver and stone-set jewels. He held them out so everyone could see. His eyes were filled with water.

"Really cool! Hold them up a little longer, Uncle Lou!" said Jeremiah. "Perfect!"

"Just wish my daddy was here to be a part of this. He spent so much effort trying to figure it out. Well, daddy," said Wafford, looking skyward, "you are vindicated twice. Your boy Louis and his friends here found it for you!"

Wafford carried the handful of jewels over to Elizabeth who cupped her hands together. Jeremiah hovered for a close-up.

"This is so wonderful," she said, "even if we can't keep a single one of them. They are so beautiful!" She fingered a necklace. "Oh, how lovely!"

Justina was surprisingly calm under the circumstances. She was taking the necklaces, rings, and other jewels out of the bucket carefully, examining them, placing them on the makeshift table, and arranging them. At least Wafford had come out of his shell and was happy for a change!

"Many of these pieces are eighteenth and nineteenth century gold," Justina said, showing an ornate gold filigree broach to Wafford. "They are exquisite. Now I understand a little how

Heinrich Schliemann felt when he discovered the Trojan jewels! But of course, there is no comparison between ancient gold jewels and these. Still, I am so pleased!"

She handed the broach to Wafford who held it for Elizabeth to see.

"And these all belonged to one family?" Elizabeth asked Wafford.

"The Austrian branch—probably half a dozen households," said Wafford, glowing proudly. He nudged her arm. "You remember seeing those papers my daddy had."

"Yes."

He looked up at Stupak. "Daddy always thought Heinrich buried the jewels here. Maybe that fella there on the table was following Heinrich when he hid the jewels in the cave. Surprised him. Ole Heinrich gave him an even bigger surprise."

Stupak stood, cigarette in hand, with an incredulous expression on his face. "You discover what you came to find!" exclaimed Stupak. "You must all be good Christian to have such luck, eh? It is truly a miracle at Easter!"

Wafford's face flickered serious for a second or two, then opened again. "I'd agree," said Wafford. "Odds of us finding anything after all these years 'bout a million to one. I'd often thought somebody had found the cache years ago."

"Is that why you seemed so gloomy yesterday and today?" asked Stupak. "You were considering the search might end in nothing, eh?"

Wafford blinked and looked toward Elizabeth. "I spose. Course, it don't matter, does it? We found it intact!"

"We will have to label, photograph and catalog all these items," said Justina. "This will take quite a while. I'll need help. Elizabeth, perhaps you would like to help catalog them with me," said Justina.

She opened her a large field case and removed a notebook, pen, a packet of string-tie labels, and packets of plastic zip lock bags.

"Edward, Lou—you both can help me."

She turned to Stupak. "I don't believe we can do more in the cave today. I will need time to set up my equipment and take photographs. By the time we finish cataloging and photographing, it will be dark. We'll also have to decide how best to secure these jewels."

"You have two choices," said Stupak. "One is the bank vault at the village or else my safe at headquarters. Whichever you would like. Of course, we'll have to include Max in this decision. He will no doubt inform the governor. These are normal protocols under such circumstances."

"Fine. Louis, do you have any suggestions?"

"I'd feel better having them jewels behind the wall of a military base 'stead of in an ordinary bank. If it's all the same to you, Miss Justina, we can trust Dimitrius to take care of them until we transfer them to proper authorities. I'll contact Homer. Let him run interference with the Athens people. We want to avoid that fella Paulas coming back too soon and stirring up a ruckus. Just wish we had more time today to explore the cave. See what else is in there."

"I'd feel better if we had proper equipment. With all we have to do today, I say we wait until tomorrow, get everything organized, and explore the cave then."

"You're in charge, Miss Justina," Wafford replied. "We'll do whatever you say."

"Thank you, Louis." Her tone was cool.

"A good plan," said Stupak. "My men have had a long day. I will dismiss them. Besides, tomorrow we have fresh start with right equipment, no?"

"Ya!"

She smiled at him and held out her hand. He shook it, then bowed gallantly and kissed it.

Elizabeth, Wafford, and Blakely spread the jewels out according to type, grouping the gold bracelets, gold necklaces, gold rings.

THE MINOTAUR   241

Stone-set jewels were in a separate group. Silver items in a different pile.

"Louis, you can create a master inventory list in my journal," Justina said, "while Edward assists me with the photography. We must be sure every piece is labeled, identified, photographed next to my ruler here, and properly stored so they will not be harmed."

Blakely glanced around. Quite a day. He looked toward the woods. The peasants were still there, watching like mutes, not showing their emotions about seeing a skeleton, jewels, a black woman in a wheel chair, or anything. Nothing stirring, not even a mouse!

Stupak was making a telephone call. He turned and spoke with his men. They began to gather materials and equipment, loading them into the truck.

His thoughts inevitably came back to Joachim. By now, Joachim's body was a couple quarts of ashes and bits of bone. Funny. He didn't feel sadness anymore. Joachim had gone home. What remained was what Justina might call an artifact of his past existence and nothing more. Unrecognizable ashes, which would easily blend with earth and become one with it. He sensed Justina looking at him. She was blushing slightly, and her eyes looked lovingly at him rather than with erotic passion. They shared an intimacy now, and he cherished it.

Justina positioned a tripod with a 35mm camera on the table above a black cloth and ruler. She placed a necklace with its identifying label next to the ruler, adjusted the aperture, focused, and clicked the camera.

"Let's take another shot using my other camera," she said, pulling a second camera up to her eye and taking an oblique angle shot of the ruler and necklace. "Now you can remove the item and place it in the container."

Blakely slipped the necklace into the zip lock plastic bag and reached for another jewel to place beneath the camera. It was a gold necklace with rubies set in a triangular pattern. He spread the necklace and turned the label so its number showed. Jeremiah had shifted the camera task to Swann and was now making notes on his clip board. It would be one helluva show to send back to Atlanta.

Everyone turned as an engine whine grew louder. The Americans in a blue ambulance had arrived. The driver pulled into the clearing, saw the covered skeletal remains on the table, swung the ambulance around, and backed toward it.

Three men in camouflage fatigues got out and walked over to Stupak, stood at attention, and saluted. He returned the salute. They shook hands and introduced one another. Stupak introduced them to the gathering.

"Lt. Smith, Sergeant Kirby, and Airman Javits."

The lieutenant started to approach the remains, but stopped in his tracks when he saw the jewels being sorted out. "Whacha got there?" he asked Blakely. "Looks like you struck it rich!"

Blakely pointed. "In the cave not far from the dead guy," he said. "We're just sorting it out for the Greek government. It'll belong to them."

"What about this fella?" asked the lieutenant, removing the wine bottles and plastic. "German officer, huh?"

"Yeah," Blakely responded.

"A triple SOB too," the lieutenant continued.

"How do you mean, triple?"

"He's an SSSOB," Smith said knowingly, grinning at Stupak.

"Didn't I tell you?" said Stupak.

"SS. Black uniform, silver here," Smith said, pointing to the collar. "Every so often we're called out to identify dead soldiers. Find Greeks, English, Indians, Australians, Canadians, Germans. Get used to differences in uniform buttons, boots, whatever. This guy's in very good shape. You say he was in that cave?"

"Yeah."

"Somebody nailed him good," said the lieutenant, putting his finger on the bullet hole. "Almost between the eyes."

"The bullet is inside the skull," said Blakely. "It rolls around when you tilt him."

THE MINOTAUR 243

"Really?"

The lieutenant grasped the skull with his bare hand, twisted it gently. The marble sound could be heard.

"Darned if it isn't," he said, looking in the cavity. "Mind if I have a look at the cave?" he asked Stupak.

"Not at all. I put plastic down so we wouldn't disturb anything."

Stupak and Blakely removed the plastic. The lieutenant flashed a light on the area. There were remnants of leather and bits of uniform in the dirt.

"It wouldn't be worth our while here," said the lieutenant, handing the light to Stupak. He strode outside. "You guys did an excellent job removing him. He's still intact. Usually when we get them, you gotta put all the parts back together like a jigsaw puzzle."

Stupak nudged Blakely. "You have a future, my friend. Become forensic puzzle solver with human bones!"

Smith approached the remains again.

"Know anything about him?"

"No."

The lieutenant asked whether anyone had a knife.

"A knife," said Stupak, pulling out a bone-handled knife and folding out the blade before handing it to the lieutenant.

"Fine knife you got, sir. A fine Cretan knife!"

The lieutenant attempted to cut along the top of the uniform. The threads gathered on the blade as he cut through the material. He lowered the point of the knife and slid it under the thin chain at the breastbone and pulled it upward, bringing a metal tag from beneath the pieces of material.

"This ought to tell us." He looked closely. "Gustav Kemft. Should be easy to trace from that." He dropped the tag and chain onto the bones.

"A son of Satan!" exclaimed Stupak. "We here on Crete are most familiar with him. It is too bad that these bones cannot be placed in the piazza of Kastelli for a day—to allow everyone to spit on him before we throw him into the bonfire. He is Judas incarnate, if ever there was one! He is the murderer of many people here. Could we not borrow him for the weekend and let God send his bones to Hell? It would save you having to bother with him."

"Well," said the lieutenant, chuckling, "I'd like to accommodate you, but I'm afraid we've got to take him straight back to the base."

He turned to Kirby and Javits. "No point in keeping him fancy. We've got an I.D., and know how he was killed."

The lieutenant turned and smiled at his audience. "Even know his reputation. Get one of the body bags and put him in it." Smith held his hand out toward the camera and Swann. "I'd appreciate it if you didn't record this for posterity, sir. Please turn your camera off there."

"Do what he says, Harry," said Jeremiah.

Harry switched it off and put the lens cap on.

The lieutenant reached over with both hands, twisted the skull and shook out the round of lead into his hand. He examined it carefully. "May be German." He looked at Stupak. "If you would like, we'll run a ballistics check, and see what it came from."

"I'd like to know that too," said Wafford, leaning against the table.

"Okay," said the lieutenant. "Load him up, gentlemen."

The two men wasted little effort in moving the remains of Gustav Kemft into the body bag. They stretched the opening of the bag over Kemft's boots and tilted the other end of the board, allowing the bones to crumple into a lump at the bottom. Elizabeth drew both hands to her face and gasped.

"Oh! I can't stand to watch!" Her eyes were as big as saucers. Justina turned her head away.

Blakely was totally amused. These guys were going through the motions—filling in time. Not too different from what the Greek guys would have done, except it hadn't taken a month of Sundays. They did the job in thirty minutes.

"Thank you, gentlemen," said Smith, nodding at Wafford and Blakely. "Sir, I'll have a report for you."

THE MINOTAUR

The lieutenant saluted. Stupak saluted and shook his hand. "We appreciate your help. Give my best to Major McDonnell."

They closed the doors of the ambulance and Gustav Kemft's whereabouts were known for the first time since 29 August 1944, thought Blakely. Stupak turned. "See how easy? That's why I like you Americans. You know how to do business and not waste everyone's time."

CHAPTER 23

Reflection

"Oh, Edward! This is so exciting! I feel like I am thirty years younger! I have so many ideas for my future! Everything I work for all these years! I discover here on this mountain a new Justina!"

She was being overly dramatic, but Blakely allowed her that. The big let-down would be tomorrow when she might discover the cave is empty and her claim to fame rests on a bucket of old jewels.

"To you and your new life!" said Blakely. He raised his glass to hers. "You looked fantastic on camera tonight—especially the shots Jeremiah took of you inside the cave."

"Ya. To think he is sending the video to Atlanta tonight."

"A new star is born! People will recognize your face and name."

"Do you really think so?" Justina sat back. She grew reflective. She leaned against the railing and smiled. She looked lovely in the twilight.

"Sure I think so." He lied. "And tomorrow, you might find the tomb of Zeus—like Stupak said."

"So much has happened. I cannot believe all that has happened so fast."

"Yeah." He thought of Joachim's death and her coming to his room with the intention of making love. The two events were entwined somehow. Was it the intimacy he felt for both of them? Or was it that the two experiences—of holding Justina and letting go of Joachim—had happened just hours apart? Whatever it was, he

THE MINOTAUR

felt changed and completed somehow. Perhaps he had grown beyond lust for the first time in his life. He wasn't sure.

"I am no longer afraid of the future," said Justina, taking his hand. "I am thinking I will take a leave of absence from the museum."

"What if you don't discover anything tomorrow?"

"It is what I discovered today that is important, Edward."

"And what is that?"

"Life can be better than any fantasy, if you are willing to risk living."

"Yeah?"

"When I came into your room the other night, I wanted to fulfill a fantasy, and we both know it was only a fantasy. I have harbored so many fantasies—about you, about Christopher, about my children—and none of them has ever come true. It has taken me forty years to understand it, Edward, and you have helped me to find my real self—a sixty one year old woman who can make a life of her own without fantasy!"

He had harbored a fantasy of Justina for forty years, too, and in an instant it was erased. The illusion had been destroyed. But what would prevent them both from creating other illusions and new fantasies?

"You talk about leaving the museum. What will you do?"

"I won't worry about that. I will do what suits me, Justina Schmidt, rather than fretting over pleasing everyone as Justina Cunningham."

"Oh? Taking back your name?"

"Ya!" said Justina. "Taking back my name and my life." She paused and contemplated the empty wine glass. "I was thinking it might be enjoyable to do some travel tapes. Mainly, I feel totally free to do what I want for the very first time in my whole life! Oh, God, Edward! The feeling is one of ecstasy!"

He glanced at his watch. It was 1945 hours. Jeremiah told him Mike would bring by a videotape at 2000 hours.

"I suppose we should be going, if you want to join everyone at the Blue Porpoise for dinner."

"You aren't coming?" She looked genuinely disappointed.

"I need to attend to some *Sea Siren* business."

"You are probably wanting rest, too."

"Yes. Thanks for understanding."

They got up from the table and left.

She put her arm through his as they climbed the steeply terraced steps. They fell into a natural rhythm, and he could feel her hip and shoulder against his. "I don't think I could have done this without you, Edward."

"Do you plan to look for Thomas soon?"

"Oh, yes. I would like to bring him back here for a holiday."

"Good. I think Thomas will like Justina Schmidt."

"I hope so."

He watched her as she crossed the cobbled intersection. Even her walk held new lightness and grace. She's going to be okay. He waved at her as she turned the corner and headed toward the restaurant where the Waffords and Stupak waited. When he arrived at the hotel, Mike was there, sitting in the van.

"Have something for me, Mike?"

"Got two cases. One has stuff Jeremiah needs tomorrow night. The other is for you."

"Good. Let's take them to my room."

They ascended the stairs, carrying the hard-shell, black video equipment cases.

"Set that one in the corner."

"Anything else?"

"No. What's it like aboard? Are King and Marchese behaving themselves?"

Mike winced. "What can I say? They've been driving Leo and Tony crazy. Double check this, do that. Marchese must have set and hoved them black receptors a dozen times today. Not only that, they were moving the spars around in all directions."

"Andy Marchese was up on the bridge operating the automated system?" It hurt Blakely to think Marchese was sitting in his place, operating Sea Siren's sailing equipment.

"Yup. Spent all day up there."

"Where was King?"

"In the comm center."

"What was he doing?"

"Said he was checking calibrations. One time I went past, the hatch was open. He had the monitors up and was using Tobok's keyboard."

"Sending messages?"

Mike shrugged. "Don't know. Next time I went by, the hatch was closed."

"And King still inside?"

"Yeah. Has Wafford said anything to you about a meeting on board early tomorrow morning?"

"No. King wants all of us there?"

"I suppose."

"News to me. I'll wait to hear from Lou. Are you going back to the ship tonight?"

"Not if I can help it." Mike ran his hand over his curly dark hair. "I was hoping to go to that disco again. Why? Do you need something?"

"Not really. Go ahead and do your thing."

"Oh, almost forgot. Tobok sent this message up for you."

Mike pulled a folded slip of paper from a pocket and handed it to Blakely.

He opened it. A message from Jenny. "Ed: Change of plans. Will arrive tonight or early tomorrow morning. Don't make any arrangements. We will make same. Looking forward to seeing you! Jenny."

Well, well. Surprise, surprise! Probably bringing Sherry White—the Balboa Bay socialite with her. Won't that be interesting.

"Any return message, skip?"

"No, Mike. See you tomorrow."

Mike left. Blakely locked the door. He opened the case and set up the recorder and mini-monitor and loaded the videotape. The split screen showed Tobok's keystrokes and the images on the monitor. Tobok opened a file and typed in a message from a handwritten note. He could not read the note, but the message on the monitor was clear. *Touchstone: Expect test score posted Saturday midnight unless you fail to show. If pass, expect visit Sunday a.m. to homeroom. Confirm. Melek.*

Several minutes went by. Tobok talked with a ham operator in Australia about a hot new heavy metal band. Tobok munched potato chips. He'll never get his weight down. He stroked the keys. A message came up. *Melek: Perfect water for baptism 11:45. Post as requested. Sunday brunch. Touchstone.*

Who was Melek? A strange name—maybe Romanian? One Tobok made up? Blakely replayed the two messages and copied them down. He went to another. It was sent yesterday at 0450 hours. *Zeb: Sea conditions dictate. Touch is in range. Know result Saturday midnight. Mel.*

So, Mel is Melek? Touch is Touchstone? Zeb is Zebulon? He replayed it and jotted down the information. The references to perfect water, sea conditions, and within range. Were they going to smuggle something on board the *Sea Siren*? Why would McCloud in Gulfport wait for confirmation of results of the broadcast test from Crete when they could obviously be obtained directly from CDN in Atlanta much faster? It didn't make any sense. Something's going to happen while the live broadcast is going on. It involves sea conditions. Maybe a ship will rendezvous? Was its name Touchstone? A bad name for a ship! He closed down the equipment, stowed the tape at the bottom of his toiletry kit, and went out to the piazza. He ordered Ouzo and a salad from George.

The air was coming out of the northwest. He went over the messages in his mind. Melek was not a code word like Touchstone or Zeb. Where had he heard it before? It was strangely familiar. Using cryptic messages on the Internet. And he supposed that

THE MINOTAUR   251

Tobok further encrypted them by using random numbers, too. What was he failing to see?

Blakely shifted in his chair, watching Polaris grow brighter and thinking of Joachim. His ashes would be returned tomorrow. The slight undertow of delayed mourning for Joachim was pleasant, somehow. A sweet sorrow of not having Joachim next to him, yet he felt Joachim's closeness anyway. When he gazed at the stars, he felt what Joachim had talked about—Joachim was gone, but not gone.

George set the platter and glass down on the table. The day in the cave had been a let-down. It probably had to do with his thinking about Joachim's death. The thrill for Blakely had been the code game—discovering a match between the marks on the relic and the symbols on the sector map. The actual discovery of the jewels couldn't compare, somehow. It was what you would expect to find at the end of the rainbow. Then, what do you do next? You can't spend it. You can't keep it. It was like the blondes the other night, looking through the binoculars for a few seconds: 'been there, done that.'

Perhaps he had truly reached the far side of paradise. He no longer needed to search for something which was nebulous or non-existent. There was no more need for illusion.

Justina. He had held onto sexual fantasies about her for years. Tonight, she was his intimate friend, and a woman he loved in a new and genuine way. They would always be best of friends, he thought. They had managed to overcome the banal for the sublime.

Would it be banality or sublimity with Jenny? He knew the answer before he could finish the question. His loins ached, yet there was this peacefulness in him which made the ache less important. Jenny was a part of the past. She would be here a day or so and then return to her corner of the world. They could only be friends.

The cave. It would be fun to explore the cave tomorrow. Maybe they would find some old stuff down there. It would be something, to touch some ancient artifacts that hadn't been felt by human hands in a couple thousand years.

He grinned at Polaris, realizing how stupid it was to think in that way when you could look up every evening and see a universe of stars which were millions of years old. Ironic. People weren't covetous about stars because they were out of reach and at the same time within reach of everyone. Yet, most people hadn't a clue about their awful power and limitless beauty.

He sensed movement behind him. Turning in his chair, he saw Wafford pushing Elizabeth across the piazza in his direction.

"Missed you down at the Blue Porpoise tonight, Ed," said Wafford, looking like he had fallen into a dark mood again. His voice didn't match his words. It was high and thin. "Had real nice fish. Max and Dimitrius and Miss Justina joined us for a real celebration."

Elizabeth looked anything but celebratory. Her face was drawn.

"I thought I'd have a bite here. I didn't sleep too well last night. I'm about ready to turn in."

"Mind if I sit with Edward awhile, Louis?" Elizabeth asked in a firm voice.

"No." He bit his lip. "I'll be in the hotel bar having a nightcap." He stopped. "Oh, before I forget it, Gresh wants you, Miss Justina, and me and the crew on the boat for a meeting about the test in the morning."

"What time?"

"Eight 'o'clock."

"Everybody informed?"

"Yes. Mike will take us down in the van."

"Very good."

It wasn't good, but he had to play the game. Wafford walked away, leaving Elizabeth bundled in a woolen cape. He looked over at her. Her face was solemn, almost morose. He had a sense of deep foreboding. She was wearing a different fragrance. Freshly ground cinnamon, some nutmeg, a pinch of ginger, with a splash of lemon. Very pleasant. He would normally tell her how nice the scent was, but that time was over. In the half-light, two rivulets of water trickled down her black cheeks. He reached over and took her hand.

"I don't know what to do," she said in a whisper, not looking at him. "Louis is acting like a dead man, Edward. It's like I told you. He is no longer my husband. I don't know who he is! And I am no longer his wife. Something bad is going to happen. I can feel it. It's like he's a walking, talking dead man."

He patted her hand. "It's time you thought about yourself."

She ran her hand over her forehead. "Louis is like a moth drawn to flame. And I am the second moth, hovering, watching Louis moving closer to the fire."

"Yeah."

She looked out across the darkness, then sighed. "Well, I suppose there's nothing to be done, is there?"

"You've got to save yourself."

"For what?" She gathered herself and retracted her hand. "I have always thought of myself as a strong person. Between my injuries and my mythology, I've always thought I understood my role in life. I even accepted my paralysis."

"Which paralysis?"

"Very perceptive, Edward," she said quietly. "Paralyzed twice. Both by white men, too. First by a white mob, and then by a white husband."

They sat without saying anything for several minutes. She was waiting for him to rescue her just like she had rescued him from Easy Ed and Captain Easy. It was different, though. She could make him believe he could become a hero, but he knew he didn't have any power to change Elizabeth's destiny or future—unless she could lift herself emotionally out of her relationship with Wafford. The words came out before Blakely could fully consider them.

"You've got to throw down the baggage, Elizabeth, and go your own way."

"One way is as good as another. When you are in my position, it hardly matters."

"Yes it does. You can't quit. You can't be a victim like Lou is. You need to leave Crete before Monday. I can get you tickets. There isn't any more you can do here. Go home and collect what you need to make a life on your own. Visit your children. Transfer to a different university. I can stay here and try to help Lou. But unless he wants my help, I don't see that I'll do any good."

She did not reply for several minutes. She looked out in the darkness. When she spoke, her voice was coldly objective.

"You sound as though you know something I don't. What's happening with Louis and his cronies?"

"I mentioned this afternoon that I had some suspicions. I confirmed them tonight. Tobok is sending and receiving coded messages. They don't make any sense, but they may involve something to be smuggled aboard the *Sea Siren* during the broadcast tomorrow night. I think it's big time. Does the name Melek ring a bell?"

"No. I don't know anyone by that name. I'd remember that one. Of course..."

She paused and put her hand to her mouth. "How do you spell it?"

"M-E-L-E-K."

"Yes. That's it."

"What's it?"

"The Bible. It's in my Bible, Edward. Melek is the Hebrew word for king."

"Gresham King."

"Uh-huh! The Minotaur raises its ugly head."

"Ironic. King hates Jews. But it makes sense. There may be a ship coming in called Touchstone. So King is saying it's a go for Saturday at midnight. I think there will be a showdown by Sunday."

"Can you keep Jeremiah out of it?"

"Yes. I won't let anything happen to him. I promise you that."

"Thank you, Edward. I am counting on you. He's too fine to

THE MINOTAUR 255

be messed over by these honkys... and that includes his uncle, too."

Her voice was flat and icy. "What will you do?"

"I'm not sure, yet."

"I know you will find a way to stop them."

"I hope I can."

She gathered her wool cape closer around her shoulders and resumed in a low, tragic voice.

"I know you will, Edward. Trust me on that." She paused, then resumed. "Once upon a time, I had a dream that all people—white, black, purple, red, yellow—could all get along and live together as one. You know—Martin Luther King's dream? So many years I believed that. You know what?"

"What?"

"I don't believe in that dream any more. Just like, if we were in love, nobody would let us be, Edward. All my years with Louis have confirmed that—even as I denied it in my heart. There are too many Homers and Kings out there. I suppose I've lived as big a lie as Louis when it comes right down to it. So, I have a new problem now. If I wanted to go back to the university and teach again, what I've always taught isn't true and never was. I just realized that. When you know the truth, you have nothing people want to hear. People hate truth."

"That sounds bitter. You and Joachim taught me how to overcome bitterness."

"It may sound bitter, but I assure you it isn't. It is merely a realization of what Joachim saw in the stars. In addition to the beatitudes, there are great calamities and violences—the harm and destruction which are eternal and part of the cosmic dance. I am simply acknowledging one of those consequences of living which nobody can change—unless there is a grand-scale altering of attitude."

"And you don't see that happening?"

"We would need some new event, like a second-coming or

another great man to rise up like Gandhi or Martin Luther King, but on an even grander scale."

"Meanwhile, Elizabeth, you and I are stuck with who we are, where we are, and when we are. You've taught me it was possible to make a change in my life. This past week, thanks to you and Joachim, I did a little slaying of dragons. I found I had to kill part of myself in order to survive. It's like you said, except now I understand. I had a fatherless boy named Easy Ed and a super boy-man named Captain Easy that Edward, the would-be man, had to fight into submission. It's like them Phyrric victories the Greeks talk about. One more victory and I'd be dead."

He chuckled. "Had it not been for you, I couldn't have done that. I guess I feel a little like I've been sick a long time and have finally awakened to see the world has changed. And here I am, feeling old and new at the same time. I'm nearly at the end of my life, starting to learn what it all means. It's like I'm cramming—like I was a kid studying to pass an examination."

There was a sad smile on her face. "You learned all of that from me and Joachim, Edward?"

"Yeah. I guess you taught me that in mythology, all things are possible."

She wiped the remnant of smile away with her hand. "Except that in the end, Ariadne always loses Theseus."

"Theseus will always love his Ariadne."

"Yes. I understand. But the myth says Theseus never sees his Ariadne again. She dies alone on an island."

"That doesn't have to be. I'd say, get off Crete as soon as you possibly can. You can change the ending, if you really want to bad enough."

She drew her head back and gazed into the blackness without blinking.

"Would you mind wheeling me over to the hotel now? I think I am ready for bed. I will let you know what I decide."

"Sure."

Blakely pushed the wheelchair to the hotel, pulled it through the door and down the hall past the desk. Wafford sat by himself, sipping what looked like whiskey. He watched their approach without smiling or changing expression.

Blakely leaned down, kissed Elizabeth on the cheek and hugged her shoulders. "Let me know soon," he whispered.

"I shall. Thank you, Edward." She gave him a gallows smile as he waved to Wafford.

"See you both tomorrow."

CHAPTER 24

Dream & Reality

Blakely felt his arms thrashing. He awoke and sat up. Gray dawn showed at the window. Somewhere off in the valley, he heard a rooster crowing. He looked at his watch. 0530 hours. His face and neck felt wet. He tried to reconstruct the dream. Jenny was naked, sitting on this swing, swooping past, up and back, in this great arc, laughing, spreading her legs, swooping again, her breasts undulating. Beneath a great tree, sitting on a rock was a hairy, naked man, his elbows out from his sides, glaring with one evil-looking eye at Blakely.

The hairy man slowly got up, keeping his eye on Blakely. Blakely tried to look away, and when he did, Jenny let go of the ropes and threw herself out into space and turned into a beautiful bird with orange, pink, and yellow plumage, flying among the branches, circling, watching the hairy man come toward Blakely, who turned, tried to run, and became heavy under a burden of rope on his shoulder, and a climbing harness from which hung iron grappling hooks. The hairy man, too, had changed into mountain climbing gear and wore a giant brown hat. They were moving through a cave and came onto a ledge overlooking emerald water within a great cavern, where the bird was now flying and circling, then landing on a ledge across from him. It turned into Jenny, sitting at the edge, laughing, pointing toward him.

The hairy man laughed, too, and began pushing Blakely. He looked at the hairy giant behind him, turned, and jumped through the air, falling two hundred feet, plunging into water, fighting for breath, coming to the surface, hardly able to stay above the water, hearing the echoes of the man and Jenny laughing above him, feeling himself drowning, gasping for breath, water filling his throat. He could see the hairy man jumping into the water, landing near him, laughing, his eye changed to two of them. Blakely felt himself sinking, reached out with his finger and touched the laughing man who immediately turned into a fish and swam away. At the same moment, Blakely suddenly felt light, able to touch bottom, breathe freely. Then Jenny dove from her high perch, splashing into the water nearby. Blakely was afraid she would be killed diving into such shallow water, and he tried to swim to her... and had awakened.

Blakely got out of bed, put on his robe, grabbed his toilet kit and towel, and headed down the hall to the shower. It was a good dream, he thought. Far better than the nightmares. He hurried through his shower, feeling Jenny's closeness.

* * * * *

Blakely strode onto the patio expecting it to be deserted at 0605 hours. A man and a woman sat in the far corner next to the potted lemon tree. No mistaking! It was Jenny. She was so intent with the guy that she didn't see Blakely until he was almost at her side.

"Welcome to Crete, Jen!" he said, not knowing what to make of the situation. The man was probably forty with rust-colored hair and a deep tan. He wasn't exactly handsome, but he flashed success. His tan sports clothes and jewelry were a walking ad for I.A. Magnum. Jenny didn't look bad either. A matching outfit. She had a new gold choker with three diamonds.

"Ed! How are you!" Jenny gushed.

She pushed her chair back and embraced Blakely. Same perfume and good hair. Only her hug was more for show than glow. Her friend stood up. She released herself from the perfunctory hug, holding onto his left arm.

"Ed, I'd like you to meet Graham Steward. Graham—Ed Blakely."

The two shook hands. Where did he know the name?

"We decided to take a vacation to celebrate," she said.

"Oh?"

Graham... She had spoken of him.

"Yes. Graham was the key to the three-way. Remember my telling you about him?"

"Oh! Oh, yes..."

It was coming back to him now. The guy from Texas—the one who owned the hotel conglomerate. What was the name? Dalgram? Yeah Dalgram, Inc. The rich guy who was buying up and the other two were buying down.

"Well..." Jenny hesitated. "Graham and I became good friends over these past months... and he's made me the real estate broker for Dalgram."

She gave Graham a smile that was more than one from employee to boss. Her eyes had the same mischief he had thought was exclusively reserved for him.

"She's done a good job for us," said Graham, in a Rod Steiger-like, slurring accent, like it was too much trouble to enunciate his words clearly. Graham exuded confidence. "She's our baby!"

He bet she was.

"Why don't you join us. Have a seat!" Graham was taking charge.

"I will."

Jenny looked tense and mischievous at the same time. No ring on her finger... yet. She sat down and looked coyly at him with tilted head.

"We just thought it would be fun to skip on over and see what you guys found."

"Well," said Blakely, picking up the pepper shaker and tapping it softly on the table, "we've lucked out with the code on the back of that old relic. We dug into a cave yesterday. Found a skel-

THE MINOTAUR 261

eton of a German SS officer and the von Etter jewels." Blakely stretched a leg across the empty chair next to Jenny.

"Wow! How neat!"

Jenny seemed incredibly happy with his luck. She held her hands together at her chin like a prayer had been answered. Her gold bracelets clicked. New, heavy gold, there.

Graham was picking at his teeth with his tongue and looked amused.

"What do you do for an encore?"

Blakely wiggled his leg back and forth. He thought the situation was amusing, too. The daughter brings home the boy she wants to marry for daddy to approve. Only, this wasn't his daughter—it was his former lover bringing her new lover for approval after he and Jenny had broken up less than two months ago! He examined the pepper shaker and put it down.

"You guys can have a ringside seat and see what happens. Maybe today we'll find some ancient Minoan artifacts. At least that's what our archeologist hopes to find."

"Yeah?" Graham's patronizing expression changed to one of interest. "Never done that. That'd be cool. You like to do that, Jen?"

Jen. He thought he owned that nickname. Jenny was relaxing, thinking all the new relationships—him and her, him and him, and her and him—would now be honky-dory.

"I'd love to do that!"

"I suggest," said Blakely, "that you change into clothes you don't mind getting dirty. It's very dusty in there."

"We don't mind," replied Jenny. She turned to Graham. "You'll get to meet Chris Cunningham—the guy I told you all about who has this cute English accent and lectures at Berkeley? He's really neat. He'll like him, won't he, Ed?"

A neat guy. The gold chain on Jenny's left wrist matched the one on Graham's left wrist. Aspiring twins, yet!

"Afraid you won't get to see Chris. He went back to Berlin.

You can meet Justina, though. She's the archeologist in charge now."

"Oh, good! I never met her." She explained to Graham. "Justina is Chris's wife."

It was like Jen could easily substitute one for the other without asking why Chris might have left or what. Same pragmatic, flexible Jenny, which until this trip he had liked in a woman. Now, he could hardly stand it.

"Is this cave far from here?" asked Graham.

"You passed it on your way up. It's at the bottom of the mountain. By the way, when did you get in?"

"We called the *Sea Siren* last night... What time was it, Graham, when we flew in?"

"Eleven o'clock?" He yawned. "Eleven fifteen?"

"Yeah. We got directions and rented a car. Had no problem getting a room."

Jenny was her old self now, resting her elbows on the table and leaning in toward the old one and the new one.

"How long will you be staying?" asked Blakely.

"Just today. We'll fly out around four thirty. We have to get back to Athens. Graham and I are shopping for some coastal property on the Pelopo... What's it called, Graham?"

"Peloponese... you may be familiar with it," replied Graham.

"Yeah. Pretty country."

"Graham wants to develop two hotel complexes on the northwest side—near a place called Patras. From the pictures, it looks fabulous. You know, do a Maui-type thing on the beach."

"Yeah," said Graham. "We anticipate lots of people will be coming there. Historic, you know? They can enjoy swimming, golf, tennis—full recreation—and get culture the same time. I figure it'll take three years to develop. Might throw in some studio and two bedroom condos, you know?"

"Yeah." Blakely didn't know, but it sounded perfect for him and Jen. Getting culture while on vacation was the in thing now.

They were a perfect match, he decided. Graham was cool and Jenny was neat.

"Sounds like you both have a lot in common," said Blakely, attempting to get at the nub of it.

Jenny turned coyly toward Graham.

"Should I tell him?"

Graham extended his hand across the table toward her.

"Why not?"

"We're thinking about getting married."

Jenny reached for Graham's hand and found it. All Blakely could do was watch and smile. Nothing like a long courtship. He supposed Jenny and Graham had been eyeing each other for months. At least they waited until the old man got out of their way! He patted their joined hands like the good father blessing the children.

"Good for you. Too bad we're not out at sea. As captain of the *Sea Siren*, I could marry you two."

"How neat! Only," she looked at Graham sweetly, "we thought we'd like a wedding in my new house on Balboa. Oh, Ed, you should see it! It's gorgeous! I've got all new furniture. And this interior decorator—I don't think you ever met her—Evelyn Price? Well, Evelyn has worked out this really neat pastel color scheme of mauves and grays and teals—even the swimming pool is color co-ordinated. Isn't that great?"

What she described had a tag between three and five million.

"Yeah. It's terrific. Listen, why don't you get some breakfast. I need to make some calls and attend a meeting in Iraklion. We can all go down to the work site later."

"Okay," said Jenny cheerily. "My God, it's good to see you again, Ed."

"I'm very pleased for you. You two seem made for each other."

Graham picked at his teeth with his tongue again. "Yeah. We think so, too."

He got up and shook hands with Graham and gave Jen a peck on the forehead.

"See you later."

He was glad to get away from all the sweetness and light. Next thing—if he'd probed a little deeper—they'd be talking about what to name their kids. Ah, well. He had done his fatherly, ex-loverly duty: approved the man Jenny would marry. Decent of her to seek his approval, he thought. He'd overlook the fact that she came over for the sole purpose of showing Mr. Rich Graham Cracker off to the over-the-hill sailor. He laughed to himself, thinking of her message. 'We did it!' Yes, they sure did it! She had scored big time.

His new life was still fragile, he realized—like Justina's was. They were both on new ground, but vestiges and echoes from the old life could still affect him. He thought he had done well with Jenny and Graham. The reality of them together was, in fact, better than his fantasy of having Jenny in bed again. He ordered breakfast from Manolis and retired to the quiet of his room and prepared himself for the reality of dealing with King.

CHAPTER 25

Severance

"Now everybody understands now..." said King, nervously pacing back and forth in front of the bar in the salon, "nobody... and I mean nobody is allowed back aboard this ship 'til I say you can come back aboard. Ya'll understand that?" King's eyes moved from one to another. "And the reason for this is, I want nothin' to be disturbed. We'll do the test broadcast tonight and—barring any transmission problems—the prospective buyers will stop by to inspect the ship tomorrow. Meanwhile, I want all personal gear removed off this here boat this morning. Everybody 'cept Harry, Gregor, Andy and me will vacate the boat before noon today. I believe y'all have discussed it, right Lou?"

Wafford rested his elbows on his knees, head down. Without looking up, he replied in a weak voice. "We've discussed it. I'll talk to them some more later."

The closest Wafford had come to a discussion was on the drive down to the boat from Kastelli. Even then, Wafford hardly seemed to know the specifics.

Justina's eyes flashed with growing anger. "In effect, then, our work here is finished at the end of the broadcast tonight?"

"That's right, ma'am. At one in the morning to be precise. What you discover in the cave today is part of Crete Enterprises. Tomorrow being Easter, you naturally wouldn't be work'n. But say you was to explore on your own Monday morning and find whatever, that's strictly between you and the Greek government.

As I recall, that was one of the conditions your attorney stipulated in the contract you signed unless I'm mistaken."

"Ya. True. So, if I wish to have support to dig on Monday, I must pay for it myself?"

"That is correct. And whatever you find doesn't involve Crete Enterprises."

"Well, good." She crossed her arms beneath her breasts. "I say that's damned good!"

She glanced at Blakely. He winked at her and held a thumb up.

Blakely fingered the envelope in the pocket of his windbreaker. It was a notice of termination given to him by Marchese at the opening of their meeting—a facsimile message from McCloud and endorsed by Wafford, thanking him for his contributions to the project. He was terminated effective 1:00 a.m., Sunday, 14 April 1996 without additional compensation or severance pay in accordance with the contract he had signed to be captain of the *Sea Siren*. Tony, Leo, Mike, and Justina had received similar terminations, except that Tony and the mates were on wages and did receive severance pay owed. Helluva shock! Not unexpected, except that it came so suddenly—and before the test was completed. Stupid management! Why not wait until they had the test results, then hit everybody in the face? They could screw up the test royally at the very moment of termination. Naturally, King had covered that, too. Any attempt to sabotage the test would result in prosecution, he said.

King continued. "And most of you have received severance pay from Andy Marchese and will not return on board. You will be free to leave out for home whenever you can obtain transportation 'cept for some who are contracted to work until one a.m. tonight. Let me say, I want to thank you for your assistance on this project. It's been my privilege to work with each and every one of you. Y'all have done a superb job!"

McCloud couldn't have lied any better. King looked around the room and began rubbing his hands.

"Are there any questions?"

Jeremiah raised his hand from the sofa arm.

"I have one. What if I need to edit some of the material I shoot today? I'd like to have it ready to send during the live feed."

King shook his head and began pacing.

"No way. You'll just have to save it and send to CDN News on Monday or so. Maybe the local station can transmit it back for you. Just follow the plan we have set up 'bout your equipment and responsibilities."

Jeremiah glanced at Blakely and Wafford. He didn't look convinced.

"Now," said King, stopping and leaning against the bar. "Let's talk more about tonight's test. Mr. Wilcox, you and Gregor can do all the testing of audio and video you want between 2230 and 2330. Would you say that gives you both sufficient time?"

"Sure," replied Jeremiah, his head down. "No problem."

"Gregor will be in contact with CDN News at 2300 hours. You'll have forty-five minutes to chat with the people at CDN, before you go on the air. That'll give everybody ample time to iron out the kinks."

Funny. Wafford was supposed to be honcho of the television side while King worried about the experimental receptors and gadgets. It was like Blakely figured. King had taken over Wafford's responsibilities.

Without raising her hand, Justina asked, "Why do you do a live broadcast so late? I can understand sending tapes at night, but why a live one so late?"

King's mouth crinkled at the edges. "So CDN can feed affiliates before the evening news. Perfect timing! Midnight here, five o'clock in the afternoon in Atlanta and New York. Just in time for prime time coverage."

Tobok raised his hand.

"Yes, Gregor."

Tobok's cherubic face was self-assured. He didn't look like one who had gotten fired. It figured. Neither did Swann. Swann sat at the dining table, flexing his right hand and making the sinewy muscles of his arm undulate like live snakes beneath his skin.

Gregor said, "I'll be contacting CDN at various times today to check our signal strength. Jeremiah, if you have questions about procedures in Atlanta, you can let me know so I can get answers for you."

Jeremiah studied Gregor, nodding at Gregor's new role. Heretofore, Jeremiah did his own transmitting and talking with Atlanta—with Gregor in the perfunctory role of computer operator. Now, Gregor was top dog.

Jeremiah said glumly, "That's cool."

"Okay," said King. He drew a toothpick from his pocket and stuck it in his mouth. He rolled it back and forth with his fingers. "You understand, the live broadcast will go from 2345 'til 2415—exactly thirty minutes. Now, I guess it's time to hear what you fellas have in mind to present. Lou? Get up here and tell us what America and the world's gonna see and hear tonight on their televisions."

Wafford raised his head. His red face was puffed, yet he had a gaunt look. He sat numbly for a minute collecting his thoughts, then slowly lifted himself to his feet. King moved over so he could stand in his place.

"We had hoped," he began, wiping across his mouth and resting a hand on the bar, "to include tape from what we find today in the cave. Hoped it might include some footage of Miss Justina discovering some Minoan treasures. Kinda mix it with the live footage so's Jeremiah and Miss Justina can take some breaks. A half hour is a long time to go live—specially..." he scowled at King, "when you can't tell what will be discovered today. Anyway, we won't be having access to the television studio here, so any mixing of tape and using the large board and monitors is out of the question. So, that means we've got to go with live footage, switching from one camera to another. Whatever Miss Justina finds in the cave today, she will be showing it to the world tonight."

Justina licked her lips and toyed with her wedding ring, sliding it up and down her finger.

"As we've already talked about," Wafford continued, "the village square up yonder is the designated broadcast site. It'd be nice to broadcast from the cave also, but Gresh tells me we'd likely encounter signal problems."

He looked down and seemed to be groping for words.

"However, they're gettin' set for a down-home kind of bonfire tonight up at the square. On Easter-Eve, these people toss an effigy of Judas into the fire. Hundreds of people will be there from around the countryside. Jeremiah thought it might be good to set up one camera on the hotel roof and maybe do interviews up there out of the way. It'd be perfect, he sez, for wide shots. Might have another camera at ground level to catch the crowd and the fire an all."

He stuck a stubby index finger into his ear and worked it back and forth before allowing his hand to drop to his side.

"Only problem is, we're short-handed on trained help, with Harry and Gregor busy down here."

Wafford was fumbling and stumbling and beginning to sweat profusely. He looked miserably at Blakely and then at Jeremiah. Blakely wanted to interrupt, but knew he must remain silent. He couldn't show his emotions now, one way or another, without risking undue attention from King. He wanted to hear all the plans King had in mind so he could figure how to counterpunch at the right time. He shifted quietly in the chair. Wafford continued in a low, uncertain voice.

"We talked some about having Colonel Stupak on the telecast. Make him look good. It would show we've done well by our Greek friends here. Beyond that, I guess I oughta let Jeremiah tell you what he has in mind."

Wafford slunk back to his seat on the sofa.

King snapped, "Ya'll haven't gone over Wilcox's shooting plan and his interview script, Lou?"

"Naw," replied Wafford, running a hand through his sparse hair, which glistened with perspiration.

King pursued furiously. "I can't believe this! You boys got just a few hours to get your act together! I can't believe you're so blasé about this, Lou? Hell, man, your future's on the line—and that of your nephew, too!"

A not so veiled threat. Wafford was writhing in quiet agony as he glared at King. Like a cornered bear, Wafford drew himself up and growled.

"When you keep changing plans on us, keeping us out of the studio, terminating everybody and all, what can you expect, Gresh? Besides, I didn't come down here this morn'n to get read out in front of Miss Justina and these men. And I won't have it... from you, Homer... or anyone! At least you can mind your manners fer Christ's sake—just a few more hours. Get this mess over with once and for all."

The mess. So, it will all be over in a few hours! What was it? Was Wafford sacrificing himself voluntarily? He sure sounded like a condemned man. For what? To save Jeremiah and Elizabeth? King had him over a barrel somehow. Why? It would all be over, and Wafford would be the scapegoat.

"We all got responsibilities," King retorted. "Yours are essential to our success..."

"Excuse me, Mr. King," said Jeremiah, defensively, "but I do have a very detailed script which Uncle Lou and I were going to go over later today. If you want to see all the shooting directions, timed segments, interviews, crowd stuff, I've got it all in the television studio. It's in my notebook, on my clipboard, and laid out on a story board."

"Glad to hear that, boy." King's face was a forced, squinting smile like one would have on discovering something that smelled bad. "You and yer uncle had me worried there."

He waved an open hand toward Jeremiah as if to dismiss a person he despised. "Nah! You don't have to show me anything. I just want to be dead certain you're prepared is all. Hear that, Lou? Yer boy, here, has it together and you didn't even know it!"

Wafford sighed, but did not rise to the bait. He slumped into

THE MINOTAUR

the sofa, allowing perspiration to trickle down his face undisturbed. Blakely held himself in check as Leo, Mike and Tony fixed their eyes on him. They were waiting for Captain Easy to step up to the plate and take a swing. And he wanted to so badly. But he couldn't afford to screw it up. If Wafford was now a sacrificed pawn in some bizarre CIA chess game, Blakely couldn't interfere. The plan King had set in motion must be allowed to play itself out. He prayed nobody else—especially Leo—would interfere. He grinned at Tony and the mates and gave them a slight 'no, it's not time yet.'

"You can count on it!" said Jeremiah firmly. "We're prepared. I just need to get a few of volunteers to assist me today and tonight."

"Tony, Leo and Mike can help, even though they are no longer paid employees," said Blakely sardonically. "We also have two guests who arrived last night. I am sure they would be happy to help this afternoon, until they fly out."

"Great," responded Jeremiah without his usual enthusiasm, looking at his uncle across the room with grave concern.

King's eyes narrowed. "What guests?"

"Tourists from California. An old friend and her fiancé."

King studied Blakely and murmured, "Good."

Justina's wedge of hair shook as she straightened up and placed her hands firmly on the chair edge. Her voice was challenging and firm.

"I have been sitting here listening to all of this," said Justina, "and I don't understand, Mr. King, why you insist on being so nasty to Louis and Jeremiah and act like we are suddenly piranha! What is your problem? Jeremiah produces wonderful videotape. Louis select and hire us. We come to Crete and find a cave. We do a dig. We discover a cache of jewels. We have a television broadcast. We are prepared to do it. We are proud of what we accomplish! What is the big deal you are making now? We do our jobs, even knowing we are all fired at one o'clock tonight!"

King raised both hands against her protest. His voice was high and conciliatory.

"I apologize if I have offended you, Miz Cunningham. I truly am sorry if I did. 'Deed I am! I 'spose none of us ought to be uptight a'tall. Fact is, I'm pleased you are so relaxed about it. Mebbe you haven't heard yet, that this here *Sea Siren's* future—and the future of some of the people in this here salon, including mine—depend on our success tonight."

Justina barked, "Oh, come on, Gresham! You are over dramatizing! Say we louse it up a little technically or don't do best program! So what? We do it again! If it's such big deal, all of CDN's competitors will want similar equipment. And I thought I heard Louis say at the party in Athens there were several interested buyers rather than one. I don't..."

Marchese broke in. "That isn't Gresham's point, Justina. We have a sale pending at this moment. He simply wants us to look as good as humanly possible."

"Ya! My point exactly. We are human beings and will act like humans. Not some robots who go through motions because Mr. King here says 'do it' and puts us all on edge. My God, Andy, you and Gresham both make me nervous, and I don't know why you want to do that just before this big test! You show no faith in us at all!"

Justina had grown balls. She was ready to tackle King or anybody else.

"Well," said King, rubbing his cheek and spitting bits of toothpick to the side, "I think I've said more'n my piece this morning. Last thing I'd wanta do today is put y'all on edge. Bad enough we have to give out severance notices. An it's like you say, Miz Cunningham, everybody's a professional here. Just go 'bout doing what you've been paid to do. Captain Blakely? You've been sett'n there real quiet-like. I know you must have something on your mind you wanna share. Wanna say something?"

The bastard was checking for any change of wind. Blakely stood up. He would play the peasant, hat in hand.

"Guess I'll use this time to thank all of you who came over here while I was captain of the *Sea Siren*. I'll write my last log entry in a few minutes and give command of the ship back to Lou Wafford. Reading the papers about companies and how they do business these days, I can understand that with the sale of *Sea Siren* slated for tomorrow, everybody has to be let go. But we all have to understand that's how companies operate, no matter how sad or bitter we all might feel. I think I speak for everybody when I say we'll do the best we can to fulfill our parts of our contracts. After that, we'll all find other pursuits and get on with our lives."

Blakely sat down. There was total silence. He hoped his little speech would keep everybody on track through 0100 hours Easter Day. King seemed as taken aback as anyone. He touched his chin and turned to Blakely.

"Well said, Captain. Meeting is adjourned."

King was attempting to leave the room when Tony grabbed his arm.

"Mr. King. If I understand you correctly and from what I read in Mr. McCloud's severance message," said Tony, "we're not to come back aboard?"

"Yes sir," said King, reaching for a new toothpick. "Those of you who got final pay checks this morning will not be reporting back here. I suggest you hop aboard that ferry next door to us today. You can be in Athens less than twelve hours and catch a flight to the states—in time to celebrate a lil' belated Easter time with your loved ones."

"But what if the test don't work out?"

King put his hand on Tony's shoulder.

"Appreciate your concern. But we're confident the test will go fine. A good test and the ship is sold. As I said, the new owner will take possession tomorrow."

"I see."

The broadcast was either cover or else a signal to Touchstone. Blakely whispered to Leo. "Tell Tony and Mike that my last command as your captain is to thoroughly inspect the ship. Keep your eyes peeled for anything unusual. Anybody asks what you're doing, tell them I ordered a final checkout as a responsible captain for my last official entry in the log before transfer of command."

*****

Blakely went below and filled in a concluding entry into the log of the *Sea Siren*, not that it really mattered. It was simply protocol at this point. Anything out of SOP would be fixed immediately. He began to write. *A final inspection of Sea Siren by me and my crew finds everything in seaworthy condition. I am relieved of all duties and responsibilities effective 0900 hours, 13 April 1996. Transferred this log and responsibility of Sea Siren to Louis Wafford on this date.*

He signed his name, thinking there are so many things in life a man does one last and final time. He carried the log book back to the salon. Wafford sat talking Marchese. They both looked up as he approached.

"This should stay with the ship, Lou. It is up to date and I have signed my last entry as captain."

Wafford took the leather bound book into his hands and placed it on his knees.

"I'll put it in the ship's safe."

So that was that. No attempt to follow any normal protocols. Without further word, Blakely went in search of his crew. They checked over the *Sea Siren* one last time, looking for anything suspicious or out of order. They were leaving a clean ship. He was okay until he ascended the ladder and entered the pilot house. A tidal wave of emotion swept over him. The *Sea Siren* was special, different from any vessel he had ever sailed. He climbed into the captain's chair and felt the places on the arms which had worn shiny and comfortable. He always felt nested there. Only one captain had ever sat in that chair. The last time! He looked out at the tall masts with their strange cowlings. It didn't seem right to be leaving her with black receptors rigged. He glanced toward the docks in time to see Wafford, Justina, Harry, Jeremiah, and Gregor loading Jeremiah's additional video equipment and some personal bags into the van.

Tony came in, looking glum. "What are our chances of getting a flight out of Athens tomorrow?"

"Good question. We'll let Manolis at the hotel find out for us."

Blakely touched the wheel, feeling the smooth, cold metal on his fingertips. "I'll miss her."

"She was a might different. You could say that for her. We sure put her through her paces, didn't we Eddie boy?"

"Yeah. And she put us through ours, too."

Tony looked toward the quay. "I see Harry's brought the launch back. I don't mean to rush you, but Leo and Mike are waiting for us down below."

Blakely climbed out of the chair and took the binoculars from their holder. He pointed for Tony to do the same. Without a word, they hung them around their necks inside their windbreakers, zipped up, and joined the two mates. Harry navigated the launch pier-side to where Wafford, Justina and Jeremiah waited.

Blakely stood up and held out his hand to Swann. "Take care, Harry. You've been a reliable guy."

Harry nodded and volunteered a limp hand. There was no sign of emotion in his yellow eyes. He was like a wild cat he'd tried to domesticate. He would always be wild and alone. Justina and Jeremiah climbed into the rear seat of the van.

"Keep serving the cobbler and kiwis, Harry."

His eyes flickered once, and that was all. Blakely stepped off the launch, and Harry pushed off, revved the motor, and returned to the *Sea Siren* without a backward glance. Blakely watched the deep wake. He'd always felt Harry had potential. There just wasn't time to develop it.

"You boys will hafta rent a cab," said Wafford. "Gresh wants the Rover here so they can come up this afternoon and see the cave."

Blakely said, "I need to talk with my crew about arrangements to fly home. You can do me a favor, Lou. You remember Jenny?"

"Yes, sir?"

" She arrived last night with her new boyfriend."

"You don't say! Miss Jenny's here in Iraklion?"

"At Kastelli."

It was the first sign of life he had seen in Wafford in three days. He managed a fairly decent hang-dog grin.

"Don't rub it in," said Blakely. "Her new beau is loaded with bucks and she is deliriously happy. And I'm trying not to show her I'm a trifle jealous. Anyway, they wanted to watch the dig today. They're at the hotel. Can you take them down to the site?"

"Miss Jenny... Sure. I'll take them as my special guests!"

* * * * *

Tony had selected a harbor front hotel with a third floor suite. The *Sea Siren*'s deck, pilot house, and gangway were in full view. There were two bedrooms and a fold out sofa in the living room. A nice kitchenette. Perfect for Tony, Mike and Leo. Blakely sat down and removed the binoculars from around his neck and put them on the table. Tony did likewise.

"They'll come in handy tonight."

Blakely unfolded some papers and passed them to Tony.

"These are the messages back and forth from the comm center. Jeremiah picked off some more last night."

The men read them.

"Seems like you oughta be reporting this to Greek authorities, Eddie," said Tony.

"It's not that simple. First, I don't want us all being kept here for months while the Greeks try to unscramble what's happening. It could turn into years! Second, we don't know this isn't a CIA thing. Marchese used to work for the CIA in Vietnam. He could still be working for them. It fits. McCloud is one of these super-patriot guys with lots of money to underwrite Contra-type projects.

And King is another right-winger who only feels important when he's helping a WASP cause."

Leo asked, "What's Wafford's role in all this?"

"Don't know. I originally thought he was a partner. Now it looks like he's been used and thrown away. He keeps complaining about the mess—kinda like Oliver Hardy, except it isn't funny. It's killing him. You notice how he's changed from the casino wheeler-dealer to a guy who expects to be hit by a sledge hammer any minute?"

"He and Elizabeth are on the outs," said Mike. "He's just damned nasty to her."

"What I'd like, Tony, is for you to stay here and watch what goes on with the *Sea Siren* today. After the broadcast, Mike and Leo can take over surveillance through the night. My guess is this broadcast test is simply a cover for something else. If there is any unusual activity, call me on your cellular phone."

"Right," replied Tony. "So what if there was to be a small boat hitching up to the gangway? You don't want us to call harbor police and try to grab 'em?"

"No. We can't interfere, because they may be good guys. See? We don't know. For as much as I dislike King and Marchese, they could be working for the Fed. And I don't want to take responsibility for screwing up a CIA operation. I don't think you want to get in their way either, do you?"

"No. Can't say I do," replied Tony. "Leastways, not in this lifetime."

"We've got to let them work their plan. Once we've got enough evidence, I think we can do our thing without hurting the wrong people."

"What kinda evidence?" asked Leo.

"Jeremiah has collected more messages. They might be what I need," said Blakely.

"All right," Tony said, stretching. "I'll make myself comfortable here at my window and keep a weather eye out."

Leo stood up and crossed his massive arms. "Just wish we could go back over there right now and kick some butt."

Blakely looked down at the *Sea Siren*. "We've got to play the game, Leo. It will all play out, and I'll be first in line with Mr. King."

Truth was, Blakely wasn't sure what his next steps should be, except to bide his time. If only Wafford would give in to the pressure and spill his guts to Blakely. The guy had to be in severe pain, and he could only stand so much.

"Well," said Blakely, "it's time we head up the hill. Let's get a taxi."

CHAPTER 26

Epiphany

Alex waved from Padopolis's office as Blakely paid the taxi driver. "Come over. I have something for you."

Blakely noticed Elizabeth sitting alone at the very edge of the piazza with her back to him. God help her! She could be thinking of rolling herself off the edge. He couldn't figure why they didn't have a railing along the edge to keep people from falling off. He entered. Padopolis was seated with shirt sleeves rolled up at his desk with two villagers looking over his shoulder. He was sketching something on paper and instructing them. It had to do with building the pyre. Alex came out of the back room holding a blue ceramic urn in both hands. An eeriness overtook Blakely as he watched Alex set it on the counter.

"They deliver it this morning to me," Alex said. "The ashes of your friend."

Blakely touched the round, cool surface of the urn, which was a little larger than a half-gallon milk jug. All that remained of Joachim.

Alex pointed to the flat lid.

"I did not open it. The lid is sealed with wax, if you wish to see."

"No. Thanks, Alex. He wrapped his left arm around it and carried the urn into the sunlight and crossed the street. Elizabeth was still sitting in the same position. A dozen elderly tourists stood in a circle around a guide who was speaking German and describing Kastelli's history. The photographer with his old camera sat on a folding chair reading a newspaper.

Blakely set the urn on a table and carried a chair to where Elizabeth sat. Edges of her bright blue and gold caftan waved in the light breeze. Her upper body flinched involuntarily as he set down the chair.

"Sorry. Didn't mean to startle you, Elizabeth."

"That's okay," she said softly, looking once more out across the mountains. "Nothing can surprise Elizabeth any more."

She lifted her head regally and folded her hands in her lap. He waited.

"Louis and I had a long talk last night."

"Yeah?"

"Nothing has changed with him."

"Too bad."

Elizabeth held her hands in supplication. "I begged and pleaded. I said, 'Let's just pack and leave in the middle of the night. Get away from King and all the mess you talk about. Fly away! Just us two. Go visit our children. Start over. Change our names! Whatever it takes.' And you know what he said?"

"No."

"He fell to his knees and bawled and asked my forgiveness. Told me how sorry he was for everything... how much he really loved me... then told me I must go... even pleaded with me to leave... and then he said that he would have to stay. He couldn't go with me... but that everything would be okay with him staying."

"So what are you going to do?"

"Leave. Get off this forsaken island. I was ready to go this morning, but Manolis checked and found the ferries and planes were booked solid with Easter tourists. So, I have to wait here until Monday."

"You'd fly out this afternoon?"

She turned and looked at him.

"I would fly out this minute, if I could sprout wings!" A semblance of smile hovered at the corners of her mouth. "A few moments ago, I even prayed for Icarus to rescue me."

"I think I can get you out of here this afternoon, Elizabeth. I need to check. It would be a private plane."

"If you can arrange it, I am more than ready."

"I know it's none of my business, Elizabeth, but did you ever have an affair after you married?"

Her nostrils flared. "I suppose Louis told you about his suspicions? He's always been paranoid about my male colleagues. I long ago gave up attempting to ally his doubts."

"Yeah."

"And the answer is no. I've never cheated. Unfortunately, I cannot say the same for him."

"I can believe that."

Elizabeth seemed to be resolved. There was no emotion he could detect. The two men Blakely had seen in Padopolis's office were starting to remove the tables and chairs. A farmer arrived with a burro laden with tied bunches of tree branches.

"I'm afraid we'll have to move, Elizabeth. They're getting the piazza ready for the pyre. Where would you like to go?"

"Take me over by the hotel, Edward. I want to watch the preparations."

He went over to the table and picked up the blue urn.

"Mind holding this?"

She took it onto her lap and looked quizzically up at him.

"His ashes?"

"Yeah."

She held the urn and examined it, rubbing her black hand lightly across the lid of the vessel. It was a weird sensation to realize Elizabeth, paralyzed as she was, was carrying Joachim's remains on her lap in a wheelchair. She must have experienced something of the same sensation, for she said, "I have never held the ashes of someone in my hands before."

"I hadn't either," he replied. He pushed her across the street and onto the slate sidewalk in front of the hotel.

"You want to go with me down to the cave later?"

"No. None of that is of any consequence to me now. I would prefer staying up here and watching them build the pyre. There is something very cathartic about the thought of building a pyre and setting it afire. Watching them, I can place my own burdens on the pile with each bundle of branches, knowing that soon, they will all be burned to ashes."

"Would you like a cold drink or something to eat?"

She seemed to be looking at him from deep within herself. Her lovely dark chocolate eyes showed no hint of anything except a resolve to be at peace.

"I'm fine. You go now, Edward."

"If I can get you the ride, I'll come back up and see you off. It'll be with Jenny and Graham."

"Oh. Yes. I met them earlier on the patio." She touched her fingers to her mouth and looked up. "I'd prefer it if you just leave word with Milos at the desk about the plane this afternoon. This can be our good-bye, Edward. I want you to go and do what you have to do. I also want to thank you for teaching me how to sail. It was always my dream. And if I never get another opportunity, I can set sail in my mind and journey wherever I want to, can't I?"

"Yes. You can. Good-bye, Elizabeth. Maybe we can sail again, sometime."

"Take care of Jeremiah for me."

"I will." She handed him the urn, and it felt to him like a burnt out torch was being passed from one to the other. The weight of Joachim's ashes still had effect. He took the urn from her hands, kissed her on the forehead, and carried the ceramic vessel through the door of the hotel. It was as though Elizabeth already knew she had a ride to Athens this afternoon—that it was preordained. There seemed to be no remorse or hurt left in her, only relief. She had risen above her paralysis and it was evident in her detached farewell.

Jeremiah was sitting in the reading room next to a vinyl equipment bag. He got up and followed Blakely up the stairs to his room.

Inside, Blakely set the urn on the dresser and watched as Jeremiah opened his case and loaded the VCR.

"What's in the pot?" asked Jeremiah.

"Joachim's ashes. I hope to have them buried at the German Cemetery at Maleme."

"That would be nice," he said. Jeremiah was already concentrating on the picture coming up on the VCR.

"This was sent last night around 0300 hours," said Jeremiah.

"Tobok?"

"Yes."

They read the message.

"*Gem: After confirmation, we'll leave church for Vatican. Arrive 1400 hours to settle. Once notified, church entry unlocked and available 1800 hours for your full use. Brother Gregory will be there for guided tour and a week of instructions. Mel.*"

"What do you make of it? All I can get is Gregor and that the church is the *Sea Siren*."

"Know what?" Blakely asked.

"What?"

"King is going to Rome tomorrow. It's about the sale. Settlement will be in Rome. The new buyer can come aboard 1800 hours tomorrow."

"Wow! Think it's the Italians are buying it?"

"Have no idea. Could be Saddam Hussein, Libyans? Iranians? Bosnians? Who knows?"

"You think they're selling out to our enemies?"

"No. It could be anybody! But your uncle Lou calls it a mess. If it's legit, why are they settling in Rome rather than here?"

"Is uncle Lou going to Rome?"

"I don't know."

"What about Auntie Elizabeth?"

"I'm hoping to get her on a plane outa here this afternoon. You might want to say good-bye. She's sitting outside the hotel.

Seems okay, but I'm not sure how she really is inside. She's definitely leaving as soon as she can get out."

"I will. I guess I'd better hustle down to the cave, too. Justina's probably already exploring. Mike and Leo said they'd pick me up at 1115 hours."

"Okay. Don't say a word about what we know. Stick exactly to what King and your uncle and you have set up. It's imperative that we let it all happen like they planned it."

Jeremiah looked in disbelief. "Why would you want to let them get away with something illegal?"

"Trust me. They can't hide a two masted brigantine. And they can't dismantle the gadgets without attracting the attention of Colonel Stupak. They are already being watched by the Greek Air Force."

"I would hope so."

"I'm taking this tape and the one you brought me last night down to put in the hotel's safe."

"You coming to the cave soon?"

"In a few minutes."

Blakely sat on the edge of the bed and watched Jeremiah leave. He switched off the VCR and emptied his leather toiletry case of its contents except the tape he had hidden in the bottom. He put the second tape cartridge in with the first, zipped it up, and placed it next to the urn.

He took out Joachim's penknife and cut around the wax seal and lifted the lid. The grayish white powder and flecks of bone were all that was left of what Joachim called the temple of the soul. He wished he had decided to sprinkle Joachim's ashes off the edge of the piazza instead of arranging with Stupak to have them interred at Maleme. Somehow, this mountain top was closer to the spirit of Joachim than a military cemetery. He replaced the lid.

A plan was forming in his mind. Tucking the toiletry case under his arm, he went down to the desk and had Milos, the day clerk, put it in the safe. He went into the sitting room and picked up the black phone. He dialed through the Iraklion operator and obtained a connection to Travis Gorton.

"Hello," a sleepy male voice said.

"Travis?"

"Yeah. Who is this?"

"Blakely, Trav. Things are happening here. I know it's short notice, but I need you to contact the FBI."

"Where are you? Still in Greece?"

"Yeah. Up to my eyeballs!"

"What do you need?"

"Get in touch with the FBI and have them stand by during the next twenty-four hours. I will try to send some computer files to CDN News."

"Why don't you let me get an FBI communication link where you can send them direct?"

"That would leave telltales. I want to make it look like one of our regular transmissions from *Sea Siren* to CDN."

"I see."

"Can I ask you to also stand by for a call? I'll let you know when the transmission is coming."

"I suppose so. We were planning on going to church Sunday, but if it is that important, I'll stand by."

"Thanks, Trav. I'll be back in touch."

"Don't do anything foolish, Ed."

"I hope I won't. Bye."

He hung up the phone and looked around. Nobody was on the patio. He went out the door. Elizabeth was nowhere in sight. Men were beginning to haul tied bundles of brush onto the piazza and stack them in a large circle under the direction of Padapolis. He went over to where Alex was cleaning the windows of his taxi.

"See Elizabeth, Alex?"

Alex pointed to the hotel.

"She is there."

Elizabeth's face showed in an open window watching the pyre.

"Good. Can you take me down to the cave site?"

"Sure."

He was about to get in when a military car came over the rise. It was Stupak, dressed in his blue uniform. He stopped and leaned his head out.

"You are very late supervisor today, Ed," he said teasingly. "The work already has commenced."

"Had other priorities."

"They have plenty caving equipment. I also called two very good cavers to assist you, should you wish to have them work with you."

"You won't be around this afternoon?"

"I have a squadron meeting. Captain Lutra is there in my place. Oh, by the way, I must remind you; we cannot furnish military guards tonight. My men will be finished at 1630 hours today and will not return to duty until Monday after Easter. You may wish to make other arrangements with Max."

"Okay."

"I received a message from the American lieutenant—the forensic one—Smith. He says the bullet which killed Kemft was from a German Schmeisser—the kind paratroopers carried."

"Doesn't surprise me. Lou hoped to get that slug back so he could do a ballistics check on Heinrich's Schmeisser."

"Yes. Well, I must be going. I will see you again tomorrow at the village feast, I hope. Everyone is invited. Lamb will be cooked. Much food and wine! Another celebration of death and resurrection! You look like you could use some resurrection, eh?" He laughed. "You are beginning to look troubled like your friend Lou. Is this a contagious disease you Americans carry?"

Blakely grinned. "Hope not."

"Me too."

Stupak shifted the car into gear and was gone in a cloud of black smoke.

CHAPTER 27

Daylight

Blakely sat watching as Alex pumped the accelerator and muttered something under his breath. With the turn of the key and a backfire, the Volkswagen came alive.

"Good Roscinante!" cried Alex.

He wrestled with the gear shift, grinding it until it caught, and he let out the clutch. Roscinante lurched down the narrow street. Burros with loads of twigs and brush plodded toward the piazza, led by farmers in mandilis and vraches.

"Our fire this year will be bigger than ever," said Alex. "Because of bigger fire, we have very big Judas to throw into the flames."

Judas, the betrayer, thought Blakely. Without a Judas, the scheme of death and resurrection cannot unfold, the pain cannot be endured, and the lesson cannot be learned. Jim Wafford had betrayed his wife, two sons, Blakely and Chris in Berlin in 1956. And here it was again, repeated. Lou Wafford had betrayed Elizabeth, his son and daughter, his nephew Jeremiah, Blakely, Chris and Justina in Greece in 1996. Must the cycle of betrayal always be repeated?

Alex maneuvered the Volkswagen up the trail of raw dirt, following the tire marks of the military vehicles. Rays of sunshine filtered through branches of pines. A swarm of gnats danced in a shaft of sunlight near the bend in the stream. Alex turned up the hill and into the open, flat space before the dark maw of cave and broad mountain stretching above it.

All work had apparently stopped. Knots of people stood around the water jug. Everyone turned as Alex swung into the clearing and parked next to Lutra's car. Blakely got out. Justina strode toward him. She looked prepared today. She wore gray coveralls and hiking boots.

"We are taking short break," she explained.

"I see that."

He waved at Jenny and Graham, who were sitting on camp chairs in the shade.

"We have slight problem, Edward," she said. "We followed the passage beyond where the cache of jewels was?"

"Yeah?"

"Approximately one hundred fifty meters past that spot, the cave opens into a large, vaulted gallery. There is a sheer drop of ten meters to bottom. We must use the trained men Dimitrius suggested."

"I take it Jeremiah and Leo won't be able to follow you in with camera and lights?"

"No. There is no reason to. I would suggest they wait until we find something."

"All right."

The red Rover swung in and parked next to Alex's taxi. Marchese was the lone occupant.

Justina put her hand to her mouth. "Oh, Gott! Not now, please, Gott!"

"If he wants to go in the cave with you, let him, Justina. It will give me a chance to check out why King didn't come with him."

"But he is such an ass!"

"I know. Stay cool."

Marchese was dressed in the same caving outfit he wore at Trieste. He unloaded harness and a nylon bag of equipment. He threw a hank of nylon rope over his shoulder, picked up the bag and harness and came over.

"Hey guys! How goes it?"

"Okay," answered Blakely. "Where's your pal Gresham? I thought he was coming up with you."

Marchese was already sweating and breathing heavily through his mouth.

"No. He and Lou are going over plans for tonight."

"They're on the *Sea Siren*?"

"Yeah, guy," said Marchese. He looked at the cave opening, shielding the sun with his hand. "That's it, huh?"

His squinting eyes moved up the mountain and back down to the entrance.

"How far have you gotten?"

Justina reluctantly replied. "We were stopped by an earthquake fault. We are about to go back in and see whether we can continue or not."

"Mind if I join?"

Justina looked momentarily at Blakely. He winked.

"I suppose. I wish to be clear with you, however," said Justina firmly. "You follow my orders here. You are not in charge. Those two men over there," she pointed, "will lead us and tell us what to do. You will follow their instructions and mine."

"Gotcha!"

Marchese did not seem fazed by his diminished role at all. He acted like a big, overgrown kid who couldn't wait to get inside the cave in whatever capacity. Blakely watched the two men she had pointed to. Both were slender, dark haired Cretans with tough, wiry bodies, probably in their early thirties. They were already fastening seat harnesses and rappel racks.

"Edward, are you ready to join us?"

"I'm taking a rain check. I need to speak with Jenny and do some chores. Have you met her and Graham?"

Justina's face lit up. "Ya! We had a nice talk—mostly about you."

He walked over and squatted down next to Graham and Jenny.

"Have a couple big favors to ask."

Jenny touched Graham's sleeve.

"Are you still flying out this afternoon?"

"Around four, we decided," said Graham. "We'll be leaving

here to check out in an hour or so."

"Elizabeth Wafford needs a ride to Athens. Any chance you could take her along?"

Graham and Jenny looked at one another.

Blakely explained. "She needs to catch a commercial flight from Athens to stateside ASAP."

"Sure. We've got a Lear with plenty of room," said Graham.

"She's in a wheelchair. Will that be a problem?"

"Oh, heavens no," said Jenny. "I met her this morning."

"She's at the hotel. Room One. You can get Milos, the day clerk, to help."

"No sweat," said Graham. "we'll take care of her. What's her name again?"

"Elizabeth. Elizabeth Wafford," said Blakely.

Jenny patted Graham's sleeve. "She's the black lady I was talking with, Graham."

"Oh, yeah."

"Lou isn't going with her?" asked Jenny.

"No. He's staying here to finish up."

"You said you had two favors to ask." Graham ran his hand along Jenny's arm. "What's the second?"

"I was wondering whether you'd like to list *Easy, Too*, the office property, the Morgan—the whole kit and caboodle—as a package and sell it for me, Jenny?"

Jenny and Graham looked at each other and laughed.

"Funny!" said Jenny. "We were talking about *Easy, Too* and the Morgan coming over."

"I collect classic cars," said Graham.

"He wants to learn how to sail, and I was telling him I would teach him. And we have a slip at my new house. Would you consider selling the Morgan and *Easy, Too* to us?"

Graham interjected, "What would you want for all your property? I'm talking about everything you got back there."

Blakely was flabbergasted. He hadn't thought what it might

THE MINOTAUR 291

be worth—especially the half-acre of Newport Beach and the business. Graham must see development potential.

"I'd go with appraised value. I'm not looking to make a killing. All my tax stuff is with Anita, my accountant. She has all the dope."

Jenny's green eyes fluttered uncertainly. "You really weren't coming back, then?"

He had to admit the truth. "No."

"What will you do?" asked Jenny, showing concern. "I mean, after this is over. Are you planning to stay here?"

There wasn't time to consider the future, he thought. Not with all that was happening. The severance effective at 0100 hours tomorrow morning did raise questions about future. But there was unfinished business ahead of him during the next twenty-four hours, and no guarantees he would have any future. What could he say?

"No. Only thing I have on my agenda after tonight is meeting Claudia for a little vacation together, sometime next week. After that, I might do some sailing among the islands... Who knows?"

Jenny asked, "What about Bumper?"

She looked down at her finger. She was wearing a large rock on a thick gold band today. Jenny said, "Jim Willis is a nice man and all, but wouldn't you like to see Bumper in a nice home?"

So that was it. "He needs the water and plenty of attention."

"We've got a swimming pool and the bay," she countered.

"Would you keep him for me until I send for him?"

"I'd love to. Wouldn't you, Graham?"

"Sure." Graham patted her arm. "What's another Lab?"

"You own a Lab?"

"Seven year old yellow bitch, named Maggie," Graham replied. "She's in Dallas. I'm planning on moving my headquarters to Irvine. She and Bumper should get along fine."

"Jen, do you have any deposit slips for my account?"

"At my office."

"How about coming up with a value on my stuff, including

appraised value of the lot and my business. Write a check and deposit it in my account."

"All right."

Jenny teared up again.

Graham said, "We leave Wednesday for California. We'll have a check in your account by the following week. That half-acre should be worth a bundle."

"Tell you what," said Blakely. "Deduct the amount of the Morgan. That'll be your wedding present from Ed Blakely."

Jenny's mouth dropped open.

She reached over and hugged Blakely.

"You always were an old softie! Thank you, Ed."

"Awfully nice of you," said Graham.

She had changed her scent, he realized. Probably some fabulously expensive stuff, but it was no longer familiar, and that was as it should be. He pushed his emotions down inside.

"I see they're getting ready to go exploring," Blakely said, getting up. "I need to take care of some things. Will you be here when I get back?"

"Probably not," said Graham, glancing at Jenny. "I think we oughta see to this lady, Mrs. Wafford." He stood up. "Don't you think, Jen?"

Jenny dabbed at her eyes with a curled finger. She always was a good crier. She got up and gave Blakely another brief hug and looked at him sadly.

"Yes."

She drew back. He thought she was more beautiful than ever. She'd always looked great when she was sad. If she hung around much longer, she'd have him crying. He looked around.

"I don't see your rental car. How'd you get down here?"

"Lou brought us. We hoped to catch a ride back with somebody."

"Alex is still here," said Blakely. "He can take you. Appreciate all you're doing for me."

"Glad to do it," replied Graham. "Good luck in the cave! And thanks again for the Morgan. I've wanted one for a long time."

"You're welcome."

He turned away, feeling strange, knowing that he had given them his Morgan impulsively. He supposed he owed Jenny for all she had put up with during their relationship. She'd tried to help him, he could say that for her. He walked across the clearing to where Marchese was adjusting his climber's harness.

"Got a favor to ask."

"Sure, pal."

"Can I borrow the Rover? I've got to take Leo and pick up some equipment for tonight."

"You'll have it back by 1700 hours?"

"How about 1600 hours?"

Marchese reached into his pocket and produced the keys. Justina was putting on her hard hat. He gave a little wave. "Good luck in there!"

* * * * *

Blakely took Leo and drove the Rover back to Tony's apartment in Iraklion. Tony was sitting, bleary-eyed at the window where they had left him in the morning.

"About time I got some relief!" he complained.

"Brought you a peace offering," said Leo, handing Tony a plate of Suflaki and a bottle of orange juice.

Blakely looked out at the *Sea Siren*. Harry and Tobok were on watch. No sign of Wafford or King.

"Any activity?" Blakely asked.

"None since Swann brought the launch dockside and took Lou Wafford across to the ship. That was around 1145 hours, according to my log here. Tobok and Swann have been switching off."

"No suspicious vessels approaching or docking?"

"None I could see."

Blakely sat down and watched as Tony set the juice on the

window ledge and attacked the Suflaki. Leo scanned the harbor with the binoculars.

Blakely said, "We've got confirmation that Tobok is in touch with unknown people about a rendezvous at midnight tonight. If all goes well, King will be leaving for Rome tomorrow to receive payment for the *Sea Siren*. The new owner is to take possession after 1800 hours tomorrow."

"What do we do, Eddie?"

Watch tonight for telltales of what they're up to. Somehow, after King leaves for Rome—if he does—we've got to get aboard and access Tobok's message files."

"Why?"

"I want to transmit them to the FBI. If these guys are legitimate, there won't be a problem. If they work for the CIA, the FBI can figure it out. Still no problem. If they are selling high-powered technology to a foreign enemy, then the FBI can fix the problem."

"You want us to sneak aboard and overpower Tobok and Swann after King leaves?" asked Leo.

"I don't see us overpowering anybody. Somehow, we've got to send the files without them knowing about it. Otherwise, we might mess up a legitimate CIA operation, big time."

Tony swigged his juice. "Beats me how you expect to do it, then. Swann or Tobok has been on watch all day."

Blakely focused the binoculars on the bridge. He thought he detected movement within the smoked windows, but it was merely reflected light. He got up and put the binoculars on the table.

"I guess I should be getting back. Marchese and Justina are probably at each other's throats by now."

Leo smirked. "Hope she tears his fat-ass to pieces."

"Tony," said Blakely, "why don't you turn in and get some sleep while Leo takes over watch. I'll check back later."

"Aye, aye."

* * * * *

Blakely arrived back at the cave at 1640 hours. No cars or trucks. Half a dozen Greek peasants lounged near the cave entrance. He drove up and spoke to a heavy set man in boots who seemed like he might be in charge.

"Where is everyone?"

The man shrugged and shook his head vigorously.

Blakely tried his Greek. "Where is the group?"

He pointed toward the mountain. "Kastelli!"

"Efharisto!" (Thank you!)

What was going on? He backed the Rover around and drove up the mountain. He parked behind the van. There was much activity on the piazza. The pyre now stood ten feet high. Men and boys were sweeping up the debris with brooms. Music blared from the taverna. He entered the hotel. Tourists crowded the lobby seeking rooms. Marchese and Mike were in the little bar having a beer. He worked his way through the noisy crowd to where they sat.

"Glad to see you, guy, I was getting worried," said Marchese. Blakely handed him the keys to the Rover.

"How'd it go today?"

Marchese started laughing heartily. "You shoulda been there. Funniest damned thing I've seen in all my years of caving!"

"What was so funny?" Blakely didn't want to hear it.

"We got in there and climbed down this shaft and then up the other side. I guess we were inside about an hour, going through these caverns and some really pretty galleries with water and all, and awhile later, I look down at my altimeter and realize we are going up more than we are going down. About this time, Stephano, one of the pros, realizes the same thing. So we ask Justina what she wants to do? Continue? Or go back and try the other passage? She sez, 'let's continue and see where it leads.' So we do that another hour. Guess where it leads?"

He hated to hear. "I don't know. Where?"

"Into this old crypt where there's a bunch of bones and skulls piled up. It's a tomb of an early Christian church. There's even a crude chapel made out of stones."

"Yeah? That sounds good. What's so funny about that?"

"Justina sits down in the middle of all the bones and all, and she says loud and clear, 'Well, God in Hell!' Only she says it in German, "Gott im Himmel! Of all the God damned luck,' she says."

"I don't understand."

"We're at the mouth of the cave, only it's been used as a burial place for an early church. It's all sealed off and all. So what does she do next? She decides to knock a little hole in the wall to see what is on the other side."

Marchese doubled up with laughter. Blakely wanted to punch him.

"So isn't that logical? You had gone that far. Why not see what's on the other side?"

"Yeah." He was laughing so hard tears were streaming down his face. "That's what we did. We punched a hole in the damned wall and guess what?"

"What?"

"There was light on the other side and then a man was looking at us with a black beard and glasses. It was the priest of the local church. We had poked a hole into the basement of his church! You shoulda seen the expression on this guy's face!"

"Yeah, I can imagine." Justina must have been mortified. Mike looked away in disgust. He had apparently heard the story before.

Marchese took a swig of beer and laughed some more. "The priest said..." He laughed convulsively. "The priest said, 'please don't make any larger hole. You are destroying my church!'" He broke off in a gale of laughter. "And Justina... Justina said we wouldn't, and she tried to plug the hole with stones, and began crying as though she had committed a mortal sin."

Marchese held his stomach and laughed uncontrollably again.

"Where is she?" asked Blakely.

"Up in her room, I believe," said Mike.

Marchese was still laughing as Blakely left the bar and climbed the stairs. He knocked.

"Go away!" Justina's muffled voice answered.

"It's Blakely, Justina. I need to talk with you."

There was silence, then a rustling. She unlocked the door and pulled it open. At least her eyes weren't puffed and bloodshot from crying. She stood there in her gray outfit, looking like a scruffy, first-day recruit in basic training.

"Come in, Edward." She beckoned him to the chair. "I suppose you've heard?"

"I got Marchese's rendition, complete with laugh track."

"Ach, it was so awful. And in front of Andy Marchese! I have never done such a thing. And when I get to the crypt, I knew what it was. I have been in many of these crypts before. I have read about them. I have seen photographs of them. One would assume there is a modern church built upon the old one. Sometimes they are four, five or more layers of church. I suppose that is what intrigued me. I thought perhaps there were other rooms above, which might lead to more cave passages." She buried her fingers in her hair and shook her head. "I don't know what I must have been thinking. It was so dumb!"

"You had good reasons. You didn't know."

"Ya. An archeologist with my experience should know. I am glad you were not there, Edward. It was the embarrassment of my life. All I could think of to say to the priest was, 'We are very sorry. We will pay for any damage and make donation tomorrow.' And the priest was very sweet. He said, 'Bless you, now please replace the rocks,' And that is what I did." She started to weep.

"It's over, Justina. No real harm done. You've got to get yourself together for the broadcast tonight. You don't want puffed eyes."

"I don't very much feel like doing it."

"We're all counting on you. Jeremiah can't do it without you. Do you know what you'll be presenting?"

"We hoped to have artifacts to show on our broadcast! What in God's name can we talk about for thirty minutes? How we explore cave and discover church?" She stood up and smoothed her hair. "Jeremiah and I have some back-up items we will do."

"Good. Are you okay?"

"I suppose. Let me rest here."

"There were peasants milling around the cave entrance when I stopped by."

"Ya. I asked them to watch over it for me. Captain Lutra could not post guards during the holiday."

"Have you thought any more what you will do after tonight?"

"I want to explore the other passage. I still have hopes of finding artifacts. I will contact my museum in Berlin on Monday. Perhaps they will provide funding for me."

"What if you said that in your broadcast tonight? Give your audience something else to look forward to?"

"Suppose I don't find artifacts?"

"Nothing lost. Crete Enterprises is kaput. But what if you were to find something? Wouldn't you want to do more videos and tell your story?"

Her face looked hopeful. "Ya. I would."

"Something to think about. See you later."

He closed the door behind him and crossed the hall to his own room. She was trying so hard. Too hard. She had to be ready to do a solid performance tonight. Maybe she should interview the priest and get his view of the dig. Perverse, Blakely. You can still be very perverse—and it's Orthodox Easter Eve, too.

CHAPTER 28

Christos Anesti!

It was 2130 hours and Wafford hadn't brought the Rover back from the *Sea Siren* with the small control board. Jeremiah was practically in tears. He used Blakely's cellular phone to call the *Sea Siren*.

"Gregor?"

"Yes."

"Is Uncle Lou there?"

"Yes."

"Can you put him on? He was supposed to bring the small control board up with him."

There was a silence.

"Let me check for you."

Jeremiah held the phone away and covered the mouthpiece.

"This is not cool, skip. Gregor isn't letting me speak with Uncle Lou."

He put the receiver back to his ear and waited.

"He won't be coming up there tonight, Jeremiah. He's sick. Mr. King says to do the best you can without it."

"Are you serious? You know it'll look like amateurville! I have no way to switch from one camera to the other! How 'bout if I send somebody down for it?"

"Just a second..."

Jeremiah covered the receiver again.

"You won't believe this! Uncle Lou is sick and can't come up.

Mr. King wants us to do the broadcast without it. I mean, like, totally beyond absurd, man. Can you talk to him, Ed?"

Blakely grimaced. "I'd rather stay out of it right now."

Gregor answered. "Mr. King says not to send anybody. Do without it."

Jeremiah held his hand to his forehead.

"Can you put Mr. King on the line?"

"I... don't think so right now. He's busy."

"Come on, Gregor! This is Jeremiah, your old crew-buddy. Can you at least ask the man if he will speak with me?"

"Hang on..."

Jeremiah tapped his mouth with a finger.

"He says he can't talk with you at all tonight."

"All right!" He sighed. "I give up. We'll do the best we can up here. Tell Mr. King for me that I really appreciate his cooperation and professionalism on this. Okay?"

"Yes. Sorry."

Jeremiah punched the off button and slumped back in the chair.

"Why can't Harry or Andy bring the board up?" asked Justina.

"Because what they're doing is more important than what we're doing," replied Blakely angrily. He wanted to intervene for Jeremiah, but knew any further discussion with King could appear provocative. King must have his way for now.

"Well, folks, that simplifies our broadcast," said Jeremiah, biting his lip. "One camera. That means we are better on the balcony than the roof or on the square. We'll use the tripod and set it so we can pan the crowd and the fire and back to announcer and guests. Can you handle the camera, Leo?"

"Sure. You give me directions and I'll do whatever you tell me."

"I've laid it out here." He handed Leo the clipboard. "I'll also give you verbal cues. Mike, can you handle the boom and get crowd noise and the music or whatever?"

"Yeah."

Jeremiah looked at his watch. "It's 2140 hours. We have plenty of time to set up and practice. By air time, everybody should be familiar with my cues and know what we're doing."

Jeremiah turned to Blakely. "I guess that leaves you free, skip, unless you want to be interviewed."

"No thanks. I'd only say something on the air that I shouldn't. I need to stand by in case Tony calls and needs me down there."

"I understand," replied Jeremiah, looking abandoned. "We can do it okay."

Blakely asked, "Can I help you set up?"

"Hardly anything to do. The three of us can handle it."

Blakely asked, "Did we get the square with the logo on it to hang behind Justina?"

Jeremiah sighed.

"Darn! That was the other thing Uncle Lou was supposed to bring with him. This whole thing's going to be totally sketchy!"

Jeremiah looked wistfully around the room. His eyes finally settled on Blakely.

"Think Uncle Lou is okay, skip?"

"Well, I hope so. In his emotional condition—and with Elizabeth leaving—he's probably had too much to drink." Blakely didn't want to think about the possibility that King and Marchese were holding Wafford against his will.

Leo seemed to sense Jeremiah's concern. "They'd call me, if your uncle were really sick," said Leo reassuringly. "I agree with Ed. He's probably suffering from a hangover."

Jeremiah nodded doubtfully.

Justina quipped, "For all his big talk this morning, Mr. King doesn't care a damn how this broadcast goes, does he?"

"I think he knows Jeremiah and you will succeed under any conditions," said Blakely.

Leo asked, "Who wants to eat before we set up? I'm famished!"

Justina and Mike raised their hands.

"What about you, skip?"

"I think I'll pass. I need to call Tony. I might join you later.

Where will you be?"

"Blue Porpoise," said Justina. "I take you men to the Blue Porpoise and we eat escargot! Come with us, Jeremiah. You should not do this program on an empty stomach."

He stood up. "Yeah. That's probably what I need. I haven't eaten all day."

They left. Blakely went up to his room. He opened the cellular phone and dialed Tony.

"Yes?"

"How's it going?"

"Marchese and Swann are standing watch. No sign of Wafford or King. No activity."

"I'll check you later. Call me whenever you need to."

"I will."

Blakely propped the pillow up and laid back. The blue urn held his attention for several minutes. He got up and looked around for a suitable container. Not finding one, he opened the chiffonier and took the white handkerchief from his blazer pocket and spread it flat. He opened the urn and grabbed a handful of Joachim's ashes and placed them on the handkerchief. He drew up the four corners and tied them in a loose knot. Yes, there would be part of Joachim on this mountain top, he said to himself.

He set the bundle next to the urn, wiped his hand across his chest and sat on the bed. If Mel was King and Vatican was Rome, then King was going to fly out to Rome early tomorrow to collect money. It probably meant Marchese would go with him, unless Andy had to stand guard. How to get into the message center? There had to be a way. He reached into his pocket and studied the transcribed messages. Touchstone. Touch stone. He put the messages back in his pocket. He adjusted the pillow against the headboard and got a pen and his yellow-lined pad from his travel case. He would write a long letter to Claudia and send it to the St. George Hotel in Athens. If he was lucky, he would get there before it arrived. He would tell her what had happened and what he thought King and McCloud were up to. In case something were to happen to him, Claudia would know how to get the story to authorities. He began to write.

Dear Claudia...

* * * * *

There was a great commotion below, with crowd noise, music and dogs barking. He had written ten pages, bearing his soul to Claudia. What time was it? My God. 2327 hours. The broadcast was about to begin! His phone was blipping. He clicked it on.

"What's happening?"

"Lights on in the pilot house. Funny, Eddie, they're sett'n all them black sails, but the yards of the squares are turned every which way along with the staysails and driver. Never seen the likes of it."

"Who's on deck?"

"Only Harry. No sign of other boats—small or large—close by."

"Deck lights on?"

"No."

"See any sign of Wafford or the others?"

"About 2310 hours, King came out the forward hatch and looked around. Checked all the sails and got on the telephone and told whoever was in the pilot house to make adjustments on the yards of the foremast. He went below and hasn't come back out. I haven't seen Wafford all night."

"Keep me informed. I'll be sending Mike and Leo down after the broadcast."

"Righto!"

He roused. He stripped off his shirt, ran water in the lavatory, and washed his face, chest, and arms. He dressed and removed the leather album from the dresser. He shoved the bundled ashes into his pocket. A bell tolled. Its voice echoed across the valley.

The hotel was deserted. A crowd of tourists and villagers stood in a packed circle around the pyre of wood and brush. Groups of men milled around the shadows or passed in dark throngs up the hill toward the church. Padopolis's voice could be heard on the other side of the pyre, still giving orders as a group of men made final adjustments to a straw and robed effigy of Judas.

The bright glare of portable television lights on the hotel balcony looked strangely out of place. Mike and Leo were positioned at one end where the camera could sweep across the piazza and back to where Jeremiah sat with Justina, their eyes shining like crystals when they looked into the lights. They were already broadcasting. Lord knows what they were talking about.

Blakely stood among the crowd in the darkness, watching for a moment, then walked to the pyre and shoved the leather album into the brush. He worked through the crowd to the other side to where Elizabeth had sat at the edge of the piazza. He pulled out the bundle and untied it, letting Joachim's ashes cascade to the bracken below. He turned and watched the television broadcast. It seemed to be going smoothly. And if it weren't, there was nothing he could do to help. He walked out of the piazza and up the hill, following the crowd of people who were moving toward the church. There was an outcropping of rocks overlooking the valley just off the road. He would go there where it was quiet and call Tony.

The church bell tolled three times, reverberating across the valley and distant mountains. He dialed.

"Yes."

"Any action?"

"Nothing new. No visitors. Nobody 'cept Swann on deck."

"I'll check back in fifteen minutes."

"Aye, aye."

Blakely moved slowly up a narrow alley, which opened onto a small square. At the far side was the silhouette of the church. Its open doorway was lit golden.

He smelled the sweet scent of burning incense and heard voices singing. He stopped and leaned against an ancient wall, listening as the patriarch of the Greek Orthodox congregation sang out the liturgy in a deep baritone. Through the open door, he could see flickers of light from candles in sconces.

He had forgotten most of the rituals his grandfather had taught him. A chime rang. The priest said something. The people answered. Two lyra and a flute played. More praising. Blakely drew nearer the door.

The priest went into a monologue, speaking of Cristos. The lyra played a haunting melody he thought might be a hymn about death. It had a brooding sound, like he had often felt in his chest. The priest chanted, his voice coming strong and powerfully through the open door.

A man standing inside the door nodded silently, beckoned him in, and handed him a candle. He took it and stood against the wall, watching as the priest in his vestments threw out his hands. It was probably the same man Justina had seen this afternoon through the hole in the wall.

Everyone stood and sang a hymn that was joyous. When it was finished, the priest said something, received a candle from a boy at the altar, and lit the candle from a large one that was burning at the foot of a giant cross. The priest turned to a parishioner and handed this candle to him. The parishioner lit his own candle. "Christos, anesti!" the priest said with deep passion, and the man repeated "Christos, anesti!" and passed the candle to the next person.

Blakely thought of Chris Cunningham, alone on Easter eve with the telegram. Christos, anesti—and he remembered: Christ Has Risen!

The man turned and lit the next person's candle, and this man did likewise, until the light of Christ was passed from one parishioner to another to the very back of the church where Blakely stood leaning against the wall.

The church bell began to toll again. Twelve times. Midnight! A young man next to him turned and Blakely held out the candle, and the man said, "Christos, anesti!" as Blakely's candle burst into flame. At that moment, he felt a resurgence of Joachim's spirit within him, and knew he would forever be connected with man and men, with the Father and with the Son. Blakely took hold of the candle and lit another man's, repeating, "Cristos, anesti!" and then he stood, waiting. A man in the far corner held up his candle. "Christos, anesti," said the man, and the congregation suddenly moved as one toward the doors and Blakely found himself unwittingly at the head of a procession.

He carried his lighted candle out of the church, pushed along the alley by the dark throng. Blakely moved slowly, falling back among them, hearing the sounds of leather shoes on the stones and watching the reflected light of candles play on dark walls and windows as they moved down the narrow way.

He stepped out of the procession when it turned onto the main road, watching the flame of his candle sputtering, and feeling hot wax collecting in the crotch of index finger and thumb. What a wonderful thing is a simple candle, he said to himself. A small flame among the many. A flicker in the firmament. He blew out the candle and put it in his pocket. It was 0010 hours. He dialed Tony.

"Yes."

"Any action?"

"All's quiet. Same as before. No visitors or leavers."

"Thanks, Tony."

He resumed walking with the people. They started singing another hymn. He hummed the tune, recalling that his grandfather would often whistle it as he sat in his rocking chair on the front porch when Blakely was a boy.

The flames of the pyre were already making a glow in the sky. Wood crackled and showers of sparks flew up at intervals to disappear in smoke. White smoke curled upward and reflected the fire glow and smelled sweetly of pine resin.

Below, in the valley, small fires were burning here and there, like the night fires of an alien army waiting to strike at dawn. Near where he figured the cave to be, there was an exceptionally large bonfire, whose flames nearly equaled the size of the fire on the piazza. The peasant farmers were superstitious about caves. It was to the caves that they had always sought refuge from invaders. He supposed the peasants had their own version of purgation and ascension. In times past, worship included the sacrifice of people as well as animals at the hand of a Cretan knife, according to what Alex told him.

He stood at the edge of the piazza, out of the glare of television lights. The priest was saying another prayer in the bright glow. Jeremiah and Justina stood at the edge of the balcony, lighted orange by the flames. Max Padopolis now held the microphone and was apparently describing the ritual. Suddenly, a group of villagers, including Alex, tossed the effigy of Judas onto the fire, and a new burst of bright flame quickly consumed the body as everyone cheered.

The heat was intolerable. Blakely moved through the crowd to the plane tree where Alex normally parked his taxi. It was 0020 hours. He dialed Tony.

"Yes, sir."

"What's going on?"

"They've struck the receptors and set the spars regular. King and Marchese are on deck with Swann. Other than that, no visitors. Haven't seen Wafford."

"Thanks."

The crowd was beginning to disburse and the television lights were off. Bits of ash floated down like small snowflakes, and a slight air swirled them in the firelight. A tired child, held in the arms of his father, began to cry. It was all over. A severance from burdens. Blakely was a free man now, without responsibility for anything or anyone except himself.

CHAPTER 29

Encore

Blakely helped Jeremiah, Leo and Mike tear down and box the equipment. They would store everything at the hotel until morning when they would haul it down to the quay. They carried the equipment downstairs to the hotel lobby and stacked it in a closet Manolis assured them was totally secure.

"Why don't we go to the patio and talk?" asked Justina. "I feel very tired, yet exhilarated!"

They followed her and sat around the large table in the center. Jeremiah looked beat, but happy. "Did you realize," he said, "that CDN kept us on the air 'til after the effigy was thrown into the fire? An extra twelve minutes!"

"They must have liked it, then," said Justina.

"Thanks to Max, people back home understood what was happening. Seeing Judas thrown into the fire was really cool! A perfect way to end the show."

"Ya," said Justina in a low voice. "Perhaps the last show."

"I thought everything worked smooth," said Jeremiah. 'Cept for the breeze. Now and then, it would shift and we got showered with sparks and couldn't see for all the smoke," he said, laughing.

Mike looked down at his jacket.

"Yeah, I got the holes to prove it." Mike's yellow jacket was riddled with brown and black holes.

"It was kind of eerie," said Leo, "seeing what looked like a real person being burned, you know?"

Blakely pulled his cellular phone out and dialed Tony. It was

0115 hours of Easter Sunday.

"Yes?"

"What's happening?"

"Not a thing right now. "

"Seen any sign of Wafford?"

"He came on deck once with King a few minutes ago. Stood at the gangway looking out for awhile, then he went back down the foc'sle hatch. King followed him inside. Last I seen of 'em."

"Nobody came or left the ship?"

"No, sir."

"Leo and Mike will be down to relieve you. I know you must be tired."

"Just a wee bit cross-eyed is all. Tell 'em to bring me some food when they come. I'm famished!"

"I will."

Blakely dialed another number.

"*Sea Siren*, Comm Center. Tobok here."

"How'd it go, Gregor?"

"Uh, fine, sir. Transmission went perfect. We got a positive confirmation from Atlanta a few minutes ago."

"Good. Did they say anything about the quality?"

"Yes, sir. In fact, they asked whether we had any more tapes to send them. Seems they could use all we have. I told them I'd check with Jeremiah."

Opportunity, said Blakely to himself. Now's your chance. Do it right!

"We've got plenty. In fact, now would be a perfect time to send it to Atlanta, don't you think? Send it while they're so positive?"

"I'll have to discuss it with Mr. King first."

"Why don't you put him on the line, Gregor? I need to talk to him about some other business, too."

"Hold on... I'll check."

Come on! Tobok, don't deny me!

"King here."

Presto!

"Gresham! Gregor tells me we scored with Atlanta!"

"Yessiree. One of them producers at CDN sent us a glowing message."

"Yeah. Gregor says they are asking us for extra videos—like the ones we recorded yesterday. Jeremiah has plenty and there are outtakes—stuff he edited out. There's also lots of footage of the villagers preparing the pyre and Judas." He lied. "I was thinking we ought to send it while they're so pleased with us. It might lead to more exposure."

"Yes, well... This sale takes priority right now, Ed. You can understand that."

"I was thinking of doing it right now—before we lose the opportunity. Jeremiah and I could come aboard and use the studio and comm center and have everything transmitted within an hour or so. Hell, we could leave here in two minutes. We wouldn't bother you or Tobok or anybody. We could also bring the equipment back on board. I'm concerned about security up here. We've got thousands of dollars of equipment and no place to keep it except in the van."

There was a long pause. He's thinking of the consequences both ways. All ways. How it would look not to respond to CDN? What if somebody did break into the van and stole everything? It was time to keep his mouth shut and let King run it through his mind. He's thinking. He's thinking!

"You talking 'bout not more than an hour?"

"Yes, sir. We'd be off the ship and back up here before 0400 hours."

"And you'd leave everything neat and clean? As you found it?"

"Yes, sir."

"Well, come on, then, but you gotta hurry. We're all tuckered out from a long day and night! Bring all the cameras and stuff, you hear?"

"Yes, sir. We'll be there."

He hung up before King could change his mind.

THE MINOTAUR   311

"Show time, Jeremiah! You and me and the *Sea Siren*'s comm center. We are doing a special, late night encore presentation for CDN News, complete with special feature of computer files."

"All right!" said Jeremiah.

"The downside is we have to haul all the equipment back tonight. I'd suggest keeping at least one camera and the transmitter. I need to make one phone call. Why don't you guys start loading the van so we can be on our way?"

"Will do," said Leo, looking a bit confused.

Blakely went to the sitting room and lifted the receiver of the black phone. He reached an overseas operator. The phone rang. A female voice answered above the static.

"You've reached the Gorton residence."

"Millie? Is Travis there?"

"Is that you, Ed?"

"Yeah."

"Just a moment, please."

"Travis. What's up, Ed?"

"Time to move. I'm going to be sending computer stuff to CDN News within one hour. Is your contact ready?"

"Have two or three available. I'll get on the phone."

"When you get to CDN, the man you need to see is Steve Summer. He's a producer."

"Steve Summer. I'll call and alert him also, if you would like."

"Please. If he isn't available, ask to speak to the station manager."

"No problem. Be careful, Ed."

"I will."

Blakely went outside. They had loaded the van, keeping a VCR, the portable transmitter, two battery packs, two portable lights, and a small video camera in the locked closet. Mike, Leo, Jeremiah and Blakely piled in the van and drove down the hill.

"Lot of smoke for this time of night," Blakely said as they rounded the hairpin curve at the bottom of the mountain. A huge orange glow reflected off trees along the road.

Beyond the trees in the clearing before the cave was a monstrous bonfire burning. Mike pulled the van to the side of the road and stopped. The sounds of lyres and flutes and voices filled the air in mysterious chants and responses. There must be fifty or more people gathered around the fire.

"They're guarding the cave all right. An all night celebration! Wish we could go join them," said Blakely, "but we have more important business. Let's go, Mike."

* * * * *

Swann was waiting in the launch at the quay. They stacked the equipment and Swann transported them to the vessel, where they off-loaded, carrying the black boxes to the television studio as Marchese watched amidships. King unlocked the studio hatch and followed Blakely and Jeremiah in and leaned against a bulwark as they stacked and secured the boxes with stretch cords.

"You won't take more'n an hour you say?"

"Yes, sir," replied Jeremiah.

"I hafta say," said King, with a wince for a smile, "that producer... believe his name is Steve... had high praise for yer work, boy!"

Jeremiah tried a big magic smile, but rendered a weak facsimile.

"If he liked that, wait 'til he sees what I got for him this morning!"

"You need Gregor to hep you?"

"No, thanks. I'll get these tapes put on and transmit from the comm center myself, if that's okay."

"That's fine!"

King was relaxed. Certainly, he wasn't suspicious. The Touchstone thing—whatever it was—must have gone off without a hitch.

"Guess I can leave you boys here. Yer uncle Lou's a bit under the weather. I need to check on him. I'll unlock the comm room."

"Is he going to be okay?" asked Jeremiah.

"Oh, yes. Gregor's with him. Guess you know yer Aunt Elizabeth left him today, don't you?"

"Yes."

"He'll be jest fine in a few days. Not to worry about him."

The toothpick rolled from one side of his mouth to another and the tick in King's jaw was as regular as a heartbeat.

"See you boys later."

Jeremiah immediately turned on the tape equipment and monitors and started a full-length, uncut tape of Friday's activities around the dig site and in Kastelli.

"That ought to do fine," he whispered. His hands were shaking as he turned the volume up on some carpet music and on a separate voice-over, so it sounded like a completed tape transmission.

"Shall we put the DO NOT DISTURB sign on?"

"Yeah," replied Blakely. "On both hatches."

They entered the comm center and locked the hatch.

Jeremiah went immediately to the computer and entered a common password. He nervously opened his notebook and followed the prompts he had copied off the split-screen. He keyed in the codes for complete access. The screen prompt asked for a verification code. Jeremiah checked and carefully typed it in and touched ENTER. A list of files appeared.

Jeremiah swung around in the computer chair.

He took a deep breath. "I feel all shook up!"

"Before we down-load, let's see what we've got," Blakely whispered.

"Which file would you like?"

"Whatever Tobok was using last."

Jeremiah turned back to the screen, scrolled down to WING and opened the file. Blakely leaned over his shoulder.

"Go to the last entry."

Jeremiah hit two different keys and the last entry, dated today, appeared on the screen. *Zeb: Leaving Vatican late tonight with Climber. Will arrive tomorrow night by vespers. Mel.*

They read the message.

"Let's see the message before this one."

Melvin: Give status of Touch. Let me know any changes. Keep Lucky under control. Zeb.

"Print that out, Jeremiah. One hard copy."

"Okay."

Jeremiah loaded the instructions for printing and sat back.

"I hate to think about it, but do you think they'll kill Uncle Lou?"

"Who can say? They're playing it like a regular up-and-up business deal right now. They don't dare do anything stupid unless he threatens them in some way."

Jeremiah switched back to the main file index.

"Okay. What would you like to see next?"

"Can you scroll down slowly?"

"Sure."

Jeremiah touched a key and the listings moved slowly up the screen.

"Hold right there. What about MIDAS. Can you open it?"

Jeremiah opened it. Several messages appeared between SPIDER and ROYAL.

"Can you move down and see if there any messages between 22 and 24 March?"

"Okay." Jeremiah and Blakely watched the screen as the messages were searched.

"Here's one," said Jeremiah, "for 22 March 1996."

SPIDER: Climber arrives your place 2455 hours 23 March. Prepared for 55 pound pack capacity. If any changes, will let you know by 2300 hours same day. ROYAL.

"Have any ideas who 'Climber' is," asked Blakely.

"Yeah. Andy Marchese."

"And who is ROYAL?"

The message copies appeared in the printer tray.

"Mr. King?"

"Yeah. And Spider?"

"I have no idea about him."

"I don't either, except he's a guy who wants to create a web. Maybe buy a communications web?"

"Too much."

"This message was sent the day we sailed up the Adriatic to Trieste. As I recall, Tobok spent the night holed up in here; he was probably watching for any message showing a change in plans. Remember how Andy Marchese disappeared after we arrived? Showed up the morning we were to set sail all worn out. Said he went climbing with a friend at Udine?"

"I remember noticing he was all scratched on his face and leg. Where's Udine?"

"Several miles northwest of Trieste. The train runs there from Trieste." Blakely realized a more logical destination would be Gorizia, which was a border town closest to Slovenia, roughly sixty miles over the mountains from Ljubljana, the capital of Slovenia. But why up there rather than making a transaction, say, down along the coast at one of those little ports? Too much chance of UN and NATO monitoring, he supposed.

"What could he carry that would be fifty five pounds?" asked Blakely.

"I don't know. Drugs? Money?"

"How 'bout gold and maybe an extra several million in greenbacks?"

"Wow! Do you really think so?"

"Have no way of proving it."

"Think it's on this ship someplace?"

"No. I think it was put aboard McCoud's jet and flown out to a safe haven. Maybe dropped by parachute over McCloud's plantation before they landed at Gulfport. Who knows? Maybe to a Swiss bank account. Gresham King probably waited for it and took it by train someplace where they could fly it out."

"That's why Mr. King got off the boat?"

"Believe so. A down payment. Looks like the rest will be paid in Rome—or else a pick-up point will be agreed upon. Then, the good ole boys will head back to Gulfport."

"My, God! And to think Uncle Lou is messed up in all this?"

"Yeah. Can you print out these messages? And after you get through with that, Jeremiah, I want you to prepare for transmission of these files."

Jeremiah took another deep breath and looked wide-eyed at Blakely.

"You really want to do this?"

"Yes. It's 0215 hours. I want you to transmit a copy of this entire file to CDN News ASAP. Send it with instructions that it be held for review by Travis Gorton and the FBI. Label it TOP SECRET. Guess that covers it. Can you do one more thing?"

"I guess so." Jeremiah was struggling to stay calm. His hands were visibly shaking.

"Can we unhook your powerbook and take it with us? It's got your split screen video stored on it. I may have to produce it as evidence."

"Okay. You know, skip, that powerbook does belong to me. I brought it on board with me."

"All the more reason you should have it."

"I don't know how you'll get it off this ship is all."

"Let's let Mr. King decide. Is there a case for it?"

"Yeah. It's in the same drawer."

"While you are preparing to transmit here, how 'bout if I go into the studio and pack it up?"

"You'll need my drawer key. I didn't turn it in yesterday. It's the second left-hand drawer of my work cabinet next to this bulkhead. You know how to save, close, and turn off a powerbook?"

"Yeah. One of the few computers I do know about. I've got one in Newport Beach."

Jeremiah pulled out his wallet and extracted a small, silver key and handed it to Blakely. The printed messages dropped into the tray. Blakely stuffed them inside his shirt.

"What else can I do?"

THE MINOTAUR   317

"Try to relax and think good thoughts, Jeremiah. There's nothing else to do, once you get the stuff ready to transmit. While you are waiting, you might check Tobok's console for anything."

"One more question, skipper. Why would Uncle Lou do this?"

"Your guess is as good as mine. Maybe when he gets better, he'll tell us."

Blakely opened the hatch and entered the television studio. He locked the hatch and unlocked the drawer. He detached the power book cables and lifted the computer out. It was now operating on battery. He moved the icon to SAVE and clicked, then to CLOSE, and clicked, and then to SHUT DOWN, and clicked.

He closed the lid and detached the other end of the cable from the power box. He opened the black leather case and slid the computer and cable inside. He gathered a few micro disks off Jeremiah's work table and put them into a side pocket. Blakely unlocked the door. The companionway was clear. He closed the hatch again and opened the comm room hatch and locked it behind him. Jeremiah sat there with beads of perspiration on his forehead and above his lip. His hands were still shaking.

He whispered. "It's ready."

"What do I do?" Blakely asked.

"Push that key. That will download and send the files to CDN. I've marked a message TOP SECRET and FOR FBI EYES ONLY. Think that'll work?"

"I'm sure it will. At least it will get their attention." He took a deep breath. "I know you are worried about Lou. We'll try to help him." He paused with his finger over the send key. "Well, Jeremiah, here goes!"

He pressed the key. The files clicked off at lightning speed. He had never seen a computer work so fast to download and transmit records. They waited. In minutes, the transmission was completed. A confirmation signal appeared.

"We've done our part. It's up to the FBI to do the easy part—determine whether they are good guys or bad guys. You can close up shop."

Blakely unlocked the hatch and checked the time. It was 0255 hours. Jeremiah sat at the console and punched several keys, which closed the special access channel.

A knock on the hatch door. Jeremiah wiped perspiration from his face with his sleeve.

"You boys 'bout through in there?"

It was King. Blakely opened the hatch.

"We just finished. Jeremiah has a favor to ask, Gresham. He forgot his powerbook yesterday. Can he take it with him?"

King touched his toothpick.

"Where is it?"

"In the television studio," replied Jeremiah.

"Well, now, let's go see 'bout this."

King left the comm room and strode into the studio like a storm trooper.

"This it here?"

"Yes, sir," said Jeremiah, breathing carefully now. "It has my name and social security number engraved on the bottom."

"Where 'bouts?"

"Just a second, sir."

Jeremiah nervously unzipped the case and lifted the computer out and turned it over.

"Well, sure 'nough. Must be yours. Whatcha got in them pockets?"

Jeremiah stuck his hand inside them, checking each. He pulled out the disks Blakely had put there and read their handwritten labels.

Jeremiah replied, "These belong to the ship. They are audios of carpet music."

"Carpet music, you say? Funny name for music."

Jeremiah handed King the disks. He immediately set them down on the bench. His slate gray eyes shifted back to Blakely and Jeremiah.

"Well, I s'pect you boys need to get back up on that there

mountain. Get some good sleep so you can travel. What time do you leave out?"

"Looks like Monday, now. Everything is booked tomorrow," replied Blakely.

"Go back and get some shut-eye. We all need it."

"Yeah. We're pretty much knocked out," replied Blakely. He felt the messages inside his shirt. They crinkled when he touched them. He zipped his windbreaker part way.

"Any chance I could say hi to Uncle Lou, Mr. King?"

"Sorry, boy. He's gone to bed. Plum worn hisself out. You can see him tomorrow, maybe. He'll be coming up there probably in the morning to collect his clothes."

They went up the companionway and out on deck. A brisk wind was coming out of the southeast.

"Looks to be a change of weather," said Blakely.

"Yes. Well, we've been mighty lucky with weather. Mighty lucky."

"Good night, Gresham."

"Good night," said King. "Happy Orthodox Easter Bunny!"

King seemed in the best possible frame of mind. Almost cocky. Swann took them to the quay without uttering a word. They got out and drove the van to the hotel where Tony and the mates were staying. Leo ran over to an all-night taverna to get Tony some supper. As Blakely climbed the steps, the impact of what he had done was beginning to hit home. He felt sick at his stomach. His hands were shaking, and he was shivering. He knocked on the door of the suite.

Tony had a funny expression when he saw them.

"You all right, Ed?"

"Yeah. I just sent a message to the FBI. It exposes the whole operation."

Tony and Mike did a high five.

"Way to go, skipper," said Mike. "Hope they nail those bastards big time."

Jeremiah sat down next to the window, biting his lip. Tears

began to stream down his face. "I can't help it, skip," he said in a broken voice. "Whatever Uncle Lou's done, he's still my uncle. And I feel so badly for him—leaving him there—not even getting to see he's all right."

"Yeah. I know." Blakely came over and wrapped his arm around Jeremiah. "We couldn't do any more tonight. I'm very proud of you. You are very brave."

Jeremiah cupped his large hands over his face and continued weeping. "I didn't feel very brave."

"Neither did I. It's natural to be scared. I'm still shaking!"

Mike retrieved some napkins and handed them to Jeremiah.

"Sorry!" said Jeremiah, taking them and wiping his face.

"No problem," said Mike. "How about some water?"

"I'm okay."

Blakely patted Jeremiah on the back. "What you need is some sleep. You've been under pressure all day."

Leo came in with Tony's food. Blakely picked up the binoculars and sat down on the couch. He lifted the glasses toward the *Sea Siren*. Swann stood at the gangway, looking across in their direction. He suddenly felt rotten about all of it. He hadn't come here to destroy people, but that's how it might turn out. It was like being punched in the stomach to realize Lou Wafford had suckered him into all this. Worse, the guy might be a traitor. He put the glasses in his lap.

"One helluva bad trip," said Blakely to no one in particular. "I've never been one who liked to hurt people."

"Not your fault, Eddie," said Tony, munching the lamb. "These people bring it all on themselves."

"Yeah, but it doesn't make you feel any better knowing that."

"I spose not. Well, if you'll pardon me, I'll finish my supper and go to bed. I'm so tired I won't be able to go to church tomorrow."

Mike and Leo opened bottles of beer and sat at the dining table. Tony turned and disappeared with his plate through a doorway.

"Jeremiah?"

"Yes, skip?"

"Do you know the number at CDN News, Atlanta?"

"Production?"

"Yeah."

"It's 404 241-1008. Steve Summer is our man."

He jotted the number down and called the overseas operator. It was 0345 hours. That meant it was 2045 Atlanta time. He waited for the connection.

Blakely looked out across the darkness of the Sea of Crete, trying to relax and allow the chaotic thoughts which were racing through his mind to settle. The sea, Blakely, look at the sea. Look beneath the sea and know that you cannot ever know it. Take hold of the mystery and embrace it. Whatever Wafford is doing to himself over there is all part of the mystery. And in order to do your part, you must understand that you cannot understand, but that you must act and do your part as it is revealed unto you. He laughed inwardly, thinking that sort of strained logic is what you were taught at intelligence school. CIA was the same: don't expect to see the big picture—your duty is the small picture, what you are asked to do. Also sounded like religion: just do what the priest and the Book say; don't argue. Believe and follow orders and everything shall come unto you.

Some calm returned, but he knew there were no words he could think of that would help him to face Lou Wafford. But he would face him later today, and he hoped he would say the right words.

"CDN News Production Department. Welcome to the World! This is Sherry. How may I direct your call!"

"Steve Summer, please."

"Who may I say is calling?"

"Edward Blakely."

"I'm afraid Mr. Summer is in a meeting right now. Is there anyone else you could speak with or would you like his voice mail?"

"Can you tell me whether Travis Gorton is with Mr. Summer?"

"Yes, sir. He is."

"It is important that I speak with him. I am calling from the island of Crete in the Mediterranean."

"Really! One moment, please."

"This is Travis Gorton."

"Ed Blakely, Trav. How's it going?"

"Thanks for the great lead time, buddy! Mr. Summer and I are waiting for two agents to come over to view the files. I've had a difficult time convincing anybody at the Bureau that time was of the essence."

"Has anybody actually looked at the files?"

"One of the technicians and Mr. Summer have seen a few message pages, but don't understand any of it. I'm waiting to see whether the agents will want me in on the viewing."

"Well, Trav, the ship is to be taken over by a foreign group later today. I don't have all the answers, but I think she may be loaded with military communications equipment. I haven't a clue as to how it will be used, but in the wrong hands it could be trouble. The players could be good guys or bad guys. Only the FBI and CIA have the means to determine that."

"Two fellas in suits just walked in who look like agents. You've given me what I need to know, Ed. Unless you have something else, I'll talk with you later."

"Nothing else to report. If I don't here from you, I'll call you tomorrow at your office."

"Meaning Monday?"

"Yes."

He hung up and looked at Jeremiah. He was sound asleep.

"Jeremiah? Time to go up on the mountain and get some sleep."

Jeremiah roused and got unsteadily to his feet.

Leo asked, "How long do you want us to stay here, skip?"

"Plan to keep watch at least until our pals over there leave and the new group takes possession."

Leo said, "We're proud as hell of what you did, Ed. We wouldn't have thought to do it that way—using the computer and all."

"Wasn't me. Jeremiah, here, did the tough part. All I had to do was punch the right key. I learned tonight that a single computer key can be more lethal than I'd ever dreamed. Kind of like pushing the button that releases a bomb."

He walked to the door with Jeremiah.

"See you!"

They got into the van. Blakely drove slowly through the dark and empty streets of Iraklion, turning onto the road to Knossos. Fires were still visible on the hillsides. Jeremiah lay back, head against the window, sound asleep.

CHAPTER 30

Orthodox Easter Sunday

A beeping noise grew louder. It was the phone. He switched on the light and grabbed it.

"Blakely."

Outside the open window, the embers from the bonfire still crackled. Wood smoke in the room had made his throat dry. He got up.

"They're leaving," said Leo. "They just got out of the launch with their suitcases and stuff."

"Who?"

"Just like you said. Marchese and King."

Blakely walked to the lavatory and opened the tap. He filled a glass with water and drank.

"What about the others?"

"Harry's taking the launch back to the boat. Tobok's standing at the gangway. Haven't seen Wafford."

He shut off the tap and carried the glass back and set it on the bedside table.

"Tell me what you see, Leo."

"King is standing on the dock next to their gear. Marchese's unlocked the Rover and starting it. He's bringing it around. Harry's tied up the launch and is walking up the gangway... King is helping Marchese load the Rover. They must be leaving for good, skip, because Marchese has all three of his climbing bags and his B-4. King has his two suitcases."

He looked at his watch. 0415 hours. "Yeah. They're on plan."

He drank some more water.

"King and Marchese are in the Rover and heading out. Tobok and Swann are headed toward the foc'sle. Now Tobok is coming back amidships. He's sitting down in a deck chair. Guess he's on watch the rest of the night."

"Good man, Leo. Will you jot all that down? Keep the log as detailed as possible."

"Will do."

Blakely lay back down and switched the light off. He supposed McCloud's jet was waiting at Iraklion Airport to whisk them off to Rome. So be it! They're probably all puffed out with their success like two turkeys.

* * * * *

The church bell clanged and echoed across the mountains. Blakely roused. It was 0600 hours. He could smell roasting lamb and special Easter cakes blending with the wood smoke of the bonfire. Alex said the baker cooked lamb for the entire village. He picked up the phone and dialed.

"Yes?"

"What's happening, Mike?"

"Nada. Rover's still gone. Tobok looks like he's asleep on deck. Swann and Wafford haven't shown their faces."

"Have you guys talked about when you'll go home?"

"We've agreed to stay on as long as you need us. We're in no hurry."

"You can head out anytime tomorrow. If you want to stay here and play tourists, that's up to you. I plan to leave in the morning myself. There's nothing left to do."

"You don't want to stick around and see what's in the cave?"

"Justina's capable of handling it, provided she gets a sponsor. Besides, I'm not sure I want to see her humiliated again. Who knows? She might break into the hotel this time."

"Uh, oh!"

"What?"

"Wafford's come on deck. He looks like a scruffy old bull that's just lost a fight. He's got Tobok out of his chair. Tobok is pointing toward the gangway. Wafford's waving his arms and ranting. He's shaking his finger in Tobok's face. Now, he's stomping back to the aft companionway. Tobok is sitting down again. The beat goes on."

"Enter it in your log."

"If we decide not to stay here," said Mike, "we could all go on the ferry together tomorrow. Be nice to have a night to ourselves and celebrate. The real crew of *Sea Siren*."

"Great idea. Jeremiah can come along. We'll talk about it later."

"See you."

At least Wafford was alive! Maybe Wafford thought he was going stateside with Marchese and King. Blakely put on his robe and went down the hall to shower.

* * * * *

"Good morning, Manolis. Do I have any messages or calls?"

"Only that Mrs. Cunningham is waiting for you to join her on the patio."

Blakely sat down with Justina and Jeremiah at one of the few clean tables. A coating of the lightest gray ash covered most surfaces, making everything appear waxen like rice paper. The leaves of the lemon trees looked frosted. Milos, the clerk, was helping Bernard, the handyman, to clean the tables in time for the tourists. A waiter brought them coffee.

"I take it," Blakely said, "you both are not partaking of the feast this morning?"

"It's after church," Justina explained. "I would like to attend it."

"I would, too," said Jeremiah.

"Neither of you has heard from Lou?"

Jeremiah shook his head and yawned. The guy was still beat.

"There was a telegram waiting for me this morning," said Justina in a resigned voice. "It was from Christopher. He is granting me my wish."

Blakely said, "Oh? You don't sound enthralled with the prospects. I thought separation and divorce were what you wanted."

She dipped her head and laughed hollowly.

"What I want! Ha! Strangely, when sometimes you get what you want, the shock is too much. I really didn't believe it would be so easy for Christopher. It rather makes me sad instead of happy."

Jeremiah sat pensively, elbows on table, resting his chin in his hands, listening.

"Would you have felt differently this morning if you had discovered a bunch of Minoan relics yesterday?"

"Ya. No doubt! That was so awful! I don't know that I will ever get over that."

"Sure you will. Monday morning, you'll be in the cave again."

"To find what? It's all been a pipe dream."

"You sound like your soon-to-be ex-husband."

She rubbed the back of her pretty neck.

"I know. I know."

Jeremiah came alive. He pulled a folded paper out of his pocket.

"You got a rave review from your performance last night, if that's any consolation."

Jeremiah handed her the paper. She read it.

"Wonderful. They suggest we continue with archeological programs!"

Blakely asked, "Who suggests?"

"I was so sleepy last night, skip, I forgot to tell you. While I was waiting, I made a copy of the message from Steve Summer. Mr. King didn't have the decency to show it to me."

She handed it to Blakely.

"Summer says he wants a series."

"Yes. Really cool!" Jeremiah's magic was back.

"He's basically offering you two a contract, right? You are under no obligations to Crete Enterprises any longer."

Jeremiah leaned back and stretched. His smile lingered. He glanced sheepishly at Justina.

Jeremiah asked, "Would you want to do some? See how it goes?"

Justina said, "Sure! What can we lose?"

Jeremiah held his hand out for a low five. She smacked his hand lightly, then raised hers. He smacked it. She held on.

"Partners?"

"Far out! Yes," cried Jeremiah.

"You guys even have a camera and some lights. Maybe we can convince Tobok to let us have the control board you needed last night."

"We could ask Mr. King if we could buy some equipment," said Jeremiah.

"Probably not cool," Blakely replied. For the first time, he shared with Justina what had transpired with King and how he had transmitted files to CDN. He brought them both up-to-date on King and Marchese leaving the *Sea Siren*, and the expectation that new owners would be boarding sometime today.

Padapolis came through the entry in a hurry, looking like a pallbearer in black suit and white flower in his lapel. He shouted. "Have you heard the news?"

Blakely was taken aback. "What news, Max?"

"The cave! The peasants hold pagan sacrifice of a bull calf and have all night celebration. They worship the old one."

"Who is the old one?" asked Justina, holding her hands prayerfully to her chin.

"Mithras. You do not know of Mithras?"

"Ya! I do know! What about Mithras?"

Padapolis's eyes opened wide as he made a sweeping gesture with his hands.

"They say the temple of Mithras—which has been lost here for nearly two thousand years—has been found. It is at the bottom of the cave! There are many bones there. An altar. Sacrifice."

Justina pushed back her chair and stood up.

"You mean they found a temple?"

"Yes! That's what I tell you. According to legend which I learn as a young boy on my father's lap, Mithras lives inside this mountain, except nobody knows how to get inside to find him. Last night, they discover the temple again. Yes. You must go down and see to it!"

Blakely asked, "Is Mithras a Minoan God?"

"No," replied Justina. "Mithras was a mysterious God worshipped by a secret cult at the time of Christ. Occasionally, one of these temples is discovered. Let's hope and pray this one has not been destroyed by the early Christians—or our recent celebrants!"

"Hey! Our first exclusive, Justina!" Jeremiah exclaimed.

"I'll call and get Leo and Tony to drive up," said Blakely.

CHAPTER 31

Mithras

Blakely pulled the van into the clearing. Some party! In the middle of the clearing were the smoking embers of a bonfire and the cleaned carcass of a calf. Two old men sat upon the ground next to the cave entrance, smoking pipes. On one side, the ground was stained with blood. Hundreds of footprints showed people had danced in a circle around the fire. Bits of wildflowers were strewn here and there. Several half-burnt fagots lay about the litter of charcoal, bones, and bits of meat. A scraggly dog lay under a plane tree gnawing a bone with meat still on it. Justina, Leo, Tony, and Jeremiah got out and unloaded the portable video equipment.

"This is really cool!" Jeremiah looked around. "Too much!"

Justina went over to the men and spoke with them. She returned, smiling brightly.

"Good news! It is approximately eighty meters down to the temple. No earthquake faults, they tell me. "

Blakely examined a burnt torch. "Too bad we don't have any good lamps. Our flashlights will be puny in there."

The two old men got to their feet and came over. The younger of the two took the fagot from Blakely, shaking his head in disgust. He threw it in the smoldering ashes and held up a finger.

"He's saying they will make you torches," said Justina.

The two men unfolded their knives and went into the brush. Tony followed, speaking Greek with them.

"While they make torches, let's us go in, no?" said Justina.

"Leo? Would you mind watching the equipment?" Blakely asked. "Jeremiah needs to check out camera shots inside."

"Suits me."

Leo sat down next to the equipment cases and rested his back against the van.

Blakely followed Justina and Jeremiah into the cave. He checked his watch. 0741 hours. It was 2441 hours, Atlanta time. Travis would be asleep. No chance he would call.

Entering the cavern where they had discovered the remains of Kemft, the passage was just wide enough to walk comfortably, much like the corridor where they found the jewels. Descending the passage, however, the cave soon opened wide enough to drive a jeep through.

"Bone fragments," she announced. Blakely came up next to where she was crouched, examining pieces of bone. "Fairly large animal," she said, taking photographs. "Perhaps a fox we have here," noting a yellow bone approximately nine inches in length. "I will return here to examine them later," Justina said.

She continued. The passage was growing larger as they descended. He could sense her anxiety. There were more bone fragments mixed in the dark gravel. Now and then, Justina would kneel down, examine them, get up, and move on. It was difficult to tell how far into the cave they had walked, but Blakely figured it must be a sixty yards or more.

"There are more and more bone fragments, Edward," said Justina.

She knelt down, and examined a thick gray bone extending out of the dirt. "A large one, perhaps the femur of a goat."

"How old do you think that bone is?" asked Jeremiah.

"Very difficult to say," Justina replied. "I would imagine at least five hundred years old, maybe much older. If early Christians sealed the cave and there are no other entrances, then it is certainly 1800 to 1900 years old."

"Too cool!"

"More bones," announced Justina. "This time of a bull."

"Large horns!" said Blakely. "Think they kept it down here?"

"Mithras favored sacrificing bulls. Perhaps this one was brought here for sacrifice." She knelt down next to the skull, which had thick, pointed horns. She took a soft brush and dusted away the dark gravel from a shoulder bone.

"Sometimes you can tell when an animal was sacrificed by finding cut marks on bones or even broken bones. I can't tell from these. Too many of the body bones are smashed."

"How would they feed a bull way down here?" asked Jeremiah.

"I don't suppose the bulls stayed alive long enough to get hungry," replied Justina.

She took photographs. The cave was chilly without being damp. The temperature appeared to remain the same. You could taste the staleness of the air in the back of your throat.

"Another bull skull," said Blakely. Ahead, the cave floor was littered with bones of every size and shape. "A regular bone yard! Some are crunched. I guess the people last night did their share of damage."

"Ya. It will be interesting to see how deep these bones are. Perhaps they represent hundreds of beasts."

Justina flashed her light into a large alcove, upon what seemed like a pile of large yellow and gray balls. They were skulls! She didn't seem at all surprised.

"Human skulls. Arranged neatly."

"Unreal," said Jeremiah, touching a skull with his finger.

"It doesn't shock you, Justina?" asked Blakely.

"Not really. I am thinking these may be victims of human sacrifice. Complete human skeletons there," she said matter-of-factly, pointing to the lower side of the alcove. She measured. "Four meters wide by ten in depth, two meters high."

She paused long enough to take more photographs. Just ahead, the passage leveled out and straightened. "Ah! Look, Edward and Jeremiah," she said, flashing her lamp ahead of them.

"A carved portal! Meinen Gott!" She exclaimed. "My prayers have been answered! And there is Mithras, depicted above the en-

THE MINOTAUR 333

trance! Yes, Christopher James Cunningham the Third, your nearly ex-wife has made a significant discovery. This is authentic antiquity! " she said, looking up at the vaulted rocks above them.

She began taking photographs as Blakely and Jeremiah stood spellbound. Stones had been fitted on either side of the nine foot wide passage to form an entrance perhaps six feet wide and ten feet high. On either side was the elongated, carved, red-painted outline of Mithras in a peaked cap holding a spear which was angled toward the opening, much like the Egyptian hieroglyphic forms from tombs. A snake entwined his body. Above the entrance, were carved outlines of various animals including a scorpion, a snake, a dog, a raven, and a bull.

"Cool! I can't wait to get my video!" said Jeremiah.

She stepped inside, flashing her light on the walls. "Mienen Gott! Look at the murals on the walls! In so excellent condition!"

Holy Moses, said Blakely to himself. Beyond the entrance was a large gallery, perhaps eighty feet long by forty wide. At the far end, a bas-relief of Mithras, stood twelve or more feet high. A frightening image. In peaked cap with a snake curled around his body, he was plunging a dagger into the neck of a bull while looking down upon a white marble slab.

"Wow," exclaimed Jeremiah, flashing his light along the walls.

To the left, another scene. Several men wearing masks of animals held knives and spears, all pointing toward a naked man who, with head bowed, knelt in the center, appearing to be waiting for them to either kill him or spare him.

On the right wall, Mithras was thrusting a dagger into a bull as blood spouted from the mortal wound. A naked man bowed before the bull, in supplication.

"Mithras initiation," said Justina, her voice hardly audible.

"Incredible!" said Blakely.

"Men were brought to be initiated into the cult of Mithras. You see? It is all explained by the murals."

"Wait 'til they see this back in Atlanta!" Jeremiah exclaimed.

"You see how the bulls were sacrificed?" asked Justina. "Perhaps the disbelieving were also sacrificed here. Ach! This is a dream come true. I never believed I would be the first to discover a temple so perfectly preserved as this!"

Justina flashed her light across the floor of the temple.

"See the shallow pit, in front of that block of white marble? It remains dark from blood. That is where the initiate and the bull were brought, just in front of the stone carving of Mithras."

Flower petals were strewn on the stone slab. Burnt fagots lay around the base. The peasants must have held their own ceremonies here last night.

Justina explained. "The white marble serves as the altar. The celebrants would stand probably on either side, wearing masks and brandishing daggers and spears just as depicted in the murals. We do not know how the initiate was tested, but you can see he would be terribly frightened. Perhaps it required that he assist in killing the bull or perhaps he had to show his faith by being unafraid. At any rate, the bull was slaughtered. It is presumed everyone taking part in the ceremony drank the blood."

"And you say this happened around the time of Christ?" asked Blakely.

"Ya," Justina replied.

"How large was this cult?" asked Jeremiah.

Justina ran her hand along the wall. "There are temples like this one found across the Mediterranean—even as far away as Scotland."

"Were women able to join?" Jeremiah asked.

"Only men, as far as we know," said Justina. "Quite an interesting change from the original Bull Goddess of the Minoans, two thousand years earlier, where bulls and human beings were sacrificed in the name of Taurus and the Minotaur."

"The beliefs changed because the constellations were changing," said Blakely, thinking of his discussions with Joachim. "But how could constellations change?"

Justina said, "Scientists say that approximately 26,000 years ago, the Earth wobbled on its axis, beginning a slow change in

THE MINOTAUR 335

how we perceive the stars and their locations. This did not become really apparent to early cultures until they began a precise study of the heavens. Cretans in 2,000 B.C., knew exactly where Taurus ought to be located in the sky at planting time. Perhaps the bull goddess culture began as a means of worship when Minoan priests observed a subtle shift in Taurus's position. By the time of the Mithras cult, Taurus had slipped further, causing astrologers serious concern."

Jeremiah asked, "Why would these people depend so much on astrology?"

"They believed the Earth was the center of the universe. It was thought that when you died, you began a journey through the Heavens to paradise. In order for you to travel through the stars to paradise, you must understand the way and obtain help from the proper God. The journey was always difficult—even when the stars seemed permanently situated. As the stars began to shift, at least some people turned to Mithras for help. Mithras had the power to move stars and make your soul's journey to paradise easier."

Blakely thought about Joachim and his belief about the soul traveling out of the body and into space, disappearing for a time, then reappearing in the form of another or possibly the same person again.

"So, these people out here," said Blakely, "still believe in the 'old one' as Alex said?"

Justina shrugged. "Ya. I am sure. There are persons who have carried on the tradition of Mithras worship. It was transmitted by oral tradition, one person to another. There are no written records of this cult. The converts were sworn to secrecy. Such a religion would continue among the illiterate, who still depend upon astrology for guidance in their lives. Cult worship from earliest times always have modern counterparts."

"I can dig that," said Jeremiah. "My great grandmother believed in voodoo."

"Of course. Today, we drink symbolically the blood of Christ, eat his flesh. We eat a sacrificial lamb and drink red wine, honoring a flesh and blood tradition."

"Too much," said Jeremiah, shaking his head.

Blakely looked at the dried, black substance in the shallow pit and gutter below the stone altar. He felt a chilling sense of dread as he was pulled back in time to imagine the horrific sounds of men wielding spears and knives against the bones and flesh of bulls and frightened men. The stench of hot blood. He could hear the screams as the victims fought against sharp metal piercing jugulars, and slowly bleeding to death. It was like any other death chamber, he thought, whether it be inside Auswitz, a trench in Bosnia, or a slaughter house in New Jersey. The fact that it was a 2,000 year old slaughterhouse didn't make any difference.

"Gott!" exclaimed Justina. "I am so excited I do nothing but talk. I must get busy."

"So this is the very bottom of the cave?" asked Blakely, flashing his light around the stone walls, looking for any kind of doorway or passage.

"There could be more passage," said Justina. "At this point, I must say I have many years of work ahead of me just cataloging and investigating all that we have seen this morning. Perhaps when I am able to remove some of the earthen floor, I will find more cave passage."

"What's Paulas going to say?"

Justina laughed. "He will be shocked! But we already have authorization from the Governor. We will have the leg up, as you say, before he finds out. After we tell the world of what we find, I will welcome assistance from Dr. Paulas and experts in Mithras research. There is plenty of work here to do."

She had it all figured out, thought Blakely. She knew she couldn't keep the glory for herself very long. He flashed his light at the ceiling. It had been hewn so that it arched like the heavens. Symbols of the constellations were marked in black outlines similar to those on the walls. Justina followed his light.

"Wonderful representations," she exclaimed. "This may be one of the best preserved Mithras temples known to date."

Jeremiah leaned down. "Mind if I just touch the marble altar? I'd like to say I touched a place where ancient sacrifices were conducted."

"Stand next to it, Jeremiah. Rest your hand on it. I'll take your photograph."

Jeremiah stood touching the flower-strewn altar with the painted God Mithras looking down upon him from the wall. He bit his lip, glanced up at Mithras, then smiled broadly for the picture. Blakely knew Jeremiah's mind was reeling with the media possibilities: Internet storefront, video releases, a veritable media gold mine.

"Can you now get the video camera?" Justina asked. "I will take my still photos. Ah!" She looked around her. "This, today, is what I work my whole life for."

Blakely hugged her.

"I need to tend to other business for awhile, so I'll check in later. I'd only be in your way down here. Tony will be available, if you need him."

"What Jeremiah and I will do today is make sure we get everything on videotape. I will also do an audio description of what you see. So I really won't need much assistance, Edward."

"Good. I'll see you later."

Jeremiah and Blakely left her and headed topside. She had found her bliss, Blakely thought, in ancient stone, old bones, and a secret ritual depicted on a cave's walls. Justina would probably write lots of articles for scholarly publications and maybe get on the lecture circuit. She would get credit for the discovery. Meanwhile, the peasants who had actually discovered the temple would remain anonymous and unrewarded.

CHAPTER 32

The Double Cross

When Jeremiah and Blakely emerged from the cave, the clearing was surrounded by peasant families dressed in their best clothes, watching the strange Americans. The two old men sat as before, except that now they were tying brush torches together with grape canes. They had assembled a dozen or more.

"I need to go down to the *Sea Siren*, Tony. I believe you and Jeremiah can handle things here."

"You going to see Uncle Lou?"

"Yeah, unless they won't let me aboard. I'll be taking Leo and Mike along. I hope to bring back your control board and anything else that's loose."

Jeremiah's eyes filled. His lip quivered.

"Take care, skip. I don't want anything bad to happen."

"See you."

* * * * *

Blakely and Leo climbed the steps to the suite. Mike was in shorts and eating potato chips.

"Nothing coming down, skip. Same as last reported, except Harry's on deck and Tobok must be sleeping. Haven't seen Wafford at all."

"Strange."

They must be waiting for the buyers. But why would Wafford want to hang around? Blakely dialed the ship. It rang several times.

"Mr. Tobok," Tobok answered.

Ah, so it is Mr. Tobok now.

"Mr. Tobok," said Blakely.

"Yes, sir."

"I need to ask you a big favor."

"Like what?"

"Like Justina Cunningham has discovered an archeological gold mine up at the cave, that's what. We need to borrow the control board and some of that stuff we brought back last night."

"I don't know, Ed. Nobody's here right now who can give you permission."

"Where's King and Marchese?"

"Oh, they had to go some place. Not sure they'll be back today."

"I see. Just you, Harry and Lou?"

"Well, yes."

"Look Gregor, I know Gresham would give us permission. He was decent enough to let us do a full transmission last night. You know he wouldn't begrudge us a couple pieces of equipment. Justina and Crete Enterprises will be famous by tomorrow morning! Might even be a job in it for you! What do you say?"

"I don't know, Ed... You're pushing the window."

"That's me, Gregor. But this is why we came here in the first place. Why don't you get permission from Lou Wafford? He's there, isn't he?"

"He's here."

"Can I speak with him?"

"He's still under the weather."

"Hey, Gregor! Then you're in charge, man! You have to make your own decisions!"

"Can you have it back by 1400 hours? The new people are supposed to arrive this evening."

"What time?"

"Sometime after 1700 hours. But you can't be here then."

Sure. It's 1000 hours now. That'll give us plenty. I promise to have it back by 1400 hours." He lied. Once they got the stuff, they'd damn well keep it as long as they needed it.

"Okay, skip—for old time's sake."

"We'll be on the dock in two minutes."

The three hustled down the steps and Mike drove them around the corner to the quay. Throngs of parishioners were entering an ancient church. Little girls in white dresses pranced about while their parents gossiped.

Tobok, instead of Swann, came across in the launch. He looked bedraggled.

"Cyberspacing again, Gregor?" Blakely asked.

"No. Not last night. Did watch."

Mike and Leo said nothing as they sat in the favored back seat. Gregor gunned the engine and they moved across the water and closed on the gangway of the *Sea Siren*. They all climbed out and moved quickly up the ladder where Harry Swann was leaning against the rail.

Harry looked different; he wore a bleached cotton outfit with a white shirt open at the collar. A turquoise ear ring had replaced the gold one on his left ear. And even more surprising, the guy was wearing what could be interpreted as a pleasant smile on his squinty face.

"Well now, look at Mr. Cool Dude!" said Blakely.

Swann's cat eyes showed merriment while his mouth pulled into a quarter-moon grimace.

Tobok led them to the television studio and unlocked it.

"Be sure to have it back in good time."

"Sure. We will," said Blakely, lying again. "Here's that small control board, Mike. We might as well take the big one too, since we'll be bringing it all back. Can you help him with that, Gregor?"

Tobok gave Blakely an impudent look.

"I suppose."

"Take these three cases, too, Leo. Might as well have sufficient equipment. Get down in the cave without something and you lose

THE MINOTAUR 341

time. Mike, ask Harry to come down here and help haul all this out. We'll use what we need and keep the rest packed."

Tobok wiped a hand across his mouth. He hadn't made a move to help carry the boxes. Time to take his mind off the equipment.

"Gregor." Blakely put his arm on Tobok's shoulder as Mike and Leo went topside. "Got another favor to ask."

Tobok looked like a he had just lost his files to a power surge.

"You already asked and got too much."

"No, Gregor. This is a tiny favor! Since we're doing a fantastic tape today, could we transmit it from here? I mean, CDN is going to go bonkers over this. As we speak, Justina is in a two thousand year old temple of Mithras—perfectly preserved—where they sacrificed bulls and human beings. God! There's human skeletons stacked everywhere! You should come up and see it! It's incredible. Anyway, it'll guarantee us an exclusive. And for what its worth, I'll give you some money for your trouble."

"How much?"

Gregor was buyable, yet.

"How much is it worth? I'm willing to pay you five hundred dollars for an hour's worth of time in the comm center and studio."

"Two thousand."

"Gregor! What's happened to the guy who once spent hours and hours on the Ham trying to locate my daughter?"

Tobok looked down. His cherubic lips stayed pursed.

"A thousand," said Blakely.

"Two thousand. One for Harry and the other for me."

"So what is it with Harry, Gregor? You share everything with him now? I thought you were in charge here."

Tobok wiped his hands and swung his arms. "I don't want him carrying stories back to Mr. King."

"I see. Okay. Can I bring you the money when we transmit the tape?"

"Yes."

"Ah! One more favor to ask."

Tobok winced. "Come on, skip. I'm not in charge. I can't do all your favors."

"This is easy. Remember the sail with the logo?"

"Yes."

"I thought it might be nice to set it, you know?"

Tobok scratched his head.

"Why?"

"Superstition. You guys have been showing them black receptors. People think the Minotaur killed Theseus. That disturbs these Cretan people. They love their Theseus. A white sail means Theseus is alive and the Minotaur is dead. You see the logic? It's Easter. And it would make everybody coming along the quay happy to see a white sail on the *Sea Siren*. It's all about mythology. Can we do it?"

Tobok looked at him like he was crazy.

"Don't see why not. You won't disturb the receptors any doing it, will you?"

"Oh, no."

Mike, Harry and Leo came back to finish hauling the second load of video boxes.

"Mike, can you come over here?"

Mike handed a box to Leo and came up the passageway.

"Go to the blue hold and get the lower-fore topsail with the logo and set it so people can see it. It's in the number four sail locker."

"Yes, sir!"

Leo smirked as he lifted a stack of boxes. Blakely took Tobok by the arm and walked him toward the salon.

"How's Lou doing, Gregor? Jeremiah is very worried about him. Fact is, he broke down and cried last night."

"All right, I guess."

"Where is he?"

"In the salon."

"You mind if I go say hello?"

Tobok shrugged.

THE MINOTAUR 343

"Why not?"

Tobok stood in the hatchway as Blakely entered. Wafford was sitting in one of the plush chairs. He was red faced from drinking. The Wafford hang-dog was sullen and covered in unshaved white stubble. Cigarette butts were in the ashtray on the cocktail table; a glass of liquor without ice, an open bottle of scotch, a pack of Marlboros and a box of matches were nearby. The table top was dusted with ashes and bits of tobacco. Blakely attempted to be nonchalant.

"Is this a private party or can anybody join in?"

Wafford looked at Blakely like an animal suddenly awakened. He tried to grin, but it wasn't working.

"Sit and have a drink," he said in a barely audible voice. He picked up his glass and looked into it as though it were a mirror.

Blakely got a glass and put ice in it. "Can I get you more ice?"

"No, thanks. Tastes better neat."

"Thought you were a bourbon and branch water guy?"

Blakely poured himself some scotch. Wafford rested his elbows on his knees so that his face was focused on the glass of liquor.

"Usually am. Do you have any objection if I drink scotch?" The voice was hostile, distant. Tobok stood observing.

"You mind giving us some sea room, Gregor? I'd like to talk privately with my friend."

Tobok blushed and vacated the hatchway.

"You can drink whatever you want, Lou. It's your life. Mind if I sit down?"

"Help yerself," he said in a low voice, gesturing toward the empty chair.

Blakely sat down and watched him for a moment. In a low voice, he said, "I think you can still save yourself. Want to talk about it?"

Wafford glanced toward the hatch and then at the pack of cigarettes. He set his drink down. He shook a cigarette from the pack and tapped the filter end of it on the table. Blakely hadn't seen anybody do that in ages. Wafford put the cigarette in his mouth and struck a match. The flame sputtered and came alive. He lifted the flame uncertainly to the cigarette. Wafford drew on the cigarette, shaking the match out and placing it in the ashtray. He blew a large puff of smoke above Blakely's head. The whole operation looked out of place for Wafford.

"Didn't know you smoked. Just take up the habit?"

"Naw!" Wafford flicked ashes in the general direction of the ashtray. "Tried to stop, but like so many other things, I just couldn't."

"Like what other things?"

Wafford's eyes narrowed. He took a breath and sighed.

"Just things, Ed. Just things."

He took another puff. His voice was lifeless.

"Nothing you need to worry yourself over. Only has to do with me."

"How 'bout Elizabeth, Lou? And Jeremiah? Jeremiah is mighty worried about you. Some of those things have to do with Elizabeth and Jeremiah, don't they?"

Wafford's jaw twitched. "That's nothing for you to worry about either, Ed. Like always, you've gotten into things which aren't your business."

"Like the messages?"

Wafford reacted as though he had been jabbed in the hand with a bayonet. "What the hell you talking about?"

He roused and mashed the half smoked cigarette in the ashtray, still avoiding eye contact.

"The messages. The ones from Mel to guys like Spider and Runner. From Melek to Touchstone. I don't have all the pieces put together, but you and your buddies seem to have some heavy duty stuff going on."

Wafford was totally alert, pulling himself sober, trying to relax and show Blakely he had missed the mark.

"I don't know what you mean. If you are referring to messages we were sending and receiving about transporting goods, that has to do with Homer's business. I wouldn't know much 'bout that."

"What about delivering a complete ship with latest technical equipment to some outfit that can't get this kind of stuff from legitimate sources?"

Wafford's chin dropped. The bayonet had found its mark again, this time closer to his heart. He sat up straighter, getting a grip on himself.

"Where'd you ever get that cockeyed idea?"

"That's what we need to talk about, except we can't do it here."

"I don't know what yer gettin' at."

Wafford stood up slowly and studied Blakely.

"I think you do," said Blakely quietly, taking a small sip of scotch.

Wafford's face was a confusion of emotions as he tried to keep his eyes and lips from betraying him further. He turned and started across the salon to the television.

"What does it take for you to get the real message, Lou?"

He stopped and turned back, hands on hips.

"What do you mean?"

Beads of perspiration on Wafford's forehead reflected silver from the skylight.

"The jig's up. You can't pretend anymore. I thought maybe you and I could go up to Kastelli and talk about it like two old friends. I know you're in over your head, but I still want to help you—if I can."

Blakely watched as Wafford picked up the channel tuner off the bar and began flicking through the channels on the television. He settled on a soccer game. He wasn't totally drunk, which was a good thing, because otherwise their talk would be useless. Wafford stopped fiddling with the tuner and turned around. His pink face radiated anger. He ran his pudgy fingers through his thin hair.

"Just a change in plans is all," he muttered. "I'm not in over my head like you think. The buyers are legitimate. They will be here in a few hours to claim the ship. You're not supposed to be here. Boat's off limits."

"I know. But Gresh was nice enough to let Jeremiah and me back on last night. I figured one or two more times before the buyers arrive is okay."

"It's not okay. You shouldn't be here."

"Seems like yesterday you and me sat here having some good talks." Blakely stroked the plush material of the chair arm. Wafford didn't respond.

"Celebrated finding the fourth piece of the relic here. You, me, Elizabeth—even old tight-ass Chris sat around that table over there and talked about how it would be, if we could vindicate your daddy. Why can't you and I talk about the good times and the bad times? Come with me to the hotel where we don't have to worry about extra sets of ears."

Wafford seemed to rally himself once more by attempting a hang-dog. It was weak.

"It's done, Ed. I'm just biding my time here 'til Homer's ole jet airplane arrives to pick me up. I'm expecting it at three."

He knew Wafford was lying as much to himself as to Blakely. They'd left him high and dry and Wafford had no earthly idea how to deal with it. The message said King was leaving Rome for Gulfport.

"And if it doesn't show?"

"I'll come up by and by and stay the night at the hotel."

"Who are the buyers?"

"Some boys from Athens. Friends of Homer."

Probably another lie.

"How come we don't just sail the *Sea Siren* over to Piraeus and deliver her to them?"

Wafford's face was reddening. He looked toward the television.

"Don't know, Ed. Not my business. I'm just following orders. Now if you'll excuse me, I'd like to watch the soccer game."

Wafford's ability to hide the truth had evaporated. He stared

THE MINOTAUR 347

at the television.

Blakely asked, "Why don't you ride back up to the cave with me? Justina's discovered an ancient temple. Your daddy's dream of finding ancient relics has come true. It's a treasure that could make you famous! Jeremiah could make a special tape of you telling your daddy's story and how, forty years later, you put this expedition together and discovered a priceless antiquity."

Wafford's blue eyes lit for a second, then faded and went out.

"No thanks," Wafford replied in a whisper. "I'd be much obliged if you'd leave now."

Wafford took a sip of scotch, while keeping his eyes fixed on the two teams competing for the ball on the huge green soccer field. Case closed. Blakely was switched off.

"If you need anything, call me on my cellular phone, Lou," Blakely said softly. "I'm leaving the island tomorrow morning. I do have something very important I want to show you before I head out. It could affect your future plans—regardless of whether King comes back to pick you up or not."

Wafford set down his drink.

"I'll leave a message at the desk," said Wafford, "if I come by."

"Good. If I don't see you, take care of yourself. I mean that."

Blakely extended his hand, but Wafford focused on the soccer and pretended not to notice it.

"See you," said Blakely. He turned and left the salon.

He felt nothing but pity for the man. McLeod had done more than twist his tail. He'd somehow double-crossed him and left him tail-less. Wafford was lost.

Blakely went on deck to the gangway. Swann stood at the rail. Blakely gave him a V for victory sign as he took two steps at a time to the landing. Leo and Mike had already loaded the van and were waiting. He jumped aboard. Tobok put the launch in motion. Blakely looked back. The white sail looked damned good. Elizabeth would have loved the irony of it!

*****

Blakely and Leo arrived at the clearing just as Jeremiah and Justina emerged from the cave entrance followed by Tony and half a dozen Cretan men with fagots ablaze.

"Skip! You won't believe the shots we got in there. The whole temple was lit perfectly with these torches! Better than any floods or fills and spots. We'd like to send it uncut to CDN this afternoon, if you can get us on board the *Sea Siren*."

"It's all arranged with Tobok."

"Cool!"

"Ya! We did an hour and a half tape, Edward, covering the murals, their symbology, the Mithras cult—we do it all—with help from these good men."

Blakely's phone rang in his pocket.

"Blakely."

"This is Gregor, Ed."

"Yeah?"

"I have a message from Mr. King. He doesn't want you back on the ship for any reason. It's off limits. He wants you to bring the equipment here on the double."

"Hold on a second, Gregor, okay?"

"Yes."

Blakely covered the phone with his hand and waved Jeremiah and Justina closer.

"Can you guys arrange to do a feed through Iraklion television and send video to CDN that way?"

"It's technically possible," said Jeremiah. "Probably from Iraklion to Athens and via satellite to CDN. I don't know any of those people, though. Why? We can't use the studio and comm center?"

"Yeah. The deal's off. The ship's off limits."

"Actually," said Justina, smoothing her hair, "a local broadcast from Iraklion could be politically good for us. We would have direct contact here. It would save us from Paulas and those other people swooping down and re-doing our story and taking it away from us."

THE MINOTAUR   349

"Too true," said Jeremiah.

"I think we try to do it! Take our videotape and deal with them. Are you willing to do that, Jeremiah?"

"Sure! I can call Steve Summer and explain our problem. He can establish us with his contacts."

"Good thinking," said Justina.

Blakely lifted his phone to his ear.

"Mr. Tobok?"

"Yes, sir."

"We don't need the studio or the comm center."

"When will you be back with the equipment?"

"Well, Gregor... That poses a little problem."

"What do you mean?"

"Looks like we'll be doing coverage of some pagan rites. The dancing could go on for a week or so."

Jeremiah and Justina began to laugh silently, holding their hands over their mouths.

"You can't do that! It's not your property! That wasn't what you agreed to."

"I know, Gregor, but you didn't have to tattle to your Mr. King either. I thought you were a big boy! Besides, I don't like the way you tried to extort money from me. You'll see the equipment when we're damned good and ready to give it back. So long, Gregor."

"But, Ed..."

Blakely folded the phone and put it in his pocket.

Jeremiah asked, "Is that what I think it is in the back of the van?"

"Seemed to me you guys needed a leg up with equipment, so we brought up enough to get you started. I wouldn't worry about getting it back any time soon. Nobody'll miss it. Tobok won't dare admit to King or the buyers that he screwed up. Besides, I doubt the video stuff would be of any interest to the new owners."

Justina laughed aloud and gave Blakely a hug.

"That is exactly what Christopher would become angry about.

When you were in the Army, you never did what you were supposed to do, and everything turn out wonderful!"

"Well, not always, Justina."

The image of Jim Wafford always reminded Blakely that he could indirectly cause a man's death. He dismissed the image, but it was replaced immediately with Lou Wafford's.

"So, you guys want to carry the equipment up to the hotel and drop it off? You can call Summer and see if he can get you set up for today or tomorrow with the television people."

"Today. It must be today," said Justina. "Paulas will be back here tomorrow. It is too late tomorrow. Which reminds me, since Crete Enterprises is kaput, we need to negotiate with Mr. Summer before we send the tape."

"True," said Jeremiah. "And we have to come up with a name for our partnership."

"What about Labyrinth Enterprises?" asked Justina.

Jeremiah considered. "That'd be cool!"

"Well," said Blakely, "let's go to the hotel. You guys can have the van and talk out your plans. I'll hang around and hope Lou pays me a visit."

"Uncle Louis okay?"

"Don't get your hopes up, Jeremiah. He's on a binge. I tried everything I could think of to get him up here. He's really not okay. He's convinced himself that King and Marchese will come back and pick him up. Maybe they told him they would. But we know different. The guy's on the ropes."

Jeremiah bit his lip and his eyes filled. "I feel so bad for him. After what he did for me, paying for me to go to Morehouse and the University of Georgia and all... and I can't pay him back by rescuing him when he needs help."

Blakely hugged him and patted him on the back. "You can't help somebody unless they want you to. Your uncle has to make the first move. When he does, we'll be there for him, won't we?"

"Yes. Always."

THE MINOTAUR

CHAPTER 33

Confession

"Back again, Milos," said Blakely as he carried a stack of video cases toward the closet across from the hotel clerk's desk. "Would you mind if Dr. Cunningham and Mr. Wilcox store this stuff here until they can get some other arrangements made?"

"No, no. As long as they like."

"Good. I'll see you guys later."

"Right, skip."

Milos said, "I have two messages for you."

Milos handed them to Blakely. One from Travis: Call him at home. The other from Jenny: Elizabeth is fine and on her way to USA. Good. Damned nice of Jenny and Graham to let him know. He waved good-bye to Justina and climbed the stairs to his room. He sat down on the bed and fished his address book out of his bag. He dialed the number through the overseas operator. 1500 hours here. It was 0800 hours in Atlanta.

"Hello!"

"Travis?"

"Yes, Ed. Thanks for returning my call so quickly. I thought you'd like to know the FBI fellas got pretty excited over those files."

"They let you see them?"

"Well, we watched them together until they figured the communications involved national security. Being a former agent myself, I could pretty much draw my own conclusions."

"So, is it CIA or a freelance black-market operation?"

"These fellas wouldn't tell me anything which I can tell you—if you know what I mean—but my impression was they thought it was black-market without CIA sponsorship."

"How could you tell?"

"It was all too blatant—even for CIA. First of all, CIA wouldn't have taken a high-tech, tall ship and challenged NATO and UN interdiction points. They'd likely haul those black receptors over by air to some private air strip and rig them on a ship already in the Med. The computers and other gismos, same thing. Have I said enough without telling you what they said?"

"Yeah, Trav. I've always appreciated your sidewise candor."

"I'd stand clear. The ship and all the players will soon be under heavy surveillance."

"They're already under close watch from the Greek Air Force."

"You're not in the line of fire, are you?"

"No. By tomorrow, I'll be gone from here. I won't have an address or phone number—temporary or permanent—if I decide not to have one."

"Not even California?"

"Nope."

"Smart man. Will you keep in touch?"

"Hell yes. I depend on you. Wouldn't know how to plan my life without checking with my old Army pal Travis Gorton first."

"Keep your powder dry, buddy."

"You, too!"

Blakely threw the phone on top of the nylon bag. He opened his wallet and counted his money. Four hundred dollars cash. Another fifty thousand drachmas. An international bank card worth close to a hundred thousand dollars. By next week, Graham said he'd have a property appraisal and a check deposited. Probably net well over a million. The telephone rang.

"Blakely."

"This is Mike. Tobok is bringing Wafford ashore."

"Any visitors?"

"No. Harry is sitting on deck paring his nails with that Cretan knife he bought."

"Is the Rover in sight?"

"Haven't seen it since King and Marchese took off."

"Stay on and tell me what you see."

"Tobok's helping Wafford out of the boat. He looks worn out, Ed. Face is bloated. He's got a suitcase. Tobok is carrying it toward the square. Wafford's following him. Tobok is waving down a taxi..."

"Yeah?"

"Taxi pulled up. Wafford's getting in. Tobok is helping the driver put the bag in the trunk... Cab's leaving. Tobok is returning to the launch."

Wafford is either going to the airport or coming here, thought Blakely.

"Mike, you can suspend all surveillance."

"How come?"

"I don't want anybody seeing you watching the *Sea Siren* with the binoculars. They're fairly easy to spot. Authorities will be swarming the area soon. So put both sets of glasses away. You and Leo can take them home as souvenirs."

"Thanks, skipper."

"Stand by in case I need you. Otherwise, see you in the morning."

Blakely sorted through the copies of the messages. He chose the one about keeping Lucky under control and the one about the Vatican. He carried them downstairs and had the clerk make copies.

"Milos, would you let me know when Louis Wafford arrives? I believe he will be coming soon to spend the night."

"Very good, sir."

He returned to his room and, using a blank CD he had procured from the studio during his last visit, began downloading the split-screen video from Jeremiah's powerbook. It was slow work, even though this computer was much faster than the one Blakely had at home. He would take the CD with him. There was a knock on the door. He opened it. Milos stood before him.

"Mr. Wafford is in his room, number one, sir. He asked me to tell you he would like to meet with you in half an hour."

"Thanks."

So Wafford was wanting him to pay a visit. That was encouraging. It would take him a half hour to finish the downloading and prepare himself to deal with Wafford.

After completing the download and turning off the computer, he placed the powerbook in the bottom drawer of the chiffonier. His body tingled with nervous excitement. Perhaps Wafford was ready for some help. He glanced at the urn, reminding himself he had to deliver it to Stupak before leaving tomorrow. He rubbed his hands. They were cold. He put on his windbreaker, feeling like he needed its warmth against the jitters coursing through his body. He folded the two copies of the messages and put them in his pocket and went down to Wafford's room. He knocked.

"Door's open."

He opened it. A table stood in the middle of the room with Wafford's jacket crumpled on it beside a basket of fruit. Wafford had made advance preparations. An open bottle of Jack Daniels and a sealed bottle of Chivas Regal sat on a small table with two glasses and a bucket of ice.

"Come in and have a seat, Ed. Make yerself at home."

Wafford leaned on the window sill with his back to Blakely. He was looking out the same window where Elizabeth had watched the pyre being built yesterday. Blakely went over and sat down.

"Like old times," Blakely said, trying to ease the tension.

"Pour yerself a drink, Ed. Not yer favorite, I know."

Blakely uncapped the scotch and poured two fingers. He dropped in two ice cubes and took a sip.

"Nice of you to get it for me. I take it they didn't come back to pick you up?"

Wafford pushed away from the sill and sat down heavily in the other chair. He had showered and shaved. His eyes and mouth were set and prepared to do battle, but his slumping body looked all but defeated.

THE MINOTAUR   355

"That's not why you're here. Now, what's all this you want to show and tell?"

Wafford did appear to have sobered a bit.

"They double-crossed you, didn't they?"

Wafford's sodden face was turning crimson.

"Make your point, Ed."

Blakely pulled the two messages from his pocket, unfolded them, and handed them to Wafford.

"Whatcha got here?"

His fat hand was shaking so that he grasped the paper in both hands and leaned his elbows on his knees for support. The papers still wavered. He scanned the top message.

"This is a bunch of damn fool gibberish."

His voice was almost a whisper, high and nasal. He looked at the second message, holding it away from him.

"Just more of the same."

He wadded the copies and threw them on the table.

"I figured out that Mel is King and Vatican is Rome. Zeb is McCloud and Lucky is Lou Wafford. Doesn't exactly take a genius to match them up."

"Where'd you get these?"

"You know where. A secret file Tobok kept for you and King and Marchese. You used it whenever you sent confidential stuff back and forth."

Wafford slowly got up and went over to the table where his jacket lay. He turned slowly around.

"You know I can pismire kill you," Wafford said, pointing a Colt 45 caliber U.S. Army automatic at Blakely. The gun must have been under his windbreaker. His entire body was shaking. His red face was sweaty and desperate; the hooded eyes wider than Blakely had ever seen them.

Blakely felt a rush of adrenaline, and steeled himself against panic, appearing totally calm. He took a breath and exhaled slowly, allowing himself time to modulate his voice so as not to show fear.

"You could if you wanted to, I guess. Not your style though, is it Lou?"

"How do you mean?"

His voice was gravelly, dangerous. His hand took a more certain grip on the automatic.

"What I mean," Blakely said, keeping his eyes fixed on Wafford's eyes, which looked despairing and puzzled, "is that you usually don't get directly involved. You hire it done."

"Keep talking like that, and I'll show you I know how to use this."

"Thought you didn't own a gun."

"Never you mind, Ed." The puzzled look changed to a plea. "Why'd you have to poke around? Dig up all this dirt?"

"Shouldn't hire an ex-military intelligence man as your personal gopher, Lou."

"I paid you well enough so's you'd be loyal and do what you were told. Leastways, my daddy thought you could be trusted."

"Well, your daddy wasn't into big time sleaze. He had his faults and obsessions, but sleaze wasn't one of them." He nodded toward the gun. "That your daddy's military issue?"

Tears welled in Wafford's eyes, not quite breaking from their rims. His face was livid purple and the veins in his throat had swelled.

"My grandaddy J.D. gave it to him before he went off with Patton."

"How'd you get it by the inspections?"

"That's for me to know."

"Why don't you put it down? Why foul it by killing somebody who fought with your dad against old Nazis? What would it prove?"

"I think I'd feel better if I destroyed you, Ed. Ever since I knew my daddy liked you more'n he did me, I think I've deep down always wanted to kill you."

"I can't help what your daddy felt or didn't feel. And it isn't your daddy's fault you've gotten into all this trouble, either."

Wafford waved the gun at him and began to rock back and

forth as he interrupted Blakely. "And now, you've helped to destroy me."

"What's the difference whether I found you out or somebody else? It's all the same. I must tell you that as we sit here, the FBI is probably searching through your private files down on your farm. The *Sea Siren* is under surveillance. All the evidence is there. Killing me won't do a damn thing except feed your ego. You still have a chance, if you come clean."

Wafford began to cry in a high, soft, steady sound of deep pain, yet he kept the gun pointed at Blakely. He stood there heaving. After a few minutes, he gathered himself in again and was quiet.

Blakely said, "Some friends you have! Homer said in that one message to be sure to keep Lucky under control. And your so-called partner Gresh? Where's he? Snuck off to Rome with Marchese. By now, they're on their way back to Gulfport."

"All that doesn't matter any more."

"Why'd they leave you here, Lou? Weren't they afraid you'd go to the authorities?"

Wafford looked away and began to sob. "They knew I wouldn't. I still hoped to save everything. My farm. The casino. You don't know the half of it. They mighta killed my children, Elizabeth and Jeremiah, too, if I snitched."

Blakely slowly reached for his glass and sipped.

"How'd they pull you into this?"

"None of your affair."

He broke off, and wiped his eyes with his free hand. He shifted his weight more onto the table without saying anything for a minute. "If you want to know, Homer agreed to cancel my debt to him."

"How much were you into him for?"

Wafford raised his eyes to Blakely's and looked down again.

"Everything I owned, plus some. Close to seven million."

"God almighty! How could you have lost everything? Elizabeth said you even drained the joint savings account."

"Elizabeth musta shared plenty with you, didn't she?"

His voice was less dangerous than bitter. He paused.

"It took all I had to invest in the casino. I borrowed from Homer. Then, the big operators came in and the casino never was able to make a profit. Five years of steady losses."

"So Homer kept loaning you money?"

"Not flat out. No, Homer would never do that. Always collateral. My boat. My horses. My savings. Everything!"

"Homer made direct loans to you?"

"Through Bobby Lee. It was all legal-like. Put on paper through Bobby Lee, with interest."

"How come the debt and mortgages don't show up on credit reports? They show you worth over six million."

Wafford glanced at Blakely, then back to the automatic, which he turned in his hand as though examining it for the first time.

In a low voice, he responded, "They were private agreements. Nobody was to know about them unless I defaulted or died."

Wafford sat with the automatic resting on his leg. His voice was small and whiny as he answered Blakely's questions.

"So what are you and Homer into?"

Tears started down Wafford's face and dripped off his chin. He wiped with his gun hand. "Can't exactly explain it."

He paused and took a deep breath.

"What's aboard the *Sea Siren* that makes it hot?" asked Blakely softly.

Wafford looked at the automatic and laid it on his lap.

"The two computers work together with them black receptors and special software. You can interrupt the programs of ground-to air-missiles and change 'em and send 'em back where they came from."

"You're serious?"

"Yes. The operator can also jam satellite signals and make false entries and the like. Send airplanes into mountains."

"Holy Hell," muttered Blakely. So it really was star wars technology!

"Tell me something, Lou. Why'd you risk hauling all this hot stuff over here on a tall ship, knowing it would attract attention of NATO and UN military? Especially in the Adriatic!"

"The deal, as I understand it, was made on two conditions. They wouldn't buy unless the ship, computers and all, could pass a UN inspection. That's why King insisted on going to Trieste. Him and McCloud knew the *Sea Siren* would be stopped and boarded by UN inspectors."

"Yeah? And the second?"

"Second was a successful test of the equipment. The buyer was to launch some kinda device and the proof would be shown by diverting it off target. That's why King didn't want anybody around when they did it."

"Who are the buyers?"

Wafford tilted his head. In a low voice he responded, "Nobody'd tell me, 'cept it was an ally of America."

Fat chance!

"So what went wrong with the deal?"

"The buyers were supposed to come here today for settlement. Colonel Stupak up yonder has been keep'n tabs on everything. King decided it'd be best to meet the buyers in another country."

"In Rome?"

"Yes."

"And not take you with him?"

"That's right."

"Why?"

"He said I needed to keep an eye on you 'til you left Crete. If you found out anything, I was 'sposed to kill you. Even gave me an unregistered .25 automatic to do it with. If all went well, I'd meet 'em back in Gulfport and Homer'd tear up the IOUs and destroy the tapes."

"The tapes?"

Wafford looked away.

"King hired a detective agency. Made some videos of me in a motel with lady friends."

"When did King let you know he had them?"

"Just before I left Gulfport. Said it was added insurance that I'd do what I was told."

He paused, set the gun on the table, and flexed his gun hand.

"King's probably left somebody to kill me either tonight or tomorrow morn'n. Make it look like suicide. I 'spect it'll be Harry Swann."

"Why Harry?"

"He's killed before. Spent time in Angola Prison."

"Why would they kill you?"

"I overheard Marchese and Gresh yesterday. I know too much. Said I was coming undone. I 'spose they're right. I don't have the stomach for it, Ed."

"When do the buyers claim the vessel?"

"A crew is to fly in tonight and leave out tomorrow night after dark."

"Hell, Lou. Let's go to the authorities. Stupak can arrange everything. We can fly you stateside in one of those C-141s at the American base. The FBI will put you under that protective witness program."

"Naw. Homer has too much of his own protection. My word against his. With his money, he can buy his way out. There's no way me and my family can be protected. I've looked into that there FBI protection business. You change your names and move and all. But if a person wants to hunt you down, he'll find you sooner or later—specially when you're white and yer wife's black. That's no way to live."

"Better than what you have now."

Wafford sighed.

"Besides, everything's different now because of what you done. You had to go and get yourself messed in this. There's no way out for me."

Wafford's mood had changed again. He pointed the gun at Blakely. "Why couldn't you mind your business and stay out of it?"

"If it were your daddy in my shoes, you know damned good

and well he'd have done the same as I did."

Wafford's shoulders slumped.

"My daddy's last letters to mama told how much he admired your intelligence skills. He thought you hung the moon, all right. Well, your curiosity's ruined everything. You haven't done me no better than you did him!"

Blakely took another swig of scotch and held the liquor in his mouth, letting its bitter flavor dissipate before swallowing. Sweat and tears trickled down Wafford's face again.

Blakely said evenly, "So you think it's somehow all my fault?"

The guy was slipping a cog. Changing from lucid to crazy in half a second. More like his old man all the time. Wafford pushed his jacket and the fruit to one side and sat more squarely on the table.

"Yes. You couldn't leave well enough alone."

Wafford shook his head up and down and began rocking.

"You're so God damned pismire smart. You and all your sailor crap. You think you're some God or Don Juan or something. Let me tell you, Captain Easy Ed Blakely, I despise your pismire ass. It wouldn't hurt me one iota to shoot you here and now for what you really are. You are a meddling sombitch bastard!"

He is trying to work up to it, thought Blakely. If he had it, Blakely'd been dead two minutes ago. Wafford didn't have it in him. Or did he? He looked across at Wafford and tried not to show any emotion at all. "Lou, you're coming apart. I saw it coming. I wasn't sure what was going on, but I was concerned mostly for Elizabeth. And she saw it coming, too."

"Elizabeth." Tears flowed. "What about Elizabeth?"

Beads of sweat covered his forehead and jowls, joining the tears in rivulets, which were turning the front of his red shirt moist and dark.

"She's been worried about you for longer than you can imagine. She's suspected you were running around, doing illegal stuff, pretending to have a grand time. She was waiting for you to come back to her and level with her. She knew you didn't have any money left. All she ever wanted you to do was tell her the truth."

Wafford turned slightly, resting the gun against his crotch.

"So you were behind that, too? 'Course, I 'spect you and Elizabeth had quite a time when I wasn't around. Never seen anything like it. You make 'em hot and crazy, don't you Ed? They all want you in their pants?"

"Sure, Lou," said Blakely dryly. "That's my reputation."

Blakely was getting his fill, but Wafford's baiting wasn't going to work.

"That musta been why you didn't want to bring Miss Jenny along? Wanted sea room, I 'spect you'd say, to navigate up any wet spot you might discover along the way?"

"Is that what you really think, Lou? For Christ's sake! Read those messages again."

He pointed to the wad of paper.

"Get real, man! Don't you have more to think about than my morals? I think our talk's gone on long enough. Either fire the damn thing or put it down—and I don't particularly care which it is. Frankly, I'm sick to death of you, your daddy, and the whole flock of your holier-than-thou pals. Just shoot or else let me leave here, so I can pack and catch the next boat out. Okay?"

Wafford dropped the gun hand between his legs, leaned over his knees and stared at the flocati rug. He began to heave silently. "Go! Get out of my sight, you fuck'n pismire. I hate the sight of you and all yer talk!"

He waved his other hand toward the door. Blakely got up without a word, walked past Wafford, and out. He closed the door and walked through the lobby to the piazza and into the fresh air. He leaned against the wall.

He took a deep breath, sucking in as much air as he could, hoping it would quell the involuntary contractions of his gut. He took another. First time he had ever looked into the hole of a loaded gun four feet away. He held his sides, trying to stop the rippling effects of nerves suddenly coming unstrung. He was shaking convulsively. He took another deep breath and drew his shoulders back. That helped.

Cadets in dress blue uniforms were gathered in clusters with pretty young women in spring dresses. Families sat at the tables drinking juices and laughing and talking. Greek Easter Day. He shivered. He had missed the feast of the lamb. A weird thing to remember. He began walking and headed down the winding, cobbled street and into the semi-darkness where the houses rose on either side and the roofs were so close above that you could see only a narrow patch of sky. He tried not to think how close he had come to death, yet now the images of Jim Wafford and Lou Wafford had fused in his mind—they were the same—the same face with the same fear and hopelessness: the face of death.

A truck was grinding its way up the hill, switching gears, and sending shrill, whining sounds like Wafford's cries of hurt and woe. The truck's lights flashed on the wall of the turn. It rounded the bend and Blakely flattened himself against the stones as it went by in a rush of sound, explosive air, and diesel stench. Shadowed faces peered out from beneath the canvas canopy. Troops. Must be a new class of cadets or support personnel, he thought, stepping back into the street and beginning to consider Wafford's predicament. It was worse than he could have imagined.

* * * *

It was dusk and the van wasn't parked where it usually was. Jeremiah and Justina must have made connections at the television station in Iraklion. The piazza and street were empty except for a military staff car parked in front of Padopolis's office. It looked like Stupak's. He entered the hotel. Manolis nodded. He went upstairs and placed the copied split-screen video CD in its case and put that into a vinyl draw string camera bag. He finished packing his clothes in a large nylon carry-all and rested awhile. At 2100 hours, when he knew the Blue Porpoise would be serving, he arose and washed for supper. He carried the camera case downstairs.

"Hello, Manolis. My friend Louis Wafford in room one is slightly ill tonight. Has he asked for room service?"

"A bottle of Ouzo and one of scotch," he said.

"No food?"

"No, sir."

"Thanks."

So Lou was in the 'let's feel sorry for Lou stage.' He wouldn't interrupt.

"Will you be here all night?"

"Yes, sir." Blakely handed the camera case to Manolis. "I'd like this stored in the safe, please."

"Very good, sir."

"I want you to inform me if anyone visits Mr. Wafford or if Mr. Wafford leaves his room. I don't care what time of night it is. It is most important that I be informed."

He handed Manolis a wad of crumpled drachmas. "Oh, I forgot," Blakely said, reaching into his jacket pocket. "I need to put these in the safe, too."

Blakely pulled out the folded messages and placed them in the bag and tied the drawstring. He watched Manolis open the safe and place the bag on a shelf next to his toiletry kit. He closed the door, pushed the lever down until it clicked, and spun the dial.

"Very good, sir."

"Know where Colonel Stupak is?"

"Yes. He's with Mr. Padapolis, having dinner at the Blue Porpoise, sir."

"Thanks. I'll either be with the colonel or else sitting in the piazza—in case you need to reach me."

"Yes, sir."

He walked down the familiar curve of narrow street to the much narrower entrance walk and avoided the pile of bicycles in the half-light. The waitress Anna saw him as he entered, wiped her hand across her mouth, and scuttled away toward the kitchen.

The large room was filled with men eating goat and lamb and drinking wine.

An old man sitting by himself in the near corner was playing his flute softly. Stupak's voice, loud and unmistakable, was coming from the far corner. He was holding forth with Padapolis and Alex, gesticulating with fork and knife, over French Fries and snails.

"Ah," said Stupak as he spotted Blakely moving toward him, "Here comes the famous American Captain, Edward Blakely, renowned archeologist, sailor, and fancier of fine ladies."

Alex moved over, leaving him a place on the long bench. They shook hands all around. Anna appeared with a place setting, a fresh pitcher of wine, and said something in the way of greeting, a little smile showing large gray teeth. When she left, Stupak leaned over in a conspiratorial manner.

"Another conquest of the American, Max. The lady is so hot for this man. I'm not so sure she won't have him right here as we watch, gentlemen. Mark my words."

They laughed.

"Sounds like the colonel has had first-hand experience with this pretty maid," said Blakely, enjoying the release of tension.

"And where is Lou this evening?" asked Stupak.

Blakely tried to appear blasé. "At the hotel. He's resting."

"And what of your lovely German archeologist, who I understand make Kastelli famous today?" asked Stupak.

"She and Jeremiah are down in Iraklion doing a program about their discoveries."

Stupak touched his cheek.

"Strange! Why not use those grand facilities I visited on Friday?"

"The *Sea Siren* is being sold. It's off limits now. As a matter of fact, everybody will be leaving tomorrow except for Jeremiah and Justina."

"It won't seem the same anymore," said Alex. "You brought us much excitement—and many American dollars."

"There will be plenty more when news of the temple gets out.

Maybe you can afford a new cab now," said Blakely.

"I think not. Rosanante have at least another fifty thousand kilometer to go. Then, I change only the engine, nothing more. I'd rather enjoy my money in other ways."

"Other ways!" Padopolis scowled. "On women over at Cheronisou."

"And why not, Max? Do you know of better place to find beautiful women?"

Padopolis punched Alex in the arm and laughed. It would be good to eat and drink with these joyful souls, thought Blakely. Get slightly drunk. Not so much that he would fall over the bikes. Just enough to pass this difficult evening. Stupak was watching him closely.

"What's the matter, my friend? You seem a little sad tonight?"

"It's the end of our journey, Colonel."

Blakely tried not to think about the reality of the matter and all the deceptions. Lou was on the verge of mayhem. There was the possibility of a hired killer lurking nearby. An illicit deal between Americans and God knows who to buy a communications ship worth millions of dollars.

He sought a better answer. "Leaving in the morning... I guess it's like when you finish a mission for NATO, and begin packing your gear to go home."

"Yes. That is an accurate observation. Speaking of which," said Stupak, "I receive a little communiqué from headquarters. A strange coincidence happen Easter Eve. While we have big bonfire and burn Judas in effigia, you have this remote test broadcast, eh?"

"Yeah."

"Another thing happen very strange! It is reported that at midnight Saturday, an object—perhaps a missile of some kind—fly up out of the sea in a graceful arc and suddenly turn as quickly and return nearly to the same place it was first seen. Isn't that a strange thing to happen on Easter Eve just as we celebrate Christo Anesti?"

"Yeah. Remarkable. Some kind of military experiment?" asked Blakely, attempting to maintain innocence.

THE MINOTAUR 367

"We don't know," Stupak replied, scratching his face. "Nobody ever see anything like it. It show up on one trajectory and then suddenly change to the opposite. A miracle on Easter Eve!"

"Probably a flying saucer from outer space," Alex concluded. "They change direction like lightning. We see such things from time to time, do we not, Max?"

"That is so."

Stupak studied Blakely and drank some wine.

"Perhaps we celebrate a little, so you will forget your sadness. Your last night on Kriti is no time to be sad." Stupak said. "I hope the reason you are sad is that you will miss all your good friends here, eh?"

"True."

Blakely knew he wasn't a good liar, and he felt Stupak's eyes watching his eyes and mouth as though he understood the real situation. Of all the Greeks he had met, Blakely felt closest to this big, gregarious air force officer. And he hated the idea of deceiving him this last night at Kastelli.

Stupak touched Blakely's arm. "I hope you will write to us now and then. I truly will miss you, Edward," said Stupak, withdrawing his hand and taking a gulp of wine.

"Same here," said Blakely. "I will miss all of you—and this place. You live in a very special village."

Alex lifted his glass. "A good send-off, for sure."

Max said, "I wish to make a toast."

He stood up, swelling in his official capacity as a province officer as he did so.

"Everybody, please give a toast to our American friend, Ed Blakely, who will be leaving our village tomorrow and who has brought us much joy and great discovery."

"Here, here!" and everybody in the room lifted glasses to Blakely.

"What time will you be leaving?" asked Stupak.

"Morning ferry. My pilot and mates and Lou Wafford will be going with me. Oh, before I forget, I have the urn with Joachim's ashes in my room. You mentioned taking it to Maleme for burial. How do you want to handle it?"

"Leave it at the desk with Manolis. No problem. I shall stop on my way to the base." Stupak paused and shook his head. "The bad one, the Nazi Kemft?"

"Yeah?"

"His bones are to be cremated also. I am told Herr Grenz and Kemft will be interred together. They make strange bedfellows, eh?"

"Yeah." Blakely didn't like the idea. The good German and the bad German sharing the same earth together. "No chance they could bury them separately?"

"No. It is no big thing. All of us end up same place. We turn to dust. It make no difference," said Stupak, nodding, a serious expression on his normally droll face.

The group ate and drank until nearly midnight without their normal frivolity. Nothing could dispel the undercurrent of sadness. Blakely finally got up and thanked them for their friendship. He turned to Anna, put a wad of bills in her fat hand, thanked her profusely, kissed her on both cheeks, and told her to keep the change from the bill. The change, he figured, would amount to a week's wages for her.

He left them there to finish off the wine and Ouzo, and carefully stepped around the bicycles as he navigated to the street. When he arrived at the hotel, he found the piazza deserted. The van was parked. He supposed Jeremiah and Justina had gone to bed after such an exhaustive day. Night noises could be heard down in the valley where a few farmhouse lamps still flickered. He walked over to a table in the lamplight and sat down.

He pulled from his wallet the tinted photograph of Joachim and himself. He held the picture close so he could study the features of Joachim's face. It was his pipe, he concluded, which made Joachim's face complete. The fire within and the fire without. It reminded him of Shakespeare's phrase, 'consumed by that which it was nourished by.' Ashes to Ashes, dust to dust.

Stupak, Alex and Max came up the hill, singing together. They said a few obscene things to one another, laughed loudly, and left without noticing Blakely sitting in the pale lamplight. Or, perhaps they were being polite, not wanting to further disturb him on his last night on Crete soil. Stupak gunned the motor and the little car churned up the road toward the base. Max and Alex disappeared inside a doorway, and he could hear them climbing the stone steps toward their respective apartments above the public offices. He would miss them all. He heard footsteps.

"Jeremiah and I were waiting for you in the bar."

Justina sat down and glanced at the photograph lying on the table. Her alabaster face was radiant.

"How'd it go?"

She put both hands on his. "Wunderbar! Steve Summer is sending contract by fax tomorrow. We have agreement with station in Iraklion. They will provide full technical support—including mobile unit."

Blakely grinned. "You've got a whole new world here, don't you?"

She squeezed his hands in hers. "Ya. It's finally good!"

"How long will you stay here?"

"I'm beginning to think many years. There's much to discover yet."

"How so?"

"We may discover a labyrinth below the temple—perhaps the Minotaur himself!"

"I don't understand."

"Remember the upper cave? Some of that passage was not wide enough for a grown bull to pass through. There must be other passages leading to the temple. There may be an entrance through the floor of the temple at the far end. It may take years to explore it."

"I thought the labyrinth and Minotaur were located at Knossos. You don't believe that?"

"Ya. I believe the architects reproduce labyrinth design at palace based upon a more primitive labyrinth one would find in caves such as this. The myth is much older than Knossos. Daedulus, the original architect in the myth, would have found the way to keep a monster inside such a cave. The depths of the original labyrinth became catacombs for the humans sacrificed there."

"H'm. Fascinating. What about your job as curator of the museum?""

"I've decided I will send a letter of resignation tomorrow and recommend Christopher as my replacement. He always envied me that position. He would continue his professorship as well, I think."

"Guilt?"

"No, Edward. Love."

"Really?"

"Ya. His love for me. I cannot deny him that. I want to do something to show our relationship mattered. Perhaps Christopher will forgive me."

"You are a lovely person."

"So are you. I see you look at photograph of you and your dear friend."

"Yeah. This piazza became our special place."

"What will you do, Edward?"

"I have no immediate plans except to spend a week or so with Claudia. Who knows?"

"Will you write to me and visit me now and then?"

"Count on it."

"I probably won't see you tomorrow; Jeremiah and I must be on the site at seven. And now, I must be getting to bed. It is very late."

"I intend to see Jeremiah in the morning. I must share some things with him before I leave and also return his powerbook."

They both stood up. Blakely held her in his arms. They kissed.

"I won't say good-bye, Edward. Not like last time. I am counting on seeing you again.

He held her tightly and stroked her hair.

"Thanks for telling me you loved me, Justina. That means a

lot."

"Ya And you, too!"

He relaxed his arms and she gave him a light peck on the cheek before turning and crossing the piazza to the hotel. Blakely watched her as she stopped at the entrance, waved, and was gone. He sat down again. Yes, he would see her again. They could both handle being closest friends now—the kind you could depend on when you needed them.

His thoughts came inevitably back to Lou Wafford and the stupid thing he had done by pulling a gun on him. Glad Elizabeth wasn't around for that show, he thought, wondering what Wafford might be doing in his room. Release. Maybe he had found release. Sleeping it off. Letting all the air out of the balloon so that tomorrow, Wafford might make better sense out of things and face up to his responsibilities. Jail time was one. He'd be arrested when he arrived stateside, taken to some federal holding facility, and it could be months before they'd figure out what to do with him. Elizabeth would be devastated, but she was a tough woman; the truth would not be a great surprise to her. You can live only so long without noticing the elephant in the living room.

You can't say Wafford didn't have some virtues. He had tried, apparently, to be a decent father. The kids were making their own way. And Jeremiah and his brothers and sisters had had a stroke of good fortune when he paid their way through college. No, Wafford wasn't all bad. Fact was, he ended up trying to save the lives of Elizabeth, the kids, and Jeremiah by sacrificing himself. That took courage.

Yeah. Never expected anything like this to happen, but like Tony said, Wafford had brought it all on himself. And once the pieces of the real Lou Wafford began to fall into place, Blakely could not stop the events which caused his downfall. They were events waiting for anybody to see and to extrapolate. When you look for the father, you find the son. Wasn't that how Christianity is set up? You can't see the father, but you can see the Son? The Sun. The Son. The Sun being the window in the sky through which you see the blazing source of energy beyond. That's what the Egyptians believed. The father is veiled in illusions, unseen, only felt, imagined, heard about indirectly, in whirlwinds, burning bushes, and in curls of ocean wave. He had to admit that sometimes he still had visions of the faceless father in shrouded, black Peacoat, standing watch in the ghostly prowl, slipping through black water on an eternal trip, without air to fill silent sails. But those visions, he knew, were only illusions which no longer mattered.

Blakely looked at the photograph of Joachim and himself again. Father and son; the son and the father. He felt coolness on his cheek, where Justina had kissed him. A fresh air was stirring, rising gently, quietly. A sailor's air by which to weigh anchor. It was a good sign, he thought.

CHAPTER 34

Absolution

Blakely looked at his watch. 0200 hours. He heard footsteps coming across the piazza. Wafford was carrying two glasses and a bottle toward him. Blakely tensed for a second, then sat back. What the hell? Might as well hear now, by himself. And if he was smart, he'd just listen. He watched as Wafford sat down wearily, looking as though he had awoken from a terrible nightmare. His face in the cool light was swollen, the hoods nearly covering bloodshot eyes. His mouth had lost all semblance of firmness, falling away under the weight of his heavy jowls. He rested his elbows on the table and pushed a glass toward Blakely.

"You couldn't sleep either?" Wafford's voice was weak.

Blakely looked at his sad face. "Didn't try."

"Care for some? It was to be a present for you." Wafford removed the cap and held the bottle of Glenfiddich unsteadily over the glass, waiting.

"Yeah."

He poured the glass half full, then poured his own and set the bottle down without replacing the cap. He looked up at Blakely. His mouth quivered slightly. He looked back down, picked up the glass slowly and drank, then held it near his mouth as though he would drink again.

A raucous noise of an engine floated up through the valley. It shifted gears at the bottom of the grade and the whining sound of the diesel grew louder, then softer, then louder again as it ascended the snake-like road and entered the village. Its lights flashed across the piazza as it made the turn and roared past and up the hill. A military truck. Blakely and Wafford watched it as the tail lights disappeared.

"Hell of a thing." Wafford's voice was a whisper. Tears rolled down his face. "All my life, I've done everything for all the wrong reasons."

He looked off toward the mountains, then turned back and took another sip and set the glass down. He lifted his eyes toward Blakely, and began turning the glass slowly with shaky forefinger and thumb.

Blakely took a good-sized swallow, feeling the liquor's heat spread inside his chest and expand into his belly. What could he say? "I don't know what I can do to help you, unless you want to turn yourself in."

"Not asking you to." He brushed the tears back with both hands. "Just came out to say I'm sorry is all. I'm very sorry for all that's happened."

"Thanks. I know you are." Unfortunately, apologies couldn't help anything, but he was still grateful that Wafford wanted to do it.

"You know, Ed?" He paused, trying to gain control of his face and hands, "You know, I didn't mean those things I said to you today." He started to cry. He calmed himself and spoke in a whisper. "I'd give everything if I could have been like you. I never did anything for the right reasons—even do'in protests and marrying Elizabeth!"

"Don't be too hard on yourself." Blakely didn't want to hear it. Once a guy gets on himself like this, it goes from maudlin to pathetic. Blakely had had enough of both.

"It's a hell of a thing, to pull off the mask and see yourself as a total liar."

"I wouldn't say that, Lou."

"I can remember the exact day it began." He took another gulp, then poured more whiskey into his and Blakely's glass.

"Yeah?"

THE MINOTAUR 375

"Second year at Riverbend Academy. I didn't want to go back. I pleaded with granddaddy not to send me. He wouldn't pay no mind. Said he was under strict orders from daddy. 'Send them back.' And he did. August 5, 1953. Sent up on the train with my brother. I vowed to myself I was gonna show momma and daddy I liked be'n away from them." Tears trickled down his face. "That first even'n after we arrived..." He broke off. "I asked Edwin to help me write a letter to my parents. We sat down and wrote them a fine letter... say'n how wonderful it was to be there and..." His voice broke. "... and that I didn't miss them one iota. That it was good be'n on my own..." He broke off again, and drew a large breath.

Blakely asked, "How old were you?"

"...I was seven at the time... I haven't stopped tell'n everybody how wonderful everything is from that day 'til this. I've lived a lie my whole life. Always wanting to be somebody I wasn't."

Blakely remembered how proud Jim Wafford seemed to be of his two boys. A damn shame he couldn't have shown it by bringing them to Germany and giving them hugs, and taking them fishing.

Blakely drank slowly, watching Wafford's thin, gray-blond hair as he leaned over his drink. Even the same hair as his old man. Wafford whispered something.

"Sorry. I didn't hear what you said."

He raised up, composed, a remnant of the old hang-dog grin playing on his thin lips. "Thanks for coming here. I'm grateful to know you. You're everything daddy said you were."

Blakely nodded.

Wafford reached out, pushed the bottle toward Blakely, and then slid his chair back. He sat for a moment, gazing at Blakely as though wanting to say more, then stood up slowly. "Good night, Ed."

"Good night, Lou."

Wafford turned absently toward the hotel, looked around as though he were confused, collected himself, and moved slowly toward the hotel entrance. Blakely took the bottle and his glass and moved out of the lamplight. He sat in darkness, thinking again of Jim Wafford and realized that Jim had gotten killed by choosing a trip to Heidelberg over going stateside to see his boys at Christmas. He had chosen the relic over his own kids. Jim's wife had pleaded with him to go with her, but he wouldn't listen. Choices.

Blakely started to pour some scotch into his glass, then stopped. Instead, he flung the half full bottle into the dark void.

"I don't need you anymore," he whispered.

Wafford's face reminded him of the gray face of Jim Wafford lying in the casket and this vision brought a myriad of other faces, including Luke, Chris, Emily, and Andrew. He wondered what Andrew would have looked like, had he grown to manhood, seeing in his mind only the image of a little brown-haired boy he still loved with all his heart. He thought of Claudia, on her way to Athens, remembering how she looked as a teenager, peeling nail polish off her toe nails and philosophizing. The scent of Joachim's pipe tobacco was almost palpable; a man Blakely knew was at peace in the firmament.

And then he thought of Jenny. He realized how incredible life is that after deep sadness of ending a relationship, one can find bliss. Certainly, he'd never seen Jenny so happy as she was with Graham.

He wasn't sure, but it seemed that he could still be of some use to himself and others. A seed was sprouting having to do with sailing and kids. Perhaps he could sell somebody on the idea of having a ship like the *Sea Siren*, where he could take kids with problems out to sea. Put in at one island or another. Show them how people are all alike, no matter where they live. He thought of Harry and Thomas and Tobok and Lou. How different they might have turned out, had someone taken them under their wing and taught them how to sail at a young age and shown them love.

Maybe Graham Steward would be interested in underwriting

such a project. Graham could afford the write-off! Anyway, it was an idea for the future.

Another military truck was grinding up the narrow serpentine road toward the piazza, shifting to lower gears, causing little shrieks as the engine labored. Its lights flashed and Blakely watched the dark monster roar past and listened to the sound slowly dissipating.

The more he thought about teaching problem kids how to sail, the more it appealed to him. They could sail in the Caribbean or the South Seas or here in the Med. Since Elizabeth was so crazy about sailing, she might consider a partnership. They could teach sailing and academics and mythology and study the stars. He would invite Claudia, Chris, Jeremiah, Tony, Mike, Leo and Justina to come aboard, too. Be a part of helping kids and helping themselves to be better people. God, would he have time left to do it? He hoped so.

The coolness wafting up from the valley brought familiar scents of wood and earth to him. There were no lights visible; all the farms were quiet. The night was totally still. Orthodox Easter night. The pagans and the Christians had eaten all the flesh and consumed all the wine. The village was silent. The only presence in the square was Alex's taxi, resting in its usual place beneath the plane tree.

He looked toward the big dipper—the plow—knowing Joachim's comet was out there, hidden for years to come, but nevertheless there in the Heavens. And he felt deeply his communion with all things living and all things dead, and all things that had ever been and all things that ever would be, reminded of Elizabeth's and Joachim's teachings about how everything in the universe is connected and nothing is ever lost.

He thought he might stay out on the piazza until daybreak and keep watch. He didn't expect Harry Swann or anyone else to attempt to kill Wafford, but you never could be sure. He would wait and watch. He felt no need for sleep.

He listened. There was the distant sound of another truck

moving unseen across the valley toward Kastelli. He watched for its lights, focusing on the moving sound. The thick, treaded wheels hummed on the paved road. It was a soothing sound. He heard a muffled pop which sounded like the truck had gone over a bump, causing the tail gate to bang. Perhaps someone forgot to fasten it properly. He listened sharply for the turn the truck would make when it passed the work-site and hit the first steep hill. There! It shifted gears and worked against the grade.

He looked back over his shoulder. A light came on upstairs at the hotel. The grinding engine grew louder. The shriek and churning of pistons reminded him of Wafford's awful crying out with pain. The shrieks increased until the truck reached the crest. Lights flooded the piazza momentarily as the truck passed by. More lights came on inside the hotel. The silence returned. He heard voices. A man in a white, half-buttoned shirt and black trousers appeared in the hotel doorway, looked around, saw Blakely, and walked toward him. It was the young night clerk he liked, Manolis.

"Mr. Blakely, sir," he said with a slight, serious bow, "would you please come?"

"What is it?"

"I'm sorry sir, but Mr. Wafford has shot himself."

"Is he dead?"

"Yes, sir."

He drained the Glenfiddich. "I'll be right there."